TUCSON MOON

ARIZONA HISTORICAL BOOK 2

RAIN TRUEAX

Tucson Moon

Arizona Historicals Book 2"
The O'Brians

is an original work of Rain Trueax.

All rights reserved.

Copyright © 2013   Rain Trueax

978-0-9898075-2-4

Paperback

113017

Prepared and presented by:
Seven Oaks
Monmouth, Or.

INTRODUCTION

Tucson Moon

Priscilla Wesley has everything going for her with wealthy parents, beauty, a privileged life. The last thing she needs is to fall in love with a lawman.

US Deputy Marshal Cord O'Brian makes his living with a gun, something she abhors. Attraction isn't enough—or is it?

Tucson Moon is about love, family relationships, the desert, and Arizona Territory in 1886-87. It's about choices and how our character can be improved, as with the choices Cord and Priscilla make, or degraded one step at a time.

CHAPTER 1

Tucson Arizona Territory, December 1886

"Oh God, no," Priscilla muttered to herself, adding a few curse words that no one was supposed to hear her saying. She looked again through the curtain to be sure she wasn't imagining it. Nope, it was Martin Matthews standing on her porch and loudly knocking on her front door.

Even though it had happened more than three years earlier, she cursed herself regularly for her stupidity in visiting El Tiradito. At the wishing shrine she had asked for that man to want her. What a fool she'd been. Her best friend, Abigail, had warned her. Would she listen? Nope. So typical.

Suppressing her irritation, she considered options. Was it too late to ask James to lie and say she wasn't home? Unfair to her loyal employee but tempting.

She could hear voices as the door opened. "Miss Wesley is lying down for a bit," James said in an officious, very butler sounding tone. He was clearly as tired as she at seeing the silly man on their doorstep.

How had she ever believed he could be her one true love?

Why had she read those ridiculous love stories? She would never forgive Jane Austen for doing this to her.

All right, she couldn't blame one of her favorite authors—at least not with fairness. Love stories were enjoyable distractions but also foolishness. Even if now and then fairy tales did come true, generally speaking, a vivid imagination led more to grief than benefit.

None of which solved the problem of Martin now moving to wait in the parlor. Putting this off would not help. She had to bite the bullet, proverbially speaking, and once and for all be forceful. Her natural reluctance to hurt the feelings of others could not get in her way—not this time.

She finished buttoning her striped yellow dress, slipped on a jacket and plopped a felt hat over the bun on top of her head. Viciously sticking in a hat pin, to keep it in place from the wind she could hear outside, she felt grateful she hadn't speared herself. Descending the stairs, ready to look surprised at a guest in the parlor, she heard Martin's whining greeting. "My dear, are you going out? I had hoped for some time together."

"Hello Martin. James, did you get the buggy ready as I had requested?"

He nodded with a wry smile. "You driving yourself, ma'am?"

She nodded. "I won't need you but thanks anyway." She saw amusement in his clear gray eyes. He liked Martin even less than she did.

"I could drive you wherever you are going," Martin suggested forcing a smile that only made him look sillier with that tiny mustache, and was that intended to be a beard?

"I'm sorry, Martin, but I have an appointment."

"Could you drop me then?"

"Where are you going?" She hoped it was the opposite way, but she wasn't prepared to be that impolite to him—not yet.

"Back to work, I guess. I had hoped for an afternoon with you, but there is a lot of work since Abigail left us high and dry."

"Good Lord, Martin." She forced a smile to hide her irritation. She was getting good at subterfuge or else Martin was so oblivious he caught no innuendoes. Poor weak little man. "Abigail has a baby and husband to take care of out at their ranch. She's been gone three years which was hardly leaving you or her father high and dry."

He shut his mouth on whatever he had intended to say but then smiled again. "I could go with you on your errand."

Her own smile disappeared. No way in Hades would she let him even know where she was headed let alone allow him to come. "I'm sorry but no."

James appeared at the door. "The buggy is ready, Miss Wesley. You sure you don't need me to drive you?"

She suppressed her amusement at James' formal address of her and shook her head as she headed out into the warm Tucson air. It would have been a beautiful December day other than the man walking alongside her, determined not to release her company until the last possible second.

"You sure it's safe for you to drive it?" he asked when they arrived at the buggy.

"Jezebel is a very reliable mare."

"What a name for a reliable horse," he remonstrated.

She gave him a look rather than saying what was on her mind. She thwarted his attempt to hand her up, by stepping into the buggy before he could do more than put out his hand.

"Well then," he said as he stepped back. "Perhaps later we will see each other."

She sighed and pretended not to hear as she flicked the reins and felt Jezebel head off leaving the want-to-be lover in the dust. Trying to settle her nerves, she looked toward the mountain that always brought her peace. A dove lit on one of the cottonwood trees. She loved mourning doves, their cooing, peaceful sounds.

A dark streak dropped from the sky. She realized with horror that a Harris hawk now had the dove in its talons as it proceeded to tear it apart. The whole thing had happened so fast she could hardly believe its reality. She looked away, hoping it wasn't an omen for her meeting.

As Martin watched her go, he felt his anger boil over. Nothing in his life had worked out right. It all went back to Abigail leaving. No, to the day Sam Ryker took her from him. Or was it when the man, who he had hired, failed to kill the desperado? Perhaps he could have forgiven it all had Ryker not looked at him with such disdain whenever their paths crossed.

Had Abigail turned Priscilla against him? If she had been willing to marry him, he'd... No, that would have never placated his wrath. He would have his revenge. Now he added Priscilla to the list of those who deserved a payback, for all who saw him as beneath them.

He watched as her buggy turned a corner and disappeared from view. With little enthusiasm, he began walking back to the office where his constantly complaining boss would be waiting, reminding him that he never did enough. At one time Martin had believed he would take over the business from Jacob Spenser. He knew now the greedy old man would never let him have it for a cost he could afford. If he wanted that business, he'd have to find another way. Manipulating the books to pull pennies from it was never going to give him the life he wanted and needed. Someday he'd find a way to get power-- and when he did, he'd settle his scores with those who had hurt him.

In the meantime, he was not going back to work and listen to Jacob whine about missing his daughter, moaning over how he'd never know his grandson, and list off all the reasons he hated Sam Ryker. No, he didn't need that. He headed instead for the Pedrales. There were women there who knew how to treat a man. He checked his wallet and had just enough for a few hours of pleasure and then to get drunk. Someday he'd deal with the rest of it-- but for today, he'd find his satisfaction as he could. He wondered if Sally would be available.

Priscilla pulled up the buggy in front of a neat frame house at the edge of Tucson. She had never met the woman inside, but James' wife, Rose, had assured her that she was exactly what she wanted. She had sent James to make an appointment and assure himself the establishment was as safe as Rose had assured them both. At least as safe as safe went.

For over a year, Priscilla had felt a nervous energy coming upon her with no explanation. She had tried to figure it out for herself. No answers had seemed right. Finally she had decided to try something unorthodox-- at least within her community's expectations.

Knocking on the door, it took only a moment for it to be swung open. The woman was in her middle years. Her reddish brown hair was pulled back and tied at the back of her neck. Priscilla supposed she had expected something exotic, perhaps a turban. The gray dress with a white lace collar was ordinary with nothing to alert anyone to her claim of being a palm reader, psychic, seer and who knew what else.

"Mrs. Sicilla?" she asked.

The woman smiled and opened the door more widely. "Please, Connie. And you are Miss Wesley."

Priscilla nodded as she walked into the pleasant parlor. "I've never had a reading from a psychic-- so I don't quite know how we begin or what to expect." She sat in the chair to which she had been ushered.

Connie smiled as she pointed to a tea pot. "Would you like a cup? I find it often helps if we start with a little light conversation."

Priscilla was a bit suspicious that light conversation was intended to get information to help with the reading, but she nodded. Part of her was wondering why she had come, while part was curious as to what might be revealed. Would this all be a fake?

Connie poured them each a cup of tea. "Rose and I are friends, but perhaps she told you that."

Priscilla took a sip before answering. "Rose didn't tell me much beyond that she likes you. When I began to discuss my own... well, restlessness lately, she mentioned that you had skills I might find of interest. I was unsure, but then I am always interested in whatever is occult, I suppose, and... I hope I didn't just insult you."

"No, not at all. The unknown always seems suspicious to us and hence the words to make it even scarier." Connie sipped her tea before she looked back up at Priscilla. "Is there something specific you want to know?"

"What kinds of things could you tell me?"

"There are assorted ways to proceed. I do tea leaves, which is what we are drinking. I can read Tarot, analyze astrology charts, or just give you what I receive from your guides. I must warn you it might be nothing. I only can reveal what is given to me."

"What do you believe about guides?"

"Interesting that you didn't ask what they were."

"I'd prefer to hear what you believe them to be."

"They are the silent voices, the manipulators of events, the incidents that we call accidents. Some might call them angels. Are they real or only a term, to explain the unknown? That is for each of us to decide."

"Purposely vague." Priscilla smiled.

Connie spread her hands. "But of course. I like you Miss Wesley, but in trying to feel your energy, I am coming up against barriers. Are you aware of those?"

"Perhaps."

"Try to relax. I won't probe into anything that you don't want. I might be able to help you more if I knew your birth date, time and place. Although that would require your coming back for it to be more than a superficial look."

"I might as well admit, even though I came, I have my doubts on any of this. I am a bit fascinated though, and it brought me past the doubts."

"Many people feel that way, but your doubts seem to come from something personal—an experience or..."

"My grandmother was involved in using the kinds of skills Rose told me that you claim. My family originally came from Georgia. Back there are voodoo queens, those who claimed to have mastered the underworld. They can cast spells for good or ill.

"Once, when I was about ten and spending the night with my grandmother, a woman came to her home who wore a brightly red, patterned scarf over her head. She was dark skinned. Her eyes were almost black, intense, with an odd light. She touched my hair, like patting it, but said nothing of what she was thinking. She whispered something to my grandmother, who only smiled. When I told my mother of the woman, she didn't let me spend the night there again."

"Did your grandmother talk about the other side, the mystical?"

"Not to me but..."

Connie smiled amusement in her eyes. "You listened."

"Yes, before the overnights ended, there had been other events that I would now say were séances but then knew little of what they were about. I did listen though."

"So you know more about this than most, and it makes you uncomfortable all while it draws you?"

"The results can be unpleasant." She knew that one well from her visit to the wishing shrine and its aftermath. Had the wish that day been responsible for Martin's sudden interest in her? How could she explain her own aversion to him when it was what she had originally thought she wanted? "My mother felt her mother was a little touched in the head."

Connie chuckled. "Then it took some courage to come despite that."

"Maybe or maybe curiosity rose over fear. I didn't fear you but more..."

"What the other side might hold for you?" Connie suggested.

"I trust Rose very much. You might think she and James are merely servants, but they are so much more than that to me. They are friends and even more family."

"And Rose suggested you come."

"She knew I had been upset, felt stress. There wasn't a physical reason for it. She thought you might have some ideas to help."

Connie nodded staring at her hands before she looked back at Priscilla. "Is it just what is-- or more what you sense is coming? Is that sense of something coming the real reason you are here?"

"Perhaps. I feel foolish though even thinking it."

"Such impressions are rarely foolish, but they can come from many sources."

"Too much imagination," Priscilla suggested.

"Well, let's see, shall we?"

"How much has Rose told you of me?" Information Rose had given her friend might make the reading less effective or seem more of a fake.

"The only thing Rose said is what a nice person you are to work for, you and your parents when they are in town."

Connie watched Priscilla with an intensity that unnerved her. It was like the woman from so many years before. Priscilla bent her head to sip more of the tea. "Your tea is excellent, mellow with something of an exotic flavor."

"I have it sent from back East. My mother lives in Boston, and she can get so many things we don't find out here. This is from the Indies."

8

"I like it very much." She supposed she was stalling, but now that she was in this cozy parlor, she was unsure what she hoped to find.

"I'll make a suggestion, Priscilla," Connie said, "that is if I may call you Priscilla."

"My friends call me Cilla."

"I hope we will be friends, Cilla. I want to explain that while I do readings, several types, I do not advertise this fact for an assortment of reasons. Not the least of which is it can force me to leave a community if certain people hear of what they see as evil. Since you saw your mother's reaction to her mother's interest or possible talent for such, you probably understand my caution."

When Priscilla waited, saying nothing, Connie went on, "People who don't understand tend to think it is insane or witch-craft. What some don't understand, they fear."

"I won't talk of it to anyone who might feel that way."

"Good, because my husband and I would like to stay here, at least as long as Del wants. My husband deals faro at the Pedrales."

"Goodness, a professional gambler and that supports you both?" Along with psychic readings she guessed.

"He also tends bar and whatever. Yes, it does."

"I didn't mean to be nosy."

"You weren't. You were wanting to know a bit about the person who might be prying into your own secrets. That's a very logical thing to want."

"Logic is not my forte." Priscilla had to work for a smile.

"Ah a person of the heart, the fire, the instinct?"

"Not that I can give that much credit either. So how do we begin?"

"One possibility is we use the cards, Tarot, to open us both to whatever information might be out there. How does that sound?"

"I am in your hands." She set down her cup.

"Now some believe that the querent, that would be you,

should cut the deck after I shuffle. I prefer nobody else touches my deck to protect its energy for my reading it." Priscilla nodded her agreement. "I also don't want you to think I am a fortuneteller. I see possibilities. I do sometimes receive visions that relate. There are the hidden voices, the symbols, which can help explain what is happening. For me, the cards help to open this process." As she spoke, she shuffled a deck of what appeared from the back to look like ordinary playing cards.

"The images on these cards were created and blessed for me by another seer. The cards and their images are merely vehicles. They aren't magical. They are pointers. The only thing that makes me different from you or anyone else is my ability to interpret and recognize how they go together."

"I see," Priscilla said not sure that she did.

"How many times shall I cut the deck?"

"Three." There was no reason for having chosen that number, but it seemed as apt as any. She watched as Connie's graceful, long fingers cut the deck three times, then dealt out three cards, placing them face down on the table between them.

"Cilla, do these cards all feel right to you? Put your hands over the top of them, don't touch but feel their energy. Does one feel out of place?"

"What would I be looking for?"

"Perhaps a coldness where another might feel warm. If they all feel cold, tell me that too."

Priscilla moved her right hand over the cards. She did seem to feel a warmth emanating up from them—no coldness. "They belong together."

Connie turned each over to reveal images that, as she had predicted, meant nothing to Priscilla. After a few moments of looking at each, Connie looked up and met Priscilla's gaze.

"These three represent where you are right now but interestingly enough, they are all male figures." She grinned. "This sometimes means a woman has a great deal of male energy either inside her or around her. Do you have a special gentleman in your life?"

"Other than my father and James, no."

"For the moment, let's assume that this energy is yours. It would tell me that you are stronger than one might think from your almost fragile looks. You are not someone who is easily broken. You stand up for what you must." Connie smiled again. "You are a fighter."

"I haven't thought of myself that way."

"If you haven't, know that it is within. When the time it is needed, it will come out. The cards though... Well the reading here does not seem to be just about your own strength." She hesitated and studied one of the cards before she added, "Yes, this card says someone is coming into your life, someone important. This might be what you are feeling, the energy. It's a man." She closed her eyes before looking back at Priscilla. "He is a leader, a strong man with the element of fire. I see power." She frowned as she studied the image. "He... might be a man who also represents danger but with him is coming love and hope."

"I know no one that could fit."

"If you don't, you will."

"To be honest, the last thing I want right now is love unless it represents family and friends."

"Want it or not, I believe it is coming. Please may I see your right hand?"

Priscilla extended it. Connie studied it before she looked up with a grin. "Ah, my dear, you have one love line. One very strong deeply engraved love line. If the one that line waits for is not yet in your life, he will be soon, very soon."

Priscilla shook her head. "I thought I wanted something like that once but... well I made a big mistake, and that person still haunts me." That was putting it mildly. "I certainly can't imagine those cards representing him." God, she hoped not.

"Cilla, does that man fit the other qualities that I mentioned?"

"Not remotely."

"Then don't worry about it being him. This man is definitely a leader. The card says he is strong... and yes, I would say he walks with fire but carries peace. An odd combination, I grant you, but there it is."

"I can't think of anyone I know who that could fit." That wasn't literally true, but it was true that there was no one possible for her that it could fit. "You're sure it's not my father."

Connie gave a humorous laugh. "Definitely not. This is a hot, passionate love." She waved her hand over her face to indicate its heat. "The two of you together will be combustible is the only word I can think of to describe it."

Priscilla frowned. "Some might consider that good news. It is not what I want."

"What we think we want is not always what we most need." She continued to hold Priscilla's hand.

"Are you reading my palm?"

"Not so much now although I will say you had a very long life line, which is no surprise considering the strength I feel emanating from you. Your aura reaches way beyond where most do. I have this feeling if you wanted to use it for healing you could. But right now I want to feel the kind of energy in you."

"You mean positive or negative?"

"Let me see what I get." She was silent for a bit as she closed her eyes. When she opened them, she again looked into Priscilla's eyes. "Your energy is a bit divided, but you know that, don't you?"

Priscilla nodded.

"When you bring all the power that is within you into force, you will not come to anyone else with questions. The answers have always been within you. You will know them and not doubt."

Not that Priscilla didn't believe her, but she also could see how that's something psychics likely told all who came to them. Flattery would get return visits most likely more than insults.

Connie smiled. "Yes, I could be flattering you-- but in this case, I am not. There is something more though. Something about which I must warn you. The cards didn't just reveal a love but a danger-- and it seems very real to me, something to be concerned about."

That didn't seem more apt than a knight in shining armor to come riding up, but Priscilla said nothing and waited.

"The card telling me this doesn't suggest what the danger is." Connie closed her eyes. "I am trying to look for symbols from your guides to help me understand what this means." She smiled. "There is a hawk. He's flying, soaring, diving and rising. A strong, powerful, beautiful bird. I am thinking he represents the man who is coming."

Priscilla said nothing. The image of the hawk tearing apart the dove flashed through her mind. She hoped Connie would not next say she represented the dove.

With her eyes still closed, Connie's face paled. She swallowed and then looked up. "There is also an owl."

"Is that bad?"

Connie frowned. "Normally, I would say not, but this time... I am not sure. The owls are often considered harbingers of wisdom or... I wish I could tell you what it all means. Symbols can be so difficult to interpret, and why the two birds, both predatory, being together, I just wish I could say."

"Perhaps they don't go together."

"Perhaps." Connie closed her eyes again. If she was acting, the act was a good one as she appeared to be intensely concentrating, trying to interpret what she saw. Finally she met Priscilla's gaze her own still looking troubled. Priscilla began to wonder if she would be selling her protection next. She realized her cynicism was coming to the fore, possibly that barrier Connie had mentioned.

Connie wet her lips, seemed to be considering before she spoke. "Leaving the symbols, what I can tell you is the deceptive card represents one wearing a mask when with you. He is a dangerous man but does not appear to be so."

"He?"

"I think it is male energy."

"I really know no one like that." Phillip was weak not dangerous.

"I keep coming back to the symbols, the hawk and the owl. They both have strong spiritual symbolisms, but both can be about being observative and aware." She shook her head again and stared out the window before looking back. "The owl... Or maybe this other card, this other entity does not relate. I don't feel good about telling you this when I can't explain it." Her mouth tightened. "I think that it won't be me though. You will be the one to figure this out."

"Let's leave it then for now. Do you have any ideas on what you feel will help me with this thing of being divided?"

Connie smiled. This was clearly more comfortable territory for her. "Of course, the obvious—meditation. Being open to your full powers. Actually you have very strong abilities toward what I am doing, Cilla. Did you know that?"

Perhaps she had always known it, been fascinated by her grandmother because of it, but she said nothing.

"Being divided is mostly due to possibly your own unwilling-ness to be all you could. Meditation sounds simple, but it really can help you to focus, figure out what is there within. Give your-self times to just be. Don't try to think through everything."

Priscilla smiled. "Easier said than done."

"True. There is something more that I hesitate to..." Connie was silent a moment. "Are you familiar with reincarnation, my dear?"

"Coming back after death as a new person, you mean?"

"Yes."

"Not much. Only that some believe in it, but I don't know that I do."

"Are you afraid to consider it?"

"Not particularly, but it seems unlikely to me."

"I think there are those around you with whom you have had past lives. Whether you believe or not doesn't matter. One of those is a very strong woman friend. She can be much help to you if a difficult time comes-- that is if you let her. Her energy is that of a powerful woman with much love to give. I feel she's been with you before as sister, friend. You have always been support for each other, as you are again in this lifetime."

Connie sighed, as she seemed to be thinking what to say or perhaps how to say it. "That lover, the one I first mentioned, he's been with you before also. He's the mate of your soul, a relationship that goes beyond the flesh. I think you do already know him but are resisting him or more accurately what he might emotionally cost you."

This was beginning to seem a little weird to Priscilla, but what should she have expected. The last time she dabbled with the occult, she got Martin. Still she had come for a reading, and she would not second guess what she was being told—not totally. Perhaps with time it would all make more sense.

"I'm not opposed to reincarnation exactly," Priscilla said finally. "I just don't know. To be honest, it seems unlikely." She gave a little laugh. "My pastor would probably say evil."

Connie laughed with her. "What we don't understand often seems evil. Now there is one more thing the guide is saying. That one, who I said you should not trust, there might be something from other lifetimes with him too."

"You see my guide?"

"Not a face but I feel the energy that entered with you today. It was feminine. I can't tell you more, but that entity is with you, wants you to know that it is with you and insists very strongly that I must warn you."

"About the second person."

Connie nodded. "This person is underhanded and always has

15

been so. One lifetime after another he's not learned anything. You trusted him once. Maybe even this lifetime, but you no longer do."

All of it was possible, but also something a psychic might say to each client. Priscilla knew she was being a skeptic. If she had come hoping to leave a true believer, it appeared it wasn't happening.

"Thank you," she said rising, but Connie put her hand out.

"I am getting something more. This is unusual in my experience as normally when I do a reading, it's for the person who has come. I think though... I am being told that that owl is meant to be the warning for the hawk." She smiled more broadly. "Yes, the hawk is the man with whom you will soon be lovers."

Priscilla resisted laughing. This was getting stranger and stranger. She couldn't resist one quip. "So I should give a warning to a man I don't even know?"

Connie, who was still looking a little pale, managed a short laugh. "I realize it sounds unlikely. That man, the one who has a hawk as his totem, he has a darkness that rides with him. He welcomes death might be a better way to express what I am feeling—although words sometimes seem so inadequate."

"So, if I do meet this man, fall in love with him, he is likely to meet a violent end?"

Connie again closed her eyes. "Jesus, Mary Mother of God, this is all sounding crazy even to me. I haven't had a reading that is so confusing ever. I..." Connie sighed. "I wish I had had something more helpful for you. It seems garbled even to me. I am so sorry."

"You gave me what you got," Priscilla said as Connie walked her to the door. "I appreciate your honesty," she said not sure how she felt about it. If she had hoped for firm answers regarding mysticism, she'd gotten instead warnings to her life, and about some man she had yet to meet. Perhaps the problem was she hadn't come with the right questions. "How much do I owe you?"

"Didn't James tell you?"

Priscilla shook her head.

"I don't do readings for money. I do it because it's something I can do, and only when I feel it's the right person. My readings are a gift. Taking money for a gift could cost me the gift. I wish I had helped you. I feel I did not. If I get something later, something that perhaps explains this all better, I will let you know. If you ever want to talk to me, ask more about this, Cilla, please come back."

Priscilla felt flummoxed by the whole experience, but said thank you again. As she left the small house, she was surprised there had been no attempt by the woman to profit from it. Who was she?

As she reached her buggy, she saw another hawk sailing high over the land looking for something. When it cried out, she felt a shiver down her spine.

CHAPTER 2

Marshal Cord O'Brian rode down the dusty street, tired and irritated at his wasted day. Why was it every time he went to the Bailey house to try and talk to them about their son, they were all gone? He had little doubt the couple hid inside to avoid him. Didn't they understand that young man was on a road to destruction? Jesse's last episode in town had nearly led to a killing. The next one might. He had no idea what was wrong with the youth. Whatever, was going on, was escalating.

When he saw the buggy turning a corner and now coming toward him, he cursed under his breath. A bad day was going steadily downhill. The last person he wanted to run into was the beautiful, useless, silly, and for some reason all too attractive to him Miss Wesley. He slowed his horse anyway to be polite and pulled to a halt when Miss Wesley stopped her buggy.

"Ah Marshal O'Brian, and what miscreants have you been rounding up today?" she teased in that faint drawl that always made him imagine mint juleps or summer evenings on a porch with a... Never mind the rest.

"Miss Wesley, did you have one to report to me?"

Her forced smile reminded him that he was not on her

favorite person list, not that he expected to be. If for no other reason, he had earned her ire when he'd been unsympathetic to her gentleman friend, Martin Matthews, who had been bedded for over a week by a paltry wound. Priscilla had served as the man's nurse and obviously had sympathy for the rascal—undeserved though it had been.

"Possibly, I might," she said. "What kind would you like?"

"The usual. Easy to arrest and then much credit to my reputation when the hombre is sealed away forever."

This time her smile seemed a bit more genuine. "Then I guess I don't know any at the moment but will be sure to report one should I come across them."

"Unlikely in your circle of superior folks," he said with a smirk that he knew would irritate her.

"Yes, you are right. People I know are all above reproach."

"Like Sam Ryker?" he asked still frustrated at the way that rustler had managed to avoid the law and settle into what looked like a respectable life, but which he knew wouldn't be. Leopards did not change their spots.

"Decidedly. He is an excellent example of a fine gentleman." She gave him a look, which said she judged him as being anything but. Well fine, he didn't consider himself a gentleman either.

He snorted. "His being married to your best friend has no bearing on your judgment does it?" He knew arguing with her was wasting both their times.

"I would recognize his character anyway. I am a good judge of character, Marshal O'Brian."

"He's a rustler and a gunman, Miss Wesley. The fact that I have not been able to prove the former doesn't make it less the truth."

"Well, such a superior lawman as yourself should consider the possibility that there is nothing to prove."

He laughed. "You still believe in Santa Claus, Miss Wesley?"

"Of course, doesn't everyone?"

He wished he was less aware of her shapely figure, the small but strong looking, finely-boned hands on the reins of her horse. He imagined those hands doing other things, and the thought made him grimace. A woman he didn't need. Even more not one like this pampered beauty. When he met her gaze, he wondered just how accurately she read his attraction. Likely she expected every man to fall to his knees at her feet. He'd be one who never would.

Before their conversation could descend into an out and out argument again, a second horseman pulled up, Daniel Jamison. "Priscilla, just the person I wanted to talk to," he said ignoring the marshal completely.

"I'm on my way home, Daniel." Her voice was cool and not welcoming. "I do have someone coming over this afternoon, however."

Jamison's face showed his disappointment. "Perhaps this evening?"

She sighed. "Perhaps." She looked toward Cord nodding her head. "Goodbye, Marshal." Flicking the reins over her mare, her buggy moved away from them.

Jamison gave his own sigh of disappointment.

"Better luck next time," Cord said with a grin as he lightly touched spurs to his gelding's side.

"Wait, Marshal," Jamison yelled, moving his own horse to catch up with him. "I needed to talk to you also." With little enthusiasm, Cord slowed Jeb's gait. "Any sign of the rustlers I reported?"

He shook his head. "Your brand hasn't shown up anywhere either."

"Like people would report it," Jamison protested.

"With a resale they would." Maybe. He understood rustling had been a way of life for this territory. With the law came a change of rules. A man wasn't entitled to brand any maverick he came across—not that it stopped them all.

"Small ranchers have no authority."

"The law sees everyone the same."

Jamison snorted. "Right, like Richard Wright has to answer to you."

"You suspect him of being the one to take your animals?"

"He's nearest."

"Seems he's on the big side to worry about a few cattle."

"Never enough for some," Jamison grumbled.

"I can't just appear at his ranch and examine every brand without a warrant. Would you like to file a complaint?"

Jamison sighed. "You know I don't have evidence, but his ranch just gets bigger and bigger since his father died."

"Maybe he's a better rancher."

"Maybe," Jamison said without much belief. "We need the law up my way. As it stands, we have no protection."

"Go up to Prescott and ask for additional men to patrol the wilder regions but don't expect much. They have a lot already on their plate with Geronimo still on the rampage."

"Tarnation."

"Pressure is the nature of the game. If you can get Wright and a couple of others to ask for more manpower down here, you might get it."

"Yeah, like he wants that. I will ask again though. Maybe Judge Emerson will listen to me. As it stands, we have no legal help north of town." He gave Cord a derogatory look.

That was a direct cut, and irritated Cord, but he held his tongue as he'd been forced to do often since becoming a Deputy United States Marshal. You could never please everybody. He got that. It seemed he often wasn't pleasing anybody. There had to be an easier way to earn a living. At least a town sheriff wasn't sent hither and yon. Although, he suspected he'd be bored with such a job.

He had hoped that would be the end of Jamison's complaints-- but as they rode into Tucson's downtown, the words didn't stop. Likely the man would follow him right into his office. The small rancher did follow him to the stable, complaining the whole time Cord rubbed Jeb down and put him into his stall with fresh hay.

"Mr. Jamison, I will do what I can when I can but..."

By that time they were at his office, the day didn't look much brighter, as there were two men waiting on the bench in front. Neither looked happy. Where the hell was Rafe? What good did a deputy do if he was always disappearing to do some Yaqui magic ritual or whatever the hell it was he did. Sighing, he walked in his office. Three unhappy men faced him when he finally sat at his desk, all of them trying to talk at once.

Priscilla pulled up the buggy behind her home, still irked at her run-in with the obnoxious, arrogant marshal, but happy to see James come out from the kitchen. "Rose has some delicious muffins she just took out of the oven," he said with one in his hand as he reached for Jezebel's harness.

"Your wife is the best baker in Tucson," Priscilla said yearning to eat one but determined to take off the five pounds she had put on, which were making the putting on of corsets less and less a pleasure and nearly a threat to her breathing. She jumped down from the buggy.

Rose would want to hear how the reading went. She didn't mind telling her. Except, her main concern was how to resist the muffins if she sat in what was bound to be a fragrant kitchen. That would undo her breakfast self-restraint where she stuck to black coffee, bacon and a thin slice of Rose's wonderful home-made wheat toast.

God, if only she had the metabolism of her friend, Abigail, who could eat anything and still lose weight. Abigail had a better figure after her baby had been born than before. Priscilla was relatively sure that if she ever had a baby, she'd balloon up like her mother. She then had better hope she had a husband who liked his wife plump.

In the kitchen, Rose's pleasing round face showed her curiosity, but she was too polite to ask. "Tea, Missy?"

She nodded looking longingly toward the fragrant muffins cooling on the counter. "How about you join me and we have it in the parlor?" she suggested as a way to avoid what she was beginning to see as inevitable. She wished she had more will power. No, not a wish, wishes had gotten her in trouble.

She sighed and left the room with a weakening determination. Was a plump figure really so bad? It would cut down on her suitors—although she suspected half of them were more interested in her father's fortune than in her.

Once the two women were settled in the parlor, Priscilla took a sip of the tea before she said, "I liked her."

"Was she helpful though?"

"I'm not sure. I'm still trying to sort it out. Out of curiosity, how much did you tell her about me?" She tried not to look at Rose's muffins now on a plate on a table safely across the room from her. At least the fragrance wasn't reaching her quite as strongly as it had in the kitchen.

Rose shook her head. "Nothing more than that you are a good woman, easy to work for, and I'd know after having worked for your family now going on fifteen years. I remember your big eyes as that little ten-year old girl, so appreciative of anything I did for you. You really have made up for me having no wee ones of my own."

Priscilla also vividly remembered the day Rose and James has shown up at the house, having been hired by her father when he heard they were in town and looking for the kind of work he badly needed for his own home. It had changed the household to have this effective couple making everything more organized. Suddenly things began to run smoothly, which was more than Priscilla's rather scatter-brained mother had ever managed or her mostly absent father could put the time into making happen.

"You know how dear you are to me, both of you."

Rose nodded. "You tell us regularly, and we appreciate that as much as the work, sweetheart."

"Okay then." She sighed. "Well, I just don't know what I think of the reading. Connie seems sincere. I can say that much. I liked her as a person. If she didn't get anything real, I don't think it's by intent. She didn't appear to be the sort to defraud."

Rose nodded with satisfaction and waited.

"She did a Tarot reading for me. Have you ever had one of those?"

Rose nodded again. "A few times. Mostly for fun as I haven't had anything I needed wisdom about. Life has sort of flowed along for me. Maybe I'm just too simple a woman to worry about much." She giggled.

"Well, do you think what she gets, the cards and all that it's... uh coming from God or... well the Devil?"

Rose nearly choked on her tea. "Neither. I think it's our own thinking—what we can't get hold of. That's what Connie says anyway. She just is a kind of path, a bit of a connector or something like that. Like it can't get through to most of us. It might be messages from angels."

"Which she calls spirit guides."

Rose nodded. "We want words. I've also heard that small, still voice. Whatever we call it. I just think she's more attuned to it than most of us—but there is one other part to it. She does appear to see things sometimes."

"Well she gave me a fair amount to think about. The main thing though was a little frightening. An enemy, near me, someone I don't recognize as dangerous."

"And just that?"

"She said it's a man."

"And no clue as to who?"

24

Priscilla shook her head. She wasn't ready to voice what she was thinking or even admit it to herself. Who else could it be but Martin Matthews? Even as she thought it, she knew it to be ridiculous. Martin was pathetic, not dangerous. It would be too much work to be dangerous.

Rose set down her tea cup. "Well that's worrisome and not much help without a name."

"That wasn't all. This might be scarier." She laughed. "The cards said love is coming in the form of a powerful man."

Rose grinned. "Any description?"

"A hawk. That's all she got."

"Goodness."

"As you well know, there was a time I wanted something like that but not anymore. Women don't have to marry. Some of my favorite authors never married. I am not convinced romantic love even exists, and I'd have no reason to marry for money. Yes, I know you found true love and Abigail, but I don't know even about my parents."

"They seem happy enough together."

"In a way. I hope their trip east will make a difference. They never fight or anything, which you know as well as me, but they seem rather disconnected. I urged them to take the train, visit Boston, New York, Washington and see old friends in Georgia. I hoped it would maybe spark a little flame between them."

"You are a bit of a romantic, no matter what you say," Rose teased.

"Maybe for others. Not for myself. I have plenty on my plate now." When her father had left, he'd given her the responsibility for the properties he had not sold. Although she'd helped for years, this had gone beyond her past endeavors. It was taking a lot of her energy. "I suppose I should have asked Connie about my parents, if they can kindle a new fire." She managed a smile that thinking about her parents' marriage didn't usually bring.

"Well a trip like that might," Rose said with a little doubt in her voice. For a woman, who worked as closely to the family as Rose, precious little got past her. Priscilla had no need to hide what was obvious-- but even so, she didn't mention the woman down on Fourth Street, who her father had been supporting. If Rose knew, she said nothing. Most likely James did, and he would have told Rose. They were that kind of close.

"But what about you?" Rose asked.

"Other than the person dangerous to me, this idea of some strong man, a mate for me, well, I don't want that or the sneaky one to be any part of my life."

"On the lover part, you have enough suitors to pick from." She grinned again as she sipped her tea.

"None that I'd want it to be." She pushed aside the dark saturnine face that came to her. Not that one. Certainly not the one who invaded her dreams with too much regularity. It made her angry just thinking about that possibility. Hawk-like he was but impossible to be anything to her.

"Sakes alive, Missy. What's wrong with all them young men coming sparking? You be so picky, you might end up a spinster."

"Not such a bad goal."

Rose shook her head and said, "Just you wait. And while you do, tell me what else Connie said."

"That was pretty much it. Not enough?" she teased. "She said I'm stronger than I know and might have psychic abilities myself. I suppose she tells everybody that. I don't know what I expected. She says she's no fortuneteller."

"Are you disappointed?"

"I quit expecting miracles a long time ago." She rose and walked to the window wondering if that was the truth. Perhaps she had hoped for more. Some kind of mystical answer to give her direction—as long as it didn't involve a man. The men courting her were none she'd consider marrying. Daniel Jamison struck her as weak, a whiner, someone who would want a wife, then constantly remind her how much she disappointed him.

"How about Mr. Wright?" Rose asked.

"He has money, and I guess that could qualify as being powerful," Priscilla agreed.

"Seems like he wanted to court you, and you turned him away."

"Going to a function more than once with him would have had us engaged."

"And that's not a good thing with him? I think he was attractive."

"In a snake oil sort of way," Priscilla said with a giggle. She supposed Richard might qualify as the powerful man in the card, but there was no way under the sun that she would want to be his wife or even friend. As for him being like a hawk, he was more like a vulture.

"Pastor Ryan has been by a time or two when you were out. He would like to have you see him as a possible suitor," Rose said reminding her of another of the potential swains.

"I had hoped he would leave Tucson when everyone said he was."

"Not interested in a pastor?"

"Well certainly not that one." Then she realized what Rose was doing. "Don't you try to marry me off, my lady. I don't need a husband—reading or no reading."

"You might need one but I agree with you, not Pastor Ryan. There is something about him that... Well he's not exactly a noble man for all his holy calling."

"I am afraid you are stuck with me."

"What about that artist fellow?"

"Joe? I like his paintings, not anything else."

"You set up a showing for him."

"As part favor to Abigail and the rest recognition that his work is excellent."

Rose giggled. "Well pretty well leaves out all the eligible young men you already know. There is only one thing to do—

take a trip to the East Coast and visit your parents, then bring back a husband."

"Of course, why didn't I think of that?" Priscilla laughed also as she gave up and picked up one of Rose's fresh muffins. "I suppose a rich one."

"Definitely and a handsome one."

"Looks are so important." She bit into it with satisfaction. "Hopefully someone who likes fat."

"Good Lord, missy, you think you are fat?"

"Pudgy?"

Rose shook her head. "Half the men in Tucson turn and look when you walk by. You have a figure women would die for with those rounded hips full breasts and tiny waist." Priscilla felt herself blushing. "And you don't know it?"

"I wish I looked like Abigail."

"Miss Abby is a beautiful woman, but she's her and you're you. You are a beautiful woman too, and that's why the young bucks come around."

"That and Daddy's money."

"They'd be here anyway. Maybe some get scared off by it actually."

"You are good for my morale, Rose."

Rose stood up. "Sweetheart, you do more for people than anybody I know. Taking food to Mrs. Gibbons, nursing folks when they got nobody. You need to think more highly of yourself is all."

"Thank you, Rose," Priscilla said as she rose and hugged her. "I need you to remind me what I have—and a lot of that is you and James."

Rose picked up the tray with the tea cups and plate of muffins. "Will we have company for dinner tonight?"

"No, just us. Maybe tomorrow night though, as Ellen arrives home. I'll be so glad to see her. It seems she's been in Dallas forever."

They walked into the kitchen just as a knock at the back door revealed Mr. Chan with his wagon and a selection of fresh vegetables for Rose to look through. "They are beautiful, fresh and in wonderful condition," Rose said as Priscilla looked over her shoulder at the squashes, bunches of spinach, and tomatoes. After Rose had made her choices and paid, they watched as the wagon with father and small son drove off for their next stop.

"I better get started on the meal." Rose said and Priscilla went to the den with the intention of working on the accounting. Several letters had arrived, a few bills and checks indicating money had been paid into her family accounts. She didn't mind so much looking after her father's interests in Tucson, but there were days she would have preferred doing anything but.

She walked to the window and looked out toward the street. In the distance she could see the Catalina Mountains. It was early for snow up there but white was edging the highest elevations. Soon it'd be winter-- even Tucson got some winter. It was more welcome than the extreme heat of the summers. She would try to talk Ellen into going up on the mountain or out to Sabino to enjoy the creek and see the last of the autumn colors. She hoped Ellen would be in the mood for such an adventure and not tired from her trip.

The face of the handsome marshal seemed to materialize in front of her. Frustrated, she tried to dismiss the vision, but it was persistent. Of all the men in Tucson, why did it have to be that one to excite her interest? The one man she not only could never have but would never want. It couldn't be him in Connie Sicilla's reading. No way could it be him, except if she knew any man who seemed like a hawk, it would have been Cord O'Brian.

With irritation she sat at her desk, opened a letter to find something to distract herself. When the words swam in front of her eyes, she knew she was going to have to work very hard to focus on something besides that dark, arrogant face.

CHAPTER 3

C ord strode back into his office, noting with some irritation Rafe's feet on his desk. "And you were yesterday?"

"Family business," his handsome young deputy said with a smug smile but did move at Cord's glare to sit on a chair in front of the big desk.

"It's always family business. How big a family you have?" he asked as he threw an unopened letter onto the desk.

"Counting those in Mexico and here?" Rafe asked as he began to count on his fingers.

A small voice at the door interrupted. "Boss, you want some vegetables today?" It was seven year old Lin Chan with a basket holding tomatoes and some fresh greens.

Cord grinned and walked over to examine the boy's wares. "They look good. What are you asking?" He didn't do much of his own cooking, but he bought something from Lin whenever he came around because he admired the small boy's work ethic.

"Good deal just for you, Boss," the dark-haired child said as he named a reasonable figure.

Cord dug into his pocket. "Where's your father?" he asked as he found the appropriate coins.

"Mama Jean's Café," he said counting the money himself before he put it into his pocket.

That was good news to Cord as it was where he took most of his meals. Maybe she'd like some fresh tomatoes to go along with whatever she had bought. Cord respected the Chan family as they were hard workers, and year round, they found ways to make their land along the Santa Cruz productive.

When the boy had gone, Cord looked again at the letter on his desk. It was from his dead wife's brother and unexpected. All communication had been through her parents when they wanted money for his daughter's care. He hoped this wasn't going to be bad news.

"Something wrong, Cord?" Rafe asked his face changing with concern.

"I don't know. Maybe."

"Why don't you open it? Find out?"

"I will." He just wanted to brace himself in case it involved Grace.

The door burst open with Jason Ridge rushing through puffing. "You got to get down to my bar."

"And the reason being?" Cord asked without looking up. Not even time to light a cigar or read a letter.

"Jesse Bailey again. He's tearing up the place. He's gonna kill somebody."

"Or get himself killed," Rafe agreed. "Want me to take this one?" He rose, loosening his gun in its holster.

Cord sighed. "No, I want you to deliver the summons to Patience Edwards."

"Damn, Cord. Anything but that. I don't do well with crying women."

"Nevertheless, a judge issued it, and someone has to deliver it. It's our job."

"She won't want to come in."

"Then arrest her."

"An old woman like that." Rafe got a sad look on his face. "You know I can't do that."

"Better that then going down to the Pedrales and getting into a gunfight with Jesse."

"Like you won't."

"Less chance of it than two young hotheads. Get."

Reluctantly Rafe headed out the door.

Cord left the letter on his desk and led the way back to the bar where inside he could hear the sounds of someone yelling and throwing things. "Sheriff Adams out of town?" he asked Ridge.

"He wasn't in his office."

"It's not strictly speaking my job, you know."

"Cord, I..."

"Never mind. Tell me what set this off."

"He's accusing Del of cheating at Faro. You know Del don't cheat. Then he got mad when some other man came up to Sherry and wanted to take her upstairs."

"That's Sherry's choice, not Jesse's."

"Yeah like we tried to tell him that. Jesse is drunk as a skunk and looking to get himself killed like your Injun friend said."

"His name is Rafael Cordova."

"Yeah, okay. Mr. Cordova."

Pushing open the bar door, Cord surveyed the room, the broken chairs, an angry young man striding back and forth while the few others remaining cowered back in their chairs.

"Jesse," Cord said with a firm voice, loud enough to carry over the youth's yelling.

Jesse turned and faced him, his hand hovering over his six-shooter. "He cheated me, Marshal. Nobody cheats me and don't have to pay for it."

"You can prove that?" Cord asked edging into the room and looking around to where Del sat calmly at the faro table both hands on it shuffling the cards.

"He wins too often."

"You gamble too much and badly. Unbuckle your gun belt."

"I ain't taking off my gun."

"Oh but you are, and it's either the easy way or hard. I was out at your folks' to try and tell them to keep you home. They scared of you or me, Jesse?"

Jesse snorted, his hand edging closer to that gun, the object that was making him feel like he was more of a man than he was or was likely ever to become at the rate he was going.

"You touch that hogleg, and it'll be the last thing you touch, Jesse. It isn't worth it."

"I'm fast."

"Like you think that's all that matters? You're a green kid with no sense. You gamble with men who do it better than you, and now you think you can take me. How many men you killed, Jesse?" He knew the answer.

"Might be there'll be a first, and it'll be you, Marshal."

Cord moved closer to him until now there was about six feet between them. "It could be a last time you try," he said. Seeing the youth reach for his gun, he lunged forward, knocking his arm down as the gun went off pointing at the floor. He slammed the youth against the bar and twisted him around until his belly was hard against it. Pulling his hands behind his back, he slapped on the handcuffs he had been hoping he'd be using instead of a coffin to end this.

The boy was struggling, but the fight was over. Ridge began cleaning up the mess. Cord shoved the kid toward the door but then stopped before going through it. He looked back at Del still sitting calmly at the table. "You cheat him?"

Del Sicilla, a still handsome, middle aged man, who had seen too much to be shaken by the threat of violence, shook his head.

"Next time he comes to the table, turn him down."

"It's a free country, Marshal."

"This boy is gambling his folks' money. They don't have

enough to keep their ranch and this kid going. Let somebody else take his dollars."

Del considered a moment and then nodded. "All right, but it won't keep him alive long if he doesn't grow up."

Cord agreed but said nothing. "No more whiskey or beer for him here either, Ridge."

"There'll be other bars," Ridge said.

"I'll talk to them too."

"You got no right to do that," Jesse snarled. "If I got money, I got a right to come in here and buy a drink."

"Well for a few days you'll be sobering up and cooling off in jail. After that, you can take your grievance up with the Judge. You're going to have to figure out how you pay off the damages as it is."

Finally with Jesse in the jail cell, now loudly snoring, Cord turned back to his letter. He had left a piece of his life back in Kansas and nothing about this letter made him feel it'd be good news from there. He ripped it open trying to make sense of the words Janice's brother had written.

Rafe shoved open the door, slumped into the chair.

"You deliver the summons?"

He nodded. "She can't be a bunco artist."

"Why not?"

"Looks like this sweet little old lady to me. No way she'd be cheating men out of their money."

"Right, like being a sweet looking lady would make it harder?" Cord shook his head.

"So what's in the letter that's got you turning white?"

Cord tried to think exactly what he'd read. "It seems my daughter is coming to Tucson to live."

"Daughter? Tucson? Live? What the hell you talking about, Cord?"

"I have a daughter."

"I thought you said had."

Cord rose and went over the stove to see if the coffee was still warm enough to drink. It was, and strong enough to grow hair even on his chest. "You want a cup?" He nodded toward Rafe, managing a faint smile when the Yaqui made a face.

"It was had. When my wife died, I was in no shape or condition to raise a baby. I had been working on the ranch her parents owned. They had me down as Satan himself. They made sure I couldn't work for anybody else in the area. I left. I could use a lot of excuses for why I didn't take her. It just seemed I did the right thing—at the time."

"They wouldn't go with you? Raise the kid out here?"

"They hated me, Rafe. Blamed me for Janice dying. Maybe it was my fault. It's not like we had much of a marriage. She got pregnant, and we got married."

"Baby was yours?"

Cord took a sip of the strong coffee avoiding the instinctive grimace. "I had no reason to think otherwise."

"What about your folks?"

"Both long dead, cholera. I guess in the beginning, I thought I could bring Grace out here sometime. Sometimes goes by awful fast. I wrote. They wrote when they wanted money. I sent them what I could." He moved to the window staring out at the street.

"You never went back?"

Cord clenched his jaw. "They did quite a number on convincing Grace I wasn't worth much. They saw me as a gunman with a badge. Predator they called me. I did go back once. Five years ago. She was cute as a button and looked at me like I was a hawk ready to tear her to bits."

"Well you do kind of look like one," Rafe teased. "Hawks aren't so bad actually, if she knew more about them."

Cord gave off a harsh laugh. "I suppose they have a mystic symbol, and you know all about it."

Rafe chuckled. "Maybe. I know more about family. Don't ever give up on yours. In the end, it's all you've got."

"Easy to say for a man with a family like yours where everybody loves everybody and you get together every chance you get."

"Yaquis believe in family."

"It's not like I don't in the abstract sense. On a personal level I don't have much reason to know it. I told you about my old man. He was mean as a skunk-- drunk or sober. He kept up a fine show for the folks in town, but around the house, he hit anybody who got in his way."

"No brothers or sisters?"

"Like she'd have let him touch her again. No, no family at all. I was fifteen when they got sick, both dead in a week. The place wasn't worth a lot, but I sold it. Banked the money and started trying to figure out a way to make a living. It was when I was punching for Janice's folks that I met her. One thing led to another."

"You a cowboy? I don't remember you saying that before."

"I liked the work, but I was better at something else." He rested his hand on his gun. "Janice's folks had their spread, nice sized place, but there was no way they wanted me on there. Not with them blaming me for her dying. I think they saw Grace as payment for... well what I cost them."

"How'd they come to blame you?"

"Big man like me. Little woman like Janice. The birthing maybe ripped her apart, maybe infection. I don't know. It seemed she birthed Grace all right, but something went wrong. She was dead within days. Doctor had no idea what happened."

Cord knew he'd never talked so much about his family, not to Rafe or anyone. He was generally a man who kept his past to himself. The letter though had blown that all away. He looked at it again trying to figure out what he was going to do. "I'm talking too much. Sorry I put this all on you."

"I didn't mind. What changed their mind about letting Grace come to you?"

"They both died." Cord walked to the pump at the back of the office and refilled the pot, poured the coffee grounds into the pot, and set it back on the stove. He put a piece of wood in the front of its door, feeling a chill that he wasn't sure came from the colder air moving in from the north.

"So who's bringing her?"

"From the letter it sounds like just Grace is coming."

"Who wrote you?"

"Janice's brother. I am guessing as to motives, but it looks like he wants the ranch. He doesn't want Grace."

"Damn. How old is she? On a train by herself. What was he thinking?"

"That he only cares about himself is pretty much how I see it. He always was a bastard." He walked to his desk and opened the box of cigars pulling one out. He bit off the tip and lit it. "She'd be nine now."

Rafe used a few Yaqui curses that Cord had never heard. His handsome face had grown harder than he'd ever seen. "Too bad he didn't come. We could've beaten him to a pulp."

"I'm more worried about Grace than him right now. She should be here tomorrow. What the hell am I going to do with a nine year-old girl?"

"You don't want her?" Rafe made an obvious effort to mask his disgust at such a thought.

"I want her," Cord said, drawing in the smoke from the cigar. "Just where do I have her? I sleep in the back of this office. I did buy that ranch down on the border, but it's deserted, definitely no place for a little girl. Not with Geronimo still out there. It's not like I can make a living on it yet either."

"You bought a ranch? Damn, man. You don't tell me anything."

"It was two years back when the Indian troubles were worse. Remember Jim McCloud?"

"Maybe."

"He came to town scared and mad that he'd bought the place. Came in here to accuse someone of fraud selling it to him and not telling him how unsettled it was out there in those mountains."

"He was a dove not interested in messing with hawks and eagles, I take it?"

"You and your symbolisms." Cord gave a short laugh. "Whatever he was, he wanted out, and I offered him a price I could afford, which wasn't much but he grabbed it. I've only been out there twice since I bought it. It has an adobe house, an outbuilding or two, barn, nothing fancy but not in bad shape—at least the last time I made it there. It's not as though I can afford to stock the place or be there enough, if I did, to protect it from the rustlers and Indians."

"Definitely no place for a little girl right now. Can't you rent a house in town?"

"I guess. Damn. I don't know."

"So what time she's coming in?"

"Like that son of a bitch told me anything more than when she left Kansas. Poor little kid. She's probably scared to death and blaming me. I'll have to go down to the depot and find what's likely."

"I wish I could help with a place for her, but you know how it is with my family. Seven in that one adobe. I usually sleep outside under the ramada."

"No, this is my problem." He cursed again as he scratched his unshaven jaw. "She didn't think much of me in Kansas. Not likely to be more impressed out here."

The first thing he'd have to do is get a shave and haircut. For a while a room at the hotel, he guessed. He tried to imagine what she would look like. He'd asked for a photograph, but one had never been forthcoming. He guessed she'd be the only little girl on the train—traveling alone, the only one with hate in her eyes for the father she probably saw as having deserted her. Son of a bitch all right. He couldn't deny it.

Adjusting her bonnet, Priscilla looked at herself in the mirror, as she tied the ribbon under her chin. For now, it was holding the overabundance of curls in some semblance of order.

She was excited at the prospect of Ellen finally coming home. She hoped it was to stay because since Abigail had moved to the distant Circle R, Ellen had been her best friend, someone to talk about her dreams or foolishness. When she had left for Texas to visit relatives, Priscilla feared she'd find a husband, but instead she was coming home to Tucson.

Walking down the stairs, Priscilla saw James at the front door. Under her breath she repeated some choice expressions as she saw beyond him was Martin. What was it going to take to convince that man to leave her alone?

"Again you are on your way out?" Martin asked with a sullen expression.

"I think that is obvious." She took her jacket from the coat rack.

"May I then join you?"

"Absolutely not."

James winked at her as he headed for the backdoor to get the buggy.

"You never have time for me anymore," Martin whined.

She decided she had to get this resolved. "Martin, I do not have time for you because you want more than I do in a relationship."

"I want to marry you."

"Yes, and that is never happening. Not ever never."

"Once you liked me."

She tried to think how to say—once I never knew you –

without being cruel. "I am really sorry, but if I led you to think more was going to happen, it's not."

For just a moment she saw the flicker of anger in his eyes. She wondered if she had been wrong about him, and he was more dangerous than she had assumed. If so, he suppressed the proof.

"You did lead me to think that. I think you once wanted more," he argued, modulating his tones to sound calmer than she guessed he felt. He adjusted his small tie and smoothed back his hair.

"I am sorry then. It is not going to happen, and frankly I want you to quit coming here."

"Not even as friends?"

"We are not friends, Martin."

"You nursed me when I was wounded."

Oh how she regretted that. She regretted a lot, and her guilt where it came to him was part of why she had been reluctant to dismiss him as abruptly as she had other young men, who had expected more than she had been willing to give.

"I nurse many people. That does not mean a relationship is about to happen with any. This last week it was Mrs. Gibbons. Surely you understand that to give someone care does not imply more."

He wasn't giving up, and she saw that in his eyes. She felt a little uneasy as he moved toward her. She stepped back into the kitchen where Rose was kneading bread. Martin followed.

"There a problem, Miss Wesley?" Rose asked with the manner she adopted when there was company in the house.

"Martin is just leaving, aren't you, Martin." Priscilla turned to face him and again caught the flicker of resentment in his eyes. She wanted him out of her house and life.

"I suppose so," he said again with an obvious effort to hide his emotion. Was he the man Connie Sicilla had warned her about? For the first time she took seriously that possibility. She didn't want to enrage him, but she also didn't want him back under her roof.

James walked through the backdoor stopping as he saw Martin in the kitchen. "Any problem here?" he asked his gaze going from Rose to Priscilla before settling on Martin.

"I thought I'd take Priscilla where she's going," Martin said with an irritating persistence.

"Martin is leaving."

"But I could."

"No, you could not." If this went on much longer, she'd be raising her voice. She hated yelling at anyone. He was inspiring a growing anger. Or was what she was feeling fear? She resented either possibility.

After Martin had finally gone, James continued to watch from the window. When he turned, his face wore a troubled expression. "You want me to go with you to the depot?"

She was not going to let a weakling intimidate her. "That will not be necessary. I just wish I knew what it was going to take to get him to stay away."

"I can take care of it for you if you wish," James said with a stern tone.

"I know you could, but I don't want you getting into trouble over this. I need to be sure he understands he's not welcome here. I've tried too hard to be polite because of an early mistake. It's gone too far though."

It wasn't as though Martin had done anything she could say was harassment. Nothing she could put her finger on. Still she needed to make certain that the man stayed away from her home. If that took being rude, it was just how it would have to be.

CHAPTER 4

A t the train depot, Priscilla tied the buggy's reins to the posts. She looked toward the hills when she heard the scream of a hawk. Were there more of them, or had she opened her eyes to what was around her? She frowned as she watched it circling before it flew away.

Walking toward the boardwalk, adding to her day's unease, she saw the tall marshal standing with his arms crossed over his chest. He looked both irritated and ill at ease. The irritated part was the expression she had come to expect, but the ill at ease was a surprise.

"Waiting for delivery of a prisoner?" she asked as she walked up behind him and saw him start—another surprise. Even more so that when he turned, there was a faint smile on that handsome face. Why did such an arrogant man have to be so good looking?

"And you," he asked, "a new gentleman friend coming in?"

"When I have so many here," she said realizing she was teasing and surprising herself. "Why would I need to import one?"

He shifted from one foot to the other. She realized his boots were polished, and he was wearing a white shirt with a string tie.

She'd never seen him so cleaned up. "Perhaps you're the one waiting for a lady friend," she suggested.

"Train's late." He ignored her implied question.

There were ten people waiting on the platform. "Hopefully it hasn't had trouble."

"Not that I heard. It passed through Tombstone a little late also."

That was reassuring. Before she could say more, someone came up behind her. When she turned, she found she was also edgy, hoping it wasn't Martin. She wasn't sure there was much improvement when she looked into Reverend Ryan's eyes.

"Ah Miss Wesley," he said with his formal manner. "Are your parents returning today?"

"No, they were ready to head for Florida last I heard, hoping for a warm winter and some lovely, sandy beaches."

"Oh my, alligators, swamps and such," he said with a tone of disapproval, "seems Arizona should be warm enough for them."

"My last letter said they were hoping to spend this winter in Saint Augustine."

"A Catholic community?"

"It is actually America's oldest city, and they thought the beaches might be a delightful change."

"Decadent." His smile was superior. "But of course, they'd not engage in decadence would they?"

"One could hope," she said hearing a snort from the marshal and leaving the pastor looking uncertain as to how she had meant it. It was then that she heard the train whistle. Glancing up into the marshal's face, she saw a clear look of fear before he brought down a hard expression that took it away. Who or what was coming in on that train?

When Priscilla saw Ellen walking toward her, she smiled rushing toward her for a big hug. She was shocked after the hug to realize there was a small girl at Ellen's side looking up at her with concern.

"Who is this?" she asked her friend as the marshal strode to their side.

Ellen looked at the marshal, a frown on her usually smiling face. "Marshal O'Brian, what in blue blazes were you thinking to let Grace ride this train alone?"

Priscilla looked from the little girl's nervous face to the marshal's, saw the resemblance, and realized the unthinkable. She remembered once hearing he had a daughter. She had thought that was past tense. Has. He has a daughter.

"Thank you, Miss Buchanan," he said his gaze now on the little girl.

"You are a son of a bitch," Ellen said cursing in a manner that was nothing Priscilla had ever heard from her. She stopped then and looked down at the waif at her side. "I mean not a good person."

The marshal still hadn't found the right words to say anything to his daughter. From what Priscilla could see from the look on her set little face, words probably weren't going to cut it anyway.

She watched as he swallowed hard, clenching his jaw while Ellen added a few more phrases depicting exactly what she thought of him. The few passengers disembarking watched for a few moments before they went on their way, finally leaving only the four of them standing on the platform.

"Does Grace have baggage?" Cord asked.

Ellen pointed to a small bag at her side. "Just this."

It didn't seem enough for more than a dress and nightgown. Priscilla felt her heart go out to the child, even as she felt some sympathy for the tall man, who had never before looked so ill at ease.

Grace looked at Priscilla, then back to Ellen, avoiding meeting her father's gaze. She seemed stoic about whatever her fate was about to be. What a lovely child, Priscilla thought, with those big blue eyes and the dark hair in curly ringlets that tumbled around her face.

"What do you plan to do with your daughter?" Ellen asked, not placated at all by O'Brian's obvious stress. It was clear she thought he deserved it.

"I took a hotel room," he managed. "Look, I didn't know Grace was coming until yesterday when I got the letter. I will figure out something better, but it'll take some time."

"Why doesn't Grace stay with me for a few days while you work this out?" Priscilla suggested, seeing surprise in his eyes at her offering such help.

"I..." He stopped still obviously stunned at the whole situation. If she had never expected to see the marshal discomfited, it was certainly what had happened. She felt sympathy for him, but even more for the quiet little girl who, although petite, had older eyes than her obvious years.

"Grace," Priscilla said dropping to her knees disregarding the dusty platform. "How would you like to come to my house for lunch? You and your father can both come. Ellen too. We can have a nice meal and talk about what happens next."

Grace looked at her with a thoughtful expression. "Are you sure you want me?" she asked with her first words. She had a sweet tone to her voice. In it, Priscilla heard her fear and uncertainty.

"Of course, I do. I have a lovely lady there who cooks the most wonderful meals. What kind of food do you like?"

Grace managed a smile. "I would eat whatever you give me."

Priscilla felt her heart go out to her. What kind of life had this little one known? How much of that was the fault of Cord O'Brian, who she had already found an irritating presence whenever she was near him, and now was more than ever annoyed to find herself feeling sympathy, wanting to make excuses for his obvious abandonment of this darling child. Of course, he'd abandon a child. That was exactly the kind of man she had always thought him to be.

She looked up then, saw the tightness around his mouth, pain in eyes that matched the color of Grace's. She looked back at Grace. "Would you like to do that? Come to my home and all of us have lunch together?"

"I... I'd appreciate that."

"Ellen, how about you?" she asked her friend.

"Pass up one of Rose's lunches? Not a chance." Ellen gave O'Brian one more dirty look. "I'd like to hear how this all came to pass."

Priscilla rose and dusted off her skirt, then took Grace's hand. "I have a buggy here. How about you ride with me? You and Ellen. Marshal, you do know where we live."

He nodded and squatted down to look directly into Grace's eyes. "I am glad you are here. I want you to know that. I hope..." He cleared his throat. "However it might've seemed to you before this... I am glad you are here."

As Cord stood on the platform, watching the buggy disappear, he felt like the biggest fool ever made. He had thought of his daughter more times than she'd ever know or believe now. He had no idea how he'd make this right for her. How much could a little girl understand of what he'd done and not done? He didn't even know how to talk to her.

He felt surprise at how Priscilla Wesley had taken charge of what was a terrible situation, and then smoothed it out. Her friend, Ellen Buchanan, who he'd only seen around town a few times, had been ready to have him hung. Not that he blamed her.

Priscilla is the one he would have expected to feel that way, given how little use she'd had for him. He realized he'd never known her at all. Now he was going to have to hope she could not only help him with his daughter but also help him find the way to explain to her what had happened. How could he do that without throwing blame onto the only parents Grace had ever known?

He swung into his saddle realizing he hadn't even thought how he'd have gotten Grace to the hotel. Some father he was. Well biology didn't make a man much of a father. He knew that through his own experience.

He nudged his gelding into a slow trot even as he realized how much he was dreading reaching the Wesley house. Damn, what kind of coward was he? He could face down a gun, but that little girl had him scared to death. By the time he reached the house, the women and child had gone in, but James was waiting for him.

"Take your horse, Marshal?" the hired man asked with a friendly smile.

Cord leaned over the pommel looking down at the hired man. "I'm thinking."

James Redman laughed. "It's a tough one, ain't it?"

Cord sucked in a breath. "Nothing I don't deserve."

"I don't know much about this. What's going on, but Rose said it'll be awhile afore lunch. Might be a good idea to give the ladies a little time to settle in."

"Right now about everything I've had has been a bad idea," Cord said swinging out of the saddle but not taking a step toward the house. He reached into his shirt pocket and took out the tobacco pouch to roll a cigarette. "Want one," he asked.

Redman smiled. "Never picked up the habit."

"Smart man." Cord flicked a match with his thumb and lit the cigarette. "Bad habit."

Redman leaned back against the rail. "Guessing by you showing up that the little one relates to you."

Cord drew in on the cigarette. "My daughter."

"Never knew you had one."

"It's a long story." Cord tied the reins to Jeb over the rail as he leaned on it smoking. "None of the blame for this is going to be something I don't deserve."

"Man can only run so long," Redman said.

"I didn't know I was but maybe so." He looked toward the house as he smoked. "I do know I did wrong here. I thought it was the right thing but maybe it was just the easy way."

"Can't never do anything but start from today."

"You ever have any children, Mr. Redman?" He drew deeply on the cigarette. It wasn't helping.

"No sir, Marshal, never got blessed that way. Not that Rose and me didn't want them. Just never happened, and call me James."

Cord couldn't explain what had happened, his choices, shouldn't even try with the hired man, but something about the unwavering older man, his cool blue eyes made him want to try.

"I thought I was doing the right thing for Grace."

"Pretty name for a pretty little gal."

"Her mother was beautiful. She died right after Grace was born. Her parents... well they blamed me for it. I had no place to take a baby. I was almost twenty-three no job, no real idea what I wanted or could do. It sounds pathetic to me now, hearing me say that. I'd kick a man from here to sundown trying to tell me the same useless reasons."

Redman smiled. "You can only start from here."

"I have no idea how."

"Trust Miss Wesley. She's got a way about her."

Cord looked at him with surprise. About all he'd had from Priscilla Wesley had been putdowns. Truth was, other than finding her maddeningly attractive, he hadn't known much about who she was. When he didn't say anything, Redman said, "Women got a way about such things. Men not so much. We can learn too though."

"If Grace'll give me a chance. I wouldn't blame her if she

didn't." Cord threw his cigarette to the dust and ground it out with his boot. "Guess I better go in."

"Might be it'd help some if you took off your gun," the hired man suggested.

Cord thought about it for a long moment. "There's not much choice for me in wearing one right now, James. It's not just part of my wardrobe but my job."

"Guns scare some folks—especially those not used to them."

"I don't know much about what Grace is used to. I don't know my daughter at all, but if she's going to accept me. I won't hold it against her if she can't. If she does, it'll have to be the whole package."

"All right then. They're in the kitchen. That's where Miss Wesley said to tell you to come."

If he had been facing a gunman in that house, Cord would have gone in with less trepidation. Knocking on the door, the hired man at his side, Cord heard steps. Rose Redman opened it without a smile. "Marshal," she said, "come on in."

He looked beyond to see Grace at the table drinking a glass of milk. Ellen and Priscilla were sitting with their backs to him but turned as he entered. "Stew will be ready in a few minutes," Rose said as she ushered him in.

"Not real hungry to be honest," he said knowing he couldn't swallow food if his life depended on it. Ellen's glare was as intense as at the depot. He couldn't read the expression on Priscilla Wesley's face. He wished he had words to cover this, but words had never been his strong suit. He was out of his element in this kitchen, with these women, but he owed Grace more than he'd given her. So he'd stick it out.

"Marshal," Priscilla said rising, "how about if you and I talk for a moment in the parlor while lunch is being readied." When he showed his doubt, she added, "Ellen and Rose will stay with Grace. He nodded and followed her through the door.

The Wesley house was finely furnished with what looked to

be expensive furnishings. The only time he'd been there was to question Martin Matthews, and then it was not into the parlor where he was being taken now. She waved him to a chair.

"Would you like a brandy?" she asked, a softness in her voice he'd never heard from her until she had used it on Grace.

He sighed and slumped into a chair. "I'd appreciate that a lot, Miss Wesley."

"I think it's time you called me Priscilla. I suspect we are going to see a bit of each other for a while." She went to the sideboard and opening the cupboard brought out a glass decanter, pouring him a generous serving before handing him the glass.

"What do you mean?" He was grateful for the bite of the liquor with the first sip.

"I think Grace should stay with me for now. Before you argue with me about it, I have the space. Rose will be wonderful with her. Although my experience with children is a bit limited, I think I can make her comfortable while you figure out more permanent living quarters."

"I wasn't going to argue. I... You are right. I know she's scared to death of me. See it in her eyes. If you are willing to have her stay here for awhile, I am sure it'd reassure her."

"I know you and Grace need help right now. I only hope I am the one who can give it to you both."

"I suppose you wonder why she wasn't with me," he said after another sip of the brandy.

"Does Grace know the reason?"

"Probably not." He told her the gist of what had happened and why he'd done what he had. "Now I think what a fool I was, but I told myself I was doing what was best for Grace."

"You never remarried?"

He shook his head. "I didn't have time to even think about that. My life hasn't been one making a family that feasible. Maybe I should have but... well by then Grace was settled, or so I thought. The Robinsons had a nice ranch, good place for raising a child. It might be hard to believe now, but I thought I was doing right by her." Even to himself it sounded like trying to justify what was unjustifiable.

He stared into the liquor. "I wasn't there for her. I look at it now and think I should have stayed closer, found a way. The jobs of sheriff and then deputy took me farther and farther west, farther from her. Damn, I'm talking too much. The truth is although a day never went by that I didn't think about her, I didn't expect I'd see her again... not until I got the letter."

"Her grandparents just pushed her out?" Her voice showed her horror at the idea.

He shook his head and finished the brandy in a large swig. "According to the letter, they both died. Close together. He had a bad accident, couldn't heal from it. Maybe the nursing wore her out. Aaron, my wife's brother, he didn't want Grace to stay there. Wanted the ranch, I guess without any strings. He wrote and said she was on the way." He tried to suppress his anger but found it impossible. "He could have given me a chance to go back there. Maybe he thought I wouldn't do it, that I wouldn't want her."

"Do you?"

"I want her. I just don't know how to make it work for her... and I am a deputy marshal. I sleep in the back of the office. My life is as uncertain as it was." He let out a breath and stared at the dark fireplace.

"No prospects for a wife?" He looked at her in surprise and then realized she was teasing.

"You offering?" he asked seeing he had surprised her with his light response. She obviously didn't expect much from him, which made it all the more amazing that she had offered to help him. He supposed though that was more for his daughter.

"Not that I felt that was a serious offer," she said with a small smile, "but I am not interested in marriage. There are other young ladies in Tucson."

"Well your friend, Miss Buchanan, looks like she'd kill me before she'd marry me. Maybe we better scratch that idea."

"Then my offer to let her stay here appears to be the best you are likely to get. For a while don't worry about it. Let her settle in. I have a very nice room up near my bedroom. I can get her some toys."

"I'd like doing that."

"All right, then you do that. And some clothes too. She doesn't have much."

"I'd also like to go back and beat Aaron to a pulp."

"I doubt it'd help much to gain Grace's trust," she snapped.

"Make me feel a hell of a lot better though."

"For a few minutes until the pain began."

"All right, we're in agreement that if Grace agrees, she will stay with you, and I guess I can visit, get to know her?"

"That would be my suggestion. You know Christmas isn't far off."

That was a holiday Cord rarely if ever thought about. It meant a few more drunks in the bars. Otherwise, it wasn't anything he had celebrated for years—if ever. It meant-- Santa Claus? He remembered sarcastically asking Priscilla Wesley if she believed in that personage. He wondered now if Grace did. Hellfire, he was so far out of his depth that he couldn't see how he could get to the surface. He rose and walked over to the fireplace staring blankly into its darkness.

Priscilla came to stand beside him reaching out to touch his arm. "It will just take time. Actually the holidays might be a good time for you with her. It's fun to put up a tree, decorate a bit, attend church, sing carols, give presents, have a wonderful Christmas dinner—which is Rose's forte. It will be a time to ease yourself into what she's like, who she is."

He whistled low as he met her gaze. "Can I take notes? I have to admit I know nothing about any of that. My world... well it's not the same as yours."

"Well, I think you better let it be for now, as you give Grace a chance to adjust to you. As much as you don't know her. She doesn't know you either."

"And what she does know has to be pretty bad given how Janice's parents felt about me."

"Well that will all change now—slowly."

He surprised himself by his urge to reach out and take her into his arms. He resisted the impulse. He realized this was going to be a test of his willpower to be close to this woman, as he got close to his daughter. He'd always found her physically attractive, challenging, but now he saw there was another side. Geesus.

Before he could say more or even think of what to say, Rose came to the door. "Lunch is ready. You two ready for it?"

"Grace is hungry now?"

"Yes, she is."

Priscilla smiled. "Maybe you can eat now too, Marshal?"

He was surprised to realize he was hungry. Although he knew it wasn't going to be easy conversation around the table, he was ready to give it a try.

As he followed the two women to the kitchen, he thought getting to know Priscilla Wesley was going to be as hard on him as trying to make peace with his daughter. He wondered if he was up to any of it.

CHAPTER 5

When Cord returned to his office, he felt drained. The lunch had been as taxing he had expected. Now and then, he had caught Grace watching him, before quickly casting her eyes elsewhere as soon as he looked at her. Fortunately she had accepted Priscilla's invitation without question. He supposed it was a relief instead of being stuck with the big bad man. He wondered if he could ever get her to see him any other way. To be honest, maybe he was the big bad man. He was beginning to wonder about that himself.

Rafe came out from the back. "How'd it go?" he asked.

"About like you'd expect." Outside he could hear the rain starting. The desert was beginning to take on the unique smell it had with the first rain after a dry spell. Inside, he heard Jesse Bailey whining from the jail cell. He opened the door and walked into the cell area. "Jesse," he said, his arms crossed over his chest as he studied the surly youth, "you have to get it together, or it's going to be the coroner with your next stop."

"You can't scare me."

"I'm not trying to scare you. I'm trying to tell you where your life is heading."

"You can't hold me here. I'm sober. You got no right to keep me."

"Oh, I could keep you. Ridge said he will bring charges if I want."

"So," he muttered.

"The courts have better things to do than mess with you. You had fifty bucks on you. God only knows where you got it, but it'll cover the damages Ridge figures you racked up over there."

"Blackmail?"

"A fact."

"All right. Keep it. I can get more."

Cord shook his head but unlocked the cell. When they walked back into the office, he gave Jesse a paper to sign turning over the money to Ridge, before he handed him his holster, gun and hat.

Jesse checked the gun before he buckled the belt around his waist. "It's not loaded."

"The shells are in your cartridge belt. The gun stays unloaded until you are out of town. I don't want to see you here for a few weeks-- and when I do, you better be sober."

"You think you're so tough," the youth sneered.

"You better worry more about you than me. Now get out of here."

After he had stomped out, Rafe observed, "He's going to end up dead before he turns twenty."

"Most likely." Cord sat in his chair looking at the mail and hoping more bad news wasn't coming.

"You know he's trouble." Rafe wasn't letting it go.

Cord slit open a letter. "Yes, but mostly to himself. He's got in mind a rep right now. He thinks he can be famous, and I guess he's had nothing in his life worthwhile otherwise."

"Thinks he's Billy the Kid," Rafe said with disgust as he slumped into the chair in front of the desk.

"You only get that reputation after you're dead." Cord slit open another letter.

"Good news or bad?"

"Neither. Politics. Damn I hate politics."

"What do they want now?"

"Warrants for Gabe Evans with some questions about some missing cattle." He hesitated a moment. "And one for Ben Albright."

"Dios, you ever seen Albright?"

Cord nodded. "He's a big man all right."

"Big? He's a giant. He must weigh three hundred pounds. Most of it's not fat, and well, you know that he's not right in the head. What's he wanted for?"

"It appears he did a job for which he claimed he was not paid. The disagreement escalated, as you might imagine, to charges of assault and attempted murder." He threw the warrants across the table for Rafe to scan.

"Overreach. I don't have much use for the jasper making the charges either," he said when he'd finished reading the particulars.

"He's got clout."

"I love justice." Rafe's smile was sardonic.

"Have you seen Ben recently?"

Rafe nodded with a smile. "The usual place."

"I was hoping he wasn't."

Rafe chuckled. "What's the other letter? More good news?"

"Better. Complaint about me demanding I deliver a written explanation for why I hit Clinton Adams."

"That scum dared make a complaint."

"So it appears. Have I mentioned I am coming to hate this job?"

"A time or two. So what are you going to do about your daughter?"

"She's going to stay with Miss Wesley as I work out something I *can* do."

"Wow, how'd she come into this?"

He described the scene as the train came in. "I swear that if Ellen Buchanan had been carrying a gun, she'd have shot me on the spot. She was mad enough to do it."

Rafe laughed again. "She's a spitfire all right. Cute little nose and bright blue eyes."

"You've been watching some."

Rafe grinned. "Some. She's pretty."

"That I didn't notice."

"Nah, you were too busy looking at Miss Wesley."

"I was more interested in the fear of me that I saw in my daughter's eyes."

"Yeah right. You do look like a bad man—with a badge." He chuckled. "She'll get used to you. And as for Miss Wesley. I've seen how you look at that woman."

"She's out of my league, even if I had such a dim-witted notion. You know how many men are courting her?"

"At one time or another, most eligible men in Tucson, but she's not giving any the time of day now is she?"

"I wouldn't know." Cord did know. He had kept track and was irked that he knew anything about her doings. To avoid being within fifty feet of her, he'd gone out of his way and now he'd be in her home or not seeing his daughter. Then he wondered again how long it'd take to win Grace's trust. If he even could.

"So what do we do about Albright?" Rafe asked taking him back to his other immediate problem.

"Where exactly did you last see him?" Cord asked without much enthusiasm, as he lit a cigar and watched the smoke curl toward the ceiling.

"Well yesterday it was Trask's place. I think it's where he hangs out."

"Evans with him?"

"Not hardly. Evans works out at Wright's ranch."

This was getting better and better. One man with a mind more like a child than the full-sized man he was—more than full-sized—who would beat him to a pulp if he didn't approach this carefully, and the other would be backed by Wright's crew.

Evans was most likely involved with the rustling that the warrant suggested, with the probability Wright was also. With the rancher's contributions to the political system, he'd be a lot harder to touch. More importantly, he would protect Evans.

He crushed out his cigar and with a humorless smile looked up at Rafe. "So where shall we start?"

~

Priscilla walked downstairs wondering how well Grace had slept. She had peeked in a few times to see the child sleeping what appeared to be soundly. She hoped that meant they were off to a good start with her finding this home to be comfortable. In the kitchen Rose was beating up batter for pancakes. Outside the skies had cleared after an overnight rain. On the distant mountains, she could see more fresh snow etching the highest points.

"How are you this morning?" Priscilla asked as she poured herself some coffee and sat at the table.

"Slept a little restless. And you?" Rose joined her at the table.

"I checked on Grace a few times. She seemed to sleep soundly at least, but she's such a quiet little thing that it's hard to tell what she's feeling."

"James said there was trouble in town last night."

Priscilla felt a chill. Trouble usually involved the marshal. She hoped she wasn't going to start feeling fear every time she heard of such, accompanied by fear for a man who should not be entering her thoughts. A man she certainly didn't want to dream about even though last night he'd invaded her dreams with a surety that left her waking half mad and unsure at what. She took a sip of coffee before she asked what had happened.

"The marshal arrested Ben Albright. It didn't go down easy."

"Good Lord. Is it the same man who helped James build our tool shed? He's huge."

"Yes, ma'am, the very same one."

"Ben is more like a child than a man. What could he have done? And uh... what did you mean about not going down easy?"

Before Rose could answer, Grace came in the door. "Good morning," Priscilla said as the little girl sat at the table without a word.

"You hungry this morning?" Rose asked her. "I am planning pancakes. Do you like them?"

"It'd be fine," Grace said quietly.

"If you don't like something, it's all right to say so," Priscilla said smiling at her.

"Really? I thought..." Grace stopped and didn't say more.

"Well, so do you like them, or would you prefer say scrambled eggs? Toast? Fruit? I think we have some apples still stored."

Grace looked around the kitchen. "Is... he here?"

"You mean your father?" Priscilla asked.

She nodded.

"No, he's busy at work today." She hoped that didn't mean beaten to a pulp-- but since she had had no chance to find out the result of arresting big Ben, she wasn't sure about that. She knew Ben was a little retarded, not understanding as others did. She hoped nobody had been seriously hurt—most especially not the arrogant marshal. Of course, that was all for Grace's sake.

"Well then," Grace said with a little smile. "Pancakes would be very nice. Do you have syrup?"

"Of course, what are hotcakes without syrup?" Rose asked as she rose to head for the stove.

"Grace, today I thought we'd do some shopping," Priscilla said. "Would you like that?"

The little girl considered a moment as Rose put a glass of milk in front of her. "I don't have any money."

"Well I do, and I'd love to buy a little girl some clothes. Such fun. Maybe we can drop by and see your father and his office."

"Would we have to?" Her lips turned down.

Priscilla decided she would have to address this situation directly. "Grace, do you actually know your father?"

"No." Her voice was barely audible.

"Then perhaps you should get to know him before you decide if you'd like him or not." She knew she certainly hadn't known him either, not until she saw the other side—the one of humility and sorrow. She'd never expected to feel pity for him, but she had —for him and his daughter.

"Grandpa said..." Grace stopped and looked down at the table.

"Maybe your grandpa didn't know him too well either. How about if you give it a chance."

"He scares me."

"I think that's coming from your grandparents, not your father. Since you don't know him yet, you can't be scared of what you don't know, can you?"

Grace shook her head but clearly wasn't sure. Priscilla decided a distraction would be a good idea to give her time to think about it. "I am thinking also that we need to look into you attending school here. What grade were you in?"

"We didn't have grades. We just did the work, and the teacher let us do whatever we could."

"Do you like to read?"

"When I can." Her eyes showed more interest in this than any topic Priscilla had yet tried.

"I have a few books here in the house that might interest you. Have you read *Little Women*?"

Grace shook her head.

"Well, how about *The Adventures of Tom Sawyer*?"

"We didn't have very many books. I read what the school had, but they were mostly primers," Grace said finally as the cakes were put in front of her, rich with butter and a pitcher of syrup set alongside them. She dug heartily into them as Priscilla tried to think who would know good books for children her age.

"As it turns out," she said as she refilled her coffee cup. "We are in luck because a few years ago we got our first library. It has a children's section-- so you and I can check that out today also."

"What would you like for breakfast, Cilla?" Grace asked as James walked in the backdoor.

What she was thinking she wanted was more information regarding what had happened when Cord arrested Ben Albright, but with Grace sitting eating and hearing everything said, she would have to wait for that. The next thing she wondered is why she cared what had happened to the marshal. Her interest was beginning to worry her. With his daughter at the house, this was going to get more complicated. Avoiding him would be impossible. Disliking him before had been easy. She was beginning to see it might not be so easy once she actually got to know him.

When Grace had finished eating and gone upstairs to dress, Priscilla found an opportunity to ask James what happened. He laughed. "I gotta say I like that marshal. He has a way of getting things done without using a gun."

"You saw it?"

He nodded. "Went down for a beer and just happened to be there."

"There was a fight?"

"Well there was some of that," James said pouring himself another cup of coffee. "He walked into the bar where Ben was standing drinking a whiskey—other end from me. He ordered one too and looked at Ben with one of those looks. You know the ones he can give."

She did know that.

"And then he said, 'you know what I'm here for.' Ben nodded. 'I didn't do nothin' wrong,' he said. Then the marshal said, 'You won't mind coming with me then to answer some questions.' 'Ain't going with you,' Ben said. 'You are," Marshal said. 'Easy or otherwise.' Ben just looked at him. "How you going to make me? In a fight?' he asked with an odd little laugh, like he didn't believe it. 'Don't need to,' Marshal said with that smile of his. That was when Rafe came up behind Ben and poked a gun in his back."

"That was it?" she asked a little surprised there wasn't more trouble than that considering what Rose had said.

"Well not exactly. Ben reached out with that big fist of his, landed it on the marshal's jaw but O'Brian ducked back and then came in low, his fist landed square in Ben's stomach before he gave him an uppercut that even raised Ben off his feet. Turns out I guess Ben has a glass jaw."

"What does that mean?"

"Hit him on the jaw, and he's out for the count. They carried him back to the jail. Ben was likely some riled when he came to, but he's in jail and reckon those bars will hold him."

"So Cord wasn't hurt?" she asked before she realized she'd used his first name, and it was too late. James just gave her a look. "Well his jaw was cut, bruised, a little swollen. God almighty, nobody can take a punch from Ben without some results."

"Have you heard why they had a warrant for Ben? I can't believe he'd do anything dishonest. He seems... well too childlike actually for that."

"Nope, but I suspect you will find out."

"I will?"

"Knowing you, you will." James grinned.

Cord sat at his desk struggling with pen and paper to explain his actions regarding Clinton Adams. The demand had come from the United States Marshal's office. He needed to find the right words for what seemed to him a straightforward approach to a man who had not only resisted arrest but brandished a shotgun. Was he supposed to let Adams shoot him and ask questions later? Admittedly he had lost his temper at being threatened and insulted. That would not find its way into his report because he had not let his temper get the better of his actions. He had done the minimum required to subdue and arrest the man without ending up dead.

He understood his boss's problem as his position was appointive, depended on the party in power in Washington, and could easily turn tenuous even with his party still running things. So what report would help both the marshal in Prescott and himself down here? He might someday face Adams again, where the results could turn even more deadly than one ending with the shotgun broken and Adams' face bearing a few bruises. Not like he broke his nose. Although that had been tempting. No, he had not gone too far. Would words make that clear?

When the office door opened, he looked up with a glower at being interrupted only to see two beautiful faces. One his daughter and the other the woman who had invaded his dreams the night before. For that matter who had been invading his dreams in sexier and sexier ways. He suppressed a smile wondering what she'd think if she knew any of what he was thinking. Likely she'd be bringing some charges of her own against the deputy marshal she made no secret of despising. This begged the question of why she was helping him with something that would have been a lot worse if she hadn't stepped into it.

"Good morning, Marshal," Priscilla said with that faint Southern drawl.

"Good morning, ladies." He rose, looking at his daughter and hoping for a smile. The best he got this time was at least she met his gaze.

"We've come to visit so Grace can see what you do all day."

"Ah and today you find me writing reports."

"So it's not all shoot and fight," Priscilla teased.

"Only on even days." He worked to match her light tone.

"How lucky we catch you on a writing day."

"So what have you been up to?"

"We visited the store and bought. What did we buy, Grace?"

The little girl looked up at her with a smile. "Two new dresses, a coat, hat, petticoats, and new shoes."

"And one other thing," Priscilla prodded.

"A doll." This time her smile was wider. "It's in a box with a beautiful dress."

"What color was her hair?" Cord asked hoping he could get Grace to smile for him. It didn't work.

"Her hair was blonde." She did meet his gaze again.

"They offered black, red, and blonde," Priscilla added. "Grace made the choice."

"I wanted it her look like you and Ellen," she said again looking up at her benefactress.

"Have you named her yet?" Cord asked trying to find something that would win a smile.

Grace shook her head.

"We thought that Rose might make her some dresses, and there might even be more dolls at Christmas from Santa," Priscilla said.

"There is no such thing as Santa," Grace said looking down. "It's a myth."

"How do you know that?" Cord asked hoping he wouldn't kill the conversation. He liked listening to his daughter talk. She seemed to have a fine vocabulary when she chose to use it.

She looked up at him. "He never gave me anything. So if there was, he didn't like me much. I was... maybe too bad."

He didn't like hearing that and sucked in a breath. He wondered what kind of life Grace had had with the Robinsons. He had thought good and safe, but was there something else there that he had not seen? God, he hoped it wasn't a secret like about his own father, who had brutalized his mother and him.

"I was told that you have Ben Albright in your prison here," Priscilla said in crisp, clearly disapproving tones.

"It's a jail, Miss Wesley, and yes, I do. As well as Gabe Evans."

"I cannot believe Ben did anything to deserve imprisonment. What are you holding him for?"

Well this was the usual from her. Nothing he did was apt to please her. Although where it came to Ben Albright, he tended to agree with her. "It was a warrant issued from Prescott. A federal warrant. I have no options on whether I serve those. You might be interested that Gabe Evans is likewise here on such a warrant. They will be transferred to Prescott tomorrow."

"I would rather that Ben not be transferred."

She was such an uppity little thing. With such beauty and seeming delicacy, he'd yet to find a time she didn't come straight at him with what she thought and expected. To the manner born. Although in her case it was likewise to the manor.

"You might discuss that with Judge Emerson. I suppose he could override such an order. He wasn't too pleased with the outcome of some of the federal trials up there."

"I will do that. May I talk to Ben about what happened?"

Although he wasn't overly pleased that would also put her in sight of Evans, who he trusted about as far as he could throw him, he had no real reason to deny her request.

"Perhaps you can show Grace around your office," she suggested as he opened the door for her to go into the back room.

"Not a lot to show but sure."

When he turned back, his daughter was watching him with a somber expression. "What are the pictures on the wall?" she asked.

He looked at the wanted posters and led her over to them. "These are all people who have done something that a judge wants to talk to them about."

"It says wanted."

"Well sometimes the people don't want to talk to the judge."

"Are there any women?"

"Sometimes but mostly men."

"And then you are the one who makes them?"

"When I am asked, yes."

She was silent a moment. "And that's dangerous?"

"Generally not." It wouldn't be fair to leave it at that. "It can be, of course."

"Do you use that gun when you do it?" She pointed to the six-shooter on his hip.

"I prefer not to, but if I need to, then yes, I might use that too."

"Grandpa didn't like guns. He said..." She stopped and didn't finish.

"It's all right to say what he told you," he reassured her. "I won't get mad."

"Well he said you were a gunman, a legal killer. That you liked to kill people."

"Sometimes people are wrong about things. I am not a gunman. But as a deputy marshal, a gun is sometimes part of my job."

"You do wear it all the time."

He smiled at that. She was certainly an observative little thing. He guessed James had been right that first day at the Wesley house. He should have left on his saddle horn. He had wanted her to understand who he was, but likely what she understood already was more about the gun than the job. "I don't wear it to sleep," he said wondering if that would reassure her. Probably not, especially if she knew he did usually have it beside his bed or under his pillow. What could a child understand of enemies?

"What did you do today besides shop?" he asked hoping to lead the conversation in more peaceful directions.

"We visited the library," Grace said still staring at the wanted posters. "That man looks pretty mean."

He looked at the image. "That one is mean."

"Might he be around here?"

"If I saw him, he wouldn't be. I suspect he's long gone. Did you like the library?"

"It was nice. It had a lot of books."

He wondered if his life would ever give him time to enjoy reading again. There had been a time when he had read a lot, set himself to reading all the classics. Now all he read were those wanted posters, orders to do something, warrants, and the reports he received as well as the ones he had to write. How much of anything did he do because he wanted to? Did he even know what he wanted anymore?

Priscilla came back through the door. "Ben said he's innocent," she said without preamble.

"Most men in a jail say that."

"I believe him. It sounds like a misunderstanding."

"Other than the broken arm part, you mean?"

"A man has to defend himself."

"Some people are more dangerous to defend yourself against than others."

"And that would be Mr. Presley, who had him work for him and then denied him pay."

"You know him?"

"A lawyer if I recall in Phoenix."

"Exactly. And he had important friends in the court system. He didn't take well to the injury."

"Which he deserved for cheating." He suppressed the smile. She was quite the spitfire herself when she got started. He well recalled her many times of putting him down. He supposed he was about to experience yet another of them.

"Isn't there anything I can do for him?" she asked.

"If Judge Emerson blocked his move to Prescott... denied

federal court jurisdiction, and levied a fine, possibly it might be the end of it on the federal side." He knew he could get in trouble for saying any of that but it wasn't as though he wanted Ben put in the federal prison system for what likely was unfairness. Worse would be if they decided he needed to be put into one of the mental hospitals that were warehouses not treatment centers.

"You think he might do any of that?"

"It's possible."

"Well then I will find out about that," Priscilla said with a wide smile. "So you won't object if such a thing should come to pass."

"Not me."

If he hadn't known better, he'd have taken those beautiful lips to have softened with a flirty smile. That look in her eyes seemed to be saying things not meant for him, other than possibly how she handled all men—wrapping them around her delicate little finger.

"Well what about another idea of mine. Will you object to that?"

"I am always cautious when I hear that kind of proposal without specifics. What kind of idea?"

"Grace and I were on our way to lunch at the Palace. Will you join us?"

He considered thoughtfully for a moment. "I wish I could, but unfortunately I have processes and writs to serve." And a warrant if Blake Johnson was home.

"Ah more abuses of the law?" she asked with a smile.

"Depends on who is being served as to who gets abused." With that teasing expression still on her face, he felt tempted to give her the kiss for which she seemed to be asking. Stupid thought. That was one thing he'd never be doing—kissing the beautiful Miss Wesley.

"I will forgive you for not joining us," she said, "if you will come to dinner Friday night."

He knew part of having Grace at her home was to allow him gradual access to her life, but dinner at Priscilla's home. That was a step beyond what he'd planned.

"There is a catch, of course," she said.

He snorted. There usually was. He looked down at Grace who was looking from one of them to another. "You know what it is?" he asked the little girl. She shook her head.

"So what is the catch?" he asked wondering if it meant he'd have to put up with Martin Matthews company for an evening.

"James was supposed to go to the mountains and cut a Christmas tree, but he's got another bout of his lumbago. I hate to ask him to do it. Do you suppose you could? We'd decorate it then after dinner."

He'd seen Christmas trees but hadn't ever cut one, or thought of decorating one. With the holiday so close, he supposed he should have expected this, but he had not. It wasn't that he couldn't do it. It would take half a day, but he knew areas where the right size pine could most likely be found. Finally he nodded. "How tall?" He felt as though his fate was sealed.

CHAPTER 6

"You're doing what?" Rafe asked with a laugh.

"You heard me and don't bother making jokes."

"No jokes but come on. Geronimo is supposedly signing a peace treaty soon, but he hasn't yet. There are always renegade bands just looking for easy pickings."

"I am not easy pickings."

"Give me a chance to adjust to this." Rafe chuckled again and leaned back on two legs of his chair. "You are going out Old Spanish Trail then up in the Rincons to cut a Christmas tree?"

"What? You heathens don't cut trees?" Cord asked finding an old scarf to wrap around his neck and cover his ears if it got too cold. Where the desert floor wasn't too bad in December, if he had to go above four thousand feet, there'd likely be snow. As he remembered it, there was a slot canyon where pines grew of the right size. It's where he'd head, hoping he could avoid going higher.

"When we cut a tree, it's to build a home. Hell, we even revere flowers as sacred. A tree oughta be more so." His smile said he took none of it seriously.

"Well it'll be decorated up real pretty until it gets cut up and burned in a fire. That seems special to me."

"Want me to go with you?"

"For what, to laugh? No, I want you to stay here and keep an eye on the town. Sheriff Adams is out of sight again, most likely drunk in the backroom of a bar somewhere or maybe in one of the girls' rooms. Whatever the case and wherever he is, he's not answering to anything."

"No surprise in that. Why doesn't the damn town get rid of him?"

Cord shrugged as he buttoned his coat. Outside the drizzle was cold. Any direction he went, this wasn't going to be much fun. Usually, when he got stuck with such hunts they were to go after a bad guy. Who'd have figured it'd be to chop down a six or seven foot pine.

"All right, I'll do it, but I'd rather ride into the mountains and let you stay here and look after town," Rafe protested one last time.

"And have you feel you had damaged some ancestor's special something? Not a chance."

"We could both go."

"I told you why we won't."

"Are they picking up Evans today?"

"Supposedly but that was supposedly yesterday too."

"I gotta admit I'm glad your girlfriend got Ben off the hook."

"She's not my girlfriend, not my friend, and yes, I am too. Judge Emerson was still chuckling as he delivered the orders."

"She has a way about her."

"The kicker was she's hiring Ben, which will work fine so long as he doesn't drink."

"James'll keep an eye on him. He likes James. He likes Miss Wesley even more."

"Hopefully it'll work out for them all." He had a few reservations mostly connected to his jaw, which had almost gone back to normal, but still hurt when he bit down wrong on something.

"Well watch out up there. See you tonight."

As Cord rode up into the hills to the south of Tucson, he appreciated once again the beauty of this country. The lower elevations were covered with multiple kinds of cactus with the mightiest being the saguaro. Then came the ocotillo and prickly pear until finally he would see the start of junipers. The line above that would be pine. The air was cold but no snow falling. In the valley, the rain had stopped with patches of clearing sky. The air wasn't much above freezing.

Time away from town and so many people with so many expectations, he had time to think about his daughter. He'd had a few hours now near her to understand how deprived she had been. He wished he had understood that earlier. It was no wonder she was so quiet, although under Priscilla's loving touch, she was beginning to talk more and even smile.

Whatever he had thought he knew about Priscilla Wesley, it was nothing to the reality. She was a beautiful woman, which was the obvious part. What he hadn't realized was what a caring person she had been to so many people. It seemed now he was told something new and good about her from someone else where maybe he'd heard it before but ignored it. Oh, he had gotten the barbs but even that now made him smile. She certainly had a quick wit. Many of the barbs she had sent his way had been to protect someone else.

His normally steady footed gelding slipped a little on the first of the ice but secured his footing, and they kept climbing. Cord needed to be paying more attention to the hazards underfoot. His mind was not on the mountain.

The last time he had dropped by Priscilla's to tell her that he would be getting the tree the next day, she had smiled as she opened the door-- but then he had seen Richard Wright in the parlor. Grace had been out in the kitchen with Rose, which meant Wright had been there to see Priscilla. Not that it was any of his business.

The cattleman was not as tall as Cord, but he was handsome in that smooth featured way women favored over Cord's own more rugged features. The slick rancher probably also knew all the right words. Cord hadn't waited around to hear any of them. If Priscilla had not invited Wright to be there, she gave no hint of how she felt about his presence. She had told Cord where his daughter was but had not come into the kitchen to be with them until ten minutes later. Long enough for a good-bye kiss—more than a few. Certainly it was her right—not like he had any rights where she was concerned.

Why it should bother him was part of what kept him from putting his mind on the trail or surroundings. Obviously a rich cattleman's son was the perfect suitor for a rich banker's daughter. The rumors, about rustling being part of Wright's fortune, were so far unproven allegations by small ranchers with reason to be jealous.

As Jeb worked his way past the big boulders, Cord forced his attention onto the uneven trail. When he finally saw the cut in the mountain, that indicated the canyon for which he was looking, he was feeling the cold clear through to his bones. Hard to believe getting a Christmas tree could be that much of a struggle. No wonder so many people bought them.

Once he entered the little canyon, he let Jeb pick his way up the creek bottom until he saw the first pines. Since this was going to be Grace's first Christmas tree, it had to be as perfect as he could find. Snowflakes were now falling more heavily, and he pulled the thin scarf up around his ears.

A nearly seven-foot pine stood right beyond the edge of a small creek. Snow frosted its branches and as Cord dismounted, he circled it, deciding it was even with nicely shaped branches. He pulled the small axe from the saddle bags. The sound of the axe striking was the only noise in the canyon. If there were any Apaches around, they would definitely hear the sound, but he wasn't sure they'd care. The likelihood of them being nearby was even less.

As the pine fell, he thought about the beliefs of his Yaqui partner about flowers and the spirit in all things. "Thank you for your sacrifice, brother," he said feeling a little silly, but something about saying it felt right.

He pulled the rope off his saddle and tied one end to the pine's trunk, the other to the pommel. He let Jeb sniff of the tree, feel the rope as it tightened a bit at his side before he stepped into the saddle. "Easy, boy," he said with a soothing tone. "This isn't a bad guy."

Slowly, they made their way back down the canyon. The gelding kept a steady pace, not bothered by what he was dragging. Cord could only hope being dragged wouldn't break off branches and ruin the symmetry, but at this point he was cold enough that he was heading down one way or the other.

Almost out of the snow, he saw two men heading toward him. Pulling his coat up a little, he loosened his gun in its holster until he saw they were Pimas. He pulled up Jeb as they came abreast.

"Good day," he said unsure if they would speak English as some did.

"You marshal?" one asked.

"From Tucson," he said nodding.

The man pointed toward the tree. "Got enemy today?" He chuckled.

Cord smiled. "Christmas tree," he said, "for my daughter." He was amazed how good that sounded. A daughter who was no longer part of his past, but a small girl back in Tucson, one who might or might not approve the tree.

"Good job," the bigger of the two said as they raised their hands in the peace sign before heading up the mountain. Cord wondered if they had a purpose like his-- and if not, what they could want up there. He was cold enough not to put much thought into figuring out the answer. A lot of things in life had no answer.

"Cord, it's perfect," Priscilla said as she came out into the yard between house and barn to see the tree.

"I hope so," he said dismounting, shivering some even though it was a lot warmer down in the valley than where he'd been. "Do I need to put some kind of base onto it?"

James had come out of the small shed with Ben Albright behind him. "No need, I can do it. Looks like a fine big tree."

"I'd have got it for Miss Wesley," Ben said looking at the marshal with some distrust.

"Next year maybe," Priscilla said, letting Cord know that his place in her life was temporary. Fine, as it was no more than he expected.

She turned back to him. "Would you like some hot coffee, Cord?" she asked arms around herself for warmth.

"No need to trouble yourself," he said knowing he should head back to his office, be sure the prisoner had been sent off to Prescott, and that there'd been no problems while he was in the mountains.

"It's ready," she said. "Just for a bit. Grace is making cookies."

He nodded, stepping down from the gelding, as James took the horse and led him to the barn. "Got some oats, bet he'll be liking. I'll give him a rub down," he assured Cord.

In the kitchen, the warmth felt incredible after the hours Cord has spent up in the cold. He wondered how long before he'd warm up if it even happened before March.

"She's making sugar cookies," Rose told him as she poured him a cup of steaming coffee.

"They look real pretty," he observed as he blew on his hands before he took the cup, hoping he wouldn't shake too much.

"Colored sugar does that," Grace said with perhaps her first voluntary response to him if he didn't count her fascination with the wanted posters.

"Pretty colors." The cookies all had different shapes formed by metal cutouts.

"I can put sprinkles on them too," Grace said absorbed in her task.

"There are some warm ones on the counter," Priscilla said, picking up a plate and offering him his choice. He took one and moved closer to the cook stove.

"Was it snowing up there?" Priscilla asked as she sat at the table.

"Some." He sipped the coffee, only slowly warming.

"You will be here tomorrow night for dinner at six, and then to help decorate the tree, won't you?" she asked. He turned to look at her, and then saw Grace stop her decorating to watch with those big, thoughtful eyes.

"Of course," he said, "but I know nothing about decorating trees."

"How did your family decorate one when you were little?" she asked

"No trees. No decorating." He didn't add no Christmas, but it didn't matter. Very few people knew holiday seasons such as Priscilla Wesley probably had taken for granted.

She must have read more on his face than he intended. "Well it'll be fun for us all. Something new for you and Grace. Kind of wonderful that you get to decorate your first one together."

He looked over to see if Grace agreed with that, but she had her head down working on her cookie designs. "I better get back to work." He set down the drained cup. "I am looking forward to seeing you tomorrow, Grace," he said. When she looked up at him, she had about as deadpan an expression as his-- when she wanted to use it. Whether she'd be glad to see him or not was her secret.

Priscilla walked him to the door where outside more rain was falling.

"Will Wright be here?" he asked and could have kicked himself right after the words were out.

"Why would you imagine that?" she asked, astonishment showing on her face.

He shrugged looking across the yard to where the alert James had brought out his gelding.

"There will be some friends, but he is not among them," she said. "I actually have nothing more to do with Richard Wright than required by business."

"Business?"

"When my father sold the bank, he didn't sell all his interests in town. A few I manage while he's gone. That was why Mr. Wright was here."

"You are doing business with him?" Now he imagined the surprise was on his face.

She shook her head. "That was what he wished but not what I wanted."

"Why?"

She smiled up at him. "I do have a bit of judgment about people, though you might not think so."

"Just because you don't like me, doesn't mean I figure you have poor judgment." He knew he should go.

"Have I said I dislike you, Marshal?"

"You've expressed displeasure more than a time or two."

"Possibly that has changed." Her smile had changed into something softer.

"Until I create another offense, of course." It was time for him to go, to step into the rain. He was reluctant.

"And what might you do that would be offensive?" she asked in a teasing tone.

His own voice dropped a bit. "I might imagine a few things."

She laughed again. "I suppose, to be fair, I should warn you, regarding Friday. There will be a few here that you know."

"Martin Matthews?"

She made a face. "Not remotely."

"I thought you were..."

She interrupted. "Whatever you had thought or were about to say, he and I were never anything."

"Ellen Buchanan isn't likely to want to sit across the table from me," he said taking another guess.

"She will be here. Beyond a few snide looks, I doubt she'll be a risk to you."

His gaze met hers. "You sure you want me here?" he asked.

"Of course. I would not have suggested it had I not." She smiled. "I am not in the habit of doing things I dislike."

He gave a little laugh and quickly walked down the steps to where his horse was waiting. He stepped into his saddle and rode off without a backward glance.

Priscilla watched until he disappeared from sight. James came to her side. She knew he was well aware how long she had watched the marshal, but he said nothing, if the small smile didn't say it for him. "How is it working with Ben?" she asked to distract him from asking questions.

"He's anxious to please. I think it'll be fine. Big help to me when I can't do the heavier work. He's nailing the tree to its stand right now."

"That's nice."

"It was a good tree. Better than anything we could have bought in town."

"Fresher, for sure," she agreed and walked back in the house.

Less than five minutes later, she heard the knock at the front door. "Don't bother, Rose. I'll get it," she said, as Rose had her head together with Grace and a new type of cookie dough.

At the front door, she was surprised and displeased to see Martin Matthews. He didn't bother with a polite greeting. "What were you doing with that man?"

"Martin, whatever man you might be talking about, it's not your concern."

"We had an understanding."

"We never had any such thing." Any guilt she had felt, at her onetime interest in Martin, disappeared. "I'm sorry, but I am busy and would like you to leave."

"You are making a fool out of yourself over him. He's beneath you, and you know it. Are you playing with him now as you once did me?" Martin asked with a sneer.

"Martin, leave my home." When she went to the door to attempt to open it and get him out, he grabbed her arms, twisting her to face him. "You are hurting me," she gasped, shocked when he shoved her hard against the wall.

"Women want to be treated rough. You and Abigail both proved that to me," he sneered and yanked her against him. For the first time she felt fear at the way he was manhandling her.

"Let me go and get out of here," she cried, raising her voice, not yet ready to scream. He lifted one his hands to tangle in her hair showing how easily he could overpower her as he pulled on it, forcing her head up. His other hand reached to cup her breast, pinching the nipple through her garments. She pushed futilely against him. Before she could resort to a scream, she heard the kitchen door burst open.

"You heard the lady," James said as he came into the room at a near run. Martin dropped his hands and stepped back.

"Lady?" he snarled. "I wouldn't say that. Not about any of them."

James was now at the front door and throwing it open. He turned and looked at Martin, with a fierce look Priscilla had never seen on his face. "You worthless, piece of... If a lady wasn't here, I'd define you more fully. Get out, and don't come back.

Next time, you'll find your face beat in. You little worm, if you ever touch my lady again, you'll live to regret it."

Martin looked from James back to Priscilla. "You will come to your senses," he snarled and stalked through the door, which James then slammed.

He turned back to Priscilla who found herself shaking. "Are you all right, Cilla?"

She lowered herself to one of the chairs and began trying to pin her hair back in place. She realized how helpless she had been against even Martin's strength. She shuddered as she imagined what might've happened if James had not been nearby.

"I am... thanks to you. If you hadn't..."

"He's a skunk, scum of the earth."

She nodded agreement. "I had no idea he could... that he would..."

James was working to steady his own breathing. "You want to have me get the marshal?"

"No, you took care of it."

"Did I?" James said, looking toward the door with an uneasy expression on his face.

"He didn't really hurt me." Except he had. He had hurt her feeling of security. She had to find a way to defend herself, if she ever faced such a thing again. For the first time she fully understood how sheltered and protected she had always been—always by someone else. She had to learn ways to take care of herself. James might not be there next time.

"James, could you teach me to defend myself?"

"Well I can teach you leverage and a few tricks," James agreed, as she rose from the chair feeling recovered enough to face Grace.

"When can we start? I mean, maybe it won't be Martin, but it could be someone else. I don't... well I don't like thinking I always have to depend on the luck of someone being near to protect me."

"I agree, but I think we should report this attack to the marshal. If we tell him, he'll take care of Martin permanently."

"You don't mean kill him surely?" She felt shocked. Just as she was trying not to see her marshal as ruthless, James said something that made him sound more than ruthless.

James managed a smile at her quick assumption of the worst. "That would work-- but no, I meant put him in jail. A few years in Yuma might get Matthews in line."

"I don't think that's necessary. He didn't hurt me and maybe." She stopped and took a breath trying to be fair and honest. "Maybe at some point this was my fault. I, well at one time, I encouraged him."

"Not for years and not that much," James argued. "I don't like the little weasel."

"I don't either-- so we won't let him in the house again."

"And you won't open the door without me or Rose if it's him there."

She nodded her agreement. "And you will teach me some self-defense. Can we start Saturday?"

"All right." His lips were pinched together, and she saw the adrenaline was still running high in him. "I better go chop some wood or something," he said. "I got a temper worked up and need to take it out on something. Might as well make it beneficial."

She stepped to him and put her arms around him. "Thank you, James. You are my hero."

He grinned. "For now," he added with a little laugh and headed out the door whistling.

She knew what he meant. She knew also why Martin had felt so threatened. Something was there between her and the marshal. It made no sense. He couldn't be anything in her life, not really but... something was there. It likely always had been and explained how often she had felt irritated at him. Whatever it was, she wouldn't let it go far. Then she wondered whom she was trying to convince.

CHAPTER 7

At the office, Rafe grinned as Cord walked in the door. "Guess who's in town?"

"The ghost of Billy the Kid," Cord said, glad Rafe had built a fire in the small woodstove. He threw his hat over the hook and spread his hands over the warmth.

"Better."

"What could be better than that?" Finally feeling a little warmer, he sat in his chair, taking a cigar from the drawer and thinking they'd keep better if he could afford a humidor.

"Sam Ryker with a herd of cattle."

"In town?" He felt irritated. He hadn't even had time to bite the tip off the cigar.

"Down at the corrals. Bold as brass."

"You didn't check for brands?"

"Figured you'd want to do that."

Like hell, Cord thought looking with regret at the cigar. He put it back in the drawer and stood reaching for his hat.

"Before you go, did you get them the tree?"

Cord was out the door without answering. At the corrals, he looked for the tallest man. When he saw him, he headed over, his mood rotten, only to be improved if some of the cattle weren't legal. Not that he imagined Ryker would be that stupid.

The tall cowboy turned to face Cord as he came up. The grin on his face was as devil may care as Cord remembered from the time he'd thought he had him on kidnapping. That had been Matthews fault for being afraid of admitting he recognized the man. Damn them both to hell.

"Marshal," Ryker said stopping to get out the makings to roll a cigarette. "What a surprise. Welcoming us to town and all."

Cord ground his teeth on the reply he wanted to make. "You know why I'm here."

"You the new brand inspector?" Ryker asked lighting his cigarette and continuing to grin. Cord tried to think what in that man's face irritated him so much. Maybe the insolence.

"When the occasion warrants."

Ryker chuckled and reached back into his saddlebag, drawing out several folded papers. "You'll see it's all in order. My brand and twenty-five head from two other ranches in my valley."

"Cold time of the year for a drive," Cord observed as he scanned the papers. He had no doubt they were in order. There was nothing stupid about Sam Ryker.

"You're telling me. I'll be lucky if I warm up before March."

That irked Cord all over again. "So why now?" He knew he had no right to demand an answer.

"Turns out a few of your stores and restaurants are not liking the prices or dealing with Wright, now that the kid is running things. They made it worth my while-- then there was Christmas shopping, don't you know."

Cord sighed reluctantly and handed back the papers. "Guess you get by this time—unless you cause trouble in town." There was still hope. How he'd love to arrest the arrogant rancher, who he knew, if not a rustler today, would be again someday—loving marriage and baby or no.

As though reading his mind, Ryker took a long draw on the

cigarette, for which Cord was wishing, before he said, "If you hoped I'd be sticking around, wanted us to have a drink or something together." Again the teeth flashed white against his swarthy skin as he smiled. "I have to disappoint you. I'm riding out as soon as I get paid, get the money in the bank, and pick up some things from the Emporium."

"I'll have to live with the disappointment," Cord retorted.

Two of Ryker's men came to stand with their boss. "Tally's done," the one Cord recognized as Joe Fox said.

Ryker nodded. "You two want to hang around town a few days, I'm fine with it. Just don't get so drunk you end up in jail. Marshal here's just waiting for that opportunity, and we don't want to give it to him, do we?"

They both shook their heads. The man built like a mountain said, "You sure you're going to be safe riding back alone, Boss?"

Ryker grinned more broadly. "I think I can manage, Rock."

Joe Fox chuckled. "Not gonna leave your lady alone a minute longer than you have to, are you?"

"Abby and Davy'll be doing fine. She's got Bull and my mom. All I got to worry about is her adopting another stray."

Rock and Joe laughed as they looked at Cord who was left wondering when Ryker had had his mother move in with him.

Ryker chuckled. "Ollie Oliver, Marshal. Mom's just his nickname beings he likes to take care of everything and mostly me." He dropped his cigarette to the dirt and ground it out with his boot.

Not having had much experience with a loving mother in his life—male or female-- Cord let that go. He nodded and headed back to his office, frustrated that once again Ryker had avoided the trouble he knew he deserved but could not prove.

Back at the office, he finally was able to smoke his cigar as he contemplated his own situation. He could count his problems on his fingers. He was not sure of their priority. He watched the smoke drift toward the ceiling as he considered his life.

There was the daughter who had been taught to fear if not hate him. He wished he could blame someone else for that, but reality was he'd let it happen and deserved all the condemnation he saw in Grace's eyes.

Then there was the attraction to a woman, whom he not only could never have but didn't want in his life. From the first time he'd seen her, he'd felt an inner jolt that he'd fought. He didn't want her. Didn't want to think about her, let alone dream about her, but there it was.

Adding to the string of what he didn't like, he had to add the invitation to dinner and worse a tree trimming. He would hate going to a highfalutin party, where he'd not only be out of his element but also with people who had no use for a man with a gun.

Finally, he was doing a job that had started out to be one of helping others but felt more and more political. Too often the law seemed to be about not offending the powerful. What kind of job was that? The recent political edict, demanding the removal of most of the Chinese in Tucson, was close to the last straw. It made him into nothing but an errand boy for the wealthy to acquire even more wealth. But what choice did he have?

Damn it to hell, he was failing in every possible way. Back to his main problem-- he had no idea how to find a way to Grace's heart. Did he even want to? Loving him was probably a bad bet. She'd be happier staying in the Wesley home where she would be given a better life than he could ever manage. Or wasn't that how he'd failed her to begin?

He thought then about the dinner party—seemingly the least of his problems but something he wasn't looking forward to doing. Maybe an emergency would crop up and save him. Although it seemed unlikely, as with the colder, wetter weather, the feistiness of Tucson's less savory element seemed to have been dampened.

For now, he had no way off the job carousel nor could he avoid Priscilla Wesley. As soon as possible, he'd try to get a small rental house with the hope Grace would be willing to live with him. Actually that made no sense. He was gone too much for a nine-year old to be in a home alone. No, it was best for her to be in the Wesley house. Maybe he'd get lucky and find seeing more of Miss Wesley would lessen his fascination with her. There was always that hope.

Rafe pushed open the door, swiftly slamming it behind him. "Damn," he grumbled as he walked over the stove and put out his hands to warm them. "Won't surprise me if we get some snow on the valley floor."

"You doing some mystical mumbo jumbo for weather forecasting now?" Cord asked with a chuckle. "Maybe some animal bones thrown onto a fire and the letters in the smoke tell you the week ahead?"

"Now how'd you know that?" Rafe asked shaking his head. "You paying more attention to my rituals than you admit?" He laughed.

"How about using one of them to figure out how we avoid rounding up the Chinese in the river bottom?"

"The powers that be want their leases?"

"Whatever looks to be profitable."

"How can they use the Chinese exclusion act to get them forced out?" Rafe asked proving to be astute about politics-- not a surprise to Cord who'd seen his deputy had been taught well by the Jesuits before his family immigrated to Tucson from Mexico.

"The argument is they have to prove they came legally. That can be hard to do, take too long, and cost too much money."

"Interesting how they pick on them instead of my people where the same argument could be made." He smiled cynically. "Probably will be made."

"It's all bigotry—one way or the other."

"So what will you do about it?"

"Get fired probably."

"It's that serious?"

"When I got into this job, I thought it'd be about catching the bad guys, protecting the good. It turns out too often it's the other way around."

Rafe smiled. "Could be I have been told of a ritual for you."

"Seriously?" Cord asked blowing out the smoke and noting it did not form any mystical symbols.

"Peyote."

"Isn't there an ordinance about that?" Cord asked with a laugh. "I am not even supposed to know you're using it, let alone me."

"It has some advantages for a man not happy, wanting direction."

"You are joking. It's a hallucinogenic, and doesn't it make you throw up?"

"You're the one knowing more about something than I thought. Yes, some throw up. Not all. They say you see answers to your problems."

"Rafael, I need a clear head, not a clouded one created by chewing on a cactus button."

He shrugged. "Talk to my uncle if you change your mind. Could be someday you'll be willing to give it a try."

"Don't hold your breath."

"I just do that when I am near your stinky cigar."

～

In the kitchen, Priscilla tasted Rose's soup. "Delicious," she decreed being careful to avoid spilling any on her dress.

"You too," Rose said. "You're pretty dressed up for a little dinner party."

"Not that much," Priscilla argued, wondering if she should change yet again. She'd already gone through three possibilities before deciding on a pink dress she'd yet to wear. Maybe it was too dressy.

A tap at the kitchen door revealed Ellen who, when she took off her heavy shawl, was wearing a beautiful yellow gown. "Think it's going to snow?" she asked as she stood by the stove to warm up.

"It could," Rose assessed. "Happens once in a great while."

"I'm a desert woman," Ellen argued. "It's not supposed to be cold here."

"Well it never lasts long. There is that comfort."

Priscilla handed Ellen a cup of hot cider. "Want something stronger in it?"

She sipped the hot beverage then shook her head. "Who is coming?"

"James is in the living room teaching Grace to play checkers. Mrs. Gibbons will come if she's up to it. She said her rheumatism was acting up though so the cold might keep her home. Joe Fox promised to come if he doesn't end up at the bar with Rock Thompson."

"Those are Sam Ryker's men?" Ellen asked. "I heard Sam was in town with a herd. Will he also be here?"

Priscilla shook her head. "Joe said he was on his way back to the ranch. Let me think oh yes, Judge Emerson and Melissa might come but that was again iffy. And, of course, Marshal O'Brian."

"Ugh! How could you invite him?"

"One good reason. He's Grace's father, but it's more than that." She hesitated a moment. "He got the tree."

Ellen put down her cider and stared at her. "He bought a tree?"

"No, he went up on the mountain and cut one for Grace."

"And you," Ellen finished, her expression contemplative.

"Well, of course, me too, and everybody," Priscilla said aware of where Ellen's mind was racing.

"How about his cute deputy, Rafael or something like that?" Ellen asked with more interest.

"I asked, but he claimed he had family business. I think he just wasn't comfortable with a group here."

"And the marshal was?"

Priscilla laughed. "Not much, but he has to do what he can to make up with Grace. You know neither of them had decorated a tree before."

Ellen's expression softened. "Well then we'll have to make this one special. Have you got popcorn to string?"

Priscilla nodded. "Grace made paper rings today. I got our ornaments from the attic. I think we can make it quite pretty."

With the leg of lamb ready, roasted potatoes tender, assorted vegetable choices depending on what Rose had found at the market, fresh rolls, and several pies for after dinner, Priscilla had little to do after she and Grace set the table.

"Is *he* coming?" Grace asked as she heard the first knock at the door.

Priscilla didn't pretend not to know whom she meant. "He was invited." There was a chance he'd not be able to come or find an excuse to avoid it. She hoped he would be here for Grace's sake—or so she told herself.

"Good evening Melissa and Judge," she said as she opened the door to see the dignified Judge Emerson and his daughter. She took their coats, hung them on hooks to dry, as she directed them to the liquor and hot cider on the sideboard. Melissa stayed close to her father. Although she was older than Priscilla by several years, she had shown no inclination to marry, if such an offer had ever been proffered. Melissa wasn't so much unattractive as very shy with few words to offer in any conversation. Perhaps the excess of weight she carried contributed to her insecurity.

Soon Joe Fox had arrived and was chatting with Ellen and James. With no children her age, Grace hovered in the background. In the future, Priscilla vowed she would get acquainted with families having daughters the right age.

At the next knock at the door, she felt her heart skip a beat. She'd never felt such a reaction to a man. She knew, before she opened the door, it would be him. He was wearing a white shirt, string tie, jacket and no gun. Her smile widened as she ushered him in. "Would you like a brandy?" she asked.

He glanced around the room, saw Grace and shook his head to the drink. Joe Fox walked over to him. "Haven't seen you in a while, Marshal," he said with a grin.

"Like a few hours."

"Not to talk though."

Judge Emerson came to them. "I was quite pleased with how you resolved the issue with Ben Albright."

"Miss Wesley and you resolved it," he said as James joined them.

"I thought Ben might be here tonight," the Judge said.

"He wasn't at ease with it," Priscilla inserted. "I did ask him. Maybe with time. He hasn't been to a lot of dinners like this. He's looking after the stock tonight."

She smiled up at him and if the expression in his eyes meant anything, he liked her dress. That pleased her as much as listening to him exchange pleasantries with Joe. She headed for the kitchen to help rose bring in the rest of the bowls.

"Please, everyone come to the table," Rose said.

"Sit where you would like. There are no place holders," Priscilla added. She put her arm around Grace and led her to sit beside her. Cord seated himself across the table from them. Joe took Priscilla's other side. Surprisingly, the shy Melissa sat next to Cord, which led to Ellen being on his other side. He looked like a cougar who had been treed, but she had to give him this much. He wasn't running—yet anyway.

As they all began to eat, Priscilla realized conversation was not moving along. Grace hadn't said a word-- of course children often didn't speak when among adults. Still.

"Grace," she said, "Joe is an artist."

The little girl looked at him with surprise. "A painter?" she asked finally.

"A very good one," Priscilla said.

Joe smiled. "I try. I do more drawing than painting, but thanks to others, I am painting more."

"What kinds of things do you paint?" Ellen asked with interest.

"I've painted Sam and Abby a few times. Drawn Sam a lot more." He looked at Cord then, who was saying nothing. Priscilla had been aware of Joe's keen powers of observation. She wondered what he was thinking. The look on Cord's face told her he didn't like it, whatever it was.

"Do you sell your paintings?" the judge asked.

"Mostly through friends," Joe said showing discomfort with the questions.

"Are you a fan of the arts, Marshal O'Brian?" Ellen asked her smug smile saying she expected him barely to know what that meant. Priscilla felt a strange desire to jump in and save him from embarrassment, but she had no right.

"No ma'am," Cord said taking a sip of the wine Rose had poured for him.

"They are beneath you?" Ellen asked.

"No, just no time. I'm too busy arresting people—innocent or otherwise."

The judge chuckled. "You keep me busy for sure."

"You like being a marshal?" Melissa asked, hanging on his every word.

"It is what I do," Cord said noncommittally. As usual, he didn't reveal much of himself. Priscilla looked over and saw Grace watching him with an expression she could not define. Looking back at Cord, she could see he was eager to leave but she would see that he enjoyed himself. She doubted he'd had much opportunity to socialize from what she knew of his life. She supposed many were apprehensive of men who wore a gun even with a badge. She had been one of them. Things could change.

In the darkness, Martin Matthews watched the lit up Wesley house feeling an equal mix of anger and self-righteousness. Yes, he should not have manhandled her. But she had driven him to it. Now she was entertaining and had not included him. She would not have even had he not lost his temper and grabbed her.

He wrapped his arms around his body glad he had a heavy coat and that it wasn't raining. He didn't know why he was torturing himself by following her, watching for what she did, but he knew it was her fault.

He heard a step behind him and a hand on his shoulder. "What are you doing watching Miss Wesley?" the big ape Ben Albright asked.

Martin smiled. "Why keeping her safe, Ben. Don't you want her kept safe?"

"You doing that by watchin' her?" Ben asked with confusion in his voice.

"I could if she needed help, then I'd be here, right?" Ben was too dumb to know otherwise, and his big hand dropped.

"What would she need help from?" Ben asked showing uncertainty as to how to interpret what he'd been told.

"The marshal is there."

Ben frowned. "He comes sometimes."

"He's not a safe man. You know that, don't you, Ben?"

"He's the law," Ben said looking worriedly toward the house.

"Ben, Ben, Ben. Law isn't always good. You do know that don't you, a smart man like you?"

Ben looked back down at him, and it was clear he was uncertain, attempting to justify two contradictory thoughts.

"The marshal is a gunman. You've seen that yourself haven't you?"

"He takes good care of his horse," Ben argued. "I saw how good his horse looks. Man takes good care of horse is not a bad man."

Martin sighed with mock shock. "Men can hire others to do that."

"That's what he does?"

"Ben, would you like a drink?"

"Miss Wesley said no drinking on the job." He clearly understood that rule.

"You wouldn't be on the job though would you? You'd be in town with me, and just one can't hurt, can it?"

Ben's face showed the warring conflicts between desire and responsibility.

"I'm watching the horses and buggies."

"You'll be back before they need them."

Desire won out. "Just one," he said holding up one finger.

Martin grinned. "Of course, let's head for the Pedrales. It's a cold night. Man needs a drink on a cold night."

Ben nodded and the two of them began walking toward town as Martin considered how he could turn Ben against the marshal. He himself couldn't take down a man of O'Brian's prowess and size, but there were other ways. He'd influenced people before to get his way. He could do it again. This time it would work better as he had an idea that couldn't fail.

At the bar, Martin stopped outside. "Oh wait, I need to get something. Be right back."

When Ben looked confused, he handed him a dollar. "You get your drink. I'll be right with you."

It wouldn't do to leave an obvious trail back to him for what he planned would happen next. He would join the dummy after he bought his drink-- then make sure Ben understood the obligations of a true friend to Miss Wesley. It'd be so easy to manipulate the big ox. He grinned with satisfaction as he imagined how it would all go down.

CHAPTER 8

W ith dinner over, dessert consumed, Priscilla said, "Now it's time to work for your supper, isn't it, Grace?"

The little girl nodded with a big smile as they headed into the parlor where the beautiful pine stood proudly in one corner. "We made chains today," she offered with one of the rare times she ventured anything without being asked.

"We did. And now we can string popcorn," Rose suggested as she brought a big bowl into the table now in the center of the room.

Priscilla looked up at the tree and then picked up a golden star. "Marshal, you are the tallest man here-- as such it's your job to put up the star."

He looked at the delicate crystal star a little dubiously but nodded. "You sure you don't worry I'll break it?"

"I trust you." He gave her a strange look, but reached up, found the hole that attached it to the tree, and set it in place.

When he stepped back, he turned to Priscilla. "How do you usually do it? As I remember your father, he's not all that tall a man."

"When I was little, he lifted me to do it. When I got too big and he got too old for that, a chair sufficed." She grinned at him.

"You did it beautifully," Melissa said standing at Cord's other side. "It's perfectly straight."

Priscilla glanced over. Clearly Melissa was mesmerized by the marshal. She wondered if that had been a long time fascination or just from that night. She didn't recall ever seeing her with a beau. Maybe she was standing beside the reason.

Ellen had come to the other side of Melissa. "I think it's a little crooked myself." She smiled smugly but stopped grinning when Cord picked her up by the waist, lifted her easily into the air and said, "Fix it."

Everyone laughed, but Ellen was a good sport and tilted it slightly to the right assuring herself it was as straight as the top allowed.

As the women set about attaching ornaments, the men gathered at the sideboard with brandy where James poured them each a small glass.

Joe stood by Cord studying his face. "You figured it out yet?" Cord asked made uneasy at the close observation.

"Not really."

"What's bothering you? The ruthless lawman look not a good subject for a painting?" Cord asked with a laugh wishing for a cigar.

"Hanging out with who I do, you know that's not it. It's... Where do you come from, Marshal?"

"A bit of a prying question, Mr. Fox," the judge inserted himself into the conversation. "Out here men aren't usually asked from where they originate. It can lead to unpleasantness."

"I have no secrets," Cord said. "I was born in Kansas. I've lived down along the New Mexico border but not long enough to call it home."

"Seeings as how you didn't punch me out for that... How old are you?"

"Is there a reason for this inquisition?" Cord asked. "I can guarantee you there are no warrants out for me. Can you say the same?"

Joe chuckled. "None that I know of. Just... you look a lot like somebody, and I was trying to figure out if there could be a distant relationship."

Priscilla had come to join them and looked from Joe to the marshal. "Who, Joe?" she asked realizing she already knew.

"Sam, of course. I've done his face so many times. Drawn him. Now painted him. The bone structure, eyes. Not so much the mouth but the rest, coloring. You two could be brothers."

"That's not possible. I don't have any brothers," Cord said not liking anything about this conversation.

"Well then just one of those things," Joe said letting it go.

Reluctantly, Cord began to put a few things together himself. He was thirty-two. It was obvious Ryker was a few years older. They did share coloring now that he thought about it. It wasn't possible-- and then he thought about his father's lifestyle, how it had been before and even after he'd married. He had never thought much about from where Sam Ryker had come. The name... He stopped, not wanting to take the thinking farther. It was impossible.

"I'm sorry, Marshal," Joe said. "I didn't mean to make you uncomfortable. It's just the way of an artist, I guess. Putting together pieces."

Cord managed a smile. "I thought that was the way of a marshal." He sipped on the brandy wishing it was stronger.

Priscilla put her hand on his arm. "Actually I do have what I am told is an excellent Bourbon-- or rather my father does, if you gentlemen would prefer." As Priscilla brought out the bottle and poured each a shot in new glasses, Cole looked uneasily at her wondering if she was a mind reader, not a good thought.

Sipping the mellow whiskey, he watched with pleasure at his daughter stringing popcorn with Ellen's help. He wished he found it easy to say the words that he knew fathers said to their daughters. Actually he knew none of that, other than what he'd read in books. The idyllic version of fatherhood hadn't been part of his life except in fiction. It looked as though it was something he and his daughter shared. Maybe he could change that—if he could figure out how. It seemed unlikely as long as he was a marshal.

"Have you met our Territory's new United States Marshal yet?" Judge Emerson asked as he moved to stand next to Cord.

"Only by reputation."

"It's a long way from a good system with marshals being replaced with every new administration. Perhaps you should consider becoming Tucson's sheriff with more job stability. You know we don't have one worth talking about right now."

That involves running for office and even more politics, which I hate."

"Can you ignore it given the nature of things?"

Cord shrugged. "More than Meade can."

"You like him?"

"He sounds like a good man. He has the experience. He won't be as disliked as Tidball."

"Life is all politics, of course. Meade will offend someone, and then it'll start all over, if he even makes it to the next administration." The Judge chuckled. "Shall we discuss this outside with a cigar?"

Cord grinned. "It's pretty cold out there."

"Gentlemen," Priscilla said, "my father smoked in the den. Please feel free to take your whiskeys in there and do likewise. Better than freezing."

Cord realized then she had been listening to the conversation, which surprised him. He had expected her to find shopping more of interest than state and city politics.

"We aren't all frivolous flowers, Marshal," she said tartly telling him his expression had again revealed too much as she turned back to helping attach ornaments with Melissa.

"I for one will take the lady up on her offer," Judge said with a laugh. "I have some fine Cuban cigars for just such a possibility."

"Enough for me too?" Joe asked and smiled as the judge nodded.

In the den, Emerson brought a small case from his coat pocket and extracted three cigars. Cord took his and sniffed the tobacco. There was no comparison to what he usually smoked. The likelihood of his ever smoking another so fine was improbable, and he meant to enjoy it as he lit it and drew the smoke into his lungs.

They smoked a few moments before Emerson said, "A young man who wished to do so could rise politically in Tucson right now. The sheriff's office might be a good beginning."

"It's not for me, Judge" Cord said studying him through the smoke.

"You really don't like politics?" Joe asked still with that intense expression in his eyes as he studied Cord's face.

"I am ill-suited to it."

"The reason being?"

"I offend too many people, too many ways. I'd never get elected. In the unlikely event I was, I wouldn't want to do what it took to stay elected."

The judge laughed. "Can't say you're wrong with that. Politics is a dirty business-- but if all good men stay out of it, where does that leave us? And my name is Robert."

"About where we are now, Robert," Cord said surprised at the offered familiarity.

"Well you think about it. Tucson will be the power center of the state. It will need those who put the needs of the citizens before the corrupt and greedy."

"I think when it lost the capitol Tucson's fate was pretty well decided."

"Prescott won't keep the capitol. That will yet be decided, and Tucson is certainly in the running to get it back, if we can prove we aren't a cow town that shoots itself up every night. Sheriff Adams isn't helping with that."

"I'm going to be honest with you, because I think you have been with me. I don't plan to stay a deputy marshal either. In the long run, I plan to be out of the town totally."

"Leaving Arizona?" Joe asked as the Judge smoked on that one.

"No, I own land south of here not far from the border. I got it a few years back, and I want to develop it into a cattle ranch."

Joe chuckled. "Not near us, I hope." He grinned at the thought.

"Why? Too much temptation?"

Joe laughed.

"It's not near the Circle R but west across the Santa Cruz valley, the other side of the Tumacacoris."

"Rough country," the Judge observed.

Cord nodded. "And it's become more uncertain with the arrival of my daughter. It's obviously no place for her as it stands."

"Is it a working ranch now? I don't think I've heard of any big ranches over that way," Joe said.

"Haven't rustled cattle that direction?" Cord asked with a smirk.

"Not recently," Joe said then looked at the Judge. "Just joking, of course."

Judge Emerson chuckled. "Taken as such."

"It was the Ramirez place before it was bought by an easterner named McCloud who didn't stay there long enough to work the place once he realized the Apache issue hadn't been settled. I have a brand in mind. It'll be the Circle O."

"You need capital to get that started," the Judge observed.

"That's true, but I don't want to borrow on the place. I've seen too many lose their land that way. I'm taking my time getting enough to start it up. So no way do I want to get into politics... more than I am."

"I just read about the demand to remove the Chinese from along the Santa Cruz, take away their leases. They after you to do that?"

"It was suggested. I have put it off and hope that Meade agrees with me."

"Unlikely that he'll have much choice if he wishes to keep his position," the Judge said smoking as he thought. "So much of this is determined by those miles from us. I don't like the idea any more than you do. The Chinese work hard and produce a lot of our food. Inevitably there are those who see that and think they can walk in and take what they didn't work for. They will fail when they see the work that goes into it, and we'll be out of fresh vegetables. So this is all very practical from my end."

"You do well in politics?" Cord asked with a little laugh.

"I am too old to care one way or the other and am well enough fixed financially that I can tell them where to go —and do."

"What's the answer then?" Joe asked as he considered a problem new to him.

"Getting our Chinese citizens proper papers would do it," Judge Emerson said. "Of course, that can require going back to China to prove they immigrated legally, and then they won't be let in or by that time, their leases will be gone."

"Is there a way to send for those papers?" Cord asked.

"If we had time."

"If pressure grows, I will delay it. I won't be taking anybody back to San Francisco to be deported. So if it comes down to that, I'll be out of this job sooner than later."

Emerson smiled. "I will see what I can do about it. For as long as I am in my position." He chuckled.

Cord wondered why he hadn't gotten to know this man sooner. He had seen him in court, of course, but never talked to him. Likely some had been his own prejudicial thoughts that anybody up the echelons of power had to be dishonest or out for only themselves. He was finding a lot of his thinking rearranged since Priscilla had come into his life. He reworded that thought— after he got to know her better. She was not in his life.

"I'm sorry I offended you earlier," Joe Fox said. "I didn't mean to. Just my words get ahead of my thinking sometimes."

"No problem."

Judge Emerson said, "I can see how you might've wondered though. Ryker does look a lot like O'Brian. I suppose there are many such likenesses in life though—twins who aren't related."

Priscilla came to the door. "Are you gentleman ready to rejoin us?" She smiled, her gaze on Cord leaving him more unsettled than Joe's suggestion that he was related to Sam Ryker, a man he despised for a lot of reasons—none of which related to what he looked like.

Back in the parlor, they had to admire the tree, which was beautiful with the combination of antique ornaments, handmade strings of popcorn, and colorful paper chains.

"We have one last task," Priscilla said pointing to the table where paper and scissors were now arranged. "No tree is complete without snowflakes. I hope you gentlemen know how to make them because we ladies have done all the work up until now—excepting getting the tree and putting up the star, of course." She smiled at Cord.

Joe picked up a piece of the paper and began folding it. The Judge, James and finally Cord followed suit, watching to see what Joe did next when he picked up the scissors. "It's easy," Joe said, "just cut out pieces and when you unfold it, voila."

"Maybe the artist should do it all," the Judge suggested, but the ladies were not letting them off the hook. They gave up with relative grace and began clipping out squares and triangles.

When the paper was unfolded, the images did bear a resemblance to snowflakes, as each was different. Cord's ended up the most intricate.

"You are an artist too," Melissa said admiring his workmanship.

"Coordination helps," Priscilla suggested. She looked at Grace. "Why don't you put your father's on the tree?" She handed her a small piece of wire.

For a moment Cord thought she might refuse, but then she delicately reached out and took the flake. She studied it a moment with wide eyes, before attaching the wire, careful not to damage it, as she found its place on the tree. Melissa did the same for Joe's, while Priscilla took James' and Ellen attached the judge's.

"It is perfect," Priscilla said, smiling widely as Grace came and hugged her as tight as she could. "You look really tired and it is way past your bedtime," Priscilla told her. "Will you all stay while I help Grace get ready for bed?"

When she came back downstairs, the judge and Melissa had left, but the others were still sitting in the parlor and talking. When she entered the room, the men rose. "This was a lovely day," Ellen said, but I should go home too." Joe offered to walk her, which left only Cord, who said he should get out of there also.

He stood and walked out onto the porch turning as he saw Priscilla coming through the door, a shawl wrapped around her shoulders. Before he could say a word, he saw a look of terror in her eyes. He swung around, but not in time to block what was coming. Ben's big fist caught him square in the throat, blocking his breathing as he was slammed back against the wall, struggling to take a breath.

Priscilla screamed as Ben moved quickly to grab the front of Cord's shirt, lifting him as though he weighed nothing, before slamming his fist into his belly, doubling him up. His next blow was against his jaw. Cord collapsed to the floor. Priscilla recovered her senses and ran, throwing herself between Cord and Ben who was determined to get at the stunned marshal.

Ben hesitated, looking confused, giving James enough time to come out and use a chunk of wood he had grabbed from beside the wood stove. He slammed it hard against the side of Ben's head staggering but not stopping him.

"Ben, stop," James yelled, lifting the wood again.

The big man looked puzzled and then stared at him. "He's not a good man," Ben said heaving for breath. "Evil."

Priscilla now had the marshal in her arms, and any future attack would have to go through her. She saw Cord's eyes blink open as he gasped for air and reached for his throat. The blow could have easily killed him. She only hoped it had not.

"He is a good man. Who told you he was not?" James asked pushing against Ben, easily now moving the huge man off the porch.

Ben looked confused. "I don't know." His words were slurred, as frowning, he now looked near to tears.

"Ben, go to the bunkhouse," James ordered. Priscilla felt relief when he obeyed. She turned then to look into Cord's face to assess his injuries. He was trying to get to his feet, but she held him back. "No, rest a moment." She turned to James. "Help me get him in the house."

Between the two of them, they managed to lift the marshal and get him to the parlor sofa. "I'm fine," he rasped, still rubbing his throat and breathing with difficulty.

"You are not fine. My Lord, Cord, he nearly killed you."

Cord managed a smile this time. "Nearly?" he said coughing. "God, he's an ox. I... never saw it coming."

"James, please get him some whiskey." She asked Rose to get

water, cloth and a bowl. "Should I send for the doctor?" she asked looking from Cord to James.

Cord answered. "No. I'll be fine. Just..." He tried to rise and then was half sitting. Priscilla kept her arms around him to assure herself he wouldn't collapse and hurt himself worse. James started to put the glass of whiskey to his lips, but he shook his head and reached for it, taking a swallow and choking again.

When Rose returned, Priscilla gently washed the blood from his face, trying to assess if he'd broken anything.

"What triggered that?" Cord managed as his voice steadied. "Usually when someone hits me, I know why."

"He was drunk, but I don't know what happened. I am not sure Ben does," James said. "Are you going to arrest him?"

"I'm... What did he say?"

"That you were a bad man. Someone told him that. He couldn't tell me who. He... he's not quite right in the head, you know, and drink, it makes it all worse," James said. "I wouldn't blame you if you wanted to arrest him."

"Let me clear my head a little. This one, who told him, you think he really existed?"

"I suppose that's a good question," Priscilla said putting down the cloth. She began to shake as she realized how easily Cord could have been killed.

He looked at her. "Are you all right? He didn't hurt you too, did he?"

She shook her head. "Just scared me but no, he wouldn't hit me." James poured himself a shot of whiskey. When he held up the bottle to ask if Cord wanted more, he shook his head.

"Shall I get your deputy?" James asked and have him arrest Ben?"

"Let me think about it. You know the places they would put someone like Ben." He shook his head. "I will talk to him tomorrow when he's sober and then decide what to do."

"He hurt you," Priscilla said in a small voice. Violence seemed to be coming closer to her, and she didn't like any part of it. She tried to steady her voice. "Whatever you decide, I will agree to. I should not have gotten him out of jail. I had no idea he would... he could..." She hesitated, guilt washing over her. "I just didn't dream he was capable of this."

Cord smiled feeling of his jaw again. "Oh I knew he was capable, but the question is, as it was before, what the law can do about it. Will he attack someone else-- and if that is the case, I won't have any choice on arresting him."

"But you'd rather not?" James assessed.

"I'd rather not, but there has to be a reason we can make sure this doesn't repeat-- otherwise, I can't let him be out there."

"I think you should spend the night here," Priscilla said forcing a stronger tone to her voice.

"That's not necessary. I'm feeling fine."

"You can't ride home after that kind of beating."

"I have before with worse," he said, managing to get to his feet and feeling a lot steadier than he had expected. "That is if James will get my horse."

Now that he was feeling more himself, Cord knew that he hated this aspect of his job as much as ever he had. He had a responsibility to the law, but he had a feeling that Ben Albright was too childlike to have come up with the idea he was a bad man. Ben could beat a man who had cheated him, but to attack for an abstract reason like evil, that took help. The one, who convinced him, that was the one to worry about—assuming it wasn't just a voice in Ben's head.

In the morning, would Ben be able to tell him who he had talked to? Maybe then he'd know if Ben was potentially dangerous to Priscilla or others? He would wait and decide when his own thinking was clearer.

Priscilla walked outside with him, wrapping her arms around herself against the cold. "I am so sorry," she said.

"It wasn't your fault."

"I interfered when I got him out of jail and brought him here."

"You were trying to do right."

"And you nearly got killed tonight."

He mounted his horse as James held the gelding's head. "The key there is nearly," he said managing another smile. "Look, don't feel bad about this. Let's work out in the morning what comes next."

She nodded with a woebegone face. He felt an urge to kiss away the tears at the edge of her eyes, but he knew how foolish that would be. "Hey," he said as he turned Jeb, "It was a nice evening right up to the end."

"All right," she said, "be brave, see if I care." She managed a tremulous smile. "If you feel worse later, please see the doctor."

He nodded with no intention of doing any such thing. As he rode, he thought over what had happened. He had to admit to himself, if to no one else, that for a moment he hadn't been sure he was going to survive that beating. The blow to his throat had seemed to strangle him, had him struggling to breathe, making him aware how easily the evening could have been his last if his windpipe had been crushed. He remembered how Priscilla had been there when he had come to, and he realized she must have put herself between Ben and him. More to wonder about a woman he now was sure he had never known.

At his office, he was about done in, but he had to take care of Jeb. He turned the gelding toward the stable only to see the office door open revealing Rafe in its light. "You all right?" Rafe asked with his usual observativeness.

"No. Can you take care of Jeb for me?"

"Sure. What happened?"

Cord slowly dismounted. "Tell you when you get back. Maybe you can help me figure out what did happen."

Rafe looked concerned, but he took the reins and walked toward the stable with the horse. Cord slowly made his way into his office, thinking he probably should have taken Priscilla up on her offer, as he felt too spent now to do more than throw himself on his bunk in the back room.

He had nearly fallen asleep when Rafe came into the room and stood over him. "The party that rough?"

Cord gave a short laugh. "It was the after party. For reasons beyond reasoning." Which, at this point didn't take much. "Ben attacked me."

"Albright was at the party?"

"No, he came at me from the dark, damned near killed me. I have no idea why. He slurred out some explanation that I was evil. He was drunk though which explains maybe some of it."

Rafe straddled his only chair. "He have a hidden bottle in the barn?"

"I don't know."

"I'll visit the bars and find out if he was there."

"When you do, ask who was with him," Cord said his eyes closing again. He didn't hear when Rafe left the room.

CHAPTER 9

W ith morning Cord had some new bruises but other than a little hoarseness, he felt little the worse for wear. As he was shaving, Rafe came in.

"What'd you find?" Cord asked as he buttoned his shirt. In his office, he poured himself a cup of the coffee he'd earlier made. The stove was putting out a good heat. It was going to be another cold day.

"Not much. Ridge said Ben was with a lot of people. Laughing, talking, drinking. There were probably ten men there while he was. The names he remembered were Jamison, Matthews, Thompson."

"Thompson as in Rock?"

Rafe nodded as he slumped into a chair. "The problem is none of them stand out as especially talking to him. Ben arrived and left alone as best Ridge remembered."

"Damn." He grimaced as he sat behind his desk.

"What are you going to do?"

Cord took the tobacco and paper from the drawer and began rolling a cigarette. "That is the question." He flicked a match and lit the cigarette. Taking a long draw on it, he considered the problem.

"Bebeje'eri."

"And that, you heathen, means exactly what?" Cord blew out the smoke.

Rafe laughed. "The demon."

"Ben?"

"Nah, it doesn't fit. Someone else. Someone you don't see. Maybe the one who didn't stand out last night."

"Always the problem. Let's concentrate on the one I do see. Ben Albright."

"What are you going to do about him?"

"What do you think I should do?"

"Glad I'm not the marshal, but if it was me, I'd hate to put someone like him in prison."

Cord nodded.

"Ready for peyote?"

Cord laughed. "Not yet. I think though I know someone where I can get some advice."

When Priscilla woke, it was late for her. She knew why. She had lain awake half the night, tossing and turning with images and feelings racing through her mind and body. She remembered the feeling of holding Cord O'Brian in her arms, unsure if the blow to his throat had killed him, realizing what it would mean to her if it had.

As she took off her nightgown, she saw bruises on her body that she'd earned by throwing herself over the prostrate lawman, unsure at that moment if she would end up being hit herself by a man she had seen as a big child. Well he was that, but his huge size meant he was a very dangerous person—childlike thinking or not.

From drawers and cupboards, she found undergarments, a

long-sleeved white blouse, and pale blue jumper. Her choices made sure no one would be seeing her bruises to ask questions.

She walked downstairs hearing Rose and Grace chattering in the kitchen. She tried to force a smile as she entered. They looked up from their task of making biscuits. "How did you sleep?" Rose asked with concern.

"Rough. How about you?"

"The same. What do you think Marshal O'Brian will do?"

Grace looked from Rose to Priscilla questions on her face that she didn't voice. She did not intend to tell the girl about what Ben had done. Still, she needed to reassure her, help build up confidence regarding her father.

"Your daddy will be stopping by this morning." She poured herself a cup of coffee. "Won't that be nice?"

"Will it?" Grace asked. "He won't make me go with him will he?"

"Why wouldn't you want to do that someday?" Priscilla asked as she sipped the strong, black coffee.

Grace looked down. "Doesn't matter what I want, does it?"

"Of course it does," Priscilla said. "Your father won't want to make you unhappy."

The child's lip stuck out, but she didn't say whatever was on her mind.

"Your father is a good man," Rose said patting the girl's shoulder. "You really didn't know him before, but you can get to know him now."

"You want me to leave here?" she asked now with a quivering lip.

Priscilla sat beside her, trying to think of the right words. "I do not want you to leave, but you do have a father, and he has needs too. Do you want to hurt his feelings?"

Grace looked up, surprise now on her face. "I could do that?"

"Of course. You already have when you act as though you don't like him or are afraid of him."

Grace mulled that over before she said, "I don't want to hurt anybody."

"Good. Now how about eggs for breakfast?"

"Where are James and Ben?" Priscilla asked Rose as she put biscuits in the oven and got plates out of the cupboard.

"James is talking to Ben in the barn, trying to get more information on what happened."

"Does he think he will get anywhere with that?"

Rose shook her head. "I think Ben is reverting to even a more childlike state. He is in a panic, and it will make it hard for him to make sense of anything until he calms down."

They had eaten by the time the marshal rode into the yard, dismounted a little more stiffly than was his wont, and walked up the steps to the kitchen door.

"Coffee, Marshal?" Rose asked. When he nodded, she poured him a cup. He took off his hat and coat and put them on the hooks by the door. Priscilla noted he now wore the gun and had on his badge. Other than a large bruise on his jaw and another nearly covering the side of his neck, he looked much as always.

"Have you eaten this morning?" Priscilla asked.

"Not hungry."

"You know, Grace," Rose said, "I think we have that project we were working on. Let's us go into the parlor and let the big people talk."

"What project?" Cord asked managing a crooked smile due to his swollen mouth.

"It's a secret, isn't it Grace," Rose said-- and when the little girl nodded, they left the room.

"How are you?" Priscilla asked.

"About like you'd expect after being put through a meat grinder," he said careful sip of coffee.

"I am so sorry."

"Because you saved my life?" he teased.

She managed a smile. "He probably wouldn't have killed you."

He shook his head. "He was berserk. Most likely he would have. I owe you and James my life. When he hit me with that first blow, I was too out of it to defend myself. At that point, it was all his choice until you interfered. I thank you for that. But how about you?"

"There are some bruises due to how fast I tried to get to you and block Ben. Nobody but me is going to see them," she said with a little laugh.

"You were brave. More than some men I've known who are trained to face what you did."

That pleased her to here. "I plan to get some training in regards self-defense. I've decided the world won't always have somebody around to protect me."

He stared into his coffee. "I wish I could say otherwise, but you're right." He looked up with a twinkle in his eyes. "I could give you some help too with that... if you'd like."

"I think we both know that wouldn't work," she said and didn't have to explain to him why it was a bad idea.

"You're probably right, but it'd be fun... for a while."

To distract them from where their thoughts were going, Priscilla said, "And now there is Ben to deal with."

"Yes."

"Are you here to arrest him?"

"I'll talk to him before I decide."

"James has him in the barn."

"A good place to talk. Thanks for the coffee." He smiled as he rose and put on his hat, gingerly working his way into his coat.

"Will you come back? I think... well it'd be good if you talked to Grace some each time you come. Maybe spent some time reading to her. Something to get her familiar with you."

"I'd like that. Thanks." With that he stepped out the door and headed for the barn. Priscilla watched as he strode with that proud, arrogant, all business tilt to his head, the broad shoulders a reminder of the power of the man. And then she remembered what it had felt like to hold him in her arms.

She sighed as he disappeared into the barn. *It'd be fun for a while.* Would it? Did she even know how to have the kind of fun he doubtless understood all too well? She could not afford to think this way, but she also couldn't stop the thoughts from coming.

In the barn, Cord saw a small room at the back lit by a lantern. He walked forward still unsure what to do-- even after a productive visit with Judge Emerson. The older man had given him several things to consider but told him, whatever he decided, he would back him. Cord felt grateful for the source of wisdom, even though in the end, it was coming down to his own instincts. He only hoped he could make the right choice for Ben and anyone who encountered him in the future.

He tapped on the door, which was almost immediately opened by James. There was a bunk bed along one wall, small table with the lantern and a pitcher of water, clothes hung neatly from hooks and big nails on the wall. Ben was sitting on the bunk his head hanging.

"A rough night?" Cord asked as he took one of the two chairs and straddled it.

"I'm sorry, Marshal. I know I done wrong. I... James told me what I did. I... don't remember much about it."

"What made you decide to do it?"

"I... I don't know."

"Did you talk to someone earlier in the evening?"

"I was at the bar. Must've there. I don't know." Ben's state was near tears. Cord saw he wasn't going to get anything from him. "You going to arrest me, Marshal? I know I deserve it. I was bad." He shuddered.

"How can we stop you drinking, Ben?" Cord asked without

answering his question. "Do you see that when you drink bad things happen?"

The weepy hunk nodded. "I done wrong. I should be punished. I know it. I know it."

"Do you know why?"

Ben shook his head. "I will go with you if you want."

"Why would I want that?"

"You thinking of letting him stay with us?" James asked.

"I'm trying to decide. Do you think he'd be dangerous to you, Rose, Grace, or Miss Wesley?" Cord asked rubbing his sore jaw.

"I'd never hurt them," Ben said with vehemence.

"I asked James, and it's his opinion I want." If Ben argued with him now, he'd have no choice.

"Yes," Ben said his voice now apologetic. "You decide. I want to do right. Don't want to do wrong again. Not ever. Never."

"What do you think, James?"

"I think it's drink that does it."

Cord looked back at Ben. "What can we do about that?"

The big man looked up. "You asking me?"

Cord nodded.

"You might let me stay?"

"It's possible, but it would take some commitments. Take care of this family. Be there for them. And swear to me, right now, that you will never take another drop of liquor so long as you live, not even one drink. Can you do that?"

"I'll swear on my heart," Ben said.

"No," Cord said, "you'll swear on James' honor. You know he's a good man, don't you?"

Ben nodded.

"If you swear on his honor, it's more binding than your own, isn't it?"

Again Ben nodded. "I swear, Marshal. I won't never take another drink of alcohol. Not listen to nobody who says I should neither."

Cord tried again. "Did someone tell you that last night?"

Ben looked confused again. "I don't know."

"If you ever remember, you have to tell James. You know he's your friend, don't you?"

Again, Ben nodded-- his expression was so childlike, that it touched Cord's heart. "So if you ever do know, at any time, you will tell James. I want you to try hard to remember what happened last night, Ben."

"I don't want to remember," he said in a childlike tone. "It makes me feel sad."

"But it might be important. So when you can, you tell James, and he'll tell me. Got it?"

The big man nodded again. "I can stay?"

"Unless you drink again. If you do that, you will have to go, because you'll have broken James' honor, you do understand?"

"Yes... I won't do that. Not never again."

"All right, I am going to trust you to remember that." He rose from the chair and looked at James. "Talk to you a minute outside?"

As the two men stood in the cold beyond the barn, Cord rolled a cigarette. "You think I did the right thing back there?"

"I hope so. I believe so."

"It puts it on your shoulders. You know that?"

"Yes, I do. I won't let you down. I'll keep an eye on him, but I think he understands."

Cord smiled. "I wouldn't like to go up against him again— ready for the fight or not." He took a long drag on the cigarette as he looked toward the house. "Miss Wesley said you were going to teach her self-defense."

"Yes."

Cord had a feeling there was more to the story than either of them was saying, but he wouldn't pry. "I think it's a good idea. You might consider getting her a derringer too."

"She don't like guns much."

Cord laughed as he remembered all his encounters with Priscilla's disapproving view of the use of firearms. "I know about that, but I think it'd be a good idea anyway. She will listen to you. Self-defense without a gun only goes so far when it's a little thing like her."

James considered that. "I'll find one for her," he said as the two men shook hands. "And thanks. You're a good man, Marshal."

Cord shook his head as he took another long drag on his cigarette. "Not that so much with Ben. Just as a marshal, I've seen the kinds of places a man like Ben can end up. I'd shoot a dog before I'd send him to such a place-- so let's hope we can make this work for Ben's sake."

"I'll do my part."

"I know you will. Try to teach him who to trust, who he can listen to for advice-- and if you ever hear who talked to him that night at the bar, let me know. I'll take it from there." His smile was a hard one.

"You can trust me to do what I can. I hope that when Ben settles down a little it'll come out little by little."

"There is a reason behind it. And that means somebody. Exactly why they sicced him on me though, that is where I'm having a hard time putting it together." He looked toward the house as he dropped his cigarette to the muddy yard and ground it out with his boot. "I guess I should go up there."

James grinned. "You sound like an attack awaits you."

"Grace still looks at me like I'm Beelzebub. I don't know if I can change that. She's had a lot of years bringing her to this place. I didn't help by not being there."

"Man does what he thinks is right. Doesn't always mean it is. Keep trying. I got a feeling that little girl wants her daddy. She just isn't sure she can trust you yet."

"She has reasons."

"Give her other ones." James clapped him on the shoulder. "I got work to do, going to get Ben off his feeling sorry for himself bed, and get it done."

"Thanks for the wisdom. Bye."

At the house, Cord didn't have to knock as Priscilla had been waiting. "Well?" she asked as she took his coat, hat and poured him another cup of coffee.

"We'll see how it goes. For now nothing changes. James will try to get more from Ben, as to who he talked to at the bar, who might've gotten his rage lit up, but for now I think he knows he can't drink. Time will tell on the rest."

"I appreciate your generosity where he's concerned."

"As I told James, it's not that so much." He looked toward the rooms beyond the door where he could hear Grace and Rose talking. "Maybe I need some generosity myself," he said after taking another sip of the coffee.

"You need time with her."

"It's hard to find. The thing is when I'm with her, she wishes I wasn't."

"I think she's being protective. Do you know much about her life with her grandparents?"

He shook his head. "I assumed pretty good but more it's looking like not so much."

"You heard about no Christmas tree. It wasn't just that. From what I can tell, and some is guesswork as Grace doesn't understand it herself. I think her grandparents wanted their daughter back. Grace was their granddaughter, but she looked like you. She was a reminder of that. They tried to turn her into their daughter. It was a rather sad situation for them all. She has been suppressed in so many ways, unable to be herself."

He felt cold. "Physically abused?"

"More emotional."

"I'm feeling guilty again," he said rising to stand at the

counter, boots crossed over as he leaned back against it considering what she had said.

"Fine as long as you don't stop with that. Understand that it's not just that she's afraid of you. She's afraid of her own self. She hasn't felt free to be who she was. At nine that's not so unusual in a child. It's just been magnified in her. She's beginning to open up, and I think more time with her will change it all, possibly very fast. She's a bright girl."

"Last night didn't seem to do much."

"It was a start, but I had too many adults here. She needs to be around children her age. Starting school will help with that. Still, even with that, she needs fun time with you."

"God, what would be fun time with me?" he asked with a disbelieving smile.

"How about coming for dinner again tonight? We'll leave out the attack." She smiled. "It'll just be Rose, James and us. Then after dinner, let's play dominoes."

"What's that?"

She shook her head. "Cord, I think sometimes that you have been as suppressed as Grace." She gave a little laugh.

He couldn't argue with that. She wasn't far off base. "All right," he said. "I should go now. More bad guys to round up and push around." He liked making her smile. "But I'll be back. Rose's cooking is worth coming for, even if I make a fool of myself with some game I never heard of."

Priscilla rose. "Well if you were counting on that you are out of luck. I'm cooking tonight. Rose is busy teaching Grace to sew and do embroidery."

"Ah so will my life be at risk again with your cooking?" he asked with a smile as he put on his hat.

"It might be. You just never know now, do you?" Her smile was pure vixen. He fought back the urge to reach out and pull her into his arms. Those lips were so kissable. No wonder half the single men in Tucson wanted her.

Being around Priscilla Wesley so often was going to require more self-control than he had imagined. He only hoped Grace would find he wasn't a big bad bear and be willing to come to live with him, before he totally lost his heart to this beautiful woman. He had once thought she'd never have him on his knees, but now he wasn't so sure. She'd only laugh and find it all a joke if she ever knew what he was feeling. It wasn't stopping the urges. Maybe a good slap would knock some sense into his head, but before he could take that thought further, Grace and Rose came into the kitchen.

Rose looked thoughtfully at how Priscilla and Cord were standing and smiled. Grace didn't look at him at all but headed straight for the pie cupboard for the promised cookie.

When Cord had ridden off, Rose gave Priscilla one of her looks.

"Don't start on me," Priscilla said with a faint smile.

"He coming back?"

"Tonight. For dinner and remember I'm cooking."

"You want to change your mind with company coming?"

"Not a chance. You've seen my embroidery."

CHAPTER 10

B y the time Cord had gotten Jeb put away and was heading back to his office, there were three people waiting outside. One, of them being Daniel Jamison, would give him a chance to ask what he had seen at the bar. Jamison was in no mood to do anything but make his own complaints.

When he had dealt with the first two by sending them to Sheriff Adams, which didn't mean he'd not see them again sooner than he wanted, he still had to listen to Jamison's continuing litany of complaints concluding with two prime steers having been taken.

It occurred to Cord that Jamison didn't just have Wright as a neighbor. "Did you try to track them?" he asked as he bit the tip off his cigar.

"It rained last night." Jamison's tone was deliberately offensive. He slumped into the chair. "No way I could tell where they went, but I know who did it."

"And that would be?"

"Wright's men, of course."

"Kind of a small number for it to be worth his while."

"What are you suggesting?"

"That you talk to your other neighbors about the loss. You sure the fence was cut and not just broken down by the cows when the grass over there looked better?"

Jamison snorted with derision. "Like I wouldn't know a cut fence. It was cut."

"All right, I'll come out and see what I can come up with. Why don't we ride out together?"

Jamison glowered but agreed. Five minutes later they were heading north toward his ranch.

"I heard you were at the Pedrales last night," Cord said.

"And so? Like a man can't get a drink?"

"Notice who else was there?"

"Lot of folks. Why?" His tone grew suspicious and a little uneasy.

"Ben Albright was there."

He nodded. "Can't miss that ape."

"He talking to anybody special?"

"Who could tell?"

"I am asking you." He pulled Jeb's reins to the side to avoid a mud puddle.

"Well I wasn't paying attention." It was going to be a long ride.

When they reached the small ranch, Cord rode to where the barbed wire had been cut. As Jamison had said, the tracks had been pretty well washed out. The obvious fact though was that the direction it had been cut would not lead to Wright's ranch. It led instead to the Bailey place. He pointed that out to Jamison.

"They're neighbors." His voice was decidedly uneasy.

"So is Wright. Let's ride on over and see if they have some newly acquired stock. If they have your brand, then they better have a bill of sale."

"They might've rebranded them." It wasn't hard to imagine his reason for concern. Accusing Jesse of rustling would be a good way to set the hothead off.

"Do you want your steers back?"

Reluctantly Jamison nodded and followed as Cord led the way to the Bailey homestead. The buildings were in poor repair. Someone was home as smoke was coming from the chimney. Cord headed for the corral where he saw a young steer. "This look like yours?" he asked as he threw his leg over the pommel and dismounted.

"Could be." He looked uneasily toward the house. "The brand is wrong."

Cord walked over to the steer-- and although it moved away, it was easy to still smell the freshly burned hair. The rebranding had been poorly done. The Lazy J was visible under the –B. "This brand is new."

"There's only one," Jamison said, his voice sounding more and more worried.

"The other is likely hanging in the barn." Cord looked toward the house, but nobody was offering to come out.

He took his rifle from its scabbard and headed for the barn where he found the skinned and gutted carcass of a beef hanging from the rafter. He looked again toward the house and considered his next move.

Jamison hadn't dismounted. "I think we should go."

"We found your beef and now you don't want them?" Cord asked without any surprise. Jamison had wanted it to be Wright, not the hothead who lived on his other side. He had not wanted to deal with it at all but had hoped the law would resolve it for him. Now here he sat with the possibility of violence not far from him.

"Yes, I want them." He swallowed hard.

Cord stalked toward the house in no mood to spend more time with this than required. He had a dinner date, and the last thing he wanted to do was face two old people who likely had stolen to get food and some money while their son was only eager to establish a reputation with his gun. Still, it was his job.

He banged on the door. "I know you are in there. Open the door before I break it down."

When it opened, Morey Bailey, holding a rifle, came out. "What you want, Marshal?"

"You know what I want. You the ones took the steer in the corral and the one butchered in the barn?"

Florence came out to stand beside her husband. "We didn't take them."

"But you know who did." They didn't deny it. "Where is Jesse?"

"He went to town."

"After he brought you the beef that you knew were rustled. You help him rebrand that one?"

Morey sunk his head. "I... yes, I did."

Morey was technically as guilty of rustling as his son who had taken the steers. If he arrested him, where would that leave Florence? Cord knew he was ill cut out to be a lawman that such thoughts even entered into his head.

He looked back at Jamison. "You want to press charges?"

The young rancher looked sick. "I want my steers back."

"The hanging carcass too?"

Jamison looked sourly at the two old people who were skinny and looked as though their last full meal had been awhile. "I can let that one go," he muttered.

To discourage this happening again, Cord knew he had to be tough. "You prepared to pay Jamison here for his steer?"

"We ain't got no money," Florence Bailey said tearfully. "We would if we had any."

"Maybe you can work it off," Cord suggested.

"That would be fine by me," Morey said looking hopefully at the younger man.

Jamison considered awhile. "What keeps Jesse from taking more?"

"Jesse gets arrested," Cord said. "There is no second chance for him. I am charging him with rustling."

"You doing it with me?" Jamison asked uneasily.

Cord's smile was hard. "No." He looked back at the old couple. "Morey, tomorrow morning, you take the steer to Jamison's ranch and fix the fence. Then show up at the Jamison place for whatever work he wants done."

The old man nodded. Florence's expression was pure mother and pure sad. "And Jesse?"

"You can talk to him in jail tomorrow."

"You won't kill him?"

He was mounting as he said, "Not if I have a choice."

Priscilla had once again chosen one outfit after another as she tried to decide what would be appropriate for a simple family dinner. She groaned as she accepted the reality that nothing would be simple where it involved Cord O'Brian. She wanted... Dear Lord, what did she want?

She had prepared a dinner that she felt wouldn't seem she spent too much time fixing except she had. Roasted potatoes, a prime rib roast, salad, even dinner rolls that she had spent way too much time shaping. She had even prepared a pie using dried apples.

As she decided on a lavender dress with long sleeves and high neckline, she knew, as she fastened the buttons, that she was only fooling herself. This man was mattering way too much to her. It could go nowhere. Whenever he managed to convince his daughter she should live with him, she would be back to rarely seeing him.

She was doing all she could to help him find a relationship with Grace for both their sakes. Whenever she could, she slipped in positive statements regarding the marshal. She felt some of it was softening Grace, who she believed secretly wanted to accept her father into her life.

When she came downstairs, she smoothed her hair and wondered how long it would be before Cord would arrive. In the parlor, Grace was watching as she walked into the room. "You are so beautiful," Grace said.

"You are pretty beautiful yourself," Priscilla said liking how the pink dress she had bought set off the little girl's coloring. She looked so much like her father, the female image of his masculine perfection. "You know, you look very much like your father."

Grace frowned. "My grandparents said that as an insult. They'd be mad at me and it's what they would say. They hated that I didn't look like my mother. She was beautiful."

"You are beautiful, Grace. You are in Tucson now, and it is different here. I think it's wonderful that you look like him."

"I thought you didn't like him," Grace said looking up with that considering expression she got when she tried to work through something.

"Why would you think that?" She smoothed the little girl's curls.

"At the train station."

"Well then I didn't know him very well."

"And now it's changed?" Grace was a very astute child. Priscilla wondered how much she had observed.

"Now I know him better. Yes, it has. He is a friend and a good man. I think you will see that yourself if you give him a chance."

Grace considered that, but didn't respond as she moved to the sofa where her doll, which she had named Rebecca, was sitting. She cuddled up to the doll and whispered in its ear.

Remembering her own days of secret friends, Priscilla smiled and knew she had to find other little girls for Grace to play games and share secrets. School would help when the new term began. It had been decided after Christmas would be an easier integration for Grace.

Since there were two schools in Tucson with children her age, the decision of which would be influenced by whether Grace moved to live with her father. With his busy schedule, she wasn't sure how long it would take him to find a home, and then there was the question of when Grace would be ready for that transition. Perhaps it would not happen until summer. Whatever, it had to be in Grace's best interests. When Grace left, she would leave a hole in her life. Priscilla had come to love her very much, almost as though she was her own child.

Finishing off the dinner, Priscilla heard boots on the porch. At first she thought it would be James until she heard the knock. Heart beating a little faster, she opened the door to see a muddy apparition.

"I just wanted to come anyway to tell you... or show you why I can't come tonight." Cord managed a small smile. "Didn't want you thinking I was ducking out on this."

"My lord, what happened to you?" she asked as she pulled him into the kitchen where she saw he had new bruises as well as being splattered with mud.

"It's a long story."

She pushed him toward a chair, where the light of the room gave her a better idea of what had happened. He had a slowly blackening eye-- his shirt was splattered with mud as well as his coat.

"Tell me," she demanded as she filled a bowl with water bringing it as well as a cloth and soap bar to the table.

"There is no cleaning this up," he said. "Sorry but I didn't plan it this way despite how you might think."

"Let's hear the story while I do what I can to make you presentable. Start with the black eye."

He told her about the rustling and his finding Jesse Bailey in one of the sleazier of Tucson's bars. "I arrested him, which led to a few hard feelings among others of Tucson's finer citizens. They expressed themselves forcefully."

"And Mr. Bailey?"

"Not a scratch on him, but he is in jail for now. He says he'll get bail posted by Wright-- so not sure if he'll even be there by morning. Not every judge is as honorable as Robert Emerson."

"You didn't kill anybody?"

He managed a laugh, which turned into a wince as she hit a sore spot on his jaw. "Despite your opinion of me, I only shoot people on Wednesdays. Since this is not, well he got off easy."

She laughed. "I can admit I have been wrong about a few things," she said as she stood back to look at that handsome but damaged face. "Well you are pretty respectable looking from the neck up. What happened to your shirt and coat?"

"That was on the way here. You know with the rain, some of our roads are hard to get around. A heavily loaded wagon was bogged down. I stopped and helped the driver push it out of the mud hole. Well Jeb helped too. The end result when it moved was this."

"You're too big for any of James' or my father's shirts," she said contemplating the problem.

"I will come another night. Just didn't want you to think I chickened out."

"You need to be here tonight. Grace is counting on you. Except for the bruises, you don't look too disreputable."

"You sure it won't just scare her more about me?"

She shook her head. "Actually it might help her to see that you work at something helpful to others. You really think Judge Ames will give him bail? And how would he pay it?"

"Ames is on the side of whatever pays best. From what he said, Jesse thinks he has a friend in Richard Wright."

"You really want me to stay even like this?" She saw the doubt on his face. Gradually, she had come to see he had been as emotionally abused at some point as Grace. She wanted to fix that for them both. She knew how foolish that urge was.

She smiled, trying not to show all she was feeling, and put her hands on her hips. "Well wash your hands at least."

"There's a lot more mud than that."

"Hey, I went to a lot of work on this dinner." She grimaced then. "Actually I didn't mean to tell you that but it happens to be so. Besides there is that game of dominoes."

"I don't know how to play dominoes."

"Oh good. Then easy pickings." She grinned. "Just in case you're a poor loser, how about putting your gun on that high peg."

An hour later after having eaten a delicious meal, answered all the questions regarding his disreputable appearance, Cord found himself at a table with a lot of black rectangles in front of him. As Priscilla explained the rules, James asked if he'd like a whiskey while they played.

"Is that allowed?" he asked with a smile.

"You better believe it. It's even needed. Did she mention she's a shark at this game?"

Cord grinned. "Somehow that doesn't surprise me." He took the glass from James and sipped the whiskey. He certainly was acquiring a taste for the finer things.

"It's really a very friendly game," Priscilla said with a saucy smile. "There is, of course, the ability to block, which can be... well a trifle testy, if someone is a poor sport. I certainly hope you're not."

Cord's smile was wolfish. "I wouldn't know. I don't lose often."

With all the tiles turned over, she explained again how they would draw, and then begin the play with the person with the highest doubles—which turned out to be Grace.

When Cord had to draw extensively to get to play, he knew this was going to be one of his times to practice being a good sport. Priscilla was down to two tiles, while Grace only had three. Rose was nearly in his position with over ten and James fell in between. Three more moves had Priscilla drawing enough to put Grace in the lead.

When Grace won, she was thrilled and didn't even protest being told it was bedtime. She and her doll, Rebecca were smiling as they went upstairs.

"You will be here when I come down?" Priscilla asked.

He nodded, his gaze on his daughter as she turned and said, "Goodnight," which for the first time included him.

"You are making progress," James said refilling his glass, when they were left alone as Rose headed for the kitchen to clean up. "Boy you sure got a shiner."

"It hasn't exactly been my week for avoiding fists," Cord said as he sat on a hard chair in the parlor. The mud was dried, but he wasn't about to take a chance on damaging one of the finely upholstered chairs. "I can go weeks without having to resort to them, and now it's been one after another. I hope Ben is not going to be waiting outside for me." He laughed, but it was half a joke and half a question.

"No, he's fine tonight. He was invited to come, but he's still feeling embarrassed by what he did. It isn't easy for him to face you. Rose took him over a meal right before we all ate. He was trying to read a book that Cilla gave him."

It was the first time he had heard Priscilla called by the nickname and liked it but doubted he'd ever be invited to use it. She was going out of her way to help him with his daughter, but he doubted her view of him had changed much. Not in the areas that mattered most.

"I don't suppose he's remembered more about what triggered that explosion?" He knew if he had that James would have already told him, but he could hope.

"He's still confused. Liquor or maybe he's scared to remember. I figured I'd wait a bit to ask him more. He does mean well."

"I'll tell you one thing, he's got a mean right hook," Cord said with another sip of the whiskey.

"Man his size could kill a person for sure," James agreed.

"He's good with the horses though, loves to feed the pigs and chickens. He just needs a chance to grow some."

"What book did Miss Wesley loan him?" he asked curious now at what level the man/child might read.

"It is mostly the pictures, of course, because Ben barely reads, but I believe he currently has one of Hans Christian Anderson's stories, 'The Tinderbox.'"

That made Cord think about what books Grace might enjoy as gifts. He thought then about all the Christmases he hadn't mailed her a gift. He had justified it at the time by feeling she was happy, and it would only confuse her. He realized how wrong he had been. He couldn't redo it though. Onward and upward or some such thing.

"You did wait," Priscilla said as she descended the stairs. "Grace went right to sleep. She had fun tonight."

"I'm glad."

James rose and said, "I'm tired and I think Rose is going to bed as soon as the kitchen is done. Good night, you two."

Priscilla sat on the sofa. "You don't look comfortable on that wooden chair, Marshal."

"I also am not exactly clean, Miss Wesley."

"A little dust never hurt anything. And you were supposed to stop calling me Miss Wesley."

"And what shall I call you then?" he asked smiling as he thought what he'd like to call her.

"My friends call me Cilla."

"Are we friends?"

"I think we are. I'd like us to be."

"I'll call you Cilla if you'll call me Cord."

"I would like that." Her smile broadened. "Is there more to your name?"

"Cordell."

"Very official sounding."

"True."

"A man who could rise up politically should he so wish. I heard what the Judge suggested to you."

"If you heard that, you heard my answer."

"You don't think much of politics?"

"I've seen it do too much damage in the name of power."

She nodded. "I suppose so. It's easier when one has a powerful person behind them."

"Like the judge?"

"Or my father. I do understand how you feel. As I think I told you, I am responsible for several of my father's enterprises while he is out of town. It gets frustrating quite quickly."

"He doesn't own any of the land down along the river does he?"

"No, I am not sure who owns those farms. Why do you ask?"

"Pressure is being brought to get Chinese farmers off the land, good people like the Chans."

"That's very unfair."

"Having powerful people behind them might delay any action."

"What involvement would you have with it?"

"The kind that will get me fired. I am not going to, as a United States Marshal, take them into custody, and force them to San Francisco where they'd be sent back to China to get papers."

"It's hard to believe anyone would want that."

"Some want land and power at any price. Short cuts are popular."

She got up from the sofa and walked to the sideboard pouring herself a small brandy. "Would you like one, Cord?" she asked using his name for the first time to his face. She liked how it rolled off her lips.

He shook his head. "I had the whiskey and have to ride back to the office."

Her smile changed, softened. "You are always welcome to stay over."

His eyes darkened. "Not likely I'd sleep much if I did."

"Oh come now. The guestroom has a soft mattress and fine bedding."

He laughed. "It wasn't the bed that would have me not sleeping."

She blushed as she realized what he meant. What he was thinking. It was all changing between them. She didn't know what to make of it.

He rose. "I should go. It's getting late. I appreciated the evening, and that you took me in mud and all."

She followed him into the kitchen where only a small lamp was burning. "You will come again?" she asked as he put on his coat and hat.

"I'll try."

"And be here for Christmas."

"I will have gifts for Grace, of course."

"Good. Then Christmas Day and dinner with us?"

"If you want me."

"Of course, I do. Why would you think otherwise?"

"It's been a lot of years since I had a Christmas dinner with a family."

"I can't believe that."

"Believe it. A lot see me as Grace's grandparents did, not better than a legalized gunman. Respectable families don't want that kind of man around—anymore than you did."

"I am sorry for that."

He smiled. "It's all right."

"No, it wasn't. I didn't really get to know you." She saw then what a lonely life he had led. It was unfair but maybe it was the way of the world. Maybe it could change. "Would you like to also come to services with us Christmas Eve?" she asked as he opened the door.

He looked back at her, surprise on his face. "Services?"

"We go to church, of course, sing carols, listen to Reverend Ryan's sermon."

"Ah yes, the righteous Reverend Ryan," he said with a bit of a sneer quickly suppressed.

She smiled. "It's good for Grace to be part of something like that—sometimes."

"Depending on what she's being taught."

"Well we don't go very often," she admitted with a small smile.

"I will see about that. Seemed to me Rafe had something he wanted me to go to that night."

"One of the Yaqui services?"

"I guess."

"Is that open to everyone?"

"I could ask. Why?"

"I was just thinking maybe that might be better for Grace than Reverend Ryan's endless sermonizing that he doesn't mean a word of." She smiled and didn't miss Cord's look of surprise.

"I'll ask."

She stood in the door as he walked across the yard to get his horse from the barn. When he had mounted, he rode back. Leaning forward on the pommel, he said, "Thank you, Cilla."

"Dinner was my pleasure."

"No, for a lot more than that. How you are helping my daughter. Me. I just want you to know I recognize all you are doing and appreciate it."

She smiled then, feeling an inner softness that she'd never experienced. "It has been my pleasure."

She watched as he rode off. Before he turned the corner, he looked back. He was too far away for her to see his expression and then he was gone. She walked back into the house thinking of the evening, of cleaning the mud from his face, of... She had to stop doing this to herself. More and more she wanted what she knew wasn't right for her or him. Logic didn't change the wanting.

In the darkness, Martin Matthews stood, long after the house lights went out. He had come by the house just by coincidence, or so he told himself. When he had seen the marshal arrive, he had stayed, lurked in the shadows-- shadows he had been forced into by that man. He hated him. He had seen how Priscilla's gaze followed the marshal as he rode off. It wasn't hard to imagine what was developing.

He had to do something to stop it. He would, but he just hadn't figured out what. Mulling it over, he headed for the Pedrales. Maybe a few drinks would clear his mind.

CHAPTER 11

When Cord woke after another restless night, not helped by the loud snoring of Jesse Bailey, he lay remembering his dream. It had been a strange mix involving Priscilla and someone else-- someone threatening. Instead of a sexy dream as he had come to expect, when she was in it, he was holding her, trying to survive, to keep her safe, not to die himself. He remembered trying to peer into the images and recognize a face. The threat was too shadowy.

"Hey Marshal, when's breakfast," Bailey yelled using a cup along the bars to accompany his words.

Cord sat on the edge of the bunk and ran his fingers through his hair before he reached for a clean—make that cleaner shirt. He'd have to give that new Chinese laundry a chance if he wanted to continue walking around the town and not scaring everyone. Without buttoning the shirt, he walked into the office.

"You slept late, Boss," Rafe said getting up from the chair behind the desk to move in front of it. "What happened to your face?"

"The cause is in the cell." He made coffee and threw in

another piece of wood before he sat down, looking for the makings for a cigarette.

"I saw he was back, but I didn't think he had it in him to mark you. That a black eye?"

"Brilliant deduction. And he didn't. It happened as he got cuffed and two miners decided they didn't like arrests or marshals."

"You took them both on?"

"By then it was more or less the whole room. Ridge pulled his shotgun, and the noise stopped it before I ended up with two black eyes. I swear those miners get testier and testier." He lit the cigarette and took a satisfying pull on it, drawing the smoke deep in his lungs.

"With the mines having problems, most likely they're edgy over what comes next. Why didn't you come get me?"

"I was not expecting the saloon to erupt. I should have gotten you."

"You figure to hold him this time?"

He shrugged. "Hard to say. Jamison isn't likely to press charges. He wanted it to be Wright and lost a lot of enthusiasm when he found out it was two near starving old people brought to that condition by their hellion son. Either way, Jesse seemed to think a lawyer will be here sooner than later to post bail—bail which Ames is likely to keep low."

Rafe whistled. "Jesse has that kind of clout?"

"We'll find out. From the sounds of it, Richard Wright is grooming him. The only reason he could want Jesse is his recklessness and supposed speed with a gun. It's sure not his cowboying skills."

"You think he's faster than you?"

"I hope I don't have to find out."

Rafe poured them each a cup of coffee.

"I was wondering," Cord said as he took the first sip. "Remember you asking me to come to something Christmas?"

Rafe nodded. "You mean you are taking me up on it?" He grinned.

"It's a little more complicated than that. Last night, I used it as a reason to avoid Ryan's excuse for a church. Priscilla then said she thought maybe Grace would like a Yaqui celebration and wondered if she could come too."

Rafe gave an amused laugh. "You serious?"

"I don't know if she is, but I am, regarding the question."

"Well then, yes, they'd be welcome. You know what our celebrations are like?"

"No peyote, I hope."

Rafe grinned. "Not for Christmas. It is though a mix of the Roman Catholic ways and ours. Deer dancing. Singing. Drumming. Nothing formal or even the same from time to time. My little brother, Gabe, will be the deer dancer this year, and he's pretty excited."

"How old is he?"

"Ten and this is his first chance to do the dance."

Cord took another drag on the cigarette. "You know that I'm not a religious man, but that sounds better than listening to Ryan."

"Well if Miss Wesley really means it, she will be welcome with your daughter as well as anybody else. It's not a closed ceremony like some. Hey, invite that cute little blonde."

"Not the first time you mentioned that. You think you'd stand a chance with someone from her world?"

Rafe shrugged his shoulders. "Who knows? Nothing ventured nothing gained or something like that. I think one of my tribal elders said that."

"If he did, he got it from Chaucer," Cord said.

"Who's that?"

Cord didn't go out of his way to let people know how well-read he was and regretted using the name before he thought. Still what did it hurt? "He was English and let me think. Almost 500 years ago. I think that one came from one of his books or poems--hell, I forget."

"Well it's a good saying whoever said it first," Rafe said as he poured them both more coffee. "And it's how I look at Ellen Buchanan."

Cord knew he was asking more than he usually ever would, but his own mind was filled with conflicting emotions. "You would want to settle down with any woman?" he asked as he blew out the smoke.

"I don't know. Haven't thought that far ahead, but I'd like to get to know her better... or have her get to know me. Maybe nada, maybe algo."

"That little woman hates my guts."

"That's your problem," Rafe said with a laugh.

"You're right. I'll mention the possibility next time I talk to Cilla—assuming even she seriously wants to go."

"Cilla?"

"Miss Wesley," he corrected. The more intimate name had slipped out, and he regretted that more than Chaucer. Damn, he was losing his grip.

"All right," Rafe said with a laugh, "and I think here comes that lawyer.

After breakfast, Priscilla, who had dressed in a pair of her father's old work pants, a flannel shirt she had bought years ago but rarely worn, and sturdy boots, followed James into the barn for her first lesson in self-defense.

"My first tip," James said, "is keep your eyes alert around you. Don't go into places where it's dark, or you don't know who might be there unless you have no choice."

She nodded. "But when it happens, when someone is being aggressive, what can I do?"

"All right, spread your legs a little. Good. Now when I grab your arm like this." He took hold of her right arm. "You reach for my nose or eyes."

"I couldn't do that."

"Cilla, if someone is grabbing you, you have to recognize one solid fact. If you lose your power, say you are wounded or tied up, you have no more choices. You have to stop them before it gets there. You cannot think of this as being a game or something that's not serious. If you never need to use any of this, good. You are doing it for the rare chance you might-- and if you do, you have to use whatever you know to do."

She bit her lip. "All right. So I'd put out my hand like this." She lifted her left hand and pushed toward his nose as he ducked back. "Well if you won't stand still," she protested, "how can I do anything?"

"You can't. So you have to be aware and ready. Surprise me-- and when you reach to gouge out my eyes or break my nose, be twisting your arm to free it. Push your hand downward, and you can more easily break my grip."

"Let me try it again." This time as James came at her, she ducked, tried to evade his grab for her arm. He got her and twisted her closer to him, while she reached with her free arm to pinch his nose.

"Better," he said with a laugh as he again danced away breaking the grip. "Now another tip is using the side of your hand. If I came at you, aggressively, you turn your hand sideways, as though it's a knife, and slash with it at my neck. A good, solid blow to the carotid artery can knock a man out, giving you time to run. Directly at the windpipe, it can kill him."

They practiced again with her getting better and more of the idea as to how she had to use her hands and body.

"Use your whole body. Two strong weapons in your arsenal are legs. Kick a man really hard in the knee when he comes at you. Hard as you can. Think in terms of breaking the joint. No light taps. I don't want you doing it to me, but you try it at this pile of hay."

She kicked out a few times, trying to get the feel for it. "I think my skirts would get in my way," she observed breathing heavily from the exercise.

"So grab them up. Free your legs. Give them plenty of room for the kick. Another move that can totally incapacitate a man is kneeing him in the groin."

"I've heard of that," she said. "Want me to try it on you?" She laughed.

He chuckled. "Nope, the hay stack is better, but you can practice that in the house. Bring that knee up but, Cilla, bring it up hard, very hard. Barely hitting a man in the groin will only make him mad. You want to put him on the floor. It's a very vulnerable spot on a male. Think you got it?"

Maybe." She saw movement and realized then that someone was in the corner of the barn. "Hi, Ben," she said when she recognized him.

"I don't like to think of someone hurting Miss Wesley," Ben complained as he came out of the darkness.

"Maybe they wouldn't," James said. "But isn't it better that she knows how to defend herself, just in case."

He nodded but obviously not certain it was.

"Ben," she said, "you, James, or Marshal O'Brian can't always be with me. You understand that, don't you?"

He shook his head. "I'd want to be though," he said in that childlike way he had.

"I know. I appreciate that, but it's also true that you can't. I need to know how to protect myself in that case."

"Knife might be better," Ben observed, his frown not lifting.

"I couldn't use such a thing," she protested.

"No, I don't think so either," James said. "Using a knife safely and effectively takes a lot of training, but I think you need to get a weapon as an equalizer. I vote for a derringer."

"I don't want a gun. You know how I feel about them."

"It would be the smart thing, Cilla. I can find one for you if you like and teach you to shoot it."

"I'll think about it."

"When we finish today, practice in the house by yourself. Practice the hard kick, the slash with your hand. And we'll work on it again whenever you have time."

When Priscilla entered the kitchen, she felt as if she had bruised herself in more places than the night she'd come between Ben and Cord. In the morning, she would have sore muscles. It was worth it, as she had learned a lot about places that were vulnerable on a man. She didn't expect to become an expert at self-defense, but she knew more than she had. She had accepted that she might have to hurt someone if she was attacked again. It wasn't a pleasant thought.

"How did it go?" Rose asked as Priscilla slumped into a chair, rubbing her shoulder.

"James is better at this stuff than I expected, and I think... it went pretty well for a first time. The only thing that bothered me is he suggested I get a gun."

"Why would that bother you?" Rose asked making them tea.

"You know how I feel about them."

Rose nodded, then added, "While it is good to be responsible with any weapon, it could be not just to save your own life but someone else's."

"I suppose, but a derringer, which is what he was suggesting, wouldn't do much against someone Ben's size anyway."

"Perhaps it would depend on where the person was shot." Rose brought the pot and cups to the table.

"Where is Grace?' Priscilla asked unwilling to continue thinking about violence.

"In the parlor. She wanted to work on a few projects in secret." Rose smiled.

"She is the sweetest girl. After the way she was raised and rejected, it's a bit amazing, but she has a softness that makes her hard to resist."

"She is that. She's excited about Christmas. I think a little uncertain starting a new school, but I know you are right. She needs to get out, make friends, and get an education."

"I've thought about whether the school here or the other across town. I am not sure where Cord can find a home for them."

"He's not going to have something that soon, I would imagine," Rose said sipping her tea. "Let's just assume she'll be with us until summer anyway."

"I'll talk to him about it. The more he can be here though, the sooner it will be to the time she leaves us. I am not looking forward to that. She already seems to belong and will leave a big hole."

"You'd miss her father too, wouldn't you?" Rose asked with a sly smile.

"He's a good man," Priscilla said knowing her voice sounded defensive. When Rose said nothing, she smiled. "All right, yes."

"And Connie said..."

"You're incorrigible. I haven't forgotten what she said, and yes, I have thought it's possible he was the man she saw. She didn't say anything about a happily ever after if that should be the case."

"She says she doesn't get predictions as for certain but directions. Events can be changed. Perhaps you should go back to see what she sees now."

"No. What will be, will be. If I wanted to go back for anything, it'd be for the one she saw as an enemy. But she didn't know who it was then. I doubt she would now."

"I guess not." Rose looked concerned. "Is that why you want James to help you learn to defend yourself?"

"It began when Martin grabbed me. Well, if James hadn't

been there, it could have been worse. I don't want to feel so helpless again."

"So, you get the derringer. You listen to what James advises, and you learn to shoot it."

Priscilla sucked in a breath but didn't argue. Maybe she had to do it. She hated the thought, but she did not want to be helpless. She knew, as a woman, her options for defending herself were limited. She would learn what she could. Despite her earlier doubts, Martin seemed more possible to be the dangerous one Connie had seen. Could she really shoot someone she knew even if they threatened her? It was still possible it was a person she had yet to meet. She realized she was taking the prophetic thinking ever more seriously.

Cord walked into the Pedrales bar, aware that half the men had turned to see what trouble he was after this time. He wasn't after any. He just wanted a beer and a few minutes to forget he was a lawman—like that could happen, at least not until the day he turned in the badge.

He needed a drink after the frustration of watching Jesse Bailey walk out of jail with that annoying smirk. What the hell good did it do to arrest anyone if money determined how long they stayed in jail?

He put the coins on the bar and Ridge handed him the beer. "You look worn out, Marshal," he said with the friendly way of bartenders.

"It's been one of those days and not getting better fast from the sounds of it," he said as he took a big swig of the beer.

Delbert Sicilla left his faro table where he'd been playing solitaire. "It's been a slow day for me," he said as he also ordered a beer. "If it keeps on like this, I'll have to move on, maybe head for Tombstone."

"I thought your wife was a seer," Cord said with a laugh.

"I thought *that* was a secret."

"Not from my deputy. At any rate, Tombstone isn't going to be growing and likely will become another ghost town. I don't need a seer for that prediction. In May they had fire destroy their fancy pump and remove their last chance of getting the water from the mines. Price of silver's going down. I'd say it's a poor direction for a gambling man."

"How come you know so much about it?" Del asked sipping his beer and watching Cord a little more intently.

"It's a marshal's job to know what's going on. That kind of thing impacts everything else. When the railroad came to Tucson, not Tombstone, that set its fate—seers or not."

"Damn, man wants to think somewhere it'll be better," Del said with a groan.

"I think that's heaven—assuming there is one," Cord said.

"Me, I believe in heaven," Ridge inserted. "Just I ain't likely going there." He chuckled. "You neither Del, not with a witch for a wife."

"Seems like me and Connie should be getting out of Tucson if that's how you folks see her. Won't be the first time we had to move on when word gets out what she does." He stared into his beer.

"Look, it's no never mind to me," Ridge said. "Hell, I'd go talk to her myself if I believed in that."

"Del, remember the night Ben Albright was in here, getting drunk. The last time?" Cord asked.

Del considered a moment. "I might. He's not one you can forget."

"What was going on with him that night? He came at me later, like to have killed me. I had a feeling somebody said something to him that set him off."

"Geesus, I'd like to help you, Marshal. I don't know though. He talked to a few. Let me think. Young Jamison was here. Not sure though if it was at the same time. I wish you'd asked me sooner. Martin Matthews was drinking, but that's nothing unusual for him. He hit upstairs with one of the girls."

"Sally. That's the one he tries to get since Sherry left town," Ridge said.

"Thanks for trying. It probably was nothing related to here anyway. Just I keep thinking Ben didn't come up with the idea without help."

As he walked out of the bar, he decided he'd never know why Ben had come after him. Not unless or until something else happened to tie it all together.

In Tucson's Emporium, Cord looked around with no idea where to start. What the hell did a man buy a little girl as a Christmas present. Mrs. Adams walked up to him. "May I help you, Marshal?" The expression on her face showed uneasiness. He was tired of people always seeing him as the one trouble followed.

"I hope so," he said. "I'm looking for something for a nine year-old girl. A Christmas present."

"Hello there, Marshal." The soft voice coming, as a door opened from the back, surprised him. As he turned, there she was, and on her face he saw none of that concern or anxiety, just a teasing smile.

"Ah Tucson's angel," he said.

She smiled. "I left my wings at home. Sorry."

"So no miracles?"

"And what you will need requires a miracle?"

He gave that one a little thought but didn't tell her what came to him. Maybe she saw it in his eyes though as she blushed. "I don't know if it will take a miracle, but I could use some help, Cilla," he said trying out the name and liking how it flowed off his lips. He saw the surprise on Mrs. Adams face.

"I will leave him in your capable hands, Miss Wesley," she

said and went back to removing new arrivals from their boxes and stacking them on the shelves.

"I am looking for something for Grace, of course," he said. "The kind of thing that can make up for nine years of neglect."

"Ah, you do want a miracle then."

"Is that what it'll take?"

"That or a big dent in your wallet."

"Hit me with your best shot."

"Well she likes books and does not have many." She led him to a section of the store with books on a table and a shelf. "We just got in this version, with wonderful drawings. *Alice in Wonderland* might be one she'd enjoy. It's magical and about a little girl." She handed it to him.

Although he wondered about the 'we', he stuck to the issue. "Is that too advanced for her?"

"From what I've seen, no. She's a very bright little girl. You or I could read it to her the first time through. It's a fun book to read aloud."

He took the copy and liked the illustrations-- so kept it. "Does she like Louisa May Alcott?" he asked before he thought.

She looked at him with surprise. "I didn't expect you to know that author."

"I might as well admit it now. I used to read a lot, Miss Wesley."

"You said Cilla before. And why would that be something you feel forced to admit. It's a good thing."

"In my world, it's not exactly something you put on a resume. At one time I set myself up to read all books they say we should have read. Dickens, Hugo, Tolstoy."

"My God," she interrupted him, shock in her voice. "You made it through *War and Peace?*"

He smiled. "Maybe not all the way."

"Goodness I am impressed. It might not work on a resume, but it's excellent for raising a daughter. And really you knew who

147

Louisa May Alcott was. How about Jane Austen?" She smiled up at him.

"You don't expect me to admit if I had."

"It is not as though it'd be a disgrace."

"I suppose you really liked her books. Especially *Pride and Prejudice*."

"You don't expect me to admit it I had," she said with a little laugh.

He felt that urge again to pull her into his arms and looked for a distraction. "What else? Does she have a teddy bear? Seems like little girls like them."

"Big girls too," she agreed, and they headed to the toy section where a beautiful, pale brown color, very soft teddy bear caught his eye.

"All right, one more thing," he said. "I think a dress. I haven't ever been able to buy her such a thing, and I'd really like that."

"A great idea and she can use some school clothes. She will be beginning the first of January."

Together they found several appropriate dresses that Priscilla felt certain Grace would love.

"I hope she won't think I'm trying to buy her," he said as he took his choices to the counter and accepted Mrs. Adams' offer to have them gift wrapped while he waited.

"She won't think that. She has not had a lot, and it's easy to want to spoil her now. Grace though has a depth to her that tells me she won't be easily spoiled. And besides, you didn't do it with these choices."

Cord smiled down at her and knew it was too late for him. This woman was grabbing his heart. He didn't see any way to stop it. He didn't have to do anything about it. He couldn't do anything about it, but for the first time in his life, he was aware of what love for a woman must feel like. It scared him at the same time he felt grateful that he would have experienced such an emotion—even when it was one he could not keep. He was a hard man. A man who had made himself hard to live the life he had to live. Little by little that hardness was cracking.

He decided he would come back to the store when she was gone. He wanted to buy something for her. He recognized she was a woman who had anything she wanted, but he needed to give her something.

In fact, for a man who had never liked Christmas, hardly remembered a good one in his entire life, he was feeling in a strangely Christmasy mood. It wasn't just for her that he desired to give presents. There were others—those, who would never dream he'd give them a gift. He felt an awareness of caring that he didn't remember-- or if he had, it'd been so long ago that he'd forgotten it. It wasn't too late for that caring—even if it was for other things.

CHAPTER 12

M artin Matthews sat at the table in the back of the Pedrales nursing a whiskey and frustrated with every aspect of his life. It had all begun to fall apart when Abigail refused his proposal. Or was it when Priscilla did? Women, they were the bane of his existence, his ruination.

He thought about the stupid little Priscilla, what a fool she had been to reject him. Watching her laughing with the marshal out front of the Emporium sickened him. He never imagined he'd see a woman, who he had thought had class, being brought down to the level of that gunman—legal though his shootings might be.

"You look like you've had a bad day," Richard Wright sat down across from him.

"A series of them." Martin was in no mood to lay out all that had gone wrong, not to a mere acquaintance, wealthy though the man might be. Wright was another example of someone who had been given much by life, none of which had he earned. Life was so unfair.

"I heard you got fired," Wright said.

"Good news travels fast," Martin said with a glower. The

unfairness of his firing would not be seen by someone born to the silver spoon like Wright. He knew who to blame it on anyway. Curses needed to fall upon Priscilla Wesley. He had known from the time she agreed to help Jacob with his books that he had to be more careful on his skimming. He had thought he had been.

Apparently not enough as he had been ordered into the office that morning, shown the figures proving his constant but small thefts. Unfortunately the receipts had been there for someone who had cared enough to balance them against the books. He was angry again as he thought about his downfall. How could he have explained their disappearance? He had assumed Jacob would never take the trouble to do any analysis. Jacob hadn't, but he had found someone who had.

Jacob had sounded sad as he said he'd have to let him go. Being himself a greedy man, the old fool had listened sympathetically as Martin pleaded for mercy. Oh how it annoyed him to beg that stupid old man, but he had done it, sworn he would pay it back. Jacob had been gullible enough to believe him and agreed at least not to contact the marshal or sheriff.

Wright walked over to the bar and came back with a bottle of whiskey, topping off Martin's glass. "I understand how you feel."

"You? How could you know it? Everything goes your way."

Wright laughed. "You have no idea."

Gabe Evans and Jesse Bailey joined them at the table. Martin had never liked any of the men, but he was past caring now. He watched as each took a slug of whiskey from the bottle. How uncouth.

"I am thinking I need to move on," Martin said. It was obvious he had no other options. No job. No woman. Very little money. No way to pay Jacob back. No plans. What else could he do except leave Tucson? Except where would he go? He didn't have enough money to buy a ticket on the train or even a horse. He took another gulp from his glass.

Wright topped it off again. "You know who is at fault

with this."

Martin studied his face wondering how much he knew. "It's the marshal's fault," Bailey answered when Martin didn't. He took another swig from the bottle. "I can take care of him. You want me to do it Rich? I'm faster, and I'd like to finish him off."

Wright chuckled. "Yeah right. Sure you are, kid."

"A better idea is to get the Marshal outside of town and bush-whack him," Evans suggested.

Martin hoped no one was overhearing this conversation. The last thing he wanted was to be tied into this kind of thing, end up in Yuma. No thanks. He had barely escaped with his hide intact as it was.

Wright was sitting back and watching Martin. His thoughts were inscrutable. After another drink, he rubbed the side of his nose. "Do you want a job with me, Matthews?"

"Why would you need me?" A job offer was about the last thing he had expected from Wright.

"I have a large ranch with complicated holdings. I could use a man... who is good with numbers." He smiled and Martin under-stood what he meant. He considered the offer.

"It would mean not skimming me," Wright said with a smile. "You would understand that I'd not be so kind as Spenser. But it would mean... creative bookkeeping, your kind of expertise."

"All right. I could do that."

When the three men left the table, Martin continued to sip at his whiskey. He was sick of losing. He knew that it had all gone wrong when he lost Priscilla. There had to be a way to get her back. Damn that deputy marshal. He was far beneath Priscilla, and yet he knew how frequently he was at her home. Maybe it was just his daughter, but more likely it was something else. When he spied from the shadows or behind buildings, he thought he saw something on her face that had never been there for him. Why would it be there for that gunman? There had to be a way to get her to see what the man was.

As he remembered the conversations at the table, his interest centered on Jesse Bailey. The youth thought he was faster than the marshal. Maybe he was. But even if he wasn't, a forced gunfight would be exactly what it might take to make the gun hating Miss Wesley see the man for what he was—a legalized killer.

If that didn't do the trick, he was beginning to think of another possibility. He needed to get Priscilla away from all the confusion that was in her life in Tucson. Once she was out of town, with him, then she'd see his value and understand her mistake. Such an action would necessarily be against her will and henceforth quite risky.

He shook his head as he thought how many ways that could go wrong. Better was removing O'Brian from her life. That would be his first plan of attack. He was good at manipulating people, and Jesse Bailey looked gullible and ready to be maneuvered by flattery into doing what he wanted. With the marshal no longer around as a distraction, Priscilla would come to her senses. If she did not, well he'd face that problem when he got to it.

For now he had a job again, possibly contact with some people he could use, and things were definitely looking up. He walked over to the bar. "Sally around?"

As the least part of her day, Priscilla struggled to make the accounting figures add up—to no avail. This wasn't the same as when she had discovered Martin Matthew's fraud. The ledger's numbers were more about what she wasn't seeing. Was it a business that would be better sold? She pressed her fingers to the bridge of her nose, tired of looking at numbers.

Grace came to the door. "May I talk to you please?" she asked with a worried expression on her face.

"Of course. Come on in." Instead of suggesting the little girl sit on one of the chairs in front of her desk, she motioned her to come and sit on her lap. Grace seemed to enjoy cuddling.

"What is wrong?" Priscilla asked.

"Just, well I wondered... I haven't been sure what I should call you. When I start school, it will be more of... well what should I say when I talk about you."

Priscilla saw the problem and was only slightly surprised Grace was mature enough to recognize it. Priscilla, as a name, was too familiar for a child to use around other people but Miss Wesley wasn't nearly close enough given how she felt.

"How about Aunt Cilla?" she suggested.

Grace smiled. "I would like that... and then... what shall I call... my father?"

"Couldn't you call him Father or Papa or Daddy? I think he'd like that."

"But he still doesn't feel like a father."

"You are more comfortable with him though, aren't you?"

Cord had been to the house every other night. Not always for dinner but sometimes to talk, play games or even read to Grace. It had felt comfortable, and she thought he was making progress. She didn't want to push that to a point of it becoming damaging. Still, he was her father.

Grace considered a bit. "I could call him Father maybe."

"Try it out tonight. And remember tomorrow night is Christmas Eve. We will be attending the Yaqui service with Rafe, Ellen and Cord. Perhaps you should call Rafe and Ellen aunt and uncle too. Would you like that as a way of showing respect?"

Grace nodded considering a moment. "We went to a regular church when I lived in Kansas. You don't go to church."

"That's true although I used to go. Would you like to go?"

"I think I'd rather go to the Yaqui Christmas. It sounds

interesting."

It did to Priscilla also. Rafe had been invited to dinner to explain what they could expect to see. With his little brother, Gabriel, doing the dancing of the deer, Grace had even more interest. For once a child had an important role in something.

The knock at her door surprised her. She looked through the side window to assure herself it was not Martin. She had been practicing every day on her self-defense, even worked with a bag stuffed with hay, which James had hung in the barn for her to practice kicking. Still she wasn't confident she was ready.

"Reverend Ryan," she said, as she showed him into the parlor. "Grace, would you ask Rose to bring us some tea?" she asked as much to get Grace from the room as for tea. The expression on the pastor's face did not bode well for a friendly conversation. This looked more like the preparation for an inquisition. She smiled.

"I have been hearing troubling stories-- very, very troubling," he said as soon as he sat.

"Goodness and you think I might be able to help you?" She forced as angelic a smile as possible, but she was in no mood to cater to the pastor, not when she had so little respect for his form of religiosity.

"Are you seeing Deputy Marshal Cordell O'Brian?" he asked wasting no time with pleasantries.

"Since his daughter lives with me, yes, I am. Did you wish me to deliver a message?" What a pompous arrogant excuse for a holy man.

"I hoped the report I received was wrong." His expression turned sad.

"Might I ask from whom that report came?"

"It would be unfair to my parishioner, but it was with the best of motives. The concern expressed was for your immortal soul, and here in Tucson, your reputation, Miss Wesley. I have been compelled to write your parents to tell them of my concern."

She took a deep breath before she responded. "You had the nerve to do such a thing without talking to me first? How dare you!"

"As shepherd of my flock, I felt it my duty."

Rose came into the room with a tray, tea pot and two cups. "I'm sorry, Rose," Priscilla said. "I put you to the work for nothing. Will you please amuse Grace in the kitchen, while I finish my conversation with the pastor?"

Rose smiled but backed out of the room. Priscilla saw that she recognized her growing rage, and even the pastor was now showing some concern, that he may have stepped in it.

"Now then," Priscilla said as she rose to her feet. "You have said your piece. You have disturbed my parents for no cause. I hope you have nothing further to say before you leave."

"Well there were two other items," the reverend said. "I heard you visited Mrs. Sicilla. That was in very poor judgment given her husband is a gambler and there is word that she is a practioner of Satanic spells. And to add to it, I've been told that you are going to the Indian celebration Christmas Eve, rather than our church. Do you think any of that is good with a small child in the house?"

Priscilla was amazed at how much information he had amassed. She walked to the door and opened it. "I think it's very good. Far better than being in a room where the pastor has been inappropriate with all the single women at one time or another and a few of the married ones."

"How dare you," he started to say and then slammed his mouth shut.

"I dare because I have firsthand experience, as well as what others have told me. Reverend Ryan, you are a fraud as a Christian or a pastor. I will thank you not to come here again. If you continue to spread gossip about me, I might be forced to tell some of what I know."

The pastor walked onto the porch, his cheeks red. "You may

someday wish you had not rejected my help," he said with as pious an expression as he could manage.

"I might, but I doubt it." She slammed the door.

Walking back into the kitchen, she saw Rose and Grace both looking at her with curiosity. "I could use that tea," she told Rose but held off explaining what had happened until Grace found something else to do. How did one explain sanctimoniousness to a child? She'd learn about it soon enough, if she hadn't already had examples in her own life.

An hour later as the three of them were working on dinner, there was a knock at the kitchen door. When Connie Sicilla entered, Rose offered her coffee or tea. "Would you two like to visit?" Priscilla asked.

Connie shook her head. "I just wanted to say goodbye. We are leaving on the train early tomorrow morning."

Rose frowned. "Oh, Connie, I am so sorry to see you go. You will be missed. Where are you heading?"

Connie shrugged. "San Diego to start, but I don't know in the long run." She looked at Priscilla.

"Grace, why don't you find those paper dolls I bought you and see if you can cut out more of them," Priscilla suggested as it looked like Connie had more to say that the child should not hear. Grace gave her a look that said she understood big people talk was about to happen, but she went.

"You aren't leaving because you have been pushed out, are you?" Priscilla asked.

"What makes you wonder about that?"

"Reverend Ryan was by here earlier today threatening me regarding a possible friendship with you."

"Had you told him anything?"

Priscilla shook her head. "Not a word, nor anyone else, as I promised. I am not sure how he knew."

"I think it's our neighbor. She was constantly spying out her window." Connie sighed. "It's not a surprise, but it is frustrating."

"You have support here," Priscilla said. "I have friends. You won't be pushed out of this town by anybody as long as I am here."

Connie gave her a strange look but then smiled. "I am glad of that, but our leaving isn't about me—this time. Del wants to move on. It appears the gambling isn't going so well. Maybe what happened to the Tombstone mines has led to less money in the territory. Perhaps it's just our time to go."

"Well, I am sorry to hear it whatever your reasons," Rose said, "but understand you have to do what is best for you, I hope you come back someday."

"We tend to wander around-- so you never know," Connie said. "I think Del is hoping the goldfields in the Sierras will be his mother lode. He always hopes for that, of course."

"You can't use your insights to figure out a good place for you?" Rose asked as she poured her a cup of tea.

Connie shook her head. "You know how that kind of thing is. It isn't very regular. I get things, but sometimes cannot interpret them. I wondered." She looked then at Priscilla. "Did anything I told you help?"

Priscilla considered that before she answered. "You did alert me to the possibility of an enemy. Although I am not sure I know who it is, I have my suspicions and am trying to prepare myself. As for a white knight." She stopped and smiled. "They are in short supply here in Southern Arizona."

"Don't give up on the white knight," Connie said. "They come up in unexpected places. Stay alert."

"Maybe she has him but isn't admitting it," Rose said with a teasing laugh.

"Sometimes they come with a few flaws. More off white than pure." Connie joined in the laughter. "As for the enemy, I don't have more to tell you except... it is good that you are being alert. I still feel danger near you. Love and danger."

"I guess that's not unusual in frontier towns," Priscilla said. "Although I have to admit I felt as threatened today by Reverend Ryan as anyone, and he's not from where I'd expect it to come."

Connie laughed again, but this time with no humor. "It's exactly where I'd expect. I won't say there aren't good men of the cloth. Of course, there are, but many of them use someone who is different, who might not see the world as they do, as a way to build their power. I've seen it before and likely will again."

"You won't refuse to use your gift?" Rose asked sipping her own tea.

Connie's eyes reflected sadness, but she shook her head. "No, I will do as I have and be cautious where I use it just for those who, I believe, deserve the help."

"I could give you some money, just to help you along the way," Priscilla said, "not as payment but as just help until you are settled again."

"Thank you, but we are fine with money. I appreciate the offer though."

"Write me," Rose said as Connie went to the door, and the two women hugged. "And if you ever need anything, let me know."

Connie looked again at Priscilla when she stood on the porch. "I do have one thing for you. That person, the one I told you about, whoever it is watches you. I am not sure if it's a woman or man right now, but that person doesn't mean you well. Keep your eyes open for that."

"I will."

"Good... and about that white knight," Connie grinned. "He might at first appear more like a black knight." And with that she was gone.

"I will miss her," Rose said as they settled back at the kitchen table.

"I bet she'll be back. Maybe not soon but someday."

"You turning into a seer yourself?"

"Lord, I hope not. I used to be fascinated by such. Now the

unseen almost scares me. I think seeing what is coming is something I'll leave for others. I have enough trouble with the world I
can see."

Rose's dark eyes were thoughtful. "We don't always ask for
that. But if it happens, that you get gifts of dreams or insights,
well don't fear it. It's not from where that reverend says."

To avoid discussing it further, Priscilla rose. "Want me to peel
the potatoes now? You never said. Are you coming with us to the
Yaqui Christmas?"

"We will indeed. I have seen the deer dancers at Easter and
will enjoy seeing them again. That young man, Rafe, seems
very nice."

"He does. I better find Grace-- so she can help us with
dinner."

Although Priscilla had invited Ellen, Rafe and Cord for
dinner, the lawmen were unable to come but promised they
would arrive later if it was possible. Later ended up past Grace's
bedtime, and she was off before Priscilla heard the knock. When
she opened it, there were two tired men, fresh from the trail.

"We better stick to the kitchen tonight," Cord said looking
down at his dusty boots and clothing. "I guess Grace gave up
on us."

"She wanted to stay up, but she was tired, and it was uncertain if you'd be here at all. She does need to adjust to a bedtime.
When school starts, it'll be easier for her. Where have you been?"

Rose poured the men each a cup of coffee as they threw their
coats and hats over the pegs by the door. "There is apple pie left.
Would you like some?"

Rafe grinned and the smile grew wider when Ellen went to
cut him a piece. Cord declined. "We were looking for five renegades reported east of Tubac. Supposedly armed, but we saw no
unshod tracks, no sign. Maybe all imagination."

"You think we will have Indian trouble again then?" James asked as he also took a piece of pie.

"General Miles is hot on Geronimo's trail. Except a few renegades, I don't see it up here," Cord said. But it didn't mean we didn't have to look."

"Tomorrow night is Christmas Eve. I hope nothing will spoil that," Priscilla said wishing she had the right to massage Cord's neck. He looked so tired, as though he had a headache. She turned to look out at the darkness of the night to resist the urge and not show what she was feeling to the others.

"I won't let it," Cord said.

"Can you tell us more what we might expect?" Ellen asked Rafe. "I am so excited at going as I have never seen a ceremony but have heard about it from others."

"It's a mix of your enchanted world and ours," Rafe said with a smile directed only toward her. His interest in the lovely little blonde was not hidden. Priscilla hoped that she was aware what she was encouraging. Ellen was dear but could be flighty.

"Your enchanted world? What is that like?" Ellen asked. If she wasn't attracted to the handsome Yaqui, she was certainly giving every impression that she was.

"Now don't quote me on this because I haven't listened as well as I should when the elders told the stories, but as I understand there are five. The wilderness, the flower world which is where little brother the deer lives, the cave world from where all spiritual power comes, the night world which is why you should look for unusual occurrences that occur at night, and finally the dream world."

When Priscilla looked across the table she saw Cord watching her. The dream world was where she met him, now almost each night. She wondered for a crazy moment if he also met her there. Did he dream of her as she did him? Was he her dark knight? It was impossible, or was it?

CHAPTER 13

W ith eagerness, Grace popped into Priscilla's room when
it was barely light. "It's today, isn't it?"

Sleepily Priscilla forced her eyes open. "Today and tomorrow.
Tonight for the ceremony and tomorrow for Santa."

"Well I don't believe in Santa. If he existed, he'd have given
me something before this, wouldn't he?" Grace asked as Priscilla
got up and dressed wishing she had a better answer for her.

"Whether they come from Santa or not, there will be gifts
tomorrow for you. Some from your father and some from me,
and who knows who else."

Grace's eyes glowed. "I am so excited I can hardly bear it."

"That's good. Now let's get some breakfast."

In the kitchen Rose was cooking bacon while James was
reading the Tucson Daily Citizen.

"Anything special going on?" Priscilla asked thinking she had
been forgetting even to look the last few days.

"Something about the Apaches south of us and the law doing
nothing about it. The usual," James said with a grin and another
sip of coffee.

"Ah fear once again sells." Priscilla read over his shoulder.

"Nothing like it."

She noted the name of Reverend Ryan with a column about the meaning of Christmas but decided there wasn't much he could say that would improve her morning. Ben knocked on the back door.

"Come on in," James said, but Ben remained outside.

"I just wanted to say I was done with the grooming."

"Ben come inside, have some breakfast," Priscilla insisted.

"Don't feel right," he responded with his head down.

"It's Christmas or will be tomorrow. Of course, it's right. You are coming to Christmas dinner, aren't you?"

He didn't look up. "Will *he* be here?"

"Certainly."

"Don't feel right."

"Ben, he understood you weren't yourself that day. He's forgiven you."

Grace looked up from her cereal with questions in her eyes but said nothing.

"I ain't forgiven me," Ben said.

"It's time you do then," Rose said. "It's what Christmas is all about. A new start. We're going to the Yaqui Christmas party tonight. You could come with us."

He shook his head. "Reverend Ryan said I should go to his church."

"Well, you do what you want, Ben."

"Reverend coming around much?" James asked with a thoughtful expression.

Ben shook his head still hiding his expression. "Not so much."

Priscilla wondered if he was lying. Was Reverend Ryan her real enemy? Ministers had ordered the burning of witches before. Was that how he saw her?

Rose came to the door, took Ben's hand, and led him into the kitchen. "It's too cold for us to keep the door open or you to stand out there. Come. Sit. I cooked plenty of bacon. How do you like your eggs?"

This time he sat and ate the food set in front of him.

"That was really good. Uh, *he* going to the Yaqui Christmas?" he asked looking at Priscilla when he had finished.

"Yes and Rafe, Ellen, all of us. Rafe's little brother is doing the deer dance."

"I'd like to see that, but pastor wouldn't like it if I didn't go to church. He said I had to go to get forgiveness."

"It is your choice, Ben," Priscilla said, "but whatever you do, I expect you here tomorrow for dinner. It's Christmas and family should be together then."

He looked at her with surprise. "Am I family?"

"Of course, you are. You work and live here, don't you?"

He nodded.

"Well then, it's settled. And *he* will be glad to see you. I am sure of that." Well relatively sure. His voice was back to normal. He didn't seem the type to hold a grudge. One way or the other, she couldn't stand the thought of Ben spending Christmas alone. Hopefully Cord would see it the same way.

When evening came, Priscilla bundled up Grace, as the night was cold especially for Tucson. It felt as though snow might fall on the valley bottom, which was a rare event. On horseback, Cord and Rafe followed the buggy. James drove the four of them to the big building where the Yaqui celebration was to be held. Rafe had explained that the secret part of the service had already been performed. This would be a welcoming of the community.

People were standing around outside laughing and talking. Some in Spanish, others English, and a few sounded to be speaking the Yaqui language. Priscilla was surprised to see people she knew.

Inside elders, at the front of the room, played drums and rattles, some singing now definitely in Yaqui. The room was rapidly filling with smiling people. Overall the feeling was warm and loving. Long tables were piled with food while on others were blankets and craft items. There was no indication whether they were for sale or to share.

She and her little group stayed close to Cord and Rafe, wanting to be sure they did nothing unfitting. She smiled as she saw Ellen making certain she was the one at Rafe's side.

As the drums and rattles grew louder, a slender boy entered the room, shuffling his feet with a little dance step, the head of a deer on his head, his chest bare. On his ankles were rattles. He moved cautiously around the room, now and then jumping in the air but always watching the edges as though for a threat. At times he stopped as though eating. As he passed near them, Priscilla glanced at Grace to see her eyes widened with wonder.

From one side came two more dancers, wearing what appeared to be wolf or coyote masks. They had bells attached to their bodies. The deer sensed the danger, reacted, and the trio stealthily circled.

When the speaker began talking in Yaqui, Rafe moved back to whisper, loud enough for Grace to also hear, "This is the struggle of the forest, the wilderness, good and evil, light and dark, that of nature. For Easter, it would go on longer, but this is Christmas, where the season is about rebirth and joy-- so the deer will not be a sacrifice and therefore escapes."

And he did, as the coyotes continued to circle, mystified where the deer had gone before they too vanished. "In some ceremonies," Rafe said, "the deer will be killed by hunters as a symbol of the sacrifice that is required for life to go on for the people."

"It was beautiful," Ellen said smiling up at him.

The people in the room moved toward the table of food, and merriment was all around them. Cord came to stand by Priscilla and Grace. "Did you like it?" he asked.

Grace was still wide-eyed. "I'd like to dance like that," she said with a wistful expression.

"You could. Make up your own steps to dance your story," Priscilla suggested. A few moments later a dark-haired boy came to stand by Rafe. Although she had only seen the bottom of his face due to the mask, she guessed it had to be his brother. She wondered if compliments were in order or was this something sacred.

"My brother, Gabriel." Rafe introduced them all.

"Your dancing was wonderful," Grace said surprising everyone as so often she stood back and shyly said nothing.

Gabriel smiled, white teeth flashing against his dark skin. "It was my first time."

"It was very good," Grace said, "especially for a first time."

"Would you like to meet my family?" Gabriel asked her and soon the two were gone.

"Perhaps she will make some friends," Priscilla said as she took Cord's arm surprising both him and herself.

"Not likely to be in her school," he observed as they moved toward the edge of the room watching as other dancers began moving to the music.

"Have you had any luck in finding a house for the two of you?"

"No, but I'd hate to force her from yours right now. Best she start school with you and by summer we can work this out. That is it meets with your approval."

"I like that idea," she agreed with a smile, as she looked up meeting his gaze. She knew where this was going and felt glad they were in an area with so many people. Had they not been, a kiss would have followed. Foolish, foolish woman. What was she thinking? But she saw the same impulse in his eyes and knew that sometime in the not so distant future they would have that kiss. Maybe it would dampen what she felt—after all, how good could a kiss be?

Rose and James joined them along the wall. "She's having fun," Rose said as they watched Grace giggling with several little girls.

"It is a generous place," Priscilla agreed. "I am glad we came." How anyone could find fault with what she saw here, she couldn't imagine. Remembering Pastor Ryan, she knew some would. She didn't care.

"Good evening, Marshal." One of the men that Priscilla recognized as earlier playing the drum had come to stand in front of their little group.

"Hello Mr. Vega," Cord said taking the elder's outstretched hand.

"Good to see you here," Mr. Vega said.

"Your nephew has been a good deputy to me."

"He's a good man."

"Yes, he is."

"You are a good man too."

"Thank you."

"You are the hawk."

Priscilla felt a cold chill as Cord smiled but said nothing. "I have a word for you," the old man went on in a somber tone. "This has come for you through me. I was asked to tell you but had waited, unsure if I should, until I saw you here tonight."

"You took that as a sign?"

The elder nodded. "There were two messages. They came to me at different times. The first is that there is something secret involving you. You do not know it, but it will be revealed in its time."

"Thank you."

"There is more. It came a different time. I know they were connected. This was a warning. An owl flew to me out of the dark sky, a sky with no moon, and spoke. You understand that in such a dream, it's not the owl, but a spirit using the owl. It said danger lies ahead for the hawk who keeps the law."

Priscilla felt as though something clutched her heart at the mention of the two birds. She looked up at Cord's face to see how he took the man's warning. He was still smiling. "That is not new."

"This will be unexpected, and it will be new. You have an ordeal ahead, possibly more than one such. Be aware, Marshal."

"I always try to be."

The old man grinned more broadly. "Like the hawk you are. Good." The old man then turned to Priscilla, nodded and smiled. "You are a good woman," he said before he turned and left them.

"Sometimes the elders get visions," Rafe said to Cord. "Don't take it lightly."

"I can't afford to worry about such."

"He wouldn't have said something if he hadn't thought this is something you don't see now, won't see then."

"It's getting late," Cord said. "Let's get Grace and take her home." Priscilla saw that he wasn't going to take it seriously, but she did. It was too much like what Connie had said, for her to dismiss it. She wished she had the capability of seeing what it all meant. Was she making too much out of the woman's vague warnings and her own seeing of hawks so much more frequently?

With Christmas morning, Grace again was waking her and rushing her to get dressed. She had been in the midst of a dream but couldn't remember anything from it.

"You can't open gifts until everyone is here," Priscilla reminded her as she chose a bright red dress with a scoop neck-- then took Grace into her room and helped her put on a red dress of her own.

"Will there be presents?" Grace asked as she finished buttoning her up.

"Of course."

"But for me?"

"We should go down and see."

"Now?"

"As soon as you get on your shoes."

In the parlor, Grace rushed in to look at the tree and see the many gifts. She was so excited that it wasn't easy getting her into the kitchen to eat breakfast.

Priscilla had urged Cord to come early, and he had promised he would if nothing arose in town. They had just finished breakfast when he and Rafe rode into the yard, putting their horses into the corral before they came to the kitchen door.

"Oh good," Grace said. "Finally you are here."

"Finally?" Cord said with a laugh as he bent to wash his hands at the sink. "It's not much past sunup."

Ben followed them in the door-- and when Cord smiled at him, he showed his relief with one of his own rare smiles.

"Ellen isn't here yet," Priscilla reminded Grace who was pulling on her skirt.

"Oh... all right."

They took their coffee into the parlor where the tree was loaded with wrapped gifts. "Shall we sing some carols?" she suggested to no one's enthusiasm. She sat at the spinet and played a few but knew she was passing time until Ellen arrived. Then her friend was there, and the unwrapping began.

Grace was thrilled by everything she opened, and she was by far the major recipient of gifts. She was delighted with the teddy bear, which she promptly named George. Her own gifts to everyone were handkerchiefs, which she had been embroidering with help from Rose. Priscilla saw the emotion on Cord's face as he saw his.

There were gifts for everyone. Priscilla had picked out plaid, heavy woolen scarves for Rafe, James, Ben, and Cord. For Rose it was a necklace of coral, which she immediately wore. Ellen's gift was a fine gold chain.

Priscilla opened one package with a scarf of her own, then one with a book she hadn't read which only Ellen knew. She waited to open the one she saw had come from Cord. It was a locket on a gold chain. "No photos," he said. "You'll have to find those for yourself."

She smiled and put it around her neck. If she had had a happier Christmas, she didn't remember. Just meeting Cord's gaze once in awhile made her glow. As she began picking up wrapping paper, she hated to see the morning end.

"I'm afraid I have to go for a bit," Cord said when she started to leave the room.

"On Christmas Day?" she asked with frustration.

"I'll be back," he said.

"Dinner is at two."

"It shouldn't take much. I got another request to check on fresh sign of rustling. I put it off to be here this morning but can't avoid it. This time there may be tracks to follow."

"Daniel Jamison is going to ruin my Christmas," she said not hiding her disappointment.

"No, this time it's another small rancher out that way."

"I hope it's not the Baileys again," Rafe said.

"You and me both."

"You want me to come?"

"No need. I am just looking for tracks. Hopefully it won't take more than an hour or two."

"We want you here," Priscilla said as she walked him to the door.

"And I want to be here too. You know that,"

"Then be sure you are," she said with a saucy smile. "There is some mistletoe here, you know?"

His eyes darkened. "I'll be back. As soon as I can."

Rose stood beside Priscilla to watch as he rode out at a fast gait. "It was a nice morning."

"Perfect right up until he had to leave," Priscilla said. "He'll be back though...or so he said."

Rose grinned. "Then let's get that dinner going so he has something to come back for."

"Oh, I tried to give him that," Priscilla said with a laugh.

When Ellen came in to offer her help, they sent her back to keep Rafe company. She didn't protest.

"You think that is going somewhere?" Rose asked as they pulled the turkey from the oven to baste it again.

"Maybe. Ellen though... she's kind of a flirt."

"She's not the only one," Rose said giggling.

"I know. And I know what you're going to tell me. It doesn't make any sense at all."

"I wouldn't be the one saying that. You are the one."

"What would my parents think?"

"I don't know but do you care?"

Priscilla smiled then pursing her lips out. "I suppose not."

"This isn't about them or anyone else. It's about you."

"It's not smart."

"It is going kind of fast," Rose said. "It wasn't that long ago you were throwing barbs his direction. What changed it?"

Priscilla realized it hadn't changed at all. There had always been something there, and it had been the reason for the barbs. "Well it can't go anywhere. I have enough commonsense to know that."

"And why not?"

"He's a man with a gun. You know how I feel about those."

"Who you trying to convince, Missy?" Rose asked as they shoved the turkey back in the oven. Priscilla knew the answer to that, but she didn't voice it.

Riding back toward the Wesley house, Cord felt nothing but frustration. He had again gone by the Bailey house after the evidence that five cattle had indeed been driven from the XT Ranch toward the Bailey place. He was convinced Jesse Bailey was taking steers, driving them down the arroyo to where the stream ran enough to hide tracks and where other cattle had been. The Baileys refused to answer their door, which came as no surprise but added to his irritation. It's not like he was thrilled to spend his morning as he had.

He remembered then how beautiful Priscilla had looked with a red dress that seemed to float around her body leaving him with mixed emotions. That dress would've cost more money than he made in a year. Unbuttoning all those buttons, letting it fall to the ground as he set about undoing all the rest of what she was wearing until she was naked was a fantasy he'd never experience for real. She was out of his league on so many levels.

He had done everything he could to stay out of her way from the time he'd first seen her in Tucson. His daughter's arrival had changed all that and left him helpless against the desires that surged. He could resist acting on them though, and he would do that.

When the day came that Grace wanted to live with him, then he'd not have to see the minx. And yes, she was that with the way she had teased him with the mistletoe. Like she'd ever really let him kiss her. He knew the way of the world. Women like her and men like him never came together for kisses and all the rest of what he could imagine with her.

When he arrived at the Wesley home, Ben was outside, and walked up to take his horse. "Been wondering if you'd get here," he said as Cord dismounted.

"You already eat?" he asked as he had no clear idea of the time.

"No, we ain't and you're why."

"Sorry," he said as he walked toward the barn with Jeb's reins in his own hand.

"I was told to take your horse," Ben said in a resentful tone.

"You going to hit me again if I don't let you?" Cord asked as removed Jeb's saddle and bridle enabling him to eat the hay in the stall.

"No. They won't let me," Ben said with his usual simple logic.

"That's good. How would I eat if you hit me again?"

"Couldn't, I guess," Ben said watching thoughtfully, as Cord gave Jeb a brushing, before he walked with him back to the house. "You still mad at me cuz I hit you before?"

"Ben, if I took offense at everybody who hits me, I'd be too busy holding a grudge to do anything, now wouldn't I?"

"Guess so."

"Of course, when you're the one who hits a man, he remembers it a little more than when some others do."

Ben looked at him, and when he saw the smile, realized he was joking. "Guess so. Well I won't do it again. Miss Wesley'd be real mad at me, and I don't want her mad at me."

"Is she mad at me for being late?" Cord asked as he stepped onto the porch.

"No, she isn't," Priscilla said as she pulled open the door. "But wash up quick. If the turkey is overcooked, we'll all know who to blame."

If it'd been a different day, a different woman, he'd have pulled her into his arms and kissed her hello, but it wasn't. Half the house watched as he washed at the sink.

Soon platters of food were carried into the dining room and set onto the table. Priscilla came in with a bottle of wine. "James, will you give the blessing since this is after all Christmas."

When he had said a few words of gratitude, James began carving the turkey, filling plates with white or dark meat as the bowls of potatoes, dressing, gravy, vegetables and rolls were passed.

"I suppose I should have gone with you," Rafe said as they began eating. He smiled down at Ellen who was sitting beside him. "Glad I didn't have to though."

"I lost the tracks before I could determine where they ended up. Just another wild goose chase."

"A lot of little rustling jobs going on out that way, are there?" James asked sipping the white wine Priscilla had poured into his glass.

"Too many," Cord said, chewing the turkey and finding it tender and moist. As he ate, he knew he hadn't had a better meal in longer than he could remember—if ever. Not the least of his pleasure came from having it with friends.

"Kind of funny that it's such small bunches. What was this one?"

"Gentlemen," Priscilla said with one of those smiles women used when they wanted their way, "can you talk business after we eat?"

They laughed but agreed. Cord knew this experience being at a table like this, a woman like her, a daughter sitting and watching him now with more approval in her eyes, it wasn't his to keep, but it was damned pleasurable while it lasted.

After dinner, the women carried the dishes to the kitchen, while the men were told to have their cigars or cigarettes in the den and dessert would be later. When Cord walked into the den, he saw a humidor on the desk, lovely silver lighter beside it. When he opened the box, the superior cigars the judge had smoked were there.

He picked one up, sniffed of the fine tobacco, its sweetness, before asking if the others wanted one. Rafe and even James took one.

"I never smoked a cigar," Ben said.

"Nothing to it if you've smoked a cigarette," Cord told him biting off the tip before he lit the end, sucking the smoke into his lungs and feeling a relaxation that seemed to flow clean through him.

Ben took one then and with some concern in his eyes

followed suit. "It's good," he assessed as he took his first puff. "Better than cigarettes."

"Costs more too," Rafe said as they found chairs to sit within reach of the ashtrays.

"About those steers," James asked. "You think Tucson has a problem?"

"From the time small ranchers came in with barbed wire and the big ranchers resented the loss of open range, yeah, there's a problem."

"So big or small ranchers doing it?"

He shook his head. "I wish I knew. Each job is small. When you tally them up, it's over fifty head reported-- with the probability more have been taken. Ranchers up that way are often iffy on exact counts for range animals. It's making them edgy, as they look at each other with suspicion. Other than when I found the brands changed at the Baileys, the cattle seem to be disappearing."

"There are a fair number of box canyons up there," Rafe said. "Should we start checking each one?"

"While they move them around as we go?" Cord asked taking another long draw on the cigar.

"So what can you do?" James asked.

"Hope we get lucky next time and get there before they have a chance to wipe out the trail."

"Sheriff doing anything about it?" James asked.

Rafe snorted with derision. "He claims any problem beyond city limits aren't his. The real issue is he's too fond of the bottle."

James sighed. "He is a nice guy."

"Nice guy or not," Cord said. "He's not doing his job, even within the city limits, and it's because he's drunk too often. Or he gets drunk because he doesn't want to do his job." He could see that possibility, as he was getting sick of his own.

Ben frowned. "Man should do what he promised."

Cord grinned. "On that we agree."

The afternoon was engaging. They played games, listened to Priscilla play Christmas songs, and were offered a choice between apple and pumpkin pie with homemade ice cream. No matter how fresh and beautiful Priscilla looked, Cord knew she had worked hard all day. He was no longer surprised that she wasn't the spoiled daughter of a rich banker, who sat around letting others serve her.

As dusk began to turn to dark, he reluctantly said he should go. Rafe had already walked Ellen home. Ben was out in the barns tending to the stock. As Cord got to the door, Priscilla said, "Did you notice what is above us?"

He looked up and there was the mistletoe hanging from a ribbon. He smiled and bent to brush a kiss on her forehead. He didn't dare do more-- but when he stepped back, he had the sense she was disappointed. He wondered what kinds of kisses she expected from her beaus. Not that he qualified as a beau.

She walked out with him to stand on the porch. "The stars are so bright," she said. "It's such a clear night." He wondered if that was what she was really thinking. For a moment, he thought about giving her the kiss, he knew they both wanted, but he wouldn't do it. He was in too deep as it was.

"That, over there, is Orion's belt," he said as he pointed toward the Catalinas. "There's a sword with it when it's fully up."

"I've always wanted to know their names. So beautiful."

He looked down at her. "Yes, beautiful."

She sighed. "I suppose you do have to go."

"You know I do."

"Could we... I was wondering if we could have lunch together later this week, Grace, you and me?"

"Only if you let me buy. You've given me too many meals, as it is these last weeks. I should be buying you lunch every day for a month."

"Where could we meet?" she asked, and he saw she was

purposely delaying his departure, not wanting the evening to end any more than he did.

"How about the Palace?"

"It's a little costly."

He smiled. "I think I can afford it, as long as it's not too often."

"Well then, yes, I'd like that and I am sure Grace would too. I think she is getting more and more at ease with you."

"I hope so. I know I am with her, and it's thanks to you. You've done so much to help her and me. I want you to know how much I appreciate that."

He could see she wanted more words from him, but he wasn't going to give them. He knew what was growing in his heart. He also knew it would never work. Priscilla Wesley was no woman for him. He couldn't be the man for her.

Ben came out from the barn with Jeb. "Horse is ready for you, Marshal," he said as he looked from Cord to Priscilla and back. Cord wondered if he had been watching them. He guessed it didn't matter. He mounted and tipped his hat to her. "Thank you for a beautiful Christmas, ma'am. The scarf," he had it wrapped around his neck, "will be much appreciated this winter."

She felt of the locket around her own neck. "As will this locket." He wondered whose pictures would someday be in it. The one thing he knew for sure-- it would never be his.

CHAPTER 14

Priscilla dressed carefully for her lunch with Cord. She wore a green suit with a hat that set off the suit as well as her. She helped Grace choose one of the new dresses Cord had bought for her. Its soft, green color worked well with Grace's intense coloring. James had hitched up the buggy, and she drove to town with a song in her heart. It might be difficult, but she felt increasing confidence that they would work out their differences. She had never met a man with whom she more wanted to see that happen.

Grace was excited at the idea of lunch again at such a fancy restaurant. "With crystal like last time?" she asked for the third time as Priscilla tied Jezebel to one of the posts.

"Of course," Priscilla said as she guided Grace across the dusty street to the marshal's office. She forced herself to ignore the scream of a hawk. Omens made no sense. Readings made no sense. A hawk was just a hawk.

"He's in back," Rafe said as they entered. "You inviting me too?"

Cord came from the back grinning. "You are tending the store."

Rafe snapped his fingers. "Lousy boss."

Grace looked with concern until she saw Rafe's teasing grin.

The three of them walked out onto the street, heading toward the Palace Hotel, when Priscilla heard the shout from behind them. "Hey Marshal!"

When she turned, she saw a young man standing in the middle of the street, his legs spread wide, his hand hovering over his gun.

"You're an ugly man, Marshal. Anybody ever tell you that. They should have. You are an ugly, old hawk always looking for something to kill. This time it's your turn"

"You two go onto the restaurant. I'll meet you there," Cord said as he turned to face the youth.

"No, we'll all go together," Priscilla said, a surge of fear traveling through her body.

"I won't be long," Cord smiled at her, but she saw the hard look in his eyes, the muscle twitch in his jaw. She didn't believe him.

"We need to all go together," she argued unwilling to move away from him.

His left hand now was on her arm. "You need to get Grace off the street." She looked into his eyes and saw that there was going to be trouble. She had no choice but to get Grace away from it.

"Please don't do anything foolish," she begged, but she took Grace's hand and crossed the street to the boardwalk. Keeping Grace on the side of her away from the street, she turned and looked back. The young man still stood as though ready to reach for his gun.

"Take it easy, Jesse," Cord said taking a step toward him.

"Marshal, it's not me gonna be dead in a minute."

"Don't be foolish," Cord said with another step

"Maybe you ain't a hawk-- more like a cowardly vulture, preying on others. You been after me. Well now you got me— want it or not."

"Jesse, you're a young man. Years ahead. Don't make a mistake now that ends your chances."

Excited laughter was his answer. "They'll be better years after this."

Cord took another step but stopped at Jesse's scream. The sound was high pitched, too much like a hawk's scream not to make Priscilla shudder. She drew Grace into her arms, using her own body to protect the girl from flying bullets.

"One more step and I draw. You are a walking dead man, Marshal." He laughed.

"Jesse, this isn't how you want to end your life," Cord said his voice even. Priscilla saw that he had his right hand out from his gun, but not so far he could not reach for it. "We can talk."

"You think I'm a rustler. You will come for me, and I might as well face it now."

"If you're not a rustler, you can prove it." Cord's voice was calming, and he had taken another step despite Jesse's orders.

"No talking, no proof, Marshal. I count to three and when I get there, I draw." Jesse gave another nervous laugh and began counting. "One ... two." But he didn't wait for three. Priscilla saw his hand dart for his gun. She didn't see Cord draw. It was so fast that she wasn't sure it had happened except for hearing two shots so close together one might have been an echo of the other.

Cord stood, tall and strong. The youth seemed to stagger, staring toward Cord with a shocked look before he crumpled to the street. Cord walked slowly forward. When he got to the sprawled form, he kicked the gun away from the outstretched hand before squatting, feeling for a pulse.

Rafe ran into the street as others came forward. "Get back to your work," Cord ordered, his voice still as level as though nothing had happened-- except it had, a man was dead.

Priscilla watched as Cord put his gun back in its holster. She avoided looking at the body and felt Grace trembling. Or was it her? Her knees felt weak. She had to hold herself together for Grace.

"We will have lunch at home," she told the little girl who had now turned to look at the street.

Cord walked to them-- his lips were pressed hard together, his eyes narrowed. At his approach, Grace shrunk behind Priscilla. She feared all the good that had been done over the last weeks had just been undone.

As much as Priscilla knew it wasn't Cord's fault, she also saw that it was who he was—a killer. She could not handle that. She couldn't meet his eyes as he stopped, standing on the dusty street below them.

"We..." She knew her voice was shaking. "Grace and I better go home."

He nodded but said nothing as he turned and walked to where she had earlier tied Jezebel's reins. He led the horse and buggy to them. "I will have things to do," he said, his voice still calm. She wondered what it meant to him to have taken a life. Maybe nothing. She couldn't bear to look at him as she lifted Grace into the buggy and then got in herself.

"Goodbye," she managed as she flicked the reins. She hoped she would never see him again, even as she knew she would have to. Whatever hope she had had for their relationship had ended with that burst of gunfire. She could not be with a man who was capable of that kind of violence. Maybe Cord had known it all along. Maybe it was why he had not kissed her, when she had tried to tempt him into it. She could at least be grateful for that.

Cord watched them drive off before he turned back to the street. He knew he had done all he could to avoid facing what happened to Jesse Bailey. It didn't make it easier. Maybe people thought he killed without a thought, but he'd taken only two other lives in his nearly nine years as a lawman. Each had been in the line of duty, not a street gunfight like this. It didn't matter how it had happened. How it ended was what counted.

Mostly as a lawman he had found ways around using the gun. Killing didn't come easy, no matter what some might think. Each time it had been forced upon him, it had sickened him. He hid his inner turmoil over it, as it wouldn't do to show weakness, not in his world.

Rafe was standing beside him, and he wasn't sure when he had come. "You all right?" his deputy asked.

"What's happened here?" Sheriff Adams asked as he joined the circle. Figures, Cord thought. Man never shows up until after something-- if then. Was there an easy way to describe what happened?

"Jesse Bailey wanted a reputation more than to keep living," he said.

"That's what I saw," Ridge said as he had joined those watching it all go down. "Jesse was in the bar talking about being picked on and going to get himself a marshal. No way Cord could've stopped him this time."

"There'll have to be an inquest," the sheriff said.

Cord's smile was hard. "You be sure and set that up, will you?" He turned then and walked with Rafe back to their office.

"You all right?" Rafe asked again.

Cord nodded, even though he knew it wasn't true. "You get the undertaker," he said forcing an emotionless voice. "I'll talk to Judge Emerson."

"Despite what that old sheriff said, you don't think anybody will blame you for this?" Rafe asked.

"His parents will."

"I saw it. A lot of us saw it. You had no choice."

"I know."

When Cord had settled the legal aspects of what happened,

arranged for someone to go out to tell the youth's parents, as it couldn't be him, he returned to his office. He took his spurs from the shelf and fastened them to his boots.

"You want to talk about it?" Rafe asked returning from his own errands as Cord came out from the back and took a rifle from the wall rack.

"Not now."

"Where you going?" Rafe asked.

"I'll be back. I just need to clear my head." He headed to the stable and threw the saddle over Jeb's back. Tightening the cinch, he had one thought—get away from town and questions.

He set the gelding on the Spanish Trail, passing wagons coming into town and those leaving, a few people walking along the edge. When he came to a wide sandy arroyo where he knew it was level without holes to break their necks or legs, he nudged the gelding. Jeb needed no further urging as he took off at a hard run.

Cord leaned forward in the saddle feeling the wind rush past, the ground blurring under the thundering hooves. As he and the gelding cleared the ground, he wished it was as easy to leave thoughts behind. Bending lower over Jeb's neck, he urged the gelding on.

As the ground got rougher and they began to leave behind the tall saguaros, he slowed their pace. High above the valley, he stopped. Absently he stroked the gelding's neck as he looked out without seeing. Finally he dismounted, loosened the cinch, and loosely tied the hackamore to a mesquite branch in a grassy area.

Taking his rifle, he walked to a good sized boulder and sat looking out at the valley so far now in the distance. Overhead, a hawk soared on the wind, in the distance, several vultures circled over what likely had been remains of a predator's kill. Predators at least killed for food. His kill had no sense to it—other than staying alive.

He didn't want to think about it, but the memory came flooding back of the first man he had killed. It had been in New Mexico after a bank robbery. He'd been a sheriff. It was his duty to stop outlaws. He had, and then looked down at a sightless, scruffy, middle-aged body, maybe the robber's first time to go bad or one of many attempts. Whatever the past of the man, Cord had been his end.

The second time he'd killed was in a scruffy border town where shots had been fired. As a deputy marshal, it had been his job to head toward them. When he got there, it was obvious the shooter was high on something. He was shooting at anything he could see that moved. Cord had tried to talk him down-- but when the gun turned toward him, he'd had no choice in what he did next—not if he had wanted to live.

Cord had faced death a lot of times. He knew he had coolness, when it happened, that got him through. Most of the time in Tucson he had avoided using his gun. His size and a tough demeanor did it for him. If you look mean enough, people back off. If he could get close to them, as he had tried to do with Jesse, he was fast enough to get their gun. Today, it hadn't been enough.

If taking a life was easy for others, he'd never found it so for himself. He saw again the moment in Jesse's eyes, that flicker, that told him he was going for his gun. It was at that point, that Cord had a choice—draw or die. So many thought they were fast, that that was all that mattered. Speed wasn't everything. Having a steady hand, being a good shot, and willing to fire fast, that often mattered more. Jesse would never learn that lesson. You had to survive for that.

For the first time he let himself think about Priscilla and Grace watching something he'd have given almost anything to keep from them. He had seen in Priscilla's eyes that she blamed him. She hadn't had to say the words.

He had known all along how this was going to be with her. It didn't help. He knew he had hoped for something, even knowing he should not. Now he figured Grace also would want nothing to do with him. He was who he was and that was not tolerable to Grace or Priscilla. Grace had been taught all her life that he was a violent man. Today she saw evidence of it. He doubted he could ever undo that.

When Cord rode back into town, it was obvious gossip was running rampant about what had happened. Such shootings were infrequent enough that the story would be bandied about and expanded. In his office was a reporter from the Citizen. No surprise Wasson would have sent him over.

"My publisher wanted your side of the killing," the man said with a pad ready to take notes.

Cord had been through such before. It never got easier. "There will be a written report," he said as he put his hat on the peg by the door.

"Certainly I'll use that, but a first-hand interview is always more meaningful." The sly look in his eyes told Cord what the man really wanted—something salacious.

Rafe came out from the back room. "I could tell you what happened. I was there. The marshal has a lot of things to do right now and as you can imagine, he's not feeling well."

"Killings make you sick?" the reporter asked writing that down.

Cord clenched his jaw against the retort he wanted to make, but he told a shortened version of what happened, enough to get the man from his office.

"It won't sound anything like that by the time he gets through," Rafe said.

"Maybe you'll end up marshal then, as I don't give a damn if they fire me."

"You sending a report to Prescott?"

"Like I have a choice?" He grimaced as he sat at the desk and began writing the bare basics of what had happened.

"Judge think there will be an inquest?" Rafe asked pouring himself a cup of the by now very stout coffee.

"He said no. We'll see. A lot depends on how Marshal Meade sees it." He rubbed his lower lip as he considered that problem. "Maybe he'll pay us a visit just to get the lay of the land down here."

"You know much about him?"

"Not a lot. You know how it works, the politics of his job. He might not be here that long."

"But for now he's got the authority?"

"That and the town, if they want to bring charges. This wasn't in the line of duty."

"Like hell. You know it related to the rustling. Wright wants you out of here, and he doesn't care how he does it."

"Frankly I can't see him sending Jesse to do it. No, this was more likely all on his own, wanting a rep, the next Billy the Kid."

"Too bad he didn't pay more attention to how it ended up with the Kid," Rafe said taking another sip of coffee.

As Cord rolled his cigarette, he thought about what he should do regarding Grace. He couldn't desert his daughter, but Priscilla wouldn't want him near her. Those easy days of dinners, playing games, spending an evening, they were done. He'd seen that in those beautiful eyes that had shown such horror and seemed on the verge of tears. He lit the cigarette taking a draw. Jesse had ruined a lot of things that day, not the least of which was his own life, his parents, and likely any chance for Cord to be a real father to his daughter.

The question of what to do was resolved two days later when James Redman showed up at the office. "How you be?" he asked as he slumped into the chair in front of Cord's desk.

"I'm sure you've heard I've had better days," Cord said leaning back and studying the older man.

"Yep. She came back, had me put away the buggy, got Grace

into the house with Rose before she broke down in tears, and told me."

"I didn't have a choice, not that it will matter in the end to her."

"She knows. But it was what she feared. Now she watched it happen. She has been holding it together for Grace not to upset her. She asked me to talk to you. She wants you and Grace to find other ways to be together."

He couldn't argue. He understood it was best all around. "Is Grace willing to see me after the shooting?"

James smiled. "You know, in that, kids are more flexible than adults."

He lit a cigarette. "So... how do we work this out?"

"Rose or I will be the go between. When you bring Grace home, the times when that might be needed, Cilla will arrange to be gone."

"All very civilized," he said inhaling the smoke.

"You know how she feels about guns."

"All right, I'll do whatever works. I would like to continue developing a relationship with Grace if she is willing."

"She might even be more so. I think it scared her, but it also scared her that you could have been hurt or worse. There are things you can do with her, maybe picnics or something. Could be with Rose and me or Rafe and Ellen. Heck, I don't know, but just time together. She starts school right after the New Year."

"That will be good. Do I have to sign papers or anything for that?"

"I think you should go to the school and meet her teacher. Best I understand it, they will test Grace to see what grade she should be in. Children benefit in schools when parents are involved."

"Then I will do that. I have been ordered to head down out of Tubac to check on those Apaches that keep popping up. I might be able to put that off until she starts school. So far there have been no attacks. Just people edgy seeing them out there."

"You have any trouble over the shooting?" James asked.

Cord walked to the stove. "Want some coffee?" he asked and got out a second cup when James nodded.

"There was an informal hearing which ruled it self-defense." No need for him to mention the Bailey's written complaint that he was out to get their son. People understood that. He tried to understand it, but it didn't make it easier, especially not after all the times he had tried to get them to keep their son controlled. "And I heard from Marshall Meade. He is supporting me. No trouble legally."

"And otherwise?"

"It's never good when a marshal kills someone. Town gets edgy. They don't feel easy about a man with a gun anyway. Miss Wesley isn't the only one who thinks I just have a badge to kill. I won't be invited to any tea socials." He grinned when James laughed.

"You have a dangerous job."

"It has its moments."

"How about me bringing Grace here tomorrow, and you figure out something for the two of you to do?"

Cord nodded his agreement, as James drank the last of his coffee and rose. "It will come out better than you think. That little girl wants her daddy. I saw how she's looked at you. She wants to believe in you."

"I hope you're right."

When he was alone in the office, Cord closed his eyes for a moment, opening them when he saw Priscilla's face. Damn, this was going to be harder than he had hoped. There was no way forward though-- except through it.

Rafe came in and slumped into the chair.

"You still seeing Ellen?" Cord asked him.

"As often as I can," Rafe said with a smile.

"She as down on me as Priscilla?"

Rafe shook her head. "No, she understood about Jesse. She said Priscilla does too, but it's more than that for her."

"It turns out James is going to bring Grace here tomorrow if Grace doesn't decide otherwise. I need to have something to do with her. How about if the four of us head out to that wash north of here-- the one with the sand and a stream? Seems like a good place for a little girl to play. We could bring a lunch. I think the café can put together something."

"I'll ask Ellen, but either way you can count on me. You think we can both be out of town at the same time?"

Cord drew in on the cigarette. "It's not that far, but I'll alert Sheriff Adams. Time he pulled his own weight for a change." He hadn't liked the mixed testimony the sheriff had offered at the hearing. Let him see how it worked to be the one who had to go when there was trouble.

"Good then. I'll talk to Ellen this afternoon. I wouldn't mind some sand fun myself." He thought a moment. "Hey and Ellen would have to roll up her stockings, right? If she was going to wade with Grace." His grin was one of youthful masculine pleasure.

Since Cord had no interest in thinking about a woman's trim ankle, he snorted and got up, pulling on his hat. "I think I'll take a look out toward Jamison's place. See if I get lucky on those rustlers." Anything was better than thinking about Priscilla. Since the shooting, he'd done all he could to fall in bed exhausted, to avoid any dreams. Sometimes it even worked.

Priscilla was washing dishes when James returned. "He agreed," he said as he sat at the table.

She had expected he would. What choice did either of them have? Whatever had been developing would be ended if they just didn't see each other. It meant nothing to him. After all when he'd had the opportunity to kiss her, he hadn't done it. He had always seen her as obnoxious and in his way. She would stay out of it in the future.

"How did he look?" She couldn't resist the question.

"Do you care?" James asked not giving an inch.

She put the dish towel down and came to sit at the table with him. "You know I do."

"Missy, you don't have to do this."

"Cut him out of my life?" James nodded. "Yes, I do. I cannot live with a man who would shoot down another human being."

"You think he had a choice?"

She felt the tears again. "Not that day, no," she said in a small voice.

"You think he didn't do all he could to prevent it? That he wanted that right in front of his daughter and you?"

"I know he didn't, but he has put himself in a position where that's part of his life. He is a man with a gun."

"And a badge."

"Legal killing."

James shook his head. "Without men like him, you tell me what you think this country would be like."

"That might be so, but I don't want to... be close to such a man."

James pursed out his lips and then gave a crooked smile. "You don't?"

She groaned. "It's what I know logically... not what I feel inside."

"Just you keep one thought in your head. Men like him don't come along all that often. He's a rare one. You know it. You know something else."

"What?" she wiped away tears.

"There's not going to be another like him for you-- ever."

She did know that, and she was torn in pieces over it. She kept reminding herself—he hadn't wanted to kiss her. Maybe her feelings weren't shared. It didn't matter either way. She could not live with a man who wore a gun. She kept seeing the street that day, a man lying dead, but it wasn't Jesse Bailey. It was Cord's intense blue eyes staring sightlessly into the sky.

No, it couldn't be. On that she was decided. So why couldn't she stop thinking about him?

CHAPTER 15

Martin sat at his favorite table nursing a beer. What to do next? His mind swirled with options. His goading Jesse into attacking the marshal hadn't led to the marshal's death as he had hoped, but it had slowed down whatever had been developing between him and Priscilla. It wasn't enough.

Gabe Evans and Clinton Adams came through the swinging doors. When they saw Martin, they grabbed beers and joined him. "Boss is looking for you," Evans said as he took a big gulp belching with satisfaction.

Coarse animals, Martin thought but managed a smile. "I am right here."

"It's not where he wants you."

Martin was in no mood to cater to these two. "Tell him I'll be out in an hour."

"I'm not your errand boy," Evans said. "Tell him yourself."

"You just were his errand boy."

"That's different. He pays me."

Martin snorted with disgust.

"He's not happy about you goading Jesse to brace O'Brian," Adams said.

"Who said I did?"

Evans chuckled. "I heard you doing it. The night before out at the ranch. You wanted the marshal gone and thought you could get him to be your errand boy there too."

"I just told him how it was, that's all." Martin didn't like this conversation. If Evans started telling that to others, it might get back to O'Brian.

"Yeah right. How dumb do you think the rest of us are? I didn't try to stop you, because Bailey, with that chip on his shoulder, was trouble waiting to happen. I wasn't sorry to see him take on a man I knew could kill him."

"So you figured the marshal would end up being your errand boy."

Evans shrugged.

"You're pretty clever then, aren't you?"

"About some things. I know what you want."

"And that is?"

"You want that marshal away from your woman."

That sounded good. Martin liked the sound of it. "My woman?" he asked anyway.

"I could help you with that." Evans' smile was sly.

That Martin didn't like at all. Any help from Evans would have a price tag attached. The more who knew what he was thinking, what he wanted, how he followed Priscilla, the more likely the wrong people would hear. "I don't need any help. I've given up on her anyway. Don't want her anymore."

Adams chuckled. "No way I believe that. If you think you've got a chance, you will go for it. Hell, for a tasty dish like her, I would myself."

"Well I won't." He went over to the bar and brought back a pitcher of beer. "I just want to do a good job for Wright, that's all," Martin said using his smoothest tone. He wasn't sure the two hands bought it, but they drank the beer and soon drifted away to find some action.

He couldn't keep going like this. People would figure it out. How could he get Priscilla to see him for the rare man he was? What would it take to have her see him the way Abigail saw Sam Ryker. Then he remembered how Ryker had kidnapped Abigail. That's what it would take. Get her away from the others, off just the two of them. Alone together, she would fall in love with him.

He swirled the beer in its glass. It would not be easy to kidnap her. She had people around her. She wasn't riding off into the desert where she'd be easy to snatch. Except as he had followed her, learned her route, there was one weak point. She was helping an old lady about a mile from her home. She went there about every other day with food, spent some time visiting and then left to walk back home.

There was a stretch on her route, where there weren't any houses. It had to be there, and he had to figure out how he could do it in such a way that he wouldn't hurt her. When he got her where they were alone, she'd be grateful to him for taking such good care of her.

He remembered then a deserted log cabin he'd heard about in the mountains. The men at the bar had been saying it'd be a good place to live except Apaches had scared everybody out of buying it.

He thought about what it would take to supply it. First, he'd have to rent a horse and ride out there—supply it with what they'd need for a week. He would use a wagon to take her and could bring more supplies with it. The more he thought about it, the more he liked the idea. It would work. Once she got away from others, he'd teach her to want him. He grew warm just thinking of how he would do it.

Cord was pleased by how it had gone with Grace. The picnic at the wash had been a winner. He'd rented a buggy allowing the four of them to ride together. Watching his daughter play in the stream, he'd earned her laughter when he tried to demonstrate how to cross the stream on the rocks. His boots slid off and he waded. Getting them wet had been worth her giggles.

Sitting on the blanket, eating their picnic lunch, Grace had even brought up some questions about death. What happened when people died, she had asked. If she had begun with something easier, he might've had more of a chance of impressing her, but this was where he didn't have answers even for himself.

Ellen had offered her own opinion. "Heaven is where the good people go."

"And the bad?" asked the thoughtful little girl.

"They say hell."

"Was the man who tried to kill Daddy bad?" It was the first time Cord had heard her refer to him as daddy and it took a moment to get past the emotional reaction.

He thought of the right words before he answered. "He was troubled more than bad. I don't think he'd go to hell."

"Do you believe in hell?" she asked not willing to let the topic go as by now all the adults wished.

Cord shook his head. "But I can't say I believe in heaven either," he admitted.

Grace then turned to Rafe. "What do you believe?"

Rafe smiled. "I am like Cord. Not sure, but my people believe in the spirits, that they hang around and can be in the area where they lived for a time after they die."

"Ghosts?" Grace asked.

"I suppose you could call it that."

Grace seemed satisfied with that, even if none of them had given her a definitive answer. After that Ellen had warmed to Cord. He had expected her to hold Priscilla's grudge, but it seemed Priscilla was still doing all she could to make it work for him with Grace and not speaking against him. What she was doing was avoiding any contact with him.

It wasn't hard to do. When Grace started school, Cord had been the one to go with her the first day, to sign the papers, talk to the teacher, and then see that she had the right supplies. Priscilla had picked her up in the afternoon. Grace very much enjoyed being with other children and back in school. It turned out she was a little ahead of what would have been expected for her age. The school had the ability to let her proceed at her own rate.

Sitting at his desk, Cord read the wire from Meade. It was a demand that he head toward the border and look for five renegade Apaches who were not coming into the reservation as had been agreed. A goat, some chickens and a calf had disappeared, which might or might not have been related. Cord realized he couldn't put this off forever, didn't expect it to be dangerous-- but more unpleasant. Winter was setting in with snow on the higher elevations.

When Rafe got back, Cord told him what he planned. "You want me to come along?"

"And leave Tucson at the mercy of Sheriff Adams?" Cord asked with a laugh. "Are you crazy?"

"Might be I should go instead of you?"

"And the logic of that would be?" Cord did not intend to agree, but it was always interesting to hear Rafe's creative reasoning.

"I can track. I am an Indian."

"One, who has been the enemy of the Apache. No thanks. And I am also fairly good at tracking. You keep an eye on things here—our girls. I already told Grace that I'd be gone for a week or so."

Rafe gave up as he obviously had no belief he could win anyway.

In the morning, Cord headed south, well-equipped for a week in the hills and warm enough clothes to go as high as need be to find the Apaches, assuming they were foolish enough to be hanging around. He had a bedroll, his saddle bags filled with food, water bags, raincoat tied to the saddle, as well as his rifle, and plenty of ammunition if he did run into trouble.

As unpleasant as the camping was going to be, he was glad to get out of town. Maybe he'd quit thinking about Priscilla Wesley.

~

Priscilla had spent an hour with Mrs. Gibbon, leaving a little later than she preferred. The elder woman was lonely, and so happy to see her, that it was hard to find a time to break away. Hearing her talk about her dead husband didn't make it any easier on Priscilla, as about all she could think about was Cord. Grace had said he left several days earlier and would be gone for a week on an expedition to capture wild Apaches. That left Priscilla both relieved she couldn't run into him as well as worried that he'd be hurt.

As she walked past the sector with no homes, she picked up her pace. Maybe she should have accepted James' offer to come with her. He had so much to do that she had said no. Still with dusk settling in, it seemed a little frightening, not that Apaches would come this close to town.

When she saw the wagon coming from the other direction she felt eased that someone else was on the road. It passed, slowed, and then stopped. She heard a step behind her, but not in time to prevent a burlap sack from being yanked over her head and pulled down to literally cover her. The smell was suffocating as she tried to push it away, but she was shoved against the back of the wagon while a strap was tightened around her arms, pinning them to her side.

When she would have screamed, a rough voice said, "Don't make a sound, or I'll have to hit you over the head. I don't want to hurt you." She struggled but could do nothing to stop the binding that was now around her ankles. In what seemed only seconds, she had been totally incapacitated.

Helplessly she was lifted and laid down in what she felt had to be the back of that wagon. Sacks of something and boxes were pushed against her body holding her more firmly in place before something was thrown over the top of her bound form. When she tried to sit up, she discovered another rope was holding her firmly into the wagon bed, as much cargo as anything else.

In moments, it could not have been more than a few, the wagon was moving forward only this time faster. Priscilla struggled against what was holding her, but she soon learned she had no hope. Even if she hadn't feared being knocked unconscious, screaming would do no good, as she heard no sounds indicating other people nearby. She had been kidnapped. The very thing she had tried to prevent had happened and so easily that she might as well have never taken a single lesson from James.

When she accepted the helplessness of her position, she took some deep breaths, grateful she was not smothered by the sack and blanket. She had to calm down. Whoever had her, they had said they didn't want to hurt her. Of course, that was probably what all kidnappers said.

Do not panic, she ordered. Sometime this would end. She would find who had her, and when she did, she had to be rested and ready for what came next. Could it be possible someone hoped to get a ransom? She felt a chill as she remembered Connie's warning.

Forcing her breathing to steady, her terror to disappear, Priscilla thought of Cord. He would save her. Except nobody would know where she'd gone. He was out of town. No, nobody would save her. That meant she had to save herself. As it darkened around her, she set herself to falling asleep. She would need all her strength for when the wagon stopped.

Cord had talked to the people of Tubac-- then headed east into the mountains. It had been three days out when he caught the tracks of unshod ponies. It would be too much luck to expect he would have already found the renegades, but he'd follow them a while and see what evolved. Their route led easterly, higher into the Santa Ritas. As the air grew colder, he unfastened his coat and put it on.

At dark, he made a simple camp for himself without a campfire, even though the air was sharp with a wind coming from the north. He ate two hard biscuits, some jerky, and drank water before he bundled up to sleep.

Waking before dawn he was still caught up in a nightmare. Sometimes he remembered his dreams, but mostly when he didn't want to. This time it was vivid. Priscilla needed him, but he was unable to help her. Someone was hurting her. He struggled to remember the person's face, but it was gone—left with Priscilla's eyes wide and pleading. Nightmares meant nothing-- still it made him edgy.

He got up and built a small fire to make coffee. He figured the tracks had been heading farther into the mountains, which meant he'd be facing snow if not in the morning by nightfall. This was becoming a fruitless venture as he worried something had gone wrong in Tucson.

Foolishness. Just a nightmare. Priscilla was well watched by James. There is no way she could be in trouble. He drank the coffee and ate another biscuit before he saddled Jeb and headed in the direction he thought the five horses had gone. He checked the load in his rifle and put it back in the scabbard. He couldn't just go shooting at Indians because they were up here in the pines. He knew a few words of their language and hoped that would be enough if he caught up with them.

As he rounded a rocky point, he heard the sound of a shot and simultaneously felt the pain of a bullet strike his left arm. He pulled Jeb to a halt and with the same movement dismounted.

Finding shelter, gun in hand, he pulled his coat off to see what damage the bullet had done.

From seemingly out of nowhere, a man hurled onto him, arm upraised with a knife, throwing them both into a dead mesquite. He reached for the man's knife hand, as he pushed his own revolver into the man's belly. Aiming it upward he pulled the trigger. The body slumped, and he pushed it off, working to dislodge himself from the dead branches, one of which he had to break off after it had speared his shoulder.

When he finally was free, he listened for more sounds. It was silent. Breathing heavily, Cord shrugged back into his coat, grabbed Jeb's reins as he drew the rifle from the scabbard and took cover behind some boulders. Snow was starting to fall. For the first time, he realized he might not make it out of this.

Priscilla had no idea how long she had been in the back of the wagon, as she had slept part of the time and plotted what she could do when the wagon stopped. It would all depend on who was driving it. She had pretty well determined it was one man, but she hadn't heard enough of his voice to know if it was someone she knew.

When the wagon stopped, she heard the man jump down and steps coming toward the back of the wagon. Instead of instantly freeing her or even picking her up, the person took the boxes and sacks that had been propped around her. He was whistling, which was annoying as it was off key. It was then that she knew who had her.

Finally, he was back. Reaching for the blanket over her, pulling it away, he untied the ropes around her ankles. When she could move her legs, he pulled her to the edge of the wagon and said, "We're here. I know you will like this."

She wondered if he was insane. What she knew she had to do was keep herself from panicking. There was a way around this.

She would find it. When she was standing, she asked, "Please free me."

"That's a nice way to ask," he said as she felt his hands on the ropes that encircled her and held the sack over her head. It took a while before she felt cold air and the ties were loosened. Where had he taken her?

When he pulled the sack from her head, he was smiling. As she looked around she could see it was likely afternoon. They had traveled through the night and a good part of the day. Snow was on the ground and tall trees overhead.

"Martin," she said forcing a pleasant tone to her voice. "What is this all about?"

"It's our honeymoon cottage, of course." He swung his arm wide so she could see the log cabin a few feet from them.

"We aren't married." She forced a smile.

"That can be fixed later. Look at how it was with Abigail and Sam when he kidnapped her. I just took a page from his book and brought you here. You and I can find the love in the mountains that they found."

Now she was sure he was insane, but she wouldn't let herself lose her head too. "Sam didn't kidnap Abigail," she said forcing a smile. "Abigail asked to go with him."

"A minor point. Come, let me show you our abode."

"Martin, I am afraid out here so far from everyone. Take me home, and we can talk about this where it's safer."

"My dearest, I can keep you safe." He pointed to a rifle in the boot of the wagon.

"I hope it's loaded."

"Of course. I am not a fool. Now let's go in the cabin."

She remembered when he had grabbed her breast. In the cabin her options might lessen. "May I help you unharness the horses?" she asked. On his belt he had a Colt. She was relatively sure it would also be loaded. One or the other gun, she would grab.

Maybe both, and when she did, she would have to find the courage to use the weapon if required. She didn't think she would have to. Martin would take her home once she had a gun to force him.

"I can take care of that," he said smiling again in the way that chilled her.

She forced a smile and moved closer to him rubbing her hand over his shoulder. She reached out to hug him, forcing herself to put her arms around him. Martin responded by taking her into his arms. "I knew it'd be this way," he said.

"Oh it will." At that point she reached for the revolver and shoved him away. Quickly she moved to the wagon. "Keep back," she ordered pointing the gun at him.

"You wouldn't shoot me." He started to walk toward her. She pulled the trigger with the bullet creasing the edge of his shoulder. He jumped back.

Without taking her gaze from him, she reached for the rifle in the boot of the wagon. "You will now take me home. This has gone on long enough."

"I can't do that."

"Oh, yes, you can. I can drive a wagon. Martin, if I must, I will kill you." She was shocked to realize she meant it. She didn't want to get too close to him for fear he'd overpower her. "Get up in the wagon and turn it around. Then we will head back into town."

He nodded and moved toward the wagon as she stepped onto the cabin's porch. She decided she could ride in the back of the wagon on the way into town, keeping both guns.

When he lunged for her, she kicked out hard with her right foot, landing it fully on his knee as James had taught her. He screamed and fell to the ground. "You broke my knee," he moaned.

"Maybe. Now using that other leg, get up in the wagon, and turn it around. We are going back to town."

He grimaced but got into the wagon, backing the horses around-- but instead of stopping when he finished, he flicked the reins hard over their rumps and took off with the wagon at a hard run.

She thought seriously about shooting him, but it was not in her to shoot a man in the back. The question of whether she would survive was not yet settled. The question of whether she'd be raped at least had been. She didn't like realizing that she had been prepared to kill a man. She could consider that later.

She took the guns into the cabin, leaned the rifle near the door, and put the revolver on the small table. The cabin had a bar to secure its door. She slid that into place. She used the small chamber pot before looking at her surroundings. The cabin had a nice sized wood cook stove. She had no idea what kind of supplies Martin had brought to their 'love nest.' In the corner was a double bed with a quilt on it. It looked as though he had been here earlier and prepared it for what he hoped would happen.

As dark was settling, she saw the snow beginning to fall heavily. She needed heat and found kindling, that perhaps Martin had left beside the stove, and matches above it on a shelf. In a few moments she had a fire going. She stood in front of it, warming her hands and wondering how she would get back to Tucson. Rose and James would fear the worst and be frightened for her. Outside she heard an animal howl and felt gratitude that at least she was within four walls.

She wished, instead of having James teach her self-defense, he had also taught her wilderness survival. It was looking as if she would need it. She lit a kerosene lamp looking around wondering what more she needed to do. Exhausted she took the rifle to lean beside the bed. She doubted Martin would be back, at least not until the snow had melted, but who knew what kind of men might be up in these mountains.

~

Firing at the moving figure, Cord knew he had hit another when he heard the grunt of pain and a figure stumbled and fell hard. Two down. Three to go. Would they continue to attack? The snow was falling more heavily. They had to be as cold as he. One of them was dead, and he thought the last likely was also if he had hit where he intended.

He had looked at his wound, but it didn't seem to be a major injury, only bleeding sluggishly. The branch that had speared him was another story. He had yanked on the end, and thought he had pulled it all out but with dead wood like that, a man could never be sure. Anything left behind would poison him more surely than a bullet. He'd heard of those who died from smaller slivers than this. It wasn't his most immediate concern.

He tried to hear if anyone was moving toward him. The only sounds were those of the wind and snow falling. Jeb was standing quietly not showing signs of distress-- maybe the renegades had taken off, cutting their losses.

Cord backed toward his horse, keeping alert. He couldn't stay where he was. Freezing to death might be less painful than a bullet, but it was just as permanent. He had to get out of the wind and find better shelter for the night.

CHAPTER 16

With morning, Priscilla woke finding it hard to believe where she was. It would have been easy to imagine it had all been a nightmare. Except, she was still in it. She built up the fire, emptied the chamber pot a few feet out from the back door, before she began looking though the boxes Martin had carried into the cabin. Flour, salt, bacon, a ham, dried beef, sacks of potatoes, carrots, cartons of eggs, and even a bottle of whiskey. Dear Lord, how long had he hoped to keep her here? Or had he ever intended she would go back to Tucson?

Outside the snow was building up-- very pretty, but making it clear she would be going nowhere until it let up. Could she walk out? Not only did she have no idea where she was-- but her walking boots were inadequate for snow. Her jacket was a light-weight one, again insufficient to walk in frigid conditions.

She sliced slabs of bacon to set frying-- then dug into the boxes to find baking soda. She could make biscuits. She wouldn't die up here, with shelter and food-- at least not for a while. Snow never lasted that long in the mountains of Southern Arizona. She hoped.

As the light increased, she knew she had to calm down and

stay put. Snow was falling in big heavy flakes. With the faint light, even in daylight, she had no clear idea of which way was north. She could survive this, if she didn't lose her head.

The biscuits were cooling on the table when she heard a horse ride into the yard. She wrapped the quilt over her shoulders, grabbed the rifle, and headed for the porch. Maybe it was someone who could help her, but equally likely it was more trouble.

Outside, she saw a rider bent over his horse. When he looked up, he was unshaven, looked exhausted, his face puzzled, as he nudged his horse closer to the porch.

"Who are you?" he asked staring at her with disbelief.

She realized what she must look like. She'd not attempted to pull her long hair up. It was probably wildly all around her face, and then there was the gun. "Your worst nightmare," she answered with a smile.

Slowly Cord dismounted, and she realized he wasn't using his left arm. "Oh you've been that all right," he agreed. "I'll take care of my horse, and then be in to see what in the hell you're doing here."

He looked pointedly at the rifle, before leading his horse to the shed where Jeb would be out of worst of the storm, Taking off bedroll, saddle bags, unsaddling, and removing the hackamore took a little more time than usual with his sore arm. He kept remembering the moment he'd ridden into the yard, then seen the door open, and she had walked out looking nothing like the fine lady from Tucson.

"Grub later," he told the gelding as he lowered his head and headed back into the storm to get to the cabin and hopefully some answers.

Priscilla, standing by the stove, turned as he opened the door. "Please put in the bar," she requested, as she watched him dump his equipment and rifle by the door. He rebarred the door, before shrugging out of his coat and removing his gun belt to hang on a peg.

"What happened to your arm?" she asked.

"After you tell me why you're in a place like this. I smelled the smoke and it's the only reason I found you."

"Want some coffee?" She held up the pot. He nodded, as he carefully lowered himself into the chair by the table. When he took the first sip of good strong, hot coffee, he felt warmed for the first time, and it wasn't all the heat of the cabin. He'd never seen her more beautiful-- wild hair, wrinkled clothing and all. If this was a nightmare, he'd take it.

"Now," he said, "explain. This doesn't make sense to me. It's crazy enough to make me think it's a hallucination."

She smiled. "I have wished that more than a few times. It does feel unreal, but it's not. Martin kidnapped me."

"Matthews?" he asked putting down the cup.

"Yes, he had some misguided idea that if he got me up here, he could convince me to marry him. I suspect rape was a factor in his thinking, but he didn't get far enough for me to be sure about that."

He clenched his jaw. "He out back and dead?"

She smiled. "I thought about it. I got his gun by letting him think I was happy to be with him. It wasn't hard. I pointed it at him and said he had to take me back to town. He had other ideas and raced the team off leaving me here-- I suppose hoping I'd die and be unable to tell anyone."

He shook his head with disbelief. "I always figured him for a coward but never a killer."

She knelt in front of him. "I didn't either, but I did have reason to distrust him and should have told you that he had tried to grab me before. James stopped him. It was why I wanted to learn self-defense. If I had told you, maybe I'd not be here now. Although... maybe it's good I am. There is blood on your sleeve."

"It's not much." He told her about the renegades and the run-in he'd had. "If they didn't leave the mountain, they could show up here." He thought about Matthews and what he had intended, how if Priscilla hadn't been tougher than he'd thought, she'd have been raped at the least. Maybe he'd have gotten here to find her dead. He let out a hard breath at the thought.

"Let me see your arm." She pointed to the dried blood.

"It'll require taking off my shirt," he protested with a smile. "Not very gentlemanly."

She gave a little laugh. "I think I can bear it. Take it off." She walked to the counter alongside the stove. When she turned back with a whiskey bottle in her hand, Cord had removed his shirt.

Priscilla sucked in a breath as she looked at what the shirt had been covering. He had a beautiful body, hard muscles, a ridged belly, strong arms, and... She swallowed hard and forced herself to look at the wound. An angry gouge on the outside of his bicep had stopped bleeding at least. "It looks painful," she said to distract herself from what she was thinking, which was she wanted those arms around her.

"So long as it doesn't infect, it's nothing."

"Martin included this in his supplies." She held out the whiskey bottle.

"For drinking or pouring?" he teased with a smile that showed him in a better mood than she'd have expected given their situation. "Hey," he teased, "I survived something I wasn't sure I would and so did you. It's a good day after all, isn't it?"

She smiled. "I'm trying to decide." She moved to the shelves and brought back a glass, pouring him a drink. As he sipped it, she cleaned his wound as best she could, pouring a little on it to his harsh intake of air. Finished, she took a sip from his glass, poured him a little more before she sat on the other chair. "They will be worried about me in Tucson, although I realize there is little I can do about that."

"Likely ready to fire me for not being back to go after you."

She looked out the window. The snow appeared to be falling more heavily. "We can't leave now." She knew despite everything, she didn't want to leave, even if the snow stopped. This was a time out, and she wanted it to last as long as possible. When she looked into his eyes, she saw the same wanting.

Confirming her intuition, he pulled her from her chair to his lap. "Remember Christmas?"

She did.

"And a kiss you promised me."

"That you didn't want," she reminded him.

"Oh I wanted it. I wanted it very much. I just knew it wasn't smart. I wouldn't have wanted it to end with one kiss."

"And now you will?" Her smile was teasing as she put her arms around his neck. She liked the feel of his skin, silky with hard muscles underneath.

"That would depend on what you wanted."

"That night I knew it couldn't be forever for us."

"Than I was right."

"What was right then might not be now," she suggested.

"You might not be thinking straight. You had quite a scare."

She nodded. "I did."

"And I thought I was going to die up on that mountain yesterday."

"So you might not be thinking straight either. I want that kiss, Cord. I want it a lot, but maybe we should give this a little time to think about it."

He grinned as she stood. "I've had some time to do that. Practically every night, Miss Wesley."

"Why Marshal, does that mean you dream about me?"

"When I don't lie awake thinking about you." His chagrinned smile told her more than his words. He didn't want to feel what he did. He stood and put his shirt back on. She noticed he winced as he tucked it into his pants.

She went back to the stove and looked at the supplies in the box alongside it. "I think I can whip up some eggs and bacon for you. Are you hungry?"

He nodded. "I'll see if I can find more wood outside. Is there an ax here?"

She looked behind the stove and there it was.

"If the storm doesn't let up, we need fuel, or food won't be our biggest concern." He looked outside at the growing wind and darkness before pulling on his hat and coat.

When he was gone, she stared at the frying pan and wished she had taken the kiss he had offered. Out of nervousness, she had missed her chance, but she would be sure she didn't again.

Of course, with them alone here at this cabin, the question was to where would a kiss lead. Cord was no callow boy. She wasn't ignorant about sexuality despite her sheltered life. A kiss was a step to something more. Biological facts didn't explain the stirrings of her own body, when he came near. How much more would his kiss do? Was she ready to take it further? If she didn't, would she end up a spinster, who never knew anything about what was possible between a man and woman?

When Cord returned, his face was strained. He had an armload of wood and without another word went out for more. She had thought one armload would be enough for the day, but he didn't quit until he had a pile of wood that she would have thought would keep them warm a week.

He took off his hat and coat sitting at the table. "Cilla, do you have any idea how to get back to Tucson from here?"

She shook her head disturbed at the expression in his eyes. "You do though, don't you?" She set eggs and bacon in front of him.

He nodded and began to eat. "I want you to know too," he said after a few bites. He took his coffee cup setting it further from the plate. The spoon formed a triangle. "The cup is Tucson." He pointed out the window as to which direction that would be. "The plate is where we are, and the spoon Tubac." Again he gestured to give her the direction.

"Martin took you a long way out, probably to be sure nobody came across you and him. Getting back to Tucson would mean covering a lot of very rough country. With snow like it is, the best bet is you head for Tubac. That's not going to be easy either because there are several. Let me think. Three dry gulches you have to cross, one with a small creek most of the year." He sketched a pattern with his finger.

"When you get to Tubac, you can have somebody take you to Tucson. I know it sounds confusing, but the main thing is stay to the left, head west toward the setting sun. There are some places where the descent is too steep and angle away from those. Damn. Do you understand?"

"I don't know. I guess so, but won't you be coming with me?"

"Of course, if I can."

"You can't think... Cord what is wrong?"

"Maybe nothing. When I had the fight with the renegade, we tumbled into a dead mesquite. It was sharp and speared right into my shoulder. When I yanked it out, I hoped I had it all but... it seems now that I didn't."

She felt a chill. She knew what he meant and had heard of those who had died from blood poisoning from something less than the branch of a mesquite. "There must be something you can do," she said.

"It's in my back. I can't reach it."

"Well, I can. Take off your shirt." This time she was less in shock at that muscular male torso and more concerned with the wound. High on his back, in the big muscle of the shoulder, she saw the entry point as well as an angry dark circle of red with streaks beyond for as much as five inches. She pressed around it, felt the heat and saw him wince at the pain. This wasn't going to be good.

"We can't go now," he said, "that snow is piling up, the wind growing. By the time we will be able, I might not be able to do it with you. Jeb will know the way though and..."

She interrupted. "You think I would leave you here?"

"God, you are a stubborn minx. I know you wouldn't want to but..."

"I think we should try to do something about it now. Get out the remaining wood. Something must still be in there with all that redness and swelling."

"And how would we do that?" His eyes were glittering, and she saw that smile that used to irritate her, but now just made her want to kiss those arrogant lips.

"You'd have to trust me to dig around in your back, I guess." She stood and put her hands on her hips. "Let me see if I can find the right tool to do it."

"You're going to enjoy this, I think," he said as she headed to the kitchen area of the cabin to see what kind of knives might have been left or brought by Martin. She went outside, got snow in a pan, and set it on the stove to melt. She had seen the doctor do such procedures, but this would be a first for her. How hard could it be?

He rose and moved to the stove. "Is there salt here?"

She looked into the box. "A small sack."

"If you can get the wood, and I don't really know if you can, then there still is infection down in there. Salt will help bring it out."

"Cord, that would be very painful." She found the narrowest knife, probably intended to do boning, which still seemed too big to be digging around in his flesh. What if she made it worse?

"It's not feeling so great right now."

"This is all I can find." She held it up for his inspection. He nodded, as she tossed it into the water to boil.

"You better have some whiskey for this," she said as she pointed to the bottle.

He shook his head smiling again. "I need to not be drunk. I am going to have to hold still or you'll put that knife clear through me." He put his hand out to take hers. "You sure you want to do this?"

"I do... but I want something for it. In payment."

He smiled. "I don't have much money on me."

She walked toward him. "I want that Christmas kiss... and Marshal, I expect you to make it a good one."

"Might be times I could do a better job." He rubbed his hand over his bristly jaw.

"Might be, but you already said I might send that knife clear through you. And I want that damned kiss."

"Sure you don't want me to shave first. Might leave you all red."

"No delays."

He laughed despite the pain he was in. "All right then, come here." He pulled her to him, but she stopped him with her fingers before his lips could descend.

"I have to warn you first."

"You gonna shoot me if don't match your other lovers?" he asked with a teasing light in his eyes.

"Cord, there've been no other lovers... and there have been no other kisses."

"None?" He stepped back to look at her.

"Never on the lips. So, make this a good one."

His smile turned warm and sensual. "I think I can handle that part. I been dreaming about it for long enough." As he bent, he lifted her chin and looked into her eyes, his own blue eyes now seeming darker. His lips lightly touched hers and then he pulled her more tightly against him as the kiss grew in intensity. His tongue pushed against her lips, parting them and thrusting in her mouth.

Priscilla felt as though warmth was surging through her whole body, as his tongue teased hers, encouraging hers to move against his. She opened her mouth wider wanting to take more of him into her, as she tightened her arms around him, stroking up his back, feeling his skin, the muscles. Her body had changed as they came together, seemingly almost melting into his. No wonder she'd been warned about such kisses.

When he finally released her and stepped back, he looked as melted as she felt. "Good Lord," she whispered. "why didn't I do that sooner?"

He managed a laugh. "Well if we get this chunk of wood out of my back, we can see if I can improve on it."

"You improve on that, and I might faint." She worked to steady her breathing as she headed back to the stove. The water was boiling nicely. "Any ideas on how I get the knife out of the water?" she asked.

He went to his saddle bag and brought out the bowie knife. Using it, he delved under the smaller knife and laid it on the stove to dry. She had found some clean towels and picked it up with one.

"I'm afraid, if you move, I'll do you harm," she said looking uneasily at the size of even the narrow blade.

"I promise. I won't move." He grinned again. "I want the rest of those kisses you are promising."

She bit her lip but nodded. She felt scared at the idea of digging into his back, but she had to do it, or this was going to turn much worse. "I don't want to hurt you."

"There is no other way. Let's give it a try," he said with the strength she had seen so often on his face. She sighed but nodded.

"I am thinking I should lie on the floor-- so we don't ruin that pretty quilt."

God, there would be bleeding. She hated every aspect of this, but he was right. Before lying down, he positioned a chair so that when he was on his stomach he could grip its legs. She knelt and studied where the wood had to have entered. Which direction had it gone?

"Don't think too much about it. Trust your instincts. To be honest, if we don't get the wood out of there, blood poisoning will most likely kill me, and it won't be pretty." He stretched out, his muscles rigid as he braced for what was coming.

She pushed the tip of the knife into the wound entrance, guessing the mesquite had to be angled some. She felt something solid and moved to get around it, using her fingers now to reach alongside the knife and trying not to think how it had to be hurting him.

Cord did not move, even as she knew this had to be agonizing. The sooner she got it out, the better. She moved the knife carefully to slide down the solid length, sensitive to where it would end. Finally she felt the space where ahead it was only soft. She moved the knife tip to edge under the chunk of wood and slowly, steadily began levering up. She tried not to think what Cord must be feeling.

When it had been raised to where she could get two fingers around it, she pulled, gently, anxious not to leave any part of it behind. Little by little it was moving, and then she had it. "It's out," she said.

"Do you see puss in the blood?" he asked through gritted teeth.

She looked more closely. "Yes."

"Pour the alcohol in the hole."

As she did that, he jerked for the first time. "Sorry," he groaned.

"I think I should bandage it."

"With what?" he asked head still down as he worked to deal with the pain.

She had to think. "You don't bring medical supplies with you?" she asked although she knew the answer.

"I try to think positive... and usually, if out by myself and something goes wrong, there's no point in them anyway."

"Let me see what I can find while this drains." As she rose, she thought of her petticoats except were they clean enough. Then she remembered the unopened boxes of Martin's supplies. He seemed to have been thinking of everything else. Surely he'd have something she could use. Breaking open one, she found cloth. "I think there's something."

It irked her to see what it was. A silky nightgown for her. Fresh shirts for him. Another pair of his pants. Those might be useful later. And wait, that shirt had a long tail, and while she could wear it, she wouldn't need all of its length.

Using Cord's bowie knife, she slit the tail of the shirt into strips. "Good old Martin," she muttered as she worked.

He was watching her. "Something about having his shirts on me is making me not like this idea."

She laughed. "They were brand new. Does that help your tender ego?"

"I'm thinking."

In a few moments she knelt and pressed some of the folded cloth against the still draining wound. "Can you sit up?" She asked.

"Last I knew." He levered himself cautiously to a sitting position, as she knelt at his side and wound the strips around his arm and shoulder to loosely hold the pad. "There is enough to do this again, when we have to reopen it."

"Wonderful," he said with that sarcastic twang that only he could do. "How about a slug of the whiskey now?" he asked as she sat back to study her handiwork. Rough but it would do. He took the bottle from her and a long swig. "You could probably use a drink too."

Thinking about all she'd been through over the last two days, she agreed and drank from the bottle, coughing as he laughed. It did make her warmer, more positive about everything. "We will both get out of this, won't we?" she asked wanting to hear it. Her fear was that the infection could still spread through his body even with the wood out—if she had gotten it all.

He shrugged wincing. "The odds are better than an hour ago."

She picked up the piece of mesquite and took it to the stove to burn. "I can't believe any of this." She looked out the window at the falling snow. "I used to think snow was pretty."

"It is." Slowly he got to his feet and moved to sit at the table. "Just inconvenient." When he started to shrug into his shirt, she came to help him.

"Did you grow up where you had snow like this? I've always lived in the south of the United States."

"Kansas and yes, it had snow, blizzards. They lasted longer than I figure this one will."

"What else can we do for the wound?"

"Make a paste of salt is about all I know. It draws out the poison."

"That would have to hurt terribly," she protested.

"Angel, letting it close up with the infection inside will hurt worse."

"Angel? Am I?" she asked teasingly as she watched him.

"You have your moments." His smile was sensual and full of promise. She wondered if any of that was wise. There wasn't just his need to recover from the infection. When they returned to Tucson, what then?

"You think too much," he said. "Why not just be where you are?"

She considered that a moment. "Is that how you live?"

"It's how I have had to live." She tried to read his expression. Whatever he was thinking, he was not revealing it.

CHAPTER 17

Whilst she convinced Cord to take a nap, Priscilla unpacked the remaining boxes that Martin had brought, for what he clearly had expected would be an early honeymoon. Foolish little man, but in terms of food, he had done well. She found dried fruit, cornmeal, tea, sugar, cheese, tartaric acid, and even chocolate. There was also a bottle of fine brandy. How had he afforded all of this? While she knew he had cheated Abigail's father, the sums had not been that great. What else had he been up to?

When Cord awoke, it was to the smell of cornbread cooking in the oven. "If years ago, I'd known you could cook like you do, I'd have been courting you myself," he said yawning as he realized he had things to do.

"You mean you weren't with all those nasty comments about my being spoiled to death?"

"I don't recall saying that." He sat up and looked around for his boots.

"It was in your eyes, Marshal."

He grinned as he pulled on the boots. "I then better watch those pesky things."

"I like revealing eyes."

"You might see something you don't want." He headed for the door and his coat.

"Where do you think you're going?" she asked in that voice he'd heard from women for other men but never one of his own. Even his mother, having been beaten down so badly by his father, had little interest in where her son went.

"I need to find food for Jeb, get him water."

"The storm is worse," she protested.

His smile was that hard one as he buckled on his gun belt. "Be right back."

Stepping out into the storm, he headed for the shed where he had secured his gelding. He found a bucket and filled it with snow, brought it back into the cabin to melt, ignored her disapproving looks, before he headed back out with the water. He had to push harder to close the door. It was really going to blow before it ended. He didn't envy anyone out in it—well for more than the few minutes he would be.

In the shed, he realized that previous owners or Matthews, thinking ahead for his own horses, had left a pile of hay in a walled off feed room. He gave Jeb several armfuls and hoped they'd be out of there before he needed more.

Back in the cabin, he rebarred the door and admitted, at least to himself, that the little bit of work had worn him out. After he had taken off his hat and coat, shaking off the snow flakes, he dropped into the nearest chair. She came across the room and felt of his forehead. "You're running a fever." Concern was back in her voice.

"I suppose it's to be expected. How about we try that salt paste?"

He looked up and saw a pained expression on her face, but she didn't argue as she headed back to the stove, dropped a handful of salt into a bowl slowly adding just enough hot water to form a paste. "How do we do this?" she asked as she brought it back to the table along with a small glass of what he discovered was brandy when he took a sip.

He stood to remove his gun belt and lay it on the table before he began unbuttoning his shirt. "I'll have to lie flat, I guess. And... you pat it onto the hole, try to work it in."

"You know how much this will hurt?"

"Once I got the mesquite stuck into me, there weren't a lot of things that didn't." He put his shirt over the chair and walked to the bed. "I hope this won't stain the quilt."

"Lie down and forget about the quilt."

He lay far enough over to allow her to sit on the edge. When she had removed the bandaging, she took a deep breath. "I'm sorry." She put the first dab of the salt paste onto the hole, working it in. He tensed, clenching his jaw against the searing pain, but managed to lie there without moving. If there was one thing life had taught him, it was stoicism.

When she had finally used all that she had, she put her hand on his back-- rubbing the muscles, stroking down nearly to his belt, and then back up, massaging, kneading and bringing warmth to his whole body. Maybe too much warmth as he began to feel a reaction he hoped he could hide.

From the moment she had told him she had never been kissed, he had known, as he should have always known, that she was a virgin. He wasn't about to do anything to change that. The next few days, until they could leave the cabin, were going to be an exercise in self-control because, while he knew what he could not do, she seemed to be doing everything possible to make that hard on him.

She applied a pad to the wound, again winding strips to keep it in place as she took the old ones away to wash. He twisted and sat up thinking some pain might not be a bad idea as way to distract him from what his body was saying it wanted—logically or not.

~

When Martin had arrived back in town, he quickly returned the wagon to its owner, thanking him its use.

"Where'd ya say ya were takin' it?" the old man had inquired with a curiosity he hadn't shown earlier.

"Just an errand for Wright. It's in fine shape and don't worry. I'll be sure you are paid a little something extra."

He went back to his rented room to debate how he could divert suspicions from himself over what had become a titillating topic-- Priscilla had disappeared. He slept on it, finishing off a bottle of bourbon before he decided the best approach was to go to the Wesley house. He hadn't seen anyone since he returned to Tucson, other than returning the wagon. He could go, pretending to know nothing of what happened. He knew it would work, as he dressed carefully in his best suit and a bowler hat.

Knocking at her door, James answered. Martin smiled. "Would you please tell Priscilla I am here to see her?"

"Where have you been not to know that she's missing?"

Martin managed a shocked look and fell back against the door. "Missing? What do you mean missing?"

"It's been over four days. She went to help Mrs. Gibbons. She got there, but somewhere on her return, she disappeared."

"No sign of anything?" Martin asked with shock in his voice. "What is the marshal doing about it?"

"Marshal O'Brian is not here."

Now Martin didn't have to fake shock. "Not here? Where is he?"

James studied his face before he said, "Where were you not to know any of this? Everyone has been looking for her."

He had thought of his alibi, but he needed Wright or Evans to back him up-- so he gave only part of it. "I was out of town, of course. How could this happen? Has a search party gone out? I remember something about renegade Apaches down south of here. Do they think... Oh dear, they don't fear they took her do they?"

"Rafe went out looking for tracks, but with all the rain we've had, he found nothing."

"What about a reward? Has that been suggested? I would certainly add to it for her return safely." Martin suppressed his smile. James would be so easy to fool.

"There is a reward already. We wired her parents. Told them not to come out. As it turns out her father is ill but hadn't told Miss Wesley in order not to worry her. They quickly offered $5,000 for her safe return."

Martin stared around the room trying to think what he could say that would deflect James' obvious suspicion. "Hadn't the marshal and Priscilla had a falling out recently, and if so, could he have done something to her?"

James snorted. "I think you better get going, Mr. Matthews. The marshal had nothing to do with this, and frankly you go saying that to someone else and it might go badly for you."

Martin saw the threat in the older man's eyes. "Of course, I was just thinking out loud is all."

"It's healthier not to do that. Now disappear." James looked beyond him and saw the little girl, O'Brian's brat, coming out from the kitchen with Rose right behind her.

"Did you find her?" the child asked tears dried on her cheeks.

"No, I didn't know about it," Martin said now wishing he'd not said that to begin. He should have come in concern but too late for that now. "I will begin looking though, you can be assured," he promised the sad looking child.

Rose met his eyes. "You do that, Mr. Matthews," she said with the same hard sound to her voice that her husband had voiced. "You just be sure you do that."

On the porch, Martin knew he had another problem. He had to talk to Wright as soon as possible to be sure his alibi was backed up. Profitable, as it had been working for Wright, he didn't want to be more under his thumb. The man would not care that he had kidnapped Priscilla, likely wouldn't care when she starved to death on the mountain. After all, he had also been rejected by her. What he would want was another hold on Martin-- one, Martin didn't want him to have. Except, he had no choice in needing his help. He had erred by not immediately going to him. It wasn't too late to fix it.

∼

As Cord's fever rose, Priscilla did all she knew to lower it. Again and again, she washed down his skin, used the salt, and pressed on the wound to force out any infection. She felt some hope when finally there was only blood, no more pus. Examining the bullet wound, she saw redness and applied the salt to it also. Nothing seemed to lower his temperature.

"It's all right," he said through shaking lips. "Body working to..." He lost whatever else he had intended to say.

She left on his pants because she felt uncomfortable going further. She washed his bare feet with cool water and finally used some of the snow cooled water to wash him down. Fearing he'd take chill, she followed it immediately with a brisk toweling off. She had to admit that having him where she could touch him freely was enjoyable despite the frightening reason for it.

After a while, when she could think of nothing else to soothe his restless movement, she began singing songs she knew, crooning, trying to reassure him that it would be all right, when she feared herself it might not.

Remembering Connie's reading and the Yaqui elder who had warned Cord of danger ahead. Was this what they had seen? Would he survive this ordeal?

She couldn't get him to eat but regularly helped him take sips of water. She continued to eat knowing she had to be strong for them both. When night fell, she crawled into the bed beside him, getting up to keep the fire going. She cuddled against his hard body as he restlessly twisted, turned, and mumbled in his sleep.

"She's a witch," he confided in a husky whisper. "I knew it from the start."

"Ah and who is she?" She wondered if he had met Connie Sicilla.

"Blonde beautiful. From the first day I saw her." His curse was graphic. "Always there, never leaving me alone... She bewitched me."

She smiled against his cheek. "Maybe she bewitched herself too," she whispered against his bristly jaw.

"Can't have her. Never can forget that," he said moaning and twisting away from her arms.

"Are you certain of that?" she asked running her hands down his torso to the line of his pants.

He smiled sadly. "Out of reach."

"Oh, not that far." She got up and found the cloth to again wash him and cool his body. With light, she would reapply the salt poultice. As she worked, she wondered if he was a little cooler. Was that good or bad? She looked up at his face, the hard set of his lips as the pain wracked his whole body. Could cooling mean his body had given up the battle, or did it mean the infection was finally being bested?

Then she heard the owl. She recognized the hoot to be that of a great horned owl, which she sometimes saw around Tucson. She also remembered the two warnings involving owls. Did its coming now mean Cord was going to die? She would not let her hawk go. She put her hands over his body-- felt her energy flowing to him. She would hold him. She would not lose him. The owl could not have him.

With light, she saw he was sleeping less restlessly and decided she better care for his horse. He had mentioned hay. She could do that as well as bring the animal water. The storm had passed on, and the sky overhead was a deep blue. With all the snow, it was beautiful.

When she got back to the cabin, Cord was shakily standing. He looked at her, a mixture of anger and fear in his eyes. "Where did you go?" he demanded forced by weakness to drop back to the bed.

"Your horse, remember?"

"You should have let me do it," he protested, clearly angry at his body's failure and lack of strength.

After she took off her coat and scarf, she got him a cup of water. As he drank, she felt of his forehead. "I think we got it." Relief surged through her. She had been afraid she'd lose him. She knew now what that would do to her life.

"You look exhausted," he complained.

"Well it hasn't been an easy two days."

"Two days? I was out for two days?"

She nodded. "Are you hungry? There were oats in the sacks I can make you oatmeal or would you like some of the cornbread?" When he shook his head, she added, "or eggs. Four are left"

"Not hungry," he muttered.

"Cord, you have to eat now that you can. You have to get your strength back."

She saw the muscle jump in his jaw. "Some white knight I turned out to be," he said angrily. "It was you saving me, wasn't it?"

She smiled at his peevishness. This was not unexpected recuperating male behavior. "Don't worry, I will submit a bill."

"I am grateful," he said in a dark tone.

"I know."

"Just don't like being weak."

"I understand. You know, about that white knight... I was

expecting a black night and that suits you perfectly. How about eggs?"

He glared at her, but she ignored him and centered her attention on fixing him food. She heard him pull on his boots and a shirt, going out the cabin's backdoor to probably take care of his bodily needs. If he was gone too long, she'd go after him, but he wasn't.

As he ate, he said nothing. She was trying to be patient with him and understood for a strong man to be brought low was hard. She decided he'd feel better if he shaved. She remembered the shaving supplies in one of the boxes. She poured some hot water into a bowl, a towel, razor and brush to return to the brooding man as he sat at the table staring out the window.

"I think it's time we removed that beard. What do you think?"

He gave her one of his looks, which no longer impacted her-- not after hearing his delirious ramblings as to how he regarded her. "Seriously, Cord. Unless you want to grow a beard, I think you'll feel better with it removed."

He looked at what she set on the table. "Matthews even brought a razor?" She saw the anger in his eyes at any thought of Martin. When he reached to take the razor, she stopped his hand. "I should do it. You're still too shaky."

His glare darkened, but he nodded agreement. She took the brush and worked the suds into his beard, enjoying doing it a lot more than he did.

"You sure you know how to do this?" he asked when she picked up the razor.

"I've shaved patients for Doc Hadley. Trust me. I can do it." Of course, she knew that had been totally different as anytime she touched Cord, she felt a warmth deep inside. She swallowed back the sensations, tilted his head to get the angle right and slowly began removing the bristles.

When she had finished, she dipped a cloth in warm water and removed the bits of suds that were left. She ran her fingers lightly over his cheek, down to his jaw. "Looks a lot nicer," she said with a smile as she bent and kissed him lightly before cleaning and returning the shaving supplies to the shelf near the stove. She felt disappointment that Cord hadn't really kissed her back, but she understood that too. Time. It would just take time. It was worth waiting for.

The third morning, she saw a rider, hat pulled low over his forehead, coming into the yard and leading a packhorse. Cord was sleeping-- so she opened the door a crack with the rifle pointed outward. When she saw the big stallion, then its tall rider, she smiled, as Sam Ryker stepped from the saddle.

"Cilla, what the hell are you doing up here?"

She propped the rifle against the wall and ran to throw her arms around him. "Lord, I'm happy to see you." When Cord stepped to the door, a revolver in his hand, she remembered the animosity between the two men. "Cord," she said, "It's Sam. We are rescued."

Probably a poor choice of words she realized instantly, but too late to take them back. By that time Sam had stalked to the door an angry expression on his own handsome face. "There better be a hell of a good reason for you being here with her," he snarled as the two stood toe to toe, each equally fuming.

Priscilla pushed between them. "Come in for some coffee, Sam, and Cord, you need to sit before you fall down." Irritated glares not subsiding-- the two did as she requested. When Sam had shed his coat, and they were both at the table drinking coffee," Sam said, "All right, let's hear it. What are you doing up here, and it better not be that you did anything to her, O'Brian."

"Now why would you think that?" Cord asked. "Who is the outlaw here?"

"Gentleman, please. If you'd let me get in a word, I can explain it and then you can tell me why you are here, Sam." She began with her kidnapping and Martin's plot.

"Damnation. I should've killed that little rodent. When I see him again, I will," Sam said with the look in his eyes that told her he wasn't exaggerating.

"You can't do that," Priscilla said. "You have responsibilities, and I've been thinking about this. How can I prove he kidnapped me if I bring charges?"

"Your word should do it," Cord retorted.

"It doesn't tend to work that way. He'll say I agreed to come and then changed my mind. You know how good he is at lying."

"Which is why you should have killed him, instead of letting him run off," Cord said with no doubt he also meant what he said.

"That doesn't explain what he's doing here," Sam said shoving his thumb in Cord's direction.

"I planned to meet Martin here," Cord jibed. "He let me down."

Sam snorted but faintly smiled. "Well if it wasn't that, how was it you ended up here?"

"Likely same reason you did. I smelled the smoke and didn't remember there should be anybody in this cabin."

"He had been out after renegades," Priscilla added. "And he was hurt."

"Shot?" Sam asked looking again at Cord without much sympathy in his cold blue eyes.

This is the part Cord didn't like admitting. "Barely grazed by a bullet," he said, "but..."

"He had been pierced by a mesquite branch and part of it remained inside and infected."

Sam looked ready to smile but instead just nodded.

"There was too much snow to travel," Priscilla said, "and he got sick with the blood poisoning and infection. Pretty much that takes us to today."

"Sorry, O'Brian," Sam said with little sound of being sorry in his voice.

"No problem," Cord said just as curtly.

"So now that Cord is recovering, my main thought is getting back to Tucson. My family must be in agony as to what happened to me."

"You aren't going straight back to town," Sam said.

"And who'd stop us," Cord snapped.

"Gulches, gullies, creeks. You know what happens after a snow this heavy and when it melts. It's been raining in the valley, flooding already down there. Now with this quick snow melt, the water's coming off the mountains in gushers. From the looks of the snow up here, it's got enough water to keep that going for a week or more. I just came from Tubac, getting supplies for the ranch, and it's a mess out there."

"Damn," Cord cursed. "I'm going outside for a cigarette and let you two old friends catch up.

"Cord, you can't do that. You'll get sick again."

He gave her a narrow eyed look, pulled on his boots and a coat before he yanked the door open and went out.

"He's a firebrand," Sam said as the door slammed.

"He's been sick. He's not himself."

Sam chuckled. "From what I've seen of him, he's exactly himself." He gave her a look then. "You used to see him that way too. Something changed here?"

"Want more coffee?" she asked going to the stove for the pot and heating up his cup.

"You didn't answer my question."

"No, I didn't. But no, I don't think my opinion has changed." She smiled at him. Sam sat back in his chair and chuckled.

"You could stay here, but I think it'd be smarter to come back to the ranch with me until this weather clears up."

"My family will be insane with worry."

He nodded. "It won't make it better if you drown trying to get back. And that talk of renegades, I might've come across the tracks of three of them about four miles from here. I think you should come with me."

"Not without Cord," she said with her arms folded over her chest.

"It's like that is it?"

"It's like that."

"Well you be the one talking him into it. I will get my pack-horse reloaded for whatever you want to take from the cabin. I think we should go as soon as possible."

"How far is this from the ranch?" she asked worried about how a long ride would impact Cord's health.

"Maybe five hours. Not a bad ride for either of you." He chuckled again as he rose from the table. "Let me know if he's coming too."

CHAPTER 18

When Sam walked outside, Cord was standing, leaning against the wall of the cabin, the cigarette dangling from his lips. "Ironic, don't you think?" Sam said with a grin as he headed to the packhorse.

Cord glared at him but went back inside with the cigarette. To hell with whether she liked it. "So you leaving with him?" he asked as he saw her kneeling on the floor, beginning to gather things into a sack.

"We are leaving with him."

"We? I go nowhere with Sam Ryker."

"You heard what he said about the flooding."

"Obviously it's unsafe for you." He took a drag on the cigarette. "I agree you should go with Ryker. I'll tell your folks in Tucson that you are safe and will be along later."

She stood up and walked over to him, thinking that at one time that arrogant expression would have infuriated her. "If you aren't going with Sam, then neither am I. We'll just take a chance on the rivers."

"Damn, we will not," Cord retorted as he felt her arms go around him.

"Oh but we will. I won't go to Sam and Abby's if you don't think it's right for us both."

He held out only for a moment before he gave up and put the cigarette onto a bowl on the stove. "It won't work. You know that." His arms went around her pulling her tightly against him.

"What won't?"

"Tactics."

She smiled as she looked up into his eyes. "They aren't tactics, Cord. It's a fact. I am going with you if you decide to go down the mountain now. Or we can stay here until the food runs out. It is your choice. Sam did say he saw tracks a few miles from here that might mean the renegades. If we go that way, we should be careful is all."

If he had been debating, that was the end of it. He would do nothing that jeopardized her life. Maybe if he had his strength, he could have believed he could keep her safe, crossing raging gullies, against those renegades, but not drained as he was.

"All right, we will go to his ranch, and I'll try to avoid killing him," he said breathing faster at the teasing smile she was giving him, her fingers now on his cheek.

"You wouldn't do that."

"I wouldn't?"

"No, Abigail would kill you then, and Abigail is my best friend. I can't have her hurting you." She reached up on her tiptoes and pulled him down for a quick kiss before she went back to the sacks. "I think," she said looking at a pair of pants Martin had brought for himself, "that I will need to wear these when we leave."

He smiled. Her in a pair of pants wasn't a bad idea... not bad at all. When she turned back to him, she said, "Would you mind going outside while I change?"

He minded, but it was sensible. He grabbed his coat and went out to finish his cigarette on the porch. Dislike though he did the idea of taking Ryker's hospitality at the Circle R, it was the best thing for Priscilla.

He watched as the man capably rearranged the load on his packhorse. He didn't trust him, although he was unsure why. He thought then about what Fox had said about them looking so much alike. Was that the real reason he had had such an instinctive dislike, one that had never lessened even when it appeared Ryker was living a straight life?

It didn't matter. He would go with him-- and when the rivers went down, he'd see Priscilla back to the safety of her home in Tucson. Whatever fascination she temporarily felt with him would be over then. He would leave Tucson because he couldn't continue living so close to her. It would be better for Grace to continue living with Priscilla. Maybe he was running. Maybe it was time to run.

He took a last draw on his cigarette before he dropped it into a puddle at the edge of the porch to saddle Jeb. If Matthews thought he was getting away with this, he'd find out otherwise. Cord wouldn't leave him alive to try again. If Priscilla didn't want to press charges out of embarrassment, he'd find another way to be sure he could not again hurt her.

As they rode away from the cabin, Priscilla felt some sadness. She had liked living there with Cord, even under dire conditions. Admittedly it had only been a few days, but for her, those days had changed everything. If Cord didn't know it yet, he soon would.

She wasn't normally a big fan of horseback riding, but riding behind Cord, the feel of his hard body against her was changing her mind. If she held on more than she had to, if her hands slipped lower, he had no way of knowing it was not out of insecurity but instead from a desire to tease him as she teased herself.

Sam led the way, as much because he knew the route, as because his stallion would tolerate no other horse in the lead.

Their easterly route climbed for a bit through the tall pines before they began to edge down the other side into mesquite and prickly pear cactus country. By a small stream, which was normally a dry bed, Sam stopped to study tracks.

"Unshod," he said.

"Heading south looks like," Cord said before turning his gaze that direction. "Can't go after them now." His voice was laced with frustration. Priscilla knew it was because of her. She was baggage that would limit them in any fight. She began to find less pleasure in the ride, partly due to sore muscles, but also concern over the possibility the Apaches might be watching them.

They rode on down through the scrub oaks and then by big cottonwoods where there were only a few patches of snow in shaded places. When they reached the ridge that overlooked a broad valley, she saw a large ranch house and outbuildings. Sam pulled his horse again to a halt. "I always like to look at it when I get here."

"Checking for rustlers?" Cord sniped.

"Sure. You never know," Sam shot back.

"You steal this too?"

"Look O'Brian, I am inviting you here as a guest, but I will only take so much from you." Priscilla watched as Sam's eyes narrowed studying the swarthy marshal who, with his bristle, again looked more like a rustler himself than a law officer.

"I'm real worried about that."

"Hey last time you were here, you got mad. Maybe you can keep your temper this time. I've got a son now, you know."

"I was mad because you were lying to me. I knew it but couldn't prove it. That worm Matthews was the fault of that too."

"That's neither here nor there," Sam said with a smile that Priscilla knew was intended to irk Cord not placate him. "The point is this will be a civil time, won't it?"

"Was that a threat?"

"Gentleman," Priscilla said in as sugary a tone as she could manage since she was mad at both of them for the way they went at each other, "can we go on? Someone here is not used to riding long hours. Plus, I've never been to Abby's home and am anxious to see her, it, and Davy. He must've changed so much in the six months since I last saw him."

"Sorry," they both said in churlish tones but nudged their horses in the side and headed down the slope.

"You won't make this difficult will you?" Priscilla asked Cord as Sam took the lead again.

"I won't have to. He will," Cord said irritation still in his voice.

"You could try."

"Oh I will try," he retorted with what didn't sound to her like any sincerity.

When they finally rode into the yard of the Circle R, men came out from the bunkhouse with guns. A tall, slender woman appeared on the front porch of the house with a shotgun. When she saw it was Sam, her smile widened as she set down the gun-- then she recognized Priscilla.

"Cilla," she shrieked as she ran forward stopping only at the bottom step as she was barefooted. Cord dismounted, by throwing his leg over the pommel, then lifted Priscilla down to where she could hobble over to her friend.

"Where on earth did Sam find you?" Abby cried as she pulled Priscilla into a warm embrace.

"It's a long story. A very long story. Can we go inside while I tell you, and I need to see Davy. I bet I won't recognize him, and he won't know me."

"Of course." Abby looked up then at Cord who was standing by his horse. "And him? What's he doing here?" Her face showed she still held a grudge, regarding past run-ins between the two men. "I hope this doesn't mean trouble."

Priscilla grinned. "Inside, my impatient friend. I need to get these boots off. Lord, I am so sore. I haven't ridden that long in years, and now I am remembering why."

Sam had dismounted and walked over to his wife with the rope to the packhorse in his hand. "Boys, unload the pack animal. I'll take care of the horses and be back."

Abby gave him a look, the kind Priscilla had seen on her face only for Sam. "And anything else?" she asked as she waited for him to come to her. "Sam Ryker," she added, "if you don't come over here right now, I'm coming after you."

He grinned. "Get those pretty feet all muddy?"

"You better know it."

He walked to her, swinging her up in his arms, and the kiss he gave Abby was as the one Cord had given her. Thinking of that, she looked at him to see that hard look on his face. If she was having tender memories of the kiss, he obviously wasn't. If she hadn't heard his delirious ramblings, she'd have felt depressed, as it was, she believed this was something she could and would surmount... but not this day. Their time however was coming.

Cord followed Ryker down to the barns with their horses. The ranch had a lot going on around it, more than he remembered from his prior visit. A cow, chickens?

"Oats in there for your horse," Ryker gestured toward some bins as he led his big stallion to a stall at the end. "Hay behind the door at the end of the barn."

Cord unsaddled Jeb feeling as uncomfortable as he ever remembered. He was about to take the hospitality of a man he had been sure was a rustler and a kidnapper.

Although Ryker seemed happily married and Abigail, obviously happy, Cord hadn't forgotten how he had come to the ranch with a posse determined to have it out with the outlaw. That had ended with his own gnashing of teeth and the whole thing dissolving into no charges of any sort. As a lawman, he counted a lot on instincts. They told him that what he had believed of Ryker was true at least at one time.

Joe Fox came over as Cord was taking a curry brush to the gelding. "Good to see you again, Marshal."

"Not been that long," Cord said not looking up from his task.

"Think over any of what I said that day?"

That he had was nothing he was going to admit. "Any new paintings?" he asked hoping to distract the questions.

Fox grinned. "Might just be there are. Maybe I'll even show you one of them." He walked off whistling while Cord clenched his jaw. This was going to be one instance after another of exercising self-control.

Ryker came to stand outside the stall. "Come on into the house. I have some good whiskey, and I bet you could use a shot."

Cord forced a smile. "Sure, I'd like that." In truth he wanted anything but to accept this man's hospitality. He had no choice. He had to get along for how many ever days he was stuck here.

In the house, Abby looked through her closet and found a skirt and blouse she felt would fit Priscilla. "Socks will have to do until your walking boots dry as mine are way too big although we had a boy here once, maybe his would work."

"Socks are fine," Priscilla said as she stripped and then reached for the clothing Abby was holding out.

"What happened? And how did you end up here with that marshal?"

As she dressed, Priscilla told her the basics of what happened.

"Oh lord. I never would have dreamed Martin would do such a thing," Abby said shaking her head. "I didn't trust him but never that he'd go that far."

"I know. I was a fool although maybe it all was for the best." Priscilla sat beside her on the bed.

"How can you say that after such a frightening experience?" Then she looked in Priscilla's eyes. "It's O'Brian, isn't it?"

Priscilla smiled but didn't answer.

"Are you sure this isn't all a reaction to shock. I mean what happened could have a woman reaching out for the first reasonable man who came along. Not that I'd define him as reasonable."

Priscilla laughed. "My dear friend, don't hold a grudge much, do you?"

"Well maybe some."

"It didn't begin in that cabin. I am going to admit something to you I barely have admitted to myself. I think it was always there but definitely from when we spent so much time together with his daughter."

"Marshal O'Brian has a daughter," Abigail interrupted. "I thought she had died or something."

"No, she was very much alive with her grandparents. It's a complicated story, but when they died rather suddenly, her uncle wrote Cord and put her on a train headed for Tucson. She arrived. He was clueless on how to proceed with her, not to mention they had been telling her bad things about him since they blamed him for his wife's premature death."

"God, this is a lot to take in all at once." They heard Davy crying, and Abby rose from the bed. "Come on and help me get him. He'll be glad to see his auntie."

"You think he'll remember me?"

"I guess we'll soon know."

In the nursery, the little boy stopped crying when his mother entered the room and contentedly let her change his diaper. When he was presentable, she lifted him into her arms. "Davy, do you remember Auntie Cilla?"

Priscilla put out her hand to let his pudgy little fingers grasp it. He smiled then and was content when Abby put him in Priscilla's arms. They walked into the kitchen just as Cord and Sam walked through the outside door.

Priscilla smiled as Davy looked toward the two men-- uncertainly at Cord but with a big smile for his father.

"I have some of mashed green beans that I just have to heat up," Abby said as she glanced past Cord as though he had been invisible.

Cord had felt pole axed at seeing a baby in Priscilla's arms. The thoughts that ran through his head left him unable to come up with a single word that made sense. When Ryker took his coat and then handed him a glass of whiskey, he thought he should say something-- but not what he was thinking, which was that the baby in Priscilla's arms could have been his for the coloring. God, why had that thought even come to him?

"Marshal, we're happy to have you here at the ranch," Abby said as she handed Priscilla the little bowl and spoon to feed the baby, now on her lap. Her voice didn't sound as though she meant it, and Cord couldn't blame her.

"Thank you for allowing me to stay. I'll sleep down at the bunkhouse, of course, if the men down there won't mind."

"I wouldn't hear of it," Abby said with what was clearly a forced but polite smile. "We have plenty of room in the house."

"It shouldn't be long anyway," he said leaning back against the wall and watching as Priscilla tempted each spoonful into the little boy's mouth.

"He's walking now," Ryker offered with a proud grin.

"He looks like a fine boy."

"You figure I rustled him too?" Ryker gibed with that insufferable look in his eyes that had Cord thinking of how good it'd feel to punch him in the mouth.

"I'd never imply such a thing... about a lady," Cord retorted leaving no doubt he would about Sam.

"You want to check brands out here?" Sam said, still grinning like a man who was itching for a fight.

"Is it necessary?"

"I can round them up, and you decide."

"You have a lot of time around here for busy work?" Cord's own smile was not friendly.

"Sam," Abby said, "if I might interrupt your snarling at each other, would you show Marshal O'Brian his room and where he can clean up." It served as a reminder to Cord that he needed to shave and must smell like he'd been on the trail a long time which wasn't far off.

Sam led Cord to the rear of the large house, past a huge living room with big stone fireplace and heavy leather furniture. "Pretty nice spread," he observed as they walked.

"I even got it legally," Sam said with that irritating way he had.

"Surprising then."

At the back there were stairs, and he was led up them to a second floor with more doors. Sam opened one. "Of course, we'd not want you sleeping on the same floor with Priscilla. You do understand."

"Of course, nothing like a good rape before breakfast," Cord muttered.

"Your style?"

"On Wednesdays. I lost track of time. Is this a Wednesday?"

Ryker snorted but didn't retort. The room he showed Cord was comfortable looking with a large double bed, dresser with a pitcher and bowl. "Want a bath?" Ryker asked

"Need is more the word. A stream nearby for that?"

"If you want to freeze," Ryker said, "but if not, I managed to get plumbing up here last year. The room at the end of the hall should have what you need. Water's not very hot by the time it gets up here. A full bath would have to be downstairs with the hot water from one of those geegaws where the pipe is behind the cook stove and runs to the bathroom. Not fancy, but it works."

The pride Ryker felt in his ranch was obvious, and for some reason that irked Cord more than it should have. He believed this man had bought all he had with ill-gotten gain. He himself had played by the rules, never even taken a bribe, and was, as a result, lucky to even own land and not remotely able to stock or live on it.

"Thanks," he said knowing it didn't sound like he meant it.

"I'll see you back downstairs," Ryker said. "Been awhile since I saw my wife and boy."

That irked Cord even more as he thought about the life he'd never know. Damnation but life was unfair. He stalked down the hall and found in the bathroom the basic facilities and a razor with soap. He appreciated the unexpected luxuries despite how rotten his mood was becoming.

Fifteen minutes later, shaved and cleaned up, he walked back downstairs, feeling churlish but trying to fight against it. He could get along here for the short time it would be required. He at least hoped he could.

CHAPTER 19

Martin faced Wright, who was sitting at his desk, with his feet on it. Why did a man like him deserve to be born into a home where everything would be handed to him? It seemed so unfair that power was distributed that way and not according to worth. The fates had not been kind to Martin, as so often they had to others. He managed a polite smile to hide his thoughts.

"So," Wright said with a smirk, "What exactly is the story you want told?"

"Just the truth... That I did an errand for you with that wagon."

"Truth?" Wright laughed. "I had Evans back you up but will decide whether I do based on you telling me the truth right now. Anything less, and I tell the sheriff and marshal you lied about the wagon. It won't take much for them to put together the reason you'd lie."

Martin had decided what his lie had to be. "Priscilla Wesley and I ran off together. We were going to be married. I took a wrong road. We got lost. Found this cabin where I thought we'd be safe as the storm was getting worse."

"Oh this is good," Wright said laughing. "And then?"

"And then... the storm grew much worse. Perhaps it frightened her. She told me she changed her mind."

"And so you brought her back home where she is now," Wright jibed.

"No, she grew angry at the whole thing. She said she'd tell everyone I raped her. I panicked and got into the wagon and left her there. If I had brought her back, she'd have had me in Yuma."

"So you just left a woman up there alone to die?" Wright was no longer smiling.

"It was a good cabin. Someone would..." He stopped, as obviously he had left her to die, and he couldn't lie his way out of that part. "Yes, I guess it's what I did. It was her or me. I was angry that she would lie about what I did. I didn't rape her." At least that part was true.

"You are a skunk, a rabid skunk, Matthews. Did you know that?"

Martin felt furious, but he hid it. He needed this man. "I did wrong. But it's too late to make it right. I can't imagine her surviving up there." He remembered all the supplies he had left, but she was ignorant and foolish. She'd have no idea how even to build a fire with her privileged life. No, she was dead. It's how he liked to think about her, suffering at the last, and wishing she'd been wiser in how she had treated him.

Wright walked around the office, his hands folded behind his back as he considered. "You've lied to me again, Matthews. I've had men killed for less. Now tell me the truth. If it's not the truth this time, I will let Gabe finish you off. Nobody will care when you end up in an unmarked grave. Nobody. You got that?"

Martin pursed his lips tightly together but realized he had no choice. "All right... I kidnapped her. I took her to a cabin I had supplied in the mountains. I thought... once we got there, she'd decide she wanted to be with me. I guess I was a fool."

"You guess?" Wright snorted. "So as best you know it, she's still there and alive?"

"It seems unlikely."

"You really don't know her at all, do you?" Again Martin felt rage build up, but he swallowed it as he watched Wright pace. "She might be grateful to a man who rescued her, mightn't she?" Wright said finally as he sat back at his desk drumming his fingers.

"I suppose but what about me? If she comes back here, I'm done in this town."

"You sleazy little worm. You're done anyway. I will see though what I am going to do for you when I get back—if she is alive."

"Back from where?"

"Why from being a white knight, of course."

"You'd go get her?"

"It's worth a chance. When I bring her back to the bosom of her loving family, I will be in with them and her. I like that scenario."

"She'll bring charges against me."

"I doubt that. Not if you stick to your original story. She won't be able to prove otherwise."

Wright's smile was ugly, and Martin knew there was more to what he was planning. It wasn't as though he didn't also have some bargaining chips. "I hope you plan to support me in this," Martin said reluctant to play his ace but feeling he had no choice. "I naturally have been keeping records for you... but not just for you. Some for insurance."

"What are you talking about?" Wright rose from the desk and reached for the front of Martin's shirt.

"I mean that if something happens to me, I have a will. With it, those records are to be opened. It might be the end of me, but it will be of you also."

Wright laughed then. "Wise little fellow, aren't you? Well, we'll see about that... when I get back with the lady."

"Have you thought about how high the rivers are between here and there? I had her up in the mountains south of us."

"Then I'll wait a day or two. It'll just make her more grateful. And whether you and I remain working together, I will think about that. Draw me a map."

When he drove his buggy back into town, Martin felt it had gone as well as possible. For now he was still alive, but he was walking a tightrope. He had to think what he could do to secure his position-- most especially if Priscilla was alive and Wright brought her back.

Maybe the best thing he could do was be sure he got back there first to ensure she wasn't. Or was that worth the risk? Most likely the mountains had taken care of her. They could equally prove the end of Wright. He smiled as he considered that possibility. Why not? It was time things finally went his way. He'd wait it out. Fate had to be on his side someday.

∾

At the Circle R, dinner was bountiful with a pork roast, baked potatoes, acorn squash, string beans and a pie for dessert. The men from the bunkhouse ate with them, and the laughter and conversation flowed with the kinds of jokes that came from long familiarity. They teased Priscilla and Abigail, but gave Cord a wide berth that wasn't unusual for him as a lawman. It seemed even if people needed the law, they didn't often have a lot of appreciation for the ones who dealt it out. No big surprise since the law wasn't always fair. These men likely had been on the other side of it for a lot of years—fair or otherwise.

When the meal was over and they were cleaning up, Ryker said, "Whiskey in the great room."

Ollie yawned. "I ain't got it in me to have a drink-- so see you all in the morning." Bull agreed which left Joe and Rock to come into the living room. Joe took a snifter of brandy and the other three whiskeys.

"How was it getting to Tubac?" Rock asked Ryker who was stirring up the fire. "Other than picking up some baggage," he added with a chuckle.

Ryker put the poker down and rose. "Not bad getting but coming back wasn't a mess. I saw tracks of unshod ponies. Maybe you should tell them about the renegades, Marshal."

"Five of them or there were," Cord said. "I was down that way to find them, but to be honest, based on the reports, was expecting mostly pilfering, not that dangerous. When I got close, it turned out they were."

"And they got away?" Rock asked with a faint sneer as though he would have expected no more.

"Three."

"Marshal got shot... and." Ryker stopped and laughed. "Got a sliver."

Cord didn't appreciate the derision. "That's about it," he said giving Ryker a look that should have quelled his enjoyment but did not.

"You boys want to see my new painting?" Joe asked.

"Sure I always like seeing your work," Ryker said.

Joe disappeared into a back room. When he came back, he had a canvas with a cloth over it. "I finished it last week but was waiting to show it to you when it was dry. Just about there but now with O'Brian here, seems a good time." He grinned and propped the canvas against the wall before he pulled off the cloth.

The painting had a mountain in the background with a Harris hawk soaring overhead, a wolf in the distance, but its subject was clearly of two men in the foreground. One, held a rifle loosely and rested his arm on the other's shoulder. The second man's right hand rested on a revolver hung low on his hip. There was no way for Cord to mistake who those two men were.

Sam stared at it for a long moment before he said, "Quite a fantasy."

"I call it The Brothers," Fox said with a little chuckle.

"Definite fantasy," Ryker repeated with a glare at Fox. "I don't have a brother."

"Nor do I," Cord said.

Priscilla and Abby walked into the room. "Baby's down," Abby said then she saw the painting. "Oh my." Priscilla wasn't as surprised by it as was Abby. She looked to see Cord's reaction. His face was stony with that muscle twitching in his jaw, which was the only sign he gave of being under stress.

"Not saying these two are brothers or anything," Joe said. "Just they made good subjects for it."

"You have a marvelous gift," Abby said as she smiled at Joe. "I don't know anybody who has painted better portraits. The lighting, the mountains behind the men, that boulder. It's wonderful."

"My Gawd," Rock said, "if they ain't brothers, not sure what the hell they could be. Look like two tough hombres. You done real good, Joe."

"Put it away," Sam said with a growl. "Good painting. Lousy subjects."

Abby went to him and touched his arm. "It was a good subject. You know how Joe likes to paint or draw you."

"Maybe so, but he ruined it by adding him." He gestured with his thumb toward Cord.

Joe looked from one surly man to the other. "Sorry. I meant no offense. Just I couldn't get the marshal's face out of my head after being in Tucson. I had to put you two together in a painting at least."

"No offense," Cord said, "on my end anyway." He smiled but with no humor. "I've had a long day. Anybody mind if I turn in?" He didn't look at Priscilla as he said good night and left the room.

"He's just tired," she said wishing she had a right to ease all she saw in Cord's face.

"He's a bastard," Sam said with a growl. Abby slapped his arm but looked sympathetically at Priscilla.

"He's been sick," she said.

Sam snorted. "Been like this from the time I met him." With a growl, he left and headed for bed.

"They do look like brothers," Abby said contemplatively.

"Probably just coincidence," Priscilla said but she wasn't sure. Still, it seemed unlikely. Wouldn't at least one of them know?

.

With the house quiet and all in bed, Priscilla lay awake, as she thought of Cord upstairs in a bed alone. She kept thinking of his kiss. She wanted more. She wanted so much more from him. Although she now was certain he wanted her, she was equally convinced that he would do nothing about it. He was a protective man who would sacrifice his own happiness for that of others. If anything were to happen between them, it would have to be her instigating it.

She thought of various ways she might do that. Nothing seemed right. Maybe Abby would have some ideas when they had a time to talk about it. Her friend had discretely avoided asking questions. Of course, between dinner preparation, Davy's needs, and her own exhaustion, there'd been little time. Perhaps in the morning there would be. She wasn't sure when she fell into a restless sleep, filled with dreams of a dark man with a sensual smile.

In the morning, she hurried into the kitchen to help Abby get the stove going. Do you raise hogs?" she asked as bacon's fragrance filled the kitchen with the promise of breakfast.

Abby shook her head. "We have some lovely neighbors. Martha Reimer does. We bought one before Christmas."

"It's a long way from town. You are fortunate to have found friends out here."

"Well it takes working on it," Abby said as she poured Priscilla a cup of coffee. "Do you still take it with cream?"

"You can't be serious? You actually have cream?"

"I have a cow--Tildy. For now, Ollie is the one milking her."

"You know how to milk a cow?" she asked with amazement.

Abby handed her a small pitcher with rich cream. "I have learned a lot of things. Martha's helped me on keeping a garden and all. This higher ground does better for growing things than Tucson or maybe I just know more how to do it."

"You are so content and yet... it's so far away from everything."

"From everything?" Abby asked with a smile. "Depends on what everything is. From a beautiful stream, birds, deer that have to be chased away from my string beans? Or from jobs that have meaning like canning and drying food for the winter, from a man I love more than life, from my baby? It's not far away from anything that matters, Cilla—except you."

Priscilla smiled as she considered that. She had also been content in the cabin but that had only been a few days. What if it had been longer? She was unsure if she had Abby's strength. Before they could talk longer, Ollie arrived with the morning's milk.

"How you be, Miss Cilla?" he asked as he put it on the counter and accepted his own cup of coffee.

"I'm doing wonderfully, and please, just Cilla. The air is so much clearer up here. It's a beautiful place."

"It shore be that," Ollie said as he snitched a piece of the bacon from the plate that Abby had been draining.

"Ollie is Sam's mom," Abby said with a laugh.

"Is his real mother alive?" Priscilla asked thinking again about Joe's questions in Tucson and the painting.

"Sam's mother was a whore," Abby said, "and died when he was a very small boy."

"Oh..."

"It's not anything to be ashamed of. It wasn't what he did."

"I wasn't thinking that." She didn't have time to tell Abby more as Sam came into the room with Cord not far behind him. The two had already been bickering.

"Boy here wants to check the brands," Sam said as he took his own cup of coffee.

"I'm no boy, and I didn't say that. I just thought I'd go for a ride, work out some kinks."

"Not breakfast first?" Abby protested.

Cord looked at the bacon and now eggs frying but shook his head. "I need the air." He also needed a cigarette.

"Won't be breakfast later for those who don't eat when it's ready," Sam said tersely.

"I have jerky left in my saddlebags."

Abby fed a stick of wood into the stove. "I suggest you both have breakfast, smoke your cigarettes right here at the table, and then go off and have a talk where you discuss this animosity you feel toward each other. I don't want this atmosphere around Davy when he wakes up."

Undecided, Cord stared blankly at her. Priscilla came to him and took his arm drawing him back to the table. "Want your coffee black or with cream and sugar?" she asked. "Turns out they have a cow."

He gave up and sat at the table, eating the food set before him, but only rolling a cigarette when he saw Ryker do the same. As they smoked, Abby headed into the bedroom to get the now fussing Davy.

"I think Abby was right," Priscilla said, drinking her third cup of coffee after taking away the plates. "You need to talk this out. You have been arguing since you met each other. Maybe if you go outside, you can talk through why you dislike each other so much."

"Talk never solved much that I know of," Sam complained blowing out smoke.

"I mean it," Abby said as she came back with the baby in her arms. "I want to breast feed Davy in the kitchen where it's warmer-- so it's a good time anyway."

The two men glared at each other but rose and walked to the door, grabbing their coats. Outside the air was a little warmer as still smoking they walked across the yard to the barn.

"Got nothing to say to a rustler," Cord said as they reached the barn and he threw his cigarette down, grinding it out with his boot.

"And a kidnapper," Ryker added, "don't forget that."

"I haven't."

Inside the barn, he gave Jeb a pitchfork of hay while Cord tended to his monster stallion. When Ryker returned, he leaned against the stall. "The truth of it is you are as much a gunman as I am. The difference is you get paid for it and feel sanctimonious as hell for it."

"You know me so well do you?" Cord said, again feeling the urge to hit that smug face.

"I know your type."

Ollie came into the barn still munching on one of Abby's sweet rolls. "Why don't you two boys head out to check that waterhole we was thinking might be iced over?"

"It's warming up," Ryker reminded him.

"Might be a good ride will cool you both off. The ladies don't need that kind of hassle inside. Cilla's been through a scary ordeal, and Abby's got a baby to tend, don't need no arguing that gets him screamin'. Go for a ride and come back better men." The old man stomped off.

"Fine by me," Cord said as he threw his saddle over Jeb's back. Ryker headed to the stall to get his stallion. Five minutes later, they were riding south toward the waterhole.

"Ollie been with you a long time?" Cord asked trying to think of something that wouldn't set off Ryker.

"Why you asking?" Ryker asked testily.

"Damn it to hell, just trying to say something that wouldn't make you mad."

"Oh, like I'm the one acting like an ass."

"Now that you admit it, yes."

They rode the next two miles in silence, until they came to the tank, which was full of water and only lightly iced. Ryker dismounted and used a club that had been left for breaking out the ice. The few cows in the area looked with some curiosity but didn't come over.

"How many acres you have?" Cord asked knowing that was a rude question to cattlemen but not caring much at this point.

"More than you," Ryker said with a sneer.

That was it-- Cord dismounted, unbuckled his gun belt and hung it over his pommel. "I been wanting to do this since I rode out to your ranch that day." He watched as Ryker also removed his gun belt.

Cord lashed out with his fist missing only because Ryker dodged back. His response in seconds sent Cord to the ground. He scrambled to his feet, lunging for Ryker and sending them both to the mud at the edge of the waterhole.

They pounded each other as they rolled on the cold ground, smeared with mud and finally missing as many punches as they landed. After landing one particularly hard blow, Cord got to his feet and stood over the rancher. "Had enough?"

"Hell no," Ryker grabbed him around the ankles and sent him back to the ground. Now bleeding from their noses, they slammed each other, with one hard blow after another, until this time it was Cord lying, and Ryker standing over him.

Cord rolled over and rose but had lost his enthusiasm for the fight. He went to the water's edge and splashed water on his face washing off blood and mud.

Ryker joined him and then sat back catching his breath. After a few minutes, he rolled a cigarette, a little unevenly with his knuckles swollen.

Cord reached into his pocket, grateful the pouch was still intact and rolled one of his own, striking a match as he watched the other man smoke.

"So is it possible?" he asked.

Ryker didn't pretend not to know what he meant. "I have no idea who my father was. I was born in a whore house that I was told later was just outside Fort Leavenworth. We moved a lot my first years, but no talk ever of a father, no name. I assume she didn't know. She died when I was four, and from then on it was trying to stay alive and not much worried about fathers, just avoiding the battles that seemed to be raging every which direction through Kansas."

"How old are you?"

"Thirty-four. And you?"

Cord drew the smoke into his lungs. "Thirty-two." He sat draping his arms over his bent knees as he considered. "It is possible," he said finally.

Ryker gave a snort. "To tell you the truth I never wanted to know who he was."

"In that you were right. He was a mean bastard-- beat my mother, me when he could catch me."

"He still alive?"

Cord shook his head. "Both my parents died when I was in my teens."

Ryker studied the tip of his cigarette. "We do look a lot alike. Joe wasn't wrong about that."

"My parents had their place not far from Fort Leavenworth. He was the kind of man, that wouldn't surprise me, if he had fathered children across the state. Using that term fathered, loosely."

Ryker laughed for the first time with some genuine humor in it. "It'd be ironic, wouldn't it?"

Cord shook his head. "Damn it'd explain why you've irked me so much."

"Too much like you?" Ryker chuckled again. "Yeah, it'd explain us both."

They rose and looked out across the range. "You really go straight?" Cord asked.

Ryker chuckled. "I wasn't all that much of an outlaw."

"Don't tell me another thing."

They mounted and rode slowly. "How we going to explain this?" Cord asked as they got close to the ranch buildings.

"We ran into outlaws?" Ryker suggested with a snicker.

"I got to say the fight was good for me but don't suppose the women will ever understand that."

"Speaking of women, you do mean right by Cilla, don't you? She's a good woman-- and if I thought you didn't, we'd be at it again."

"I know what she is, and what I am. I mean to leave Tucson."

"Running?" Ryker asked with another chuckle, but more one from a man who understood than from ridicule.

"Call it what you will, but it's the right thing to do."

"What seems like the right thing isn't always right," Ryker said as they got to the barn, dismounted and led their horses back inside.

"It would be this time," Cord said. "I do have a favor to ask though."

"Brother to brother?" Ryker asked with a flash of white teeth.

"Man to man. I can't leave those renegades up there as it stands. I think I can go back and pick up their tracks. When I didn't think they were dangerous, I wasn't so concerned. Now I am. I'd like to take Priscilla back to Tucson, but in case... I am gone longer than I expect, would you do it?"

Ryker's smile broadened. "Nope."

"Why the hell not?"

"Because I'll be going with you." His smile was the arrogant one that used to annoy Cord, but which he now saw as a lot like his own.

"You got a child and wife."

"Oh thanks for reminding me. I clean forgot."

"I just mean these renegades are hanging around, looking for trouble now. They won't be so easy to take."

"And I should let them either kill you or come on my ranch when I'm not around, when the boys are out. No thanks. I am coming." Ryker's expression brooked no argument.

"In that case, all right." Cord laughed and shook his head. "Now what's our story about the fight?"

CHAPTER 20

In the house, Cord and Sam tried to come up with a logical reason for their damaged state, Priscilla and Abby laughed. "Doesn't look like anybody got hurt much," Abby judged. "And you both appear in a better mood-- so maybe it was just boys will be boys."

"Women," Sam said leading Cord into the great room where he poured them each a snifter of brandy and they sat on hard chairs to protect the furniture. "Who can figure them?"

"You must've, been married how many years now? Good brandy."

"Not a clue most of the time. And it's three years, counting an unorthodox beginning."

"You didn't really kidnap her, did you?"

"More like the other way around. Actually we both wanted the same thing but just didn't agree on how to get there. We worked it out. You will too."

"It's different for me."

Sam chuckled. "It's always different when it's you." He looked up when Abby entered the room.

"When you two get through commiserating over the ills of

women," she said, "Come back in the kitchen where we can clean up those abrasions that you didn't get in a fight."

After a nice dinner, the four of them sat by the fire in the living room. Priscilla had cuddled against Cord's side. He realized he needed to head for bed, reluctant as he was to leave her.

"I'll be leaving before first light-- so have to get some sleep." Like he would with the way Priscilla cuddled against his side.

"Where are you going?" Priscilla asked moving away from him.

"I can't leave those renegades up there. If I find out they took off for Mexico, I'll have some peace about it. The thing is I don't feel it's what they did. I think they will hang around and be marauding when they can. I need to return them to the reservation if possible."

"You think they'll go peaceably?" He didn't believe that but said nothing. "You can't go alone," she protested.

"He won't be. I am going too," Sam said. Then it was Abby's turn to get upset.

"Indian hunting? You have to go Indian hunting? Since when?"

"Since my brother is going."

Abigail's mouth dropped open. "So Joe was right."

"It's more likely than not."

"Then neither of you should go. Get the law." She stopped when she realized what she said. "The military."

"Now is the right time. By the time the army gets here, they could be gone or already hit someone else. You'd rather I left them hanging around to maybe come to the house sometime when I'm not here—or hit Reimers?"

She gave him one of those looks. "Who else are you taking?"

"Cord and I should be plenty. I want the boys here, alert, and sticking close to the house."

That was when Cord heard the two of them go at it. Abby was

clearly no submissive wife who did whatever she was told. "You should take Rock and Bull. Ollie can stay with us." Her beautiful face turned forceful and anything but soft.

Sam snorted with a gleam in his eyes that said she'd not be running this outfit. "You have to be joking. Listen, I know what I'm doing and clearly so does Cord."

"Minus being shot, you mean," Priscilla added gaining herself a glare from each man.

The argument went on a few more minutes but there was no way to stop them from going, and eventually Abby only wanted to go to bed with her husband.

"You will be more careful," Priscilla asked, as soon as they were alone.

"You know I will."

"You probably thought you would last time too."

She had had him there. "I got careless, didn't understand what I was up against, and it was a fluke that I got speared."

"Like the bullet wound was the expected?"

"More than what actually laid me out. Look, Angel, I will be back to take you to Tucson. Trust me on this."

"Looks like I have to," she said before she pulled his head down and put her lips against his. As her arms went around him, she opened her mouth and pressed beyond the chaste kiss he intended. When her tongue entered his mouth, he was lost and the next moments were a blaze of kissing and caressing.

Finally he pulled away, because going any further would have had him carrying her upstairs and taking what he had no right to have. When they kissed good night, he knew what she wanted. He wouldn't do it. Forever for them was not in the cards.

The next morning, as Sam and Cord rode into the mountains, they learned they had a similar way of working when on a trail, not a lot of conversation, hand gestures that indicated what they were seeing, and where they needed to head.

Cord watched the hills for unusual movements, birds being flushed but also thought about Priscilla. He knew distractions could prove fatal at a time like this, but he couldn't help himself.

"Are you paying attention?" Sam asked as he pointed to the tracks.

Well he hadn't been, but he was when he saw fresh unshod tracks. "What's down there?" he asked as he looked around for further sign.

"A dependable waterhole and beyond, Mexico. They could be leaving the country and heading for the Mexican hills."

"I can't take that chance." He would follow them at least to the border if that truly was where they were heading.

"I agree."

They picked up their horses' paces, keeping the tracks in sight, their eyes peeled on the scrub oaks for any movement. The chatter of a coatimundi stopped Cord for a moment. The little animal was up a tree and complaining at their interruption of its peace.

"He's looking for a sweetie," Sam said with a grin. He looked around as they headed forward again. "You know about a mile from here, there's a little box canyon. It'd make a good shelter and might be where they've holed up."

"So what's the plan?"

"You do much fighting 'paches?"

"No more than I had to. You?"

"Same, but when I have, I felt like they have a kind of sixth sense. They know what's coming."

"So you think they'll be expecting us?"

Sam nodded.

"How do you think we should do it then?"

"We come at this from two directions. One of us ride on in like a pigeon. The other circles around like a wolf and gets above them."

"Sounds good to me. You circle around."

Sam gave him that narrow-eyed look. "Being the pigeon is most dangerous. I should do it."

"Why?"

"It's nearest my land."

Cord snorted. "With that kind of logic no wonder you became an outlaw."

"I told you. Hell, never mind."

'Look, you have the fastest horse and know this country. How good are you with a rifle?"

"Good enough."

"Then it's settled."

"I don't like it."

"Like that's something new?" Cord said with a sardonic laugh.

"All right, but little brother, I don't want you getting shot. You got that. I just got a brother, obnoxious son of a bitch though he might be, and I don't want to lose him."

"Then be a good shot."

Sam gave him that look again before nudging his stallion in the side. He took off to the south faster than any man had a sane right to ride over rough ground. Satan might have a vicious temperament for anybody but Sam, but he was a horse in a million for his agility and strength.

Cord kept the tracks in sight, but mostly watched the high ground for any movement. As he got nearer to where he judged the canyon to be, he realized how hard it would have been to find if someone hadn't known it was there. He took his Winchester 76 from its scabbard, levering in a cartridge, and rode on at a slow pace angling back and forth to make it harder to get a shot at him if they were watching as Sam expected.

When he saw the first movement, he brought up his rifle but waited until he was sure it was one of the renegades. His shot caught the man as he was bringing his own rifle to bear.

Quickly Cord levered in another round when he heard a

second shot, not sure if it was the other two or Ryker. Two more shots and then all was silent.

He nudged Jeb into a run. Two bodies were sprawled at the mouth of the small canyon. A third was not far beyond on a rise. He approached more cautiously not sure if this was all.

Sam was riding his horse down the ridge at his usual break-neck speed. They got to the bodies at almost the same time. Cord dismounted to be sure they were dead while Sam kept his rifle at the ready.

"Sam, look at this." He pointed to a fresh scalp on one of the men's belts.

"Ugh. Where you figure they got that?"

"Just guessing, last night. There any cabins around here?"

"Not a lot. You know until Geronimo gives it up, and they round up all the strays, folks aren't much for being isolated out this way."

"I need to backtrack to find out what happened."

Sam gave him a look. "Need to?"

"It's my job." He didn't much like the idea either.

"Look anybody out here in these hills oughta know it's dangerous." When he saw the determination on Cord's face, he gave up. "That means we'll be stuck out all night, you know that?"

"You go back and tell them it's all right."

"Oh sure and leave you out here in case there are more. Sorry, but if you stay, I stay which means we better follow those tracks as far as we can, and then find a good place to camp. It's not snowing but it's still damned cold."

"You are as stubborn a man as I know, Sam Ryker," Cord said mounting his horse.

"But likely not more than those who know you, Cord O'Brian."

When Priscilla and Abby realized there was no chance Cord and Sam were coming back that night, they fixed a quiet dinner, got Davy asleep, and then settled into the great room with glasses of wine.

"So now you can tell me about you and Cord," Abby said curling her legs under her.

"Not a lot to tell. He isn't going to ask me to marry him if that's what you are wondering."

"Wow, you are thinking marriage? I am kind of surprised. Wait. I said that wrong. I am totally shocked."

"What'd you think this was?"

"I didn't know. An affair maybe."

"It's not even that. Cord hasn't touched me that way. I am as pure as the driven snow... not quite as ignorant, of course."

Abby laughed. "Ah so you have awakened. Good." She shook her head. "I would've never guessed it'd be him to do it."

"Me either but what's wrong with him?" she asked as she took another sip of her wine.

"Not a thing but weren't you the woman who didn't want a man with a gun? Seems like I recall that."

"I know." She sighed as she thought about all her expectations. "I had a lot of ideas once upon a time. Foolish ones where it came to some things."

Abby laughed. "No more faith in wishing shrines?"

"God in heaven, that was the most foolish of all. It ended up a curse considering what Martin eventually did."

"No way could you have known that."

"No, not back then, but more recently, well I did have a hint. I... uh visited a seer."

"Oh Cilla, no."

"Oh Abby, yes."

"What did she tell you?" Her eyes showing her interest despite herself.

"She told me that I had a secret enemy, which pretty well describes Martin. She also said a white knight was on his way. Actually more of a black knight."

Abby laughed. "Well that fits your marshal."

"Go ahead and laugh. He's your brother-in-law now." She thought about telling her of the hawks that Connie and the Yaqui elder had mentioned, of her own more frequent sightings of them, but she wasn't sure it meant anything-- so decided against muddying the waters.

"Their being brothers really did shock me. I suppose I should have seen it, but to me he was just a threat to Sam. It took Joe seeing the strong resemblance, but now it seems obvious."

They both sipped their wine. "The problem I have," Priscilla said finally, "is he doesn't want me, not that way."

"It looks to me like he wants you but can't see it working. You said he had a daughter, maybe he's been burned before."

"That and we are from different worlds."

"So were Sam and I. That can be overcome."

"I have no idea how."

"Be forceful. Don't wait on him for this. It's time little Cilla stood up for herself."

"He won't think that's pushy?"

Abby laughed. "Who cares? It will settle it one way or the other. It's what it took with Sam." She poured more wine into their glasses. "Fortunately since I don't breast feed again until morning, I can have some more too."

"Do you really like living out here, Abby?"

"As I said, the only thing missing is you. I love it."

"I've thought about it... Well that if Cord gave up being a lawman, maybe he'd consider farming or ranching. He said he worked on the ranch where he met his wife, but her parents didn't have any use for him after she died. They blamed him."

"Was it his fault?"

"No way could it have been. I guess she had the baby but something went wrong. He didn't know why she died, but I can see how parents might look for someone to blame."

Abby nodded with understanding.

"The thing is I've wondered if he'd want ranch life again-- or even if he did, how it'd be for me. I guess, if it's not that, he'd have to stay with lawmaking. Judge Emerson suggested running for some office. The look on Cord's face pretty well left that out. I can't see him working in a bank or store."

Abby giggled. "Heavens no, definitely not that. Well I guess that's something you and he can work out if you get him past the fear point."

"You think that's what it is?"

"I don't know him that well. Maybe he likes being a marshal, and you have to decide if you can live with that."

When she went to bed, Priscilla thought about that. Could she live with a man who used a gun and wore a star? There was a bigger question. Could she live without Cord O'Brian?

Cord and Sam had built a small fire and warmed up a can of beans. The night was dark and cold around them as the trees glistened with ice. "It's going to be a cold one," Sam decreed

"I've been out in worse."

"You could be lying in a soft bed."

"Not a choice by now."

"You like being a marshal that much?" Sam asked as he rolled a cigarette.

"Lately about like hitting myself over the head with a hammer."

Sam laughed. "Then why do it?"

"It's all I know other than cowboying years back. You know I have a daughter, don't you?"

Sam nodded. "What's her name?"

"Grace."

"That means I have a niece. Where has she been?"

Cord shook his head. "It's a long story, but I have her now. That has to be a consideration for whatever I do." Except running. How did Grace fit into that?

264

"You can work on my ranch if you want."

Cord gave a laugh. "Thanks, but I own a ranch. It's west of here, across the Santa Cruz valley and up in the mountains."

"Rough country but pretty if I recall. The other side of the Tumacacoris?"

"You rustle over there?"

Sam laughed. "I've done nothing in this country that is illegal, and nothing anywhere that wasn't the way of the land before the law rushed in to make rules."

"Mean old law." Cord rolled a cigarette. "It's pretty country, but I have only been there a few times. A good mix of hills and a few meadows. Not as big as your place, just fifteen thousand acres or so but good grass most of the year if it's not overstocked anyway."

"So why aren't you there?"

"Money. I was lucky to afford it, because of someone who bought it with no idea what he was getting into. Even before Grace arrived, I didn't have the money for stock and living there. It wasn't like I could leave it with cattle on it, given the conditions as they've been." He gave Sam a pointed look.

"I told you I didn't rustle anywhere in the Territory. And any cattle I might have sold, from whatever source, were to big ranchers like Wright."

"You know much about him?" Cord asked as he thought about the rustling going on to the north of Tucson.

"He stiffed me. The deal was with his father, and the old man had a heart attack. I was lucky to get out of that one with my hide intact, missing the cattle I'd brought up, of course."

"It looks like he's involved in penny ante rustling but can't be proved."

"Sounds like small shakes for him, but maybe it amuses him. Watch your back around him, Cord."

"Don't disagree."

"Might be better running cattle down in the Arivaca country. At least less rustlers, and they say Geronimo is about done."

"No money for cattle and what about Grace?"

"Makes it tough." They smoked in companionable silence. "I could give you a start."

Cord laughed. "You go from wanting to beat my brains in to wanting to help me stock a ranch?"

"You weren't my brother then. I never had a brother."

"Me either."

"I never had any relatives actually. Raised by Annie, a whore, after my mother died. She was mean as a snake-- but as long as I worked to suit her, she kept me eating. As soon as I could, I took off and made my own way."

"We didn't have such different paths. Kansas was tough country to grow up in before and after the war."

"You're telling me. Quantrill's raiders not the least of which. You never got into that, did you?"

"Too young for the war and no interest in being a desperado."

Sam chuckled. "I keep telling you I wasn't as much of an outlaw as you make out. I worked for big ranches in New Mexico, learned how to handle a gun. They taught me about Mexico and loose, unbranded cattle. Don't get that look on your face. I know it was wrong legally speaking."

Cord smiled.

"The man, I worked for on the Circle R, who sold me the ranch when he decided to leave it, taught me about another side to life. Until Abby, I couldn't see how I'd get there."

"Sometimes a woman can do that for a man." Cord smoked thinking sometimes not too.

"Here's one for you," Sam said. "Duty is important to you, isn't it?"

"I've said so, wouldn't be here tonight cold and about to spend a miserable night if it wasn't."

"What are you going to do about Matthews?"

Cord snorted. "Why do you ask?"

"It's a logical question, you being a lawman and all."

"If the legal system takes care of him, nothing."

"You think if she brings charges, they will believe her?"

"She's a woman of quality."

"She's still a woman. Women get short changed where it comes to our courts, and you know it. Women and children," Sam added pointedly.

Cord took a long draw on the cigarette, blowing out the smoke as he thought about how much he was willing to tell Sam. "I'd have to follow the law," he said finally, and with what he hoped was a sincere tone.

Sam chuckled. "Sure you would, so he could do it again."

"Possibly."

"Going to tell you a story, son, about something like this. Man told me the story... There was this minister in a town, who had been abusing boys for years. The bastard had tried to rape this man when he was young, but he'd gotten away-- barely. Years later, the man came across a boy who was in the same straits he'd been. Vulnerable, poor, no family to protect him. It had been easy pickings back in Kansas for a predator like this supposed holy man was."

When Sam hesitated, Cord waited, saying nothing, smoking, knowing there was more.

"So when this man came across the reverend, with another boy, he knew no court of law would do right for what was going on. The boy wouldn't be believed. He could have gotten this victim away, but there'd always be another." His voice grew hard. "So the man, he killed that pastor, all the while the bastard was begging for his life. He shot him dead-- in cold blood, most would call it murder."

Cord understood what Sam was telling him. "Some men," Sam went on, "they can do something like that and live with themselves. Some can't."

267

"What makes you think this story would apply to me?" Cord asked, even as he was well aware of the reason for the telling of it.

"Just saying that maybe you should let somebody else take care of Matthews. Somebody who can kill without it bothering him. Kill when he knows it needs doing, and he won't let guilt tear him up later."

"I stomp my own rats."

Sam chuckled. "All right."

"And it's not like I want to kill somebody... or even saying I will... but if it needs doing, I won't ask another man to take that on." He smiled then and gave Sam a hard look across the campfire. "Especially not a brother."

"Hell's fire, you're an obnoxious man."

"Not disagreeing."

"You come by that from our father?"

"Could be."

"What was the old man like?"

"We look a lot like him. Tall, dark haired. Personality like a wolverine. A mean bastard. I know you might've wished for a father, but that one, you wouldn't have wanted."

"I stopped wanting that years ago."

"One more question," Cord said. "Where'd you get the name—Ryker?"

"Annie said it was my mother's. Why?"

"It was something I wondered about after Joe first said we might be related. I knew some Rykers near where my parents lived. The story was one of those adults whisper about. I wasn't supposed to, but I heard pieces. There had been a daughter. I don't know what she looked like. They said she was young, when she got in trouble by some son of a bitch.

"She had more honor than he did and wouldn't say who the father was. The family turned her out without a nickel. I'd hear talk once in a while about wondering what happened to her. Whether the wolves got her. She was a mystery as she seemed to disappear. It seems most likely it was our father. He didn't stand by her. It might be she had no choice but to do what she did to survive."

Sam said nothing for a while. "Men are bastards."

"We're men," Cord said staring into the dying fire.

"I know."

CHAPTER 21

Martin nursed his third beer or maybe fifth. He had lost count. The one thing he had known was he wasn't going back to that cabin. He had wanted to, but then he got afraid of what he'd find. It wasn't actually in him to kill Priscilla. What if she was alive, angry, and had been waiting for him? He had talked himself out of going and instead had gotten drunk. Two nights in a row.

Someone was playing the piano badly. There were only five or six men in the bar. He wondered where Sally was. She was so beautiful. Likely she found a new customer. One who paid better. Morosely he stared into the amber liquid wishing he hadn't borrowed money to supply the cabin he had hoped would be a love nest. Damn Priscilla. Damn all women. They were unfaithful harlots.

He only looked up when the bar door swung open. Richard Wright and Clinton Adams walked in, ordered whiskeys and came to Martin's table. Glumly they downed their shots while Adams went back to the bar for the bottle.

"You didn't tell us there were Apaches up there," Wright said.

"Apaches? I didn't know that. I thought they had Geronimo cornered or signing a treaty or something."

"Whatever they thought they had, we got attacked, full on attacked. Gabe was killed."

Martin winced thinking how lucky it was that he hadn't gone. That could have been him. He had no sympathy for Evans. What was he-- just a gun hand who got what he deserved by going up there to effect a phony rescue.

"Is the marshal back?" Wright asked gulping another whiskey.

"How would I know?"

"Ask Ridge."

"How could I do that without--" He saw the look on Wright's face and yielded to the demand.

At the bar he ordered another beer. "I haven't seen Marshal O'Brian around. He out looking for Miss Wesley?"

"How the hell am I supposed to know?" Ridge asked. "Not like he reports to me. Ask his deputy."

"How about Sheriff Adams?" he added to make this all sound less directed.

"Likely drunk as usual. Since when did you want the law?" Ridge looked at him suspiciously.

"I am logically concerned about Miss Wesley being lost. Do they think she wandered off?"

Ridge gave him one of those looks, which said he'd had all the questions he wanted. Martin took his beer back to the table wishing Sally would come downstairs. He should have asked where she was. He began to feel angry that she wasn't there when he needed her. Women. Who could count on them for anything?

"You'll have to talk to Cordova. Ridge knew nothing and cared less."

"You will talk to Cordova. I want to know where that marshal is."

"Why?"

"Just a feeling I got. Meet me back at the ranch tomorrow morning. Come with the answers about O'Brian. Then we'll discuss the deal you were concerned with."

Martin looked at him uneasily. "Deal?"

"You know the one relating to your bookkeeping." With that, Wright rose and stomped out of the bar with Adams at his heel like the dog he was.

"Jesus H. Christ," Martin muttered. He walked back over to the bar. "Where's Sally?"

"Am I the keeper of the girls?" Ridge asked as testily as before.

Martin tried to manage a glare such as he'd seen the marshal do, but it was beyond him, especially as drunk as he was. He decided he'd go back to his room, sleep it off, and worry about Wright in the morning. He hoped he had covered his butt with Wright. With that Wright couldn't touch him—at least not without hurting himself.

The bigger problem was if Priscilla wasn't dead and showed up. Maybe if he got lucky the Apaches had gotten her. He smiled for a moment at the thought. It would be just what she deserved. Then he sighed. Luck wasn't running with him. She would show up, and he better be ready with his own story and a lot of confidence.

He'd handle Wright in the morning. That was less of a problem, even though he was sure Wright thought he had all the answers. What he didn't have were brains. Martin smugly thought it was where he excelled. And then he thought about what Wright wanted to know. What could O'Brian have to do with any of it?

~

It was close to dusk when Priscilla saw Sam and Cord ride into the ranch yard. She and Abby went out to the barn where the two were unsaddling their horses.

"Did you get them?" Ollie asked.

Sam nodded. "But not before they got someone else."

"Anybody we know or make that knew?" Joe asked.

"More or less," Cord answered. Priscilla didn't like the cold look on his face.

"Gabe Evans. You saw him too that time you visited the jail. He was killed not that far from the cabin."

"You mean..." She stopped unwilling to finish her thought.

"From the looks of it, three of them were heading for it. They didn't make it. Gabe got shot and the others ran back to their Tucson holes."

"You think the cabin was their destination?"

"It would be the logical assumption, but unless I figure out who the other two were, I won't know for sure." She wondered if Martin had been one of them. He had no reason to want her rescued and to tell her story—so unlikely.

As they ate dinner, Davy playing in the corner with some blocks, Ryker's men had questions as to what had happened. Was more trouble likely? With neither Cord nor Sam much in the mood to answer questions, the hands left after dinner leaving just the family.

"That was very good, Mrs. Ryker," Cord said as he rolled and lit a cigarette.

"Why thank you, Cord. Cilla fixed most of it though as Davy was wanting to be held a lot today, and you better start to call me Abby, don't you think?"

"Well you ladies fixed a fine meal however you did it." He took a long draw on his cigarette before he turned and met Priscilla's gaze. "I think the rivers are down enough to cross safely."

"So we have to leave?" Priscilla understood her family must

be desperate, but she worried how she'd be received home and now adding to it-- why had someone come to that cabin? What had their intention been? She was very fortunate she hadn't been there.

There was another thing. Nothing was settled between her and Cord. It would be easier settling it away from Tucson. Once they got back, the world would close around them and make it all more complicated than she had come to believe it had to be.

"Tomorrow morning," Cord answered.

"Can we talk about that?" she asked him.

Sam got a grin on his face. "Why don't you two head into the great room where you can get the fire going, Cord. I'll help Abby with the dishes and getting Davy to bed.

When Abby had been going to protest, he stopped her with a kiss. "They need to talk."

Cord built up the fire in the fireplace as Priscilla settled onto the big sofa. She was wearing a yellow dress that likely had belonged to Abby as it was too long for her and tight across her straining breasts. She was beautiful with her long hair clipped back with combs.

When he would have sat on one of the big chairs, she said, "Here, where we can talk better."

He threw his cigarette into the fire and gave up as he came to sit beside her, his arms around her as she cuddled against him.

"I don't want to leave tomorrow," she said.

"It won't make it easier putting it off."

"I know, but I want us to have time to talk, and it's easier here than it will be back there. I expect a lot of questions. When we show up together, what will people think?"

"Then we better not show up together. I'll take you to Benson where you wait for the train, while I ride into Tucson and make sure to be there before you."

He saw by her expression that she didn't like that. "And so

what do you want?" he asked, as she caressed his bristly jaw with her fingers.

"You need a shave again," she observed.

"Pretty much every day."

"I want us to have some time to talk about us."

"Angel, there can't be an *us*. You know that."

"I do? How would I know that?" He looked into those big eyes and wished he could see a way. "What will one extra day hurt?" she asked.

He let out his breath. He wasn't sure what it could hurt, but he had an uneasy feeling about it. The more time he had with her, the worse this was going to be for him when it was over.

"All right. If they'll have us."

"You know they will. Sam is liking this idea of having a brother. You can see that. And I like time with Abby and Davy. Maybe... we could go on a picnic or something."

He laughed. "Is this the season for it?"

"Isn't it always?" Her smile was sweet, but seemed to have something behind it. It wouldn't matter. They had to go back sometime, but actually he was no more eager to go home than she was.

"You two work it out?" Sam asked as he and Abby came in.

"If you will have us, we'll stay an extra day," Priscilla said with a big smile.

"Hey, you're family," Abby said. "Of course, we'll have you. Do you two play whist?"

"Oh God, not that," Sam protested with a groan.

She swatted his hand. "You know you like it always once we get started."

"I never even heard of it," Cord said. "How about poker instead?"

Sam laughed. "Now that's more like it."

It turned out that Priscilla was very good at poker, surprising them all. Using match sticks for their bets, she cleaned their clocks. "It's all that accounting," she said with a pleased smile as she pulled in the last pot and counted up her winnings at a penny a stick.

"You are good at numbers for sure," Abby agreed. "Better at it for Father than I ever was."

"It probably added to Martin's hate of me," Priscilla said. "And I have to think hate played a role in what he did. It certainly wasn't love."

"What do you mean?"

"As I went over your father's books, I saw that in the last year or two, Martin had been cheating him. He was adjusting the books to give himself a steady income as he changed numbers from receipts and bills to the books. I told Mr. Spenser, and he fired him."

"Too bad he didn't bring charges," Cord said as he accepted a whiskey from Sam.

"I guess he hated to do that after all the years Martin had worked for him."

"Martin has skimmed by too many times. He shouldn't this time," Cord said giving Priscilla a questioning look.

"I am thinking about it, but there is a lot to consider. I think he will lie, and who will believe me? He can say I wanted to go with him and changed my mind. He can make it sound like it's all me. I don't know though why I care." She gave a little laugh. "My reputation is shot anyway after disappearing as I did. When I turn up, what will they think in town?"

Abby laughed. "That you were off cavorting," she suggested, "and with the marshal no less."

"Hey, I suggested a way for her to avoid that by taking the train back."

"And arriving there alone?" Priscilla asked. "No thanks. What if Martin shows up before you do?"

He walked over to the fireplace, putting a boot onto the raised hearth as he stared into the flames. She knew he was considering what he could do within the law. She didn't want any of it to cause him trouble. She'd have to deal with it.

"Why don't we all go to bed and think about it," Abby suggested with a yawn. "It might be obvious tomorrow."

Cord smiled and opened his hands in agreement. "I am tired. See you all in the morning." He turned and walked into the darkness to head upstairs. Priscilla watched him go, met Abby's questioning eyes but shook her head. She didn't have answers, not yet.

She went to her room but with no plan to go to bed. Of course, after going after the renegades, Cord was doubtless exhausted. She thought about that for a few seconds as she stripped out of her clothing, dove into the bag she had brought from the cabin, and pulled out a lacy nightgown.

Martin had intended it to be what she wore for him. Maybe Cord wouldn't appreciate that or maybe his sense of humor would see it for what it was—ironic justice. As she dropped it over her head, she didn't bother to look in a mirror as she loosened her hair letting it fall down her back. Rather than taking the kerosene lamp, she lit a candle and slipped out her door, silently padding up the stairs. She tapped lightly on the first door she came to as she recalled how Cord slept with a gun nearby and startling him wasn't smart.

"Yeah?"

"May I come in?" she asked.

"Angel?" he asked his voice sounding more awake. "What's wrong? Yes, come in."

She opened the door and saw him lying on the bed, covers to his waist and bare above it... most likely below.

"I wanted to talk," she said taking the candle to the nightstand and then perching on the edge of the bed.

"Dressed like that?" he asked a smile in his voice that she saw when she looked up and met his gaze.

"Marshal, it's chilly out here, mind if I get under the covers."

"God, do you know what you're asking?" His voice now sounded ragged.

"I think so." She didn't wait for his permission, as she lifted the covers enough to slide under them. "You are warm." She moved to lie close, their bodies touching.

"Hot would be more accurate," he said lifting one of his knees to hide what she realized had to be an erection. Yes, this was going to go as she hoped.

"I thought we could talk about a lot of things," she said running her hands over his muscular chest. That felt good.

"Is that what you thought?" he muttered. She teased one of his nipples into an erect little button. She wished she knew more about this. Then he came up on one elbow and over her, claiming her lips with his as his tongue delved into her mouth.

"Oh yes, I like that kind of talk," she whispered against his lips.

"You know nothing is going to be changed by this. You sure it's what you want?" Even now he was holding off giving her a chance to change her mind.

"Definitely. I know what I want but may not know how to get there. Think you can help," she teased as she ran her fingers down his back to his firm buttocks then squeezed.

"Babies come from this kind of play," he warned.

"Not at this time of the month." She looked back at him, saw the indecision in his eyes change to one of determination. He slipped her nightgown from one shoulder, then the other, sliding it down to her waist and leaving her breasts bare to take into his mouth, sucking on first one nipple and then the other.

"Oh yes, Cord. Mmmmm," she moaned as he continued to use his mouth and hands to move over her upper torso, sliding the nightgown lower.

She thrust her hips against him. "You want more?" he whispered.

"I want everything," she whispered against his mouth as he

claimed hers again, his tongue delving within, making her whole body sing for him.

"You sure you can take it all?"

She smiled then. "Let me think about that." She pushed him from her and as he lay back, sucking in a breath, she removed the blanket that had been covering his lower body. He was fully erect and seemed very large. For a moment she wondered if she could take all of that inside her. She ran her hand down his chest to his belly and then the hair that surrounded that swollen male organ. "Can I touch you?" she whispered, stopping just shy of grasping him.

"If... you want." His body was rigid with the control he was exerting as she grasped him and stroked a little, unsure of the right way to proceed. As she played with him, finally, he groaned. "Enough," and laid her on her back as he pushed her nightgown from her. When she was naked, only the candlelight to illuminate her body, he began to touch her, stroking down her belly, her inner thighs and finally to her most private places, creating a need so great she thought she'd go mad if he didn't do something about it.

"Angel, you can still change your mind. You can't give this night twice."

"Are you insane? Take me now before I go crazy." She reached up and pulled his head down where they could kiss again. She was writhing with a need that was moving through her. She wanted something. Some kind of release, but it seemed he wanted to play as he spread her legs, pushing his fingers inside where she most wanted him to be. She groaned as she tried to take them deeper. She realized he had been stretching her.

When he shifted to come over her, she felt his hard erection, and her own excitement grew. She lifted her hips to take him within, feeling some discomfort, but not enough to stop. "Mmm-mmm, more," she begged. He was filling her completely. She had never felt anything better than his naked body moving against hers, and him inside her.

As he moved and she thrust up against him, the feelings increased until she felt as though he and she were one, moving as one body. The feeling of ecstasy grew until she exploded with lights and glorious sensations. She heard him groan and felt him pulsing within her.

She wanted the feelings to last forever, but when they subsided, it was still good. The sensations of warmth and relaxation seemed to be in every part of her body. When he would have withdrawn, she held him to her. He turned them to their sides-- so they could stay connected, their bodies now sweaty and hot.

As she finally felt the cooler air, he drew the blankets up over them, holding her in his arms. She slept and only was aware later that he had pulled out of her as they still lay curled together.

When she woke, she ran her hands over his torso. She loved his muscular length, the masculine feel of him, his bare skin under her fingers.

"You sorry?" he asked, his eyes staring at the ceiling. The candle had long gone out, but the moon was sending light over them, a kind of unearthly light.

"Do I look sorry?" she asked as she kissed his chest.

"I never want to hurt you."

"I know that, and don't give me that nothing else can be between us. I am not going to argue with you about it. I want what I can have of you, Cord. If this is all, then so be it. But I want you and as often as it's possible."

"It will be complicated."

"I know that too, but it will also be worth it."

"I hope you feel that way tomorrow."

"There is no reason I won't. I thought about it before I came up."

"I figured you had-- considering what you wore."

She grinned, taking his big hand into hers, kissing his fingers. "I hope you won't be mad about this."

"Why would I? You look so beautiful in it... Of course, more beautiful out of it. Was it Abby's?"

She smiled as she nipped a finger. "No, it was something new that Martin had bought and taken to that cabin evidently hoping I'd wear for him. I took it when we left because I already knew who I wanted to wear it for."

She heard him chuckle and felt relieved.

"You probably need to wake up in your own bed," he said kissing her.

"I don't intend to hide this. Abby won't be surprised that we are now lovers. She advised this actually."

"Advised it?"

"She told me to be forceful. Take the situation in hand." She reached down playfully touching him again, liking how it caused him to suck in a breath. For a man who always liked to be in control, who was tough in every way, she enjoyed making that control disappear.

"When I came up here," she whispered against his ear, "the only thing I worried about was how to do it. I am glad you knew."

"My angel."

"Yes, I am... and Cord..."

"What?"

She stroked him feeling his organ growing hard as her body was also heating up. "Can we do it again?"

CHAPTER 22

In the morning, Priscilla woke to find Cord already gone. She washed in the upstairs bathroom, then slipped down the stairs with the quilt wrapped around her. Although she didn't care if Abby knew about her night, she didn't want to run into Sam while wearing that revealing nightgown. When she had fully dressed, she went into the kitchen smiling, until she saw the expression Cord's face. Cigarette dangling from his lips, he stared out the window. Sam was sitting at the table drumming his long fingers as he watched his brother through narrowed eyes.

What were those two angry about now? She walked over the stove where Abby had breakfast cooking. Pouring herself a cup of coffee, she smiled. "And how is your morning going?" she asked as she nodded her head toward the two surly brothers.

Abby chuckled. "See the solution I found for Davy?"

Chairs had been placed on their side to keep the toddling baby from anything hot and dangerous while it let him practice walking. "Good going," Priscilla said. "He's on the move for sure."

"Walking today, running tomorrow, and on horse next week," Abby said with another laugh.

"What's with those two?"

"A minor disagreement... but it's been decided and for assorted good reason. We're going with you to Tucson."

"How can you do that?"

"Easy we hitch up the buckboard, saddle some horses, take along enough supplies to sleep out one night, if we have to go farther south to get to the shallowest ford, and we leave Bull, Rock and Joe here even though they will be complaining to high heaven. Somebody has to protect this place."

"You are putting yourself out for me?"

"It's you but other reasons also. Ollie has been off his feed, as the men say here. He needs to see a real doctor to find out what's going on."

"So he could come without you. Won't this be hard on Davy?"

"Not really. He's a tough little customer. And there are reasons for us to come. We want to meet our niece, of course."

"She'll be thrilled-- and a baby to play with, nothing will make her happier. Although I suppose she'll be set back some, by it seeming her father and I deserted her for so long."

"So all the more reason for us all to come and make it fun."

When Priscilla saw the troubled look appear in Abby's eyes, she knew that wasn't all. "What else is going on?" she asked.

"The source of the argument between those two stubborn men and I'll let them explain it to you."

Priscilla knew Cord had been listening to their conversation but had said nothing. She walked over to where he still stood smoking. "Did you sleep well?" she asked pertly.

He looked down at her and his eyes softened. "Woke up a lot."

"Oh you poor man. Maybe you'll need a... nap." She smiled with what she hoped was a provocative look.

"No time for naps," Sam said. "He's going out with me to help round up some of the cattle south of us. I don't want to leave them that close to the border with less of us on the ranch."

"So don't come to Tucson," Cord said turning and the hard look on his face was back.

"Oh I am coming."

"Maybe I'll have to arrest you."

"Could be. Think you're up to it?" Sam snapped back.

"If need be."

Abby came over from the stove. "Start eating or I throw it to my chickens."

Cord moved to the table and took several hotcakes, which he lathered with butter and syrup while Sam did the same.

Priscilla looked from Sam to Cord as she sipped her coffee, thinking how much those hard, sullen faces looked alike. "What are the other reasons you are coming?" Priscilla asked Sam as she sipped her coffee.

"Just some unfinished business."

"Which is why you should not come," Cord said as soon as he swallowed.

Priscilla topped off both their coffee cups. "I think I should know what's going on here."

"So you can worry?" Cord asked.

"So I can be prepared with a lie when required," she shot back with a saucy look.

"Like you think a marshal would ask you to lie for him?" he asked with a bit of a sanctimonious touch to the words.

"Some might," she suggested, reaching over and kissing him hard on the lips. If that surprised Sam or Abby, neither said a word.

"Finish eating," Sam told Cord, rising, kissing Abby, his son, and then grabbing hat and coat. "I'll be saddling the horses. Let's see what kind of cowboy you'd make."

"Yeah like that'll ever happen," Priscilla said when Cord also rose and took a last gulp of coffee.

"I own a ranch," he retorted shocking her and Abby, "so you never know." He bent then and lifted Priscilla's chin for another kiss, which let her know he hadn't forgotten the night they had had.

Moments later, they heard the two men thunder out of the yard on their way south. "He didn't want to take the crew?" Priscilla asked Abby as she picked up dishes to take to wash.

"I guess he thought they'd be enough. Or maybe he's still concerned about Apache trouble. He's been a lot more protective since Davy was born."

Ollie came in through the back door, coughing as he handed Abby a pail of milk before depositing his coat on the peg. "Dad blasted cold is hard on my lumbago," he complained as he sidled up to the cook stove.

"Want some hotcakes?" Abby asked as she took him a cup of coffee.

"Might try one."

"Did Sam tell you about taking us to Tucson-- so Sam can meet his niece?"

"Said we was going, as he rode out, but no explanations. He's in a mood again, ain't he?" Ollie sat at the table as he watched Davy play with blocks, creating a tall structure that tumbled with the last block. The little boy patiently set about doing it again.

"Son shore don't take after his pappy," Ollie said with a chuckle. "Got his mama's sticking to it."

"He has his days," Abby said handing a plate with two hotcakes as she sat at the table.

"I was thinking I'd like to help feed the chickens and things today," Priscilla said. See how you do it."

Abby looked at her with shock. "You planning on chickens or a cow in town?" Abby asked.

Priscilla tried to essay an innocent smile. "You never know. We have space."

"I heard that about Cord owning a ranch. That wouldn't be what this is about, would it?"

"Not at all," Priscilla said, knowing she was a terrible liar. Abby just laughed at her.

As Ollie ate, he listened to their conversation. "Wind comin' from a new direction here, ain't it?" he said.

"I thought the same as always," Priscilla said hoping they weren't due for more snow in the high country. She'd had her share of snow for the year or even a couple of years. She wondered at what elevation Sam's ranch was.

Ollie chuckled. "Not meanin' the weather, girlie."

"Oh." She played innocent with a smile that usually had men forgetting their questions but didn't work with Ollie.

"You ain't thinkin' of hookin' up with that marshal, are you, gal?" Ollie asked looking at her pointedly.

"And if per chance I was?" Priscilla asked defensively before she could get her voice under her command, "not saying I am, of course."

Ollie chortled. "You got any more coffee left in that pot, Abby?"

"Enough for you to have one more cup but are you sure it's good for you?"

"I am." He gave her a gimlet eyed look similar to what Sam and Cord did.

He turned back to Priscilla. "Now about that boy, the lawman. He's not for you and you know it. The first time I saw him ride onto this ranch, he was r'aring to shoot or arrest Sam—and I don't think it made no never mind to him which. In town, it ain't never been no different. I seen the two of them ride out a bit ago, and they were still looking ready to get into a brawl."

"It's their nature," Abby said. "And them being brothers, not real surprising."

Ollie choked on his coffee. "Brothers? Like as in blood brothers?"

"The kind who had the same father. Sam is actually an O'Brian."

"I thought Joe was just blowing hot air with him doin' that painting and all. Brothers? For real?"

"You look at them together and you wouldn't ask that," Abby said.

"Man, I can't hardly believe it but now that you say it, guess they do look alike. Both got the disposition of a rattler."

When he saw he had offended both women, he chuckled. "All right. All right. I am just getting' myself used to the idee of it." He hesitated than gave Priscilla one of his wise old man looks. "It don't change a thing about you not setting your sights for that one. He won't be alive long enough to matter."

Priscilla felt a chill. "Why would you say such a thing?"

"Him being a lawman down here, and the kind who don't take payoffs from all I seen. Looking for trouble, bracing it when he could walk around it. Nah, he ain't gonna live to be an old man."

"Sam thought the same thing once," Abby protested. "Men can change."

"Some... Well all right, you think you want to marry that one, guess nobody's gonna stop you with commonsense logic and any hows."

"Marriage probably isn't in the cards," she said as she looked into her tepid coffee.

"Why not? Don't wanta marry him?" Ollie asked being as nosy as the old woman, which some claimed he acted where it came to Sam.

Priscilla laughed and met his eyes squarely. "So you going to teach me how to milk a cow and whatever else goes on outside?"

"Skirts ain't much for such jobs."

"I have pants. I'll be right back... Oh, and on that cough, do you have any onions in that garden?"

Abby looked blankly at her. "Why? But yes, we do."

"I've been working some with Doc Hadley and there is this cough syrup I learned about made with onions. We could give it a try."

"Sounds terrible," Ollie said making a face even at the thought.

"Well I don't expect it tastes good but isn't what matters whether it works, and he swears by it. Better than the stuff with opium that addicts so many people."

"We'll give it a try," Abby said. "What do I do?"

"Bring them in, slice them and pour some of that honey I saw on your shelf on top of them. Then put them in the oven, low heat until the onions turn clear. Strain them getting all the juice and bottle it. Makes a person tear up, but Doc says it works. Lemon is good with it too."

"Well no lemon here, but Davy and I'll head for the garden and give this a try. It sounds easy, while you and Ollie visit Tildy. She loves attention... kind of."

As Sam and Cord rode across the grasslands, they didn't talk even though they both felt the need to clear the air. When they saw the first cows and steers, Sam signaled with his hand for Cord to head to the right while he circled left.

Little by little they began rounding them up, forming a bunch, then gathering more. Cord hadn't done this kind of work for years, but he found it coming back as he used the rope Sam had loaned him to make enough noise and movement to keep the cattle moving.

Racing to the edge of an arroyo, he cut off five heading for the hills, forcing them back to the main herd. After that they decided he and Jeb meant business and stayed with the herd. After two hours, fifty head grazed in the middle of the meadow.

"You think this is all?" Cord asked as he scanned the hills looking for movement.

"Pretty near. Any stragglers will follow us in. Cattle like a herd."

"You don't run as many head as I'd have figured," Cord said as they began driving the cattle back toward the ranch, keeping them from cutting away.

"It's the grass. Look at it," Sam said.

"It looks good. Rich grassland."

"Because it's not overgrazed. I move these cattle around to make it stay that way. I learned a lot working for the ranchers I did through the years. Some abused the land, and they were out of business. Those that cared for the grass, they could make it through droughts and tough times. The grass. That's what it's all about."

It was more than Sam generally spoke, and Cord could hear the love of his land in his voice. It was good wisdom. He'd remember it if he ever got a chance to work his own place.

"You don't want me going with you to Tucson, do you?" Sam asked in a voice that said he already knew the answer.

"It'll just make it more likely that there'll be trouble."

"You don't look like an optimist."

"You don't look much like a man who'd know that word," Cord quipped.

"I know a lot of them like retribution, revenge, settling of scores."

"Yes, Wright cheated you, but you can't do anything about that now."

"Nope, but I know him better than I think you do."

"So?"

"So he will have hired more hard cases by the time you get back to Tucson. He lost Evans-- so he will need more if he wants to maintain or even build his power. For that, you eventually will stand in his way. It's sure not that poor excuse for a sheriff that they've got. You say he's hitting the small ranches. I say he'll be ready for trouble."

"I have a deputy."

"Good, that'll make three of us."

"Don't you ever take no for an answer, you bastard," Cord snapped.

Sam chuckled. "With me it's a fact of birth, but you on the other hand are a self-made man."

Cord tried not to laugh, but it was impossible. "All right. You come, but you don't start anything."

"Haven't you figured out yet that I won't have to? Wright will want to take you out. What else stands in his way in Tucson?"

"Judge Emerson."

"He much of a gunman?"

"Not that I know of."

"Well, when you get back, tell him to watch his back."

"You really do see Wright as a back shooter. It seems to me he has a lot to lose by going that route." Cord had to wait for the answer as Sam nudged Satan to bring back a wayward cow.

"Not the way he'll try to do it... And whatever sneaky route he has to take, that's what he'll do. I doubt he's been hiring cowboys to run that ranch of his. He doesn't need those cattle he's been taking. So why's he been doing it?"

"Game playing?"

"Most likely. It's sure not about the money of which he has plenty. He could have paid me off for the cattle I brought up, but he didn't because it amused him. I let it go three years ago because I knew I couldn't do much about it considering where I'd... er found those cows." White teeth flashed in his swarthy skin. "And I also didn't want a fight."

"You do now?"

"Even less. I have more to lose now than I had back then. The thing is I want a brother."

"Did you tell Ollie about the doctor?" Abby asked Sam as after dinner they had settled into the great room with Cord and Priscilla.

"Why?"

"I think you should. Better to deal with that here than wait until we get there."

Sam considered that a moment. "You sure?" He chuckled.

"Is he likely to agree to see a doctor once we get there, if you don't face it now? You know what he's said about sawbones."

"I think he knows something is wrong. He will go along when the time comes. Better though that he's already there."

"He could still refuse."

"How many days will it take us to get there?" Priscilla asked.

"We'll take supplies for two nights," Sam said, "but unless the gulches are still running full from snow melt, which I don't think will be the case, I'd guess just one night out."

"This trip is getting more and more complicated," Cord said from the chair where he was slouched, smoking his cigarette. He had resisted sitting near Priscilla with the idea he needed to fight the physical relationship she wanted, which he believed would be a disaster for them both. The farther he was from her, the easier that was to do.

"It doesn't seem too complicated to me," Priscilla said, still wearing the pants she'd used to get instruction on care of chickens and milking of cows. The revealed rounded hips made him far too aware of what was under them. She was sitting on the raised hearth with the warmth of the fire on her back. "In fact, I like the idea a lot. Traveling with a family is something I've never done."

"And who is Ollie in this family?" Cord asked with a sullen tone to his voice again. His mood had gotten worse during the day until he felt ready to argue with anybody about anything.

"My mother, of course," Sam said with grin. The worse Cord's mood had grown, apparently the better his had become.

Cord snorted. Priscilla moved from the hearth to Cord's chair and to his shock plopped down on his lap. "What do you think you're doing?" he asked with that look which usually worried people if it didn't scare them.

"I think I'm sitting on your lap," she said as she put her arm around his neck. "Want to know what comes next?"

"No."

Sam and Abby laughed. He rose pulling his wife to her feet. "I think it's time for us to go to bed and let them... argue this out."

When they were gone, Priscilla said, "That was very understanding of them."

"There is no arguing it out."

"There isn't?" she kissed his ear running her tongue along his jaw line.

"What do you think you are doing now?" He took a breath to try and steady himself.

"Did you think we'd go back to Tucson and take up where we had left off, arguing, avoiding each other, pretending nothing happened between us?" she asked running her fingers through his silky hair.

"Anything else will end with the first gunfire."

"I don't like thinking of you being in danger. I admit it, but after what I've been through, I might be a bit tougher, don't you think?" She took the cigarette from his mouth and threw it into the fire.

He studied her smiling face wanting to believe but knowing he couldn't. "You're not tough enough."

"And you aren't tough enough to take the risk to find out that I am?" She bent then and took his lips in a hard kiss. She pushed his mouth open with her tongue delving inside. He sat there, his hands gripping the chair arms, not letting himself touch her, all too aware of what she had learned about his body. Slowly she unbuttoned his shirt to bare his chest.

"Have I ever mentioned how much I love your chest," she whispered as she pushed the shirt off his shoulders. She brushed her fingers over his skin. "So strong, so muscular. Oh my, your nipples are already tight." She wiggled again. "As well as something else. This is encouraging."

"Angel," he warned as she teased one of his nipples with her teeth.

She lifted up her head and met his gaze, the expression in her eyes determined. "I don't intend for you to pretend you don't know who I am to you," she said as she kissed him again and then moved down his chest.

"God," he muttered giving up as he lifted her, carrying her up the stairs to his room. He pushed the door open with one booted foot. Inside, he saw the lamp had been lit... and on the bed was the nightgown.

"I moved my things today," she whispered against his ear as he laid her on the bed.

"And what will Abby and Sam think?" he asked not that he gave a damn.

"She helped." Kisses and caresses ended further conversation.

In the morning, Cord didn't argue with her that they would go downstairs together. In the kitchen, an argument was ongoing. Ollie was sitting sullenly at the table.

"Ain't goin' to no doctor," he muttered making it easy to understand what had been the disagreement.

"You'd want us to go if we were the sick ones," Abby retorted.

"I ain't sick." Ollie coughed.

Sam snorted. "You have been down, and you know it. You're not eating right, and what's that cough about?"

"Little touch of pleurisy maybe," the old man suggested.

"Doctor Hadley is a good man," Priscilla said as she poured Cord a cup of coffee. "He won't be diagnosing anything that isn't there."

"They're all quacks," Ollie grumbled.

"Not him," Cord said sipping the coffee. "He patched me up twice." He glanced over to see Priscilla's face tighten. "Minor things, of course," he added, "but he's a good doctor."

"You are going, and you will see the doctor," Sam said with a tone that brooked no room for disagreement. He looked over at Abby. "Told you we shouldn't have told him until we got there."

Abby gave him one of her own looks, which had him grinning at her.

"When are we leaving?" Cord asked as he dug into the eggs Abby set in front of him.

"Right after breakfast," Sam said. "I got the wagon ready, just a few supplies left to load. Ollie will drive it. You and I'll ride but take a spare horse in case we need one."

"Which way?"

"Under the uncertain conditions, safest with less chance of problems will be taking that lower divide and then up the Santa Cruz valley. It looks to me like our rain is gone. We might even make it to Tubac to spend the night which would be a hell of a lot easier than camping with Davy."

"He'll be fine either way," Abby said, looking at her son as he was trying to find a way around the chair barricade.

"Mamamama," he protested and put up his arms to be held.

"Do you think that's a word?" Abby asked Priscilla who grinned.

"Like I'd know." Then she realized she did have interest in knowing. She had been sure that it was a safe time of the month for what she and Cord had done-- but that would change. Was she ready to have a baby? She decided she'd have to keep a little better track of her periods. When she looked back at Cord it looked as though he was wondering some of the same. They would work it out. She felt confident about that. She loved him too much to believe otherwise.

CHAPTER 23

When Martin arrived at Wright's ranch, he saw more men hanging around than he had expected. A meeting of some sort? He looked more closely at the new faces. They were not cowboys but rather hired guns. Was a range war brewing? Or something else?

Inside the house, he was shown to the office and left alone with Wright.

"What's up?" Martin asked as he sat in the big chair in front of the desk.

Wright glared at him. "You tell me. Did you betray me, Matthews?"

"Why would you ask that?"

"Are you trying to blackmail me? Are you such a fool as to think you can play that game? It won't work. I can guarantee you will pay a price for it. A price you won't much like." His smile showed no humor. "You have already caused me more losses and trouble than you can be worth."

Martin felt uneasy but was still confident he had this situation in hand. "I would never think of doing anything to hurt you or your interests. You must understand, being a man of wisdom, of course, I had to assure my own safety. Unless something happens to me, there is no problem. You have paid me well. I don't want anything more—except to stay alive."

"You think I'd kill you?"

"If you thought it benefited you, of course."

"You aren't an insignificant person in this town. You have friends. I have no interest in bringing more trouble onto myself by murdering you." His tone was a little less aggressive.

Martin felt increasing confidence. "Then we neither one have a problem. I would like to know though why you have brought in the type of men you have."

"What do you mean?"

"You know what I mean. Those aren't cowhands."

"Life has risks. I need to assure that my future is secure. Hired men make certain of that."

Martin barely suppressed his grunt of disbelief. "Well that's good then," he said instead. "You don't want trouble though, do you?"

Wright smirked. "Might be trouble has found me already. From now on though, no more double books, Martin. Anything like that I'd consider very unfriendly."

"I wouldn't need to do that."

"So what'd you find out about the marshal? He back yet?'

"I stopped by the office. Cordova said he's out chasing renegade Apaches but due back soon."

"Seems like a long stretch for him to be out of town."

Martin shrugged. He'd thought the same thing but wasn't about to bring up his own concerns to a man he didn't trust.

"Any talk about what happened to Miss Wesley?" Wright asked mockingly.

"Those things do happen. People disappear. It's how life goes... or not."

"What do you think happened and I don't mean in town—out at the cabin?"

"You were there. Didn't you see any indication?"

"We got hit a mile before we should have gotten there. With Gabe dead, we weren't about to keep going and get ourselves killed. With the Apaches that close, seems likely they have, or should I say had her."

"It's possible." Martin's mood brightened. "Ellen Buchanan was in the marshal's office. She appears to have a thing going with his deputy."

"Jesus Christ, what is it with this attraction to lawmen?"

Martin had no idea, but it irked him too. With Priscilla gone, Ellen was the most likely female for him seriously to pursue. It was not as though Sally, beautiful though she was, could ever be more than a diversion. What reputation he had in Tucson would be gone if he were to be seen with a whore. No, Ellen was the right choice, but what was she doing with that redskin? "Women show no judgment," he said when he saw Wright was waiting for a response.

A knock at the door interrupted them when Wright's Chinese cook entered. "Man at back door, want talk to you," he told Wright.

"Show him in."

"Him here?" the cook asked gesturing to Martin.

"No secrets from Mr. Matthews." Wright snickered. A few moments later Judge Ames entered looking a little surprised and displeased to see Martin.

"Martin get up. Let the judge have your chair. You can take that wooden one."

Martin felt resentful but obeyed. The judge sat, the worried look not disappearing.

"I've had several complaints about cattle being taken, Richard. I can't keep stalling this."

"Judge, this is my accountant, Martin Matthews. He can assure you by the records that I haven't been taking cattle. Actually I've had losses too."

The judge looked with disdain at Martin but nodded. "You can prove that?"

"Of course." Wright smiled.

"What are all those men outside? I've never seen you with so many hands out here."

"Hey it's dangerous times. I think maybe some rustler is working us all. I need to protect my spread. Isn't that right, Martin?"

Martin smiled. "It certainly is. These are dangerous, dangerous times. I mean someone must have kidnapped Miss Wesley right near town. With the marshal disappearing as he did, who knows if he's been killed too."

"I don't know..." The judge, fear clearly showing on his face, turned back to Wright. "I just can't afford anything that ties me to trouble. You do understand my position."

"Of course, I do, but as Martin said, these are dangerous times."

And about to get more so, Martin thought, trying to figure out how he could profit from it, while not being sucked in. When Wright met his gaze, he smiled. "Very treacherous indeed," he repeated with what he hoped was a concerned expression.

"And Judge," Wright said. "I need to know you are on my side... on anything that might possibly come up. Can I count on you?" His look was piercing. "I know you were always there for my father."

The judge continued to look uneasy, but he nodded. "Of course, and I will be for you too. Just nothing that could cost me my position, would there be?"

"That didn't sound like a very firm yes." Wright had moved forward in his chair and the expression on his face didn't bode well for denial.

"Of course, of course, my boy. It was a very firm yes."

Wise choice, Martin thought, because the alternative would

be a new judge being appointed due to a vacancy brought on by an unexpected accident.

As Martin drove his buggy from the ranch, he knew he was walking a very thin line. He considered again leaving Tucson. But he didn't have the money to do that at least not yet.

Then he thought about Sally and wondered if she finally would be free. He felt a mix of anger and satisfaction, as he thought about her curvy figure and all the things she knew how to do to a man. Why was she avoiding him? She wouldn't pull what the other women had. She had better not.

The closer they got to Tucson, the edgier Priscilla felt. She had alternated driving the wagon with Ollie as her experience with her buggy had made her pretty good at handling the team. Abby spent her time distracting and keeping Davy content. He was restless and tired of sitting or being held.

They had spent a night in Tubac, which by necessity had separated Priscilla from Cord. As an unmarried couple there was no way they could have slept together, but as it turned out there was only one available room at the small hotel. The men slept under the wagon while she, Abby and Davy took the room.

No one had questioned Priscilla-- and so she assumed they hadn't realized she was the woman on the poster offering so much money for her safe return. That night she had lain awake a long time before falling asleep, unable to talk to Abby about her fears, as it would have awakened the sleeping baby.

Cord was riding a bit ahead of the wagon. Seeing his easy grace in the saddle, the way he kept his eyes constantly looking for problems, made her want to be with him. Cord didn't want that, and she would have to let thoughts of happily-ever-afters rest for the moment. The important thing was they continue to see each other. The rest would take care of itself—eventually.

Behind them Sam rode and looked as edgy as she felt. There would be trouble in Tucson. She felt sure of that. Was Cord right, and she wasn't up to it? Once she got back where life was comfortable, would she be able to stand beside him? Would he even want her?

"You don't look excited to be home," Abby said when they changed drivers to let Ollie bring them into town.

"I'm nervous about getting back… about all of it."

Abby smiled. "I do understand."

"They might blame me for it happening."

"Those who love you won't. They'll just be glad you are home. What about charges?"

"I will talk to Judge Emerson and explain it. He knows Martin and me. He will understand how it will play out in a court of law. You know over the years Martin has done all he can to establish himself as a legitimate and important member of Tucson society. He's friends with other young men in town. The thefts were never revealed as your father felt sorry for him, and it was, of course, his choice." She shook her head. "For all people know about him, he's a young man who a young woman might want to snag for herself."

"Then no charges again?" She didn't sound condemning.

Cord dropped back interrupting their conversation. "I better head the other way now," he said, "but I'll see you later tonight… when I investigate your disappearance." He smiled at her, but the expression on his face was impossible to read before he nudged his gelding and took off at a gallop toward San Xavier.

Priscilla watched until he disappeared from view and then turned back to Abby. "I will bring charges, if Judge Emerson thinks there is any chance at all that they will even get to trial. I am not even sure who would hear the case. Whose jurisdiction will it fall under? If It's Judge Ames, I don't think there's a chance he'd bring it to trial."

"I have to admit I was ignorant about the politics of Tucson even when I lived there. You think he's that crooked?"

"My father thought so. He warned me about staying out of his court where it comes to our business dealings. Anyway I will bring charges if there seems to be a chance to make it stick. If it seems hopeless, I don't know yet. Maybe I will, but I will have to think if it's worth the problems that it could bring."

"You know what Cord will do," Abby said as she wiped some drool from Davy's mouth. He had just begun getting a new tooth.

"What?" She hadn't thought of that angle. What could he do? He was a lawman. He would have to stick to what the law said.

"Never mind. We can talk about it later." They began passing other wagons and people on horseback, burros or walking as they neared Tucson's population center—such as it was. Priscilla thought a few looked at her questioningly, but she wasn't sure it wasn't just her general sense of unease. The last time she had been here, she'd been kidnapped. She still found it hard to believe it had happened.

She was clenching her jaw so much that her teeth hurt, and she worked to loosen up—after all, the worst was over. She hoped this wouldn't have set Grace back on trust issues. Then she wondered would even Rose and James be glad to see her? Would they blame her for the worry they had been put through? Perhaps it was her fault-- for being blind to Martin's true nature.

Whatever the case, there was nothing she could do now except face them and be forced to tell her story one more time— or more than once. She hated depicting herself as a victim, and yet she had been. They would at least believe that even if nobody else did. Still, if she had done as James had asked that day, he'd have been with her. No one would have been put through what they had.

From her own perspective, she could not say, frightening as it was, that she was sorry it had happened. If Martin hadn't done what he had, she'd never have had that precious time with Cord. Would Cord have died alone and untended in the mountains. If he had survived the infection, would they have ever found their way to each other? Had Martin unknowingly done her a favor?

Whatever might have been, now she had to look forward, facing the future with the courage she had learned was within her.

As the wagon pulled into the barnyard behind her home, Priscilla turned to Abby. "I forgot to ask if you were staying with me. I hadn't thought about your father being here and just assumed you would be here. I understand if you feel otherwise."

Abby put her hand on her arm. "I'll visit Father, but we'll all stay with you. Sam wants time with Grace. I suspect Davy would make Father nervous, and he's yet to forgive Sam for stealing me away—as he still sees it. Besides, you need me here for support."

Priscilla smiled in gratitude. She had that right.

As Ollie pulled the team to a halt, James and Ben came out from the barn. It took a moment for them to recognize her as she stepped down from the wagon.

"Thank God," James yelled with a huge smile as he ran forward. "We were afraid you were dead. Where you been, Missy?" He had her in his embrace before she could answer.

Ollie threw the reins to Ben-- then stiffly got down and helped Abby with the baby.

Rose was out of the kitchen door as soon as she heard the yelp from James. Tears were running down her cheeks as she threw her arms around Priscilla.

"Is Grace in school?" Priscilla asked also crying.

Rose nodded. "We tried to keep her from worrying, but that poor little mite is going to be so glad to see you and..." She turned then to where Sam had dismounted and was walking toward them. "My Lord in heaven, did you bring her back to us?" she asked him.

"Where have you been?" James repeated.

"I'll explain it all after we get inside," Priscilla answered as she took Davy from Abby's tired arms.

"We'll take care of the horses," James said signaling for Ben to help. The big man had looked confused at first but now was smiling broadly.

In the kitchen, Ollie accepted the coffee Rose offered as he sat at the table coughing.

"You need to lie down, Ollie," Abby told him taking the squirming toddler back from Priscilla.

"If it's made up, he can have the bedroom at the head of the stairs," Priscilla told Rose. Rose nodded and led the tired looking old man from the kitchen.

James and Sam came in from outside where Sam, with a smile, took a cup of hot coffee.

"I figured Ben could finish up with the horses," James said, "and maybe better he not listen to whatever was going on that took you from us." He sat at the table watching Priscilla with concern in his eyes.

Priscilla nodded her agreement and gratitude. There was no easy way to say it, "I am so sorry you have all been so worried. I was... kidnapped. Martin Matthews and it just took a while to get back."

"Did that son of a bitch hurt you?" James asked anger flashing in his eyes.

"No, he thought—at least it's what he said, that it would cause me to love him."

"I should have killed him the first time he touched you," James said his voice tense.

"Me first," Sam said, as he sipped the coffee.

"So then Sam saved you?"

"Not exactly. By the time Martin got to the cabin where he'd intended to take me, he let me out of the sack he'd used to hold me. I managed to get his gun, but had no idea where I was other than high in the pines. I tried to force him to take me back immediately, but he raced the team off and disappeared leaving me there alone. Fortunately, he had unloaded the supplies before he unloaded me."

James cursed using a few words Priscilla had never heard

RAIN TRUEAX

from him. "He's a worse devil than I figured," Rose said as she entered the kitchen, "and I figured he wasn't worth much."

"So then Sam came along?" James asked.

Davy began to fuss, and the recital ended until he was given a buttered slice of fresh-baked bread, which he hungrily ate. With curiosity, he looked around the kitchen.

"I should probably put him down for a nap," Abby said.

"Take the bedroom next to Ollie's," Priscilla said. "It's the one you usually use when you stay over."

"Good, I'll be back when he falls asleep but don't stop telling what happened. I do already know."

When the kitchen had again settled down, Priscilla said, "It was Cord who came first. He had been up in the mountains looking for renegade Apaches. He smelled the smoke and went to check, as it was supposed to be a deserted cabin."

"The marshal?" Rose asked, her voice sounding as surprised as she looked.

"Where's he now then?" James asked. "Still going after the Apaches?"

None of this was easy to explain. Priscilla realized it would be even harder when she eventually faced a courtroom full of those who didn't know or love her. Determinedly she went on with what happened, finishing with where Cord now was.

"That's quite a story," Rose said. "I guess we need to tell you. We've had a little issue here too."

"Grace is all right, isn't she?"

"Healthy, worried about where you were, but it does involve her," James said. "Two days ago, her uncle showed up. He claims he wants her back."

"Oh my God."

"Exactly."

"She isn't with him, is she?"

"Not a chance. We said she wasn't going anywhere until her father got back. He went to Judge Emerson, but the Judge sided with us. So now with Marshal O'Brian back, he'll have to deal with that question."

"Well, he can't take her," Priscilla said, tears in her eyes. This was the last straw. She would not lose Grace, and she realized then how much she had come to love that sweet child.

"I am not sure how the law will see it, but I think Cord can fight it."

"What kind of uncle would send her off on a train by herself, and then show up here?" Priscilla felt irrationally angry, more at this than anything that had happened to her.

"Judge Emerson said he'd be finding out about that. He's got some resources in Kansas, and he was contacting them."

"I might have a talk with this uncle," Sam said standing and looking as though talking would be the last thing he'd have in mind.

"Let Cord do it first," James suggested. "We don't want you in jail now do we?"

"Surely Grace doesn't want to go with him," Priscilla said unsure how Grace might see that since they had seemingly abandoned her.

"No, she does not. She's liking her school and living here. She knew her father was out taking care of a responsibility. Ellen has been by a lot to reassure her that you would be back."

"What a mess. I will talk to the judge as soon as I can."

"You look exhausted," Rose said, "and should lie down after a nice hot bath."

"I'll let the Emerson know you're back," James said. "We'll see if he can come by tonight."

"I think I'll go see if Cord is in his office by now," Sam said rising and taking his cup to the counter.

"You and Cord not going to fight again, I hope," James protested.

"Maybe some," Sam said with a grin. "Turns out that Cord is my brother."

James looked flabbergasted for a moment and then grinned broadly. "Well, I'll be damned. Fine then, I'll see about Judge Emerson while you see if O'Brian is in."

When they had gone, Priscilla sat while Rose made a pot of tea. "This isn't all, is it?" Rose asked as she looked back at her.

Abby came back into the kitchen. "Finally he went down. What isn't all? And where's Sam? Hopefully not off getting into trouble."

"That man of yours good at that?" Rose asked teasingly.

"He does have a way about him."

"James was going to let the judge know Priscilla is back and Sam went to see if Cord had arrived back at his office yet. Hopefully the Judge will come by tonight and we'll know better what's going to happen next."

"What's going on?" Abby asked.

Priscilla explained about Grace's uncle.

"It never rains but it pours," Abby observed as she took a cup of tea from Rose. "What else can go wrong?"

"Don't even think of asking."

When Cord had unsaddled Jeb, given him hay, oats, and a grooming, he had several things on his mind. He ran his hand over his bristly jaw and knew he needed a shave, haircut and bath at the barbershop. Unfortunately it couldn't come first as he would have to check at the office, with no feeling there'd be good news waiting. He hoped all had gone well with Priscilla's arrival home, but finding out would have to wait. He considered picking Grace up at school, but on the chance it would upset her, he wouldn't do that either.

When he walked through the office door, Rafe came out from the back. "Good God, you look like hell. Where you been?"

"Good to see you too," Cord said sitting at his desk and looking in the drawer to see if he had any cigars left. When he found one, he tore off the tip and lit it taking a relaxingly deep draw. "So tell me what's gone wrong in order."

"Miss Wesley disappeared, no sign of her."

"She's home."

Rafe sunk into the chair with a disbelieving look. "How do you know?"

"I know. So what else went wrong?"

"Grace's uncle, Aaron Robinson showed up. He wants to take her back to Kansas."

Cord let out a hard breath. "Well he can't have her."

"That's what James and Rose told him. He went to Judge Emerson."

"He won't let him have her either."

"Judge Ames might."

"God damn. That bastard. All right, what's the rest of the bad news? I won't let Robinson have her-- so he can go through all the courts he wants."

"You got the money to fight it?" Rafe asked with concern.

"I won't let him have her—one way or another. What else is going on?"

"Wright has been hiring guns. He claims he's also been rustled and needs them to protect his spread."

"Yeah right." Out the open door, Cord saw Sam ride up front and tie his stallion's reins to the rail.

"Guess I was wrong," Rafe said as he watched the tall man walk through the door. "More can go wrong."

Cord laughed while Sam sat in the other chair in the office and began rolling a cigarette.

"Kind of pushy, aren't you?" Rafe asked him clearly surprised that Cord was saying nothing.

"Runs in the family," Sam said with a hard smile. With Sam also needing a shave, Cord knew they looked like a couple of hard cases.

"You here to file a complaint?" Rafe asked when Cord still hadn't said anything.

Sam flicked a match with his thumb and lit his cigarette. "I'm here on a matter of blood."

"Someone got killed?" Rafe asked still showing surprise that Cord was only smiling.

"Nah, blood kin." Sam blew out the smoke.

"We're brothers, Rafe," Cord said.

Rafe's mouth dropped. "Brothers?"

"Disreputable as he looks," Cord said, "yep."

"Me disreputable?" Sam chuckled.

"We both need a shave, bath and haircut," Cord said blowing out smoke.

"You being the little brother means, no orders," Sam retorted. "I was thinking more of a shot of whiskey myself."

"We do have a problem where we need to look like less than gunslingers," Cord said. "Grace's uncle is here to try and take her back to Kansas."

Sam exhaled loudly. "He can have her—the day after hell freezes over."

CHAPTER 24

J ames picked up Grace from school as he had every day. When she arrived home, Priscilla greeted her in the kitchen.

"Where have you been?" Grace asked as she threw down her book bag and ran to Priscilla for a big hug. "I missed you so much."

"Me too, sweetheart. I'm here now though."

"Don't go away again," Grace demanded with tears rolling down her cheeks.

"I don't plan to."

"My daddy is gone too," Grace said her lip trembling.

"He was out chasing away Indians, right?" Priscilla asked not wanting to give away too much of her knowledge on where Cord was but also wanting to reassure Grace.

"That's what Aunt Rose said."

Rose poured her a glass of milk and put a plate of cookies on the table. "I heard now that he just got back, but he had work to do," Rose said. "I'm sure he'll be by as soon as he can."

Grace frowned. "Uncle Aaron wants me to go back to Kansas," she told Priscilla as she ate an oatmeal cookie.

"Your daddy won't let that happen," Priscilla reassured her.

"I don't want to go back to Kansas," Grace said drinking some of the milk.

"Then you won't. Do you have homework tonight?"

Grace nodded looking up when Abby walked into the kitchen with a squirming Davy in her arms.

"Who's that?" Grace asked her eyes intent on the dark-haired toddler.

"Your cousin Davy, and Aunt Abby," Priscilla answered. Abby sat Davy on the floor.

"I have a cousin and aunt?" Grace hadn't taken her eyes from the boy who was now working his way to being on his feet.

"And an Uncle Sam," Abby said as she walked over and gave Grace a hug.

Grace smiled broadly. "Where's he then?" She looked around the room but quickly back at Davy who was toddling toward her now with a big smile.

"He'll be back as soon as he can."

When Davy reached Grace, she smiled. "Could he have a cookie?"

"Why don't you give him one?" Abby suggested.

When Grace held out the cookie, Davy grabbed it, lost his balance and ended up plopped back on the floor where he began eating it.

The door opened again. This time it was Ollie. "Can't believe I slept during the day," he muttered, "Like a baby." He looked down at Davy. "No offense meant."

"Grace, this is Uncle Ollie," Abby said. "Ollie, Grace O'Brian."

The little girl looked a bit awestruck by her riches in new relatives, but she smiled as Ollie shook her hand.

"Coffee or tea?" Rose asked him. When he gestured to the coffee pot, she brought him a cup. "You take anything in it?"

"Ain't that much of a sissy," Ollie said as he began drinking the coffee as though it was life blood.

"Where's Sam?" he asked.

Abby frowned. "Good question."

Looking a lot more presentable after Cord and Sam had agreed to get the shave, haircut and bath before they hit the saloon for the whiskey, they entered the bar. Cord was aware that, even without his badge, their height, dark coloring and guns still would make a lot of men step back.

"Good to see you, Marshal," Ridge said. "Been gone a spell."

"It took a while," Cord said ordering the whiskey. "I'm paying," he said to Sam.

"Like hell. I'm paying."

"I see nothing has changed with you two," Rafe said as he came from the other end of the bar bringing his glass of beer.

Ridge grinned. "No fights in my bar." He brought the club out from behind and brandished it.

"Wouldn't think of it," Cord said. "You see a jasper by the name of Robinson in here?"

"Don't ask names. What's he look like."

"Last time I saw him he had thinning hair, about yea tall." He put his hand just below his neck. Kind of round faced, blondish hair, soft voice."

"Sounds like a guy come in but not today. He wanted for something?" Ridge asked wiping down the bar, as he refilled their glasses. "This one's on the house-- so you can skip the argument."

"We just want to talk to him," Sam said. "For now... and thanks."

"God, you two look like gun hands yourselves. You see what the Wright spread is taking on?"

"Heard about it," Cord said rolling a cigarette. "They come in here?"

"Nah, they don't like my club, and we're too close to the marshal's office. "They hit Shady Bell."

"Seen anything of Martin Matthews?" he asked, lighting the cigarette.

"You're out of luck there too. He was coming, but he got into a snit with Sally. She threatened to bring charges against him."

"For what?" Sam asked with a neutral tone.

"She told me that he hit her. She wasn't taking that guff off him and told him to stay away. Not sure if he has, but he avoids my place whatever the case."

"She bring charges?"

Ridge shook his head. "Unlikely."

"Shady Bell's where Wright hangs out when he's in town—him and his toughs," Rafe said.

"Matthews works for Wright now. I don't mind losing business of somebody like him. Always sat in a corner glowering. His kind of mood does my till no good."

The piano player came downstairs and began playing Stephen Foster as more customers drifted in, a few to play cards. "Ain't been the same for cards since Del left," Ridge complained. "I got to get myself a new dealer. Any of you a gambler?"

"Not with cards," Sam said with a humorless smile, as they finished off their drinks and went outside. The sun was sinking below the horizon, beginning to turn the whole western sky a bright orange.

"There aren't that many hotels in town where he could be staying," Cord said. "what if we split up and see who finds him first? I don't want to face Grace until I have this settled."

"How do you figure to settle it?" Sam asked with that expression that often sent men running.

"Nicely, of course," Cord said with an innocent grin. "I'll take the Palace. You take the Occidental, and Rafe, you check the San Xavier."

"Meet you back at Cilla's then," Sam suggested.

"Good. How about you, Rafe? You coming over tonight too?"

"Like I'd miss it," Rafe said with a rakish smile. "Ellen will be there too. She's been coming over to help Grace with her homework. She'll be right glad to see Priscilla. Been a long time, her away and all. You never did say how you know she's back."

"Nope," Cord walked off, loosening his gun in the holster. He didn't expect trouble, if he was the one who braced Aaron Robinson. He didn't remember him as a man prone to violence. What he most wanted to know is why Robinson had changed his mind, after dumping Grace on a train going to meet a father she didn't know. There had to be a reason. One of his skills as a lawman had been finding out what that was.

Priscilla was helping Rose fix dinner when Sam rode into the yard, took his big stallion to the barn, before coming to the kitchen and washing his hands. "Did you see Cord?" she asked.

"Yep."

Abby came into the room and gave him a welcoming kiss feeling approvingly of his freshly shaven jaw. "Nice," she whispered in his ear.

"Where's Davy?" he asked.

"With Grace and James. Grace is mesmerized by her cousin, and he likes a smaller person to play with."

Sam grinned. "Well introduce me to her."

Rose took Priscilla's arm when she would have followed them. "I think there is a lot you are not telling me."

"I will later, but I want to see this."

In the living room, Grace was looking up at Sam with amazement in her big dark eyes. "You look like my daddy," she said.

"That's because he's my brother," Sam told her. "That makes you my niece. Do you like that idea?"

She nodded and then grinned. "Are you any good at mathematics?"

He laughed. "Some."

"I could use some help with mine. Miss Albertson gave us a really hard assignment, and Uncle James says he can't help me with it."

"I'll give it a shot," Sam said following her into the den.

When Priscilla returned to the kitchen to peel potatoes, she heard Cord's horse coming in the yard. "Thank God," she whispered but loud enough that Rose heard her. He took care of his horse before he came into the kitchen. As soon as he was through the door, she had him around the waist. "Where have you been? Wasn't it your job to find that poor kidnapped woman?" She reached up to kiss his jaw. "Oh, I like that. You shaved."

"Superficial little thing, aren't you?" he suggested as he headed for the sink. "How are you, Rose."

"Glad to see you, Marshal," Rose said with a smile as she poured him a cup of coffee.

"Did you see Grace's other uncle?" Priscilla asked as he was washing his hands.

"We had a little conversation." He bent then to give her the kiss for which she had been waiting.

"Tell me."

"Only after I talk to Grace. Be back in a bit."

After he was gone, Priscilla said, "That was so frustrating."

"Just like a man to never give us all we want. But which part you talking about—the lack of information or the kiss?" Rose giggled.

"Both." She sighed and went back to her potatoes, as she heard Grace's squeal of delight.

Ten minutes later, with the potatoes onto boil, she heard the door open, and it was Cord. "Mathematics. What would I know about that? Sam's got it though."

"You can help with other things," she reassured him as she put her arms around his lean waist. "Like me."

When he bent to kiss her, his tongue thrusting into her mouth, she felt herself melt into him and her knees grow weak. When he would have ended the kiss, she clung, and he kissed her again. He ended it by pushing himself away and straddling a chair to sit at the table.

"Want a whiskey, Marshal?" Rose asked with a sly smile.

"Something cold would be more like it," he retorted.

"Tell me now about Aaron Robinson," Priscilla asked catching her breath and trying to get control of her wayward body. "Uh what is he going to do?"

"I don't think there's much he can do. I did talk to him, and no, I didn't beat his face in like I was thinking. We sat very civilly in the hotel lobby and talked. He said he'd take us to court for her, but I doubt he can get very far. I am Grace's father. She said she wants to stay here. I don't know what his motive is, but whatever the case, he'd have had to grab her to have any possibility, and then back in Kansas, maybe. He missed his chance for that. We won't let him take her."

She wished she felt more confident he was right. "How long will he stay?"

"Not sure. I'd just like to know why he suddenly wants her."

"Ellen and Rafe are coming to dinner. I needed to explain all that had happened to her and she and Rafe are seeing a lot of each other right now."

"Seriously?"

She smiled. "I don't know about that. Ellen and I haven't had much chance to talk since I returned. Also, Judge Emerson will be here later for dessert. I wanted to ask him my odds on being successful if I bring charges against Martin, and we can also discuss this issue of custody."

"Good." He grinned. "So, miss me?"

"You desperado you," she said slapping his chest. "You know I did. And what are you going to do about it?"

"Any more kisses like that last one," Rose said, "and the two of you will be going upstairs before dinner, I'm betting." She giggled. "Why don't you go in and visit with the others while I finish up supper? Might keep you from getting into trouble."

An hour later with the meal eaten and dishes cleaned up,

Abby and Priscilla took the children up to bed. Grace protested that she should be allowed to stay up longer with her father and new uncle, but she was reminded she had school the next day.

When Priscilla came back downstairs, she heard James say, "I take her to school and can alert them that nobody but us is to pick her up."

Sam was standing by the fireplace with a booted foot on the raised hearth. "I should go too, so those teachers know who I am."

"Like it'd be hard to miss you being related to her and Cord," James said with a laugh. "She's a little chip off the block so to speak. She's sure going to be a beauty when she grows up. That's when your real trouble will start."

"I think we can handle it," Sam said with that wolfish smile of his.

Priscilla reached into the sideboard for the good brandy. "Anyone like one of these?"

"Nothing stronger?" Sam asked, and so she brought out the good whiskey. A knock at the door stopped her from pouring as the judge came in shrugging out of his greatcoat.

"Colder'n Beelzebub out there," he complained.

"Been getting' to my rheumatism something fierce," Ollie agreed, then looked at Sam. "Course, it ain't that bad."

"I didn't know hell was cold," Ellen said cuddled next to Rafe.

The judge chuckled. "Depends on who you read explaining it," he declared. "Now Christians see it as fiery, but Buddhists as cold. Dante had various levels of hell. The ninth and last of which was a frozen lake."

"Oh my," Ellen said. Whether from fear of hell or amazement of the varieties, Priscilla was unsure.

"Judge," Priscilla said as she handed him a glass of what she knew to be his favorite brandy, "You know Abby but have you met her husband, Sam Ryker?"

"In passing is all." He shook Sam's hand before settling into one of the chairs. "I was relieved when James came today and told me you were back, my dear. We were all so worried."

"I know, and I'm so sorry. I didn't choose to leave."

"And I am assuming there is something involving that story with which you are seeking advice."

"That was the original reason, but now something more important is concerning me. Rose said you backed them about not letting Aaron Robinson take Grace. We would like to know where that stands if her uncle takes it to civil court."

He swirled the liquid a little as he considered. "That would put it under Judge Ames which has always been a problem since the man is crooked as well as taking money for whatever benefits him. The town council, will, of course, be supporting you given how much sway you have here thanks to your father's businesses which are now under your control."

"So he should have no real chance?"

"I didn't say that. The question then would be does Robinson have that kind of money behind him."

"What I am trying to figure out is why he changed his mind on wanting her," Cord said. "He sends her off on a train, and then when she's settled here, suddenly he turns up. It doesn't make sense. I talked to him today, but he gave no reason that made sense."

"He might not have wanted to admit his reason," the Judge said. "I sent some inquiries back to Kansas, as soon Rose and James came to me. Grace is heir to the ranch there. Robinson didn't know there was a will. The lawyer who had it safely secured, filed it in court. He can't fight the terms. Grace now owns the family ranch, and all other holdings in Kansas, which included a bank account. It appears to me that he wants control of her assets."

Cord let out a whistle. "Well that figures. So Grace is an heiress."

"For whatever the ranch is worth."

"It would be more than enough to fund her going to a fancy school back East when she is ready," Cord said.

"Maybe she won't want to do that," Abby reminded him as she had come down the stairs listening to the last of the conversation.

"Well she can do what she wants," Cord said. "I can probably arrange for selling the ranch and putting her money into some kind of investment or a trustworthy bank."

"Sounds like a plan to me," Sam said. "Judge, what do you know about the crew that Richard Wright is putting together?"

"Just that it can't be about good. I'd say it's unlikely we can get more U.S Marshals here-- without more than suspicion anyway. Sheriff Adams is not a help if Wright wants to gain power through intimidation or worse. Tucson is growing fast, and the days of a gang like the Cowboys in Tombstone pulling something like that here are probably past."

"It occurs to me that you should be watching your own back," Cord said as he sipped his whiskey. "Taking you out and replacing you with someone corrupt, would fit right into Wright's style."

"I've thought of that." The Judge took a derringer from his jacket pocket. "I am careful these days."

"Good."

"There is another thing," Priscilla said, uneasy at the possible danger Cord and Sam would face if Wright really was meaning harm to anyone standing in his way. When the judge looked her way, she told him her own story. When she finished, she asked, "My question is, if I bring charges against Martin, what are my odds of it being successful?"

"With a jury you mean?" the Judge asked.

"Would it even get to one? I've thought about this some-- and although Martin took me in town, he took me out of it. Who would have jurisdiction?"

He cleared his throat, as he considered. "I see your concern.

Yes, it would be our sheriff and again Judge Ames, and if so, it's quite probable he wouldn't let it go to any trial if you are assuming Martin will lie when questioned."

"I have to assume that he will have his story ready in the remote case I ever returned to Tucson. He likely hoped I would die up there, but he won't take the chance of not having those ready to back up his version."

"Your reputation would help, of course. You are a young woman of fine character from a powerful family."

"My father though is no longer here. Martin has worked to make his character show up well to the town. To be honest, my own might have some questions." She mentioned the visit to Connie Sicilla, the Yaqui Christmas. "I was warned by Reverend Ryan that my ethics have been in question. If he was called to testify, it's not hard to see what he'd say."

"Being Yaqui didn't make it not a Christian celebration," Rafe snapped.

"You know that, and I do," Priscilla said, "but it wasn't how the reverend painted it."

Sam's lip curled as he said, "I could have a little talk with him."

Abby came to stand beside him, putting her hand on his arm. "I know how you feel about phony pastors. You're not the right one to have that talk." Sam gave her the kind of look that caused most men to back up but only had his wife smiling. "You know I'm right," she said without giving an inch.

"I feel fine with my choices," Priscilla said, looking at Cord then, "but I realize how they may seem to others. I see a problem regarding it if Judge Ames was the one deciding Grace's guardianship. Maybe it would be best if you found a home for her with you, Cord," she finished.

"Robinson won't bring it to court," Cord with a steely tone. "He will be on a train within a day or so to head east, or he'll lose even more than the ranch."

The judge chuckled. "I did not hear that. I am thinking a cigar would be good about now. Gentleman, shall we adjourn to the den?"

"Pie in a few minutes," Rose said as she headed for the kitchen, with Abby, Ellen, and Priscilla just behind her to make coffee and tea.

In the den, the Judge reached for his cigars, but Cord stopped him. "Cilla has some. Let's smoke hers."

"No thanks on the smelly things," Sam said rolling a cigarette. Ollie shook his head as the others lit their cigars.

"Fine tobacco," the Judge said with a sigh of pleasure as he took the first pleasurable puff, holding and then releasing the smoke.

"So what did you want to say that you didn't want the women to hear?" Cord asked as he contemplated the older man.

"Several things. One Wright. I might sound complacent on it, but I am not. I see Wright as a dangerous man. Spoiled all his life, selfish to the core, and totally amoral-- which all makes him more dangerous. What he is doing now about the cattle makes no sense. Bringing in hard cases-- then riding them through town to parade their power, also makes no sense. He will do something that makes no sense-- and for us, who are logical men, we have to be prepared and yet how can we?"

He looked then at Sam. "I take it that you and Cord are now friends."

"In a manner of speaking."

"What I'm wondering is how long can you really be here? You change the dynamics for Cord and Rafe but for how long? Can Wright wait you out?"

"He might not want to wait me out. He might want me too," Sam said as he drew on the cigarette, staring at its glowing tip.

"I won't ask the reason to that," the Judge said with a smile. "Sometimes a man, who deals in the letter of the law, is better off

320

not to know, but I take it you know what you are saying. You do not strike me as a man to speak without thought."

Sam said nothing-- his hardened expression said it all.

"So then, it's the three of you against I'd guess it was ten last I counted but might be more by now."

"Don't count me out," Ollie protested coughing.

"Or me," James said.

"Ollie, you aren't well, and you know it," Cord said, "and James, you're no gun hand. It would have us worrying more about you, than who we were supposed to be protecting the town from."

"Wait a minute here," Rafe asked. "You seriously thinking he might brace us in town?"

"If you want to quit, I understand," Cord said knocking ash from the cigar into the crystal ashtray as he sat on the desk.

"Not a chance. Just wondered what to expect." His voice said that while he might be young, he wasn't about to run from a fight.

The judge then looked from Cord to Sam. "How long have the two of you known you were related?"

"Just recently," Cord said, "you saying you knew it."

"It made sense. Both from Kansas, then what you look like. The way you have been at each other's throats. I figured something. What is it?"

Cord explained, and the judge chuckled. "Well good enough. Then that gives you something over Wright."

"And what would that be?" Sam asked blowing out puff of smoke.

"You will stick to each other, and his men won't. Cord, you might see if there are any warrants on some of those men. Keep an eye out when they come to town. If there are, you might be able to reduce the odds."

"Will Martin stand with his boss?" James asked from where he was sitting back on the bench at the wall of the den.

The judge snorted. "Martin?" He laughed as he took another sip of his brandy. "Only if he can't run." Then he looked at Cord.

"I told her I don't think it'd do her any good to bring charges-- but you know if she does, I'll stand with her and do what I can. The question is, if he gets off anyway, putting her through that, what will you do about it?"

Cord looked at him, the narrowed eyes and hard-set lips said it all.

CHAPTER 25

Priscilla had been disappointed that when the Judge, Ellen and Rafe had left, Cord had also gone. She had hoped he and she would have time to talk... or so she told herself.

Upstairs in her room, she put on an older nightgown thinking how much this room, which as a girl had been her safety, now was a barrier against the man she loved.

The light tap at her door surprised her, wondering what Abby could want-- but when she opened it and saw his tall form, she threw herself into his arms before she pulled him into the room. "How did you get in?" she whispered as she drew him toward the bed.

"Have James get better locks," he ordered as he unbuckled his gun belt and tossed it and his coat on the chair. "Tomorrow."

She smiled feeling the reality of him clear to her toes. "I'll also get an extra key." He began to unbutton his shirt. "Stop," she said still keeping her voice low. When he did, she began undoing the buttons, oh so slowly, and brushing her fingers against his bare skin. When she had it unfastened, she undid the cuffs and then walked behind to pull it from him.

She sighed and breathed against his bare back, the muscles

gleaming in the light from the lamp. So beautiful. He was so beautiful. She slid her arms around him to the front and reached for the belt buckle. It took her a little longer but when she had undone it, she threw it on the chair. Now for the buttons on his pants. He was leaning back against her now, letting her have her way with him, which she fully intended to do.

When his erection sprung out virile and ready, she stroked along its length, ran her fingers then over the ridged muscles on his belly.

"Angel," he said hoarsely, "we better take this to the bed."

She watched from the bed as he sat on its edge pulling off his boots. "I wanted you to be here," she whispered when he came to her. She raised herself over him kissing his cheek, neck, chest and down.

Caressing as he went, he pulled her nightgown off. "Now," she begged. "I want you in me now."

"Just a minute." He reached for his pants and came back with a small rubbery looking object. "Want to help?" he asked meeting her gaze teasingly.

She had heard of condoms, but it was the first she had ever seen.

"I figured we better not push our luck."

She took the rubbery tube and smiling sheathed him with it. This time, instead of waiting for him to come over her, she straddled him and lowered herself, encompassing him. She was so moist and ready. She knew she had been ready for him her whole life.

She bent to kiss him, feeling his tongue in her mouth, then hers in his, as he began to lift his hips. It was all she could do to not moan, but with Abby and Sam only one wall over, she restrained herself as much as possible. Long moments later, when they had both exploded with their climaxes, he lifted her to lie beside him, got hold of the quilts and covered them.

"Tomorrow," he said still holding her in his arms. "Get a lock for this room too."

She wasn't sure how she'd explain that to James, but she nodded her agreement. "How did you happen to get the condom?" she asked sleepily.

"Wondering how often I do this kind of thing?" he teased.

"Well a little."

"Big brother suggested it. I had heard of them but never had a reason to find out." He kissed her forehead. In the morning, when she woke, he was gone.

Sitting at his desk, sorting through the mail that had been piling up, Cord alternated sipping on a cup of coffee and smoking. When the door opened, it was Aaron Robinson.

"It's cold out there. Shut the door," Cord said. "Coffee's on the stove and clean cups on that shelf."

When the older man had a cup, he sat and met Cord's gaze. "I wanted to talk to you."

"You decided what you want to do then."

"I won't sue for her. I recognize you do want her, and she's settled here. I... Well before I leave, just wanted you to understand what it has been like for me."

Cord sat back smoking and waited.

"You took off when Janice died," Robinson began.

"Was driven off. Your folks made it impossible to find work nearby. I had no way to care for a baby. They didn't want me anywhere near Grace. Their friends didn't either. But you know that."

Robinson shook his head. "I knew part but not all. It makes sense considering." He drew in a breath and exhaled loudly. "It wasn't easy being around them. I worked that ranch for them but nothing was ever enough. I wasn't what they wanted. Never did anything right. I tried but it was always missing their mark."

"You got kids?"

"No, Mary and I... well it never happened. The old man, he found fault with me on that too. When Mama died and him right after, I got to admit, I thought, it's mine. All mine. Grace was a reminder of the past and how my sister always was the one they wanted. I decided I could have a clean slate. I thought that you'd just left her and your responsibilities-- so I put her on a train. I think I was a little crazy when I did it. I thought I'm finally my own man, finally free."

"Then you found out about the will."

Robinson managed a smile. "There was that. Mary was nagging at me. She had been mad all along about what I had done. She kept saying poor little mite. She's the one bought her that little straw hat. I thought maybe you hadn't wanted Grace, weren't going to be a good father to her. I remembered that time you showed up when she was what four and then took off again."

"By then she was scared to death of me with all they'd told her. Yeah," Cord said, "you put her on a train to a man she saw as a monster."

"Not my finer moment," Robinson agreed with another sigh. "Anyway I can at least go back and tell Mary that it all worked out. I can't blame you for how you see me. It seems she's happy. I'll head back to Kansas and find something else to do."

"Why?" Cord asked as he smoked, thinking ahead.

"Kansas is my home."

"I mean why find something else to do. Why not work that ranch?"

"As a hand for someone else? No thanks."

"I was thinking more... You buy the ranch from her, but at a low enough price that you can afford to make payments. That old man had a mean streak. He didn't help Grace either with how he browbeat her. What if we took the view you were entitled to half and Grace the other? So you start paying off Grace, which by the time she needs it for say college, there will be enough money there for her to go or get a start in a business or whatever she decides she wants."

"You serious?" Robinson's mouth dropped open. "Why would you do that?"

"So that Grace has two uncles. She doesn't need the money now, but an uncle in Kansas, whoever knows when that might come in handy." Cord smiled for the first time.

"How would we do it?"

"I suspect Judge Emerson will have some ideas. He had some associates in Kansas, which is how I knew about the will. Let's talk to him."

"It sounds good to me. I'll get a train ticket after we figure it out."

"One more thing."

"And the kicker is?" Robinson asked with some doubt in his voice.

"Dinner tonight at the Wesley home. Grace needs to see you as being good with us. More stability for her. Dinner with her two uncles-- that is if Miss Wesley agrees, and I think she will. She's a believer in family."

Robinson grinned widely as he rose and put out his hand. Cord stood to take it. "Thank you. Thank you so much. Grace is lucky to have you for her father. Maybe you can undo some of the damage my folks did."

"I'll give it my best shot," Cord said knowing he had a lot of things to work out in his own life before he could offer her the stability she needed. His ranch? Would that give her security or make it even harder? Could he keep working as a marshal, a man with a gun in a dangerous time, if he hoped to give her any kind of quality life?

And then there was Priscilla. If he had thought he could walk away from her, he had learned otherwise the night before when he had started to ride off and realized he had nowhere else he wanted to be. He had put Jeb back in a stall and slipped into the house, used his knife to open the lock and told himself all the way up the stairs that he was being a fool. Fool or not, he needed her. There would come a time she'd end it, but until then, he'd take what he could have. It was more than he'd ever known or expected to know with a woman.

The Wesley house was in an uproar. Priscilla had convinced Doc Hadley to drop by to talk to Ollie, but Ollie had resisted any such notion. "You will do it or you don't come back to the ranch," Sam had ordered.

"I'll let you stay here," Priscilla offered knowing the old man would hate that. "We could get chickens," she added with a teasing smile.

Ollie saw no humor in any of it. "Don't see why I need no sawbones." Slowly he was worn down and argued less vehemently.

"So I let you go back with us," Sam finished it off, "and you get really sick making me either take you back here or to Tombstone with calving coming up in a few weeks."

Ollie grimaced. "All right, but I ain't got nothing wrong." He coughed again as an accent.

In the parlor Doc Hadley had been drinking coffee and waiting patiently. "All right, you damned quack," Ollie said sullenly.

Doc, who was a vital man in his mid-fifties, grinned. "Where can we do the exam?"

"Upstairs bedroom would work where Ollie's been staying," Priscilla suggested. And up the stairs the two went as the others sat in the parlor waiting for some kind of diagnosis.

Finally they came back downstairs. "So?" Sam asked anxiously.

"I would say he's had lung congestion, a touch of pneumonia, but he beat that off and likely the cough is just the remnant. His lungs sound clear. Heart beat regular and strong as an ox, but I find it hard to believe he hasn't been complaining of pain in his mouth."

Sam gave Ollie one of his looks. "Not a word."

"Just cuz weren't no reason," Ollie snapped. "Hurts some but so what."

"Teeth can be the end of you faster than some other things," Doc said. "Without a doubt he will have to have two molars pulled and maybe a third canine, but I am not an expert on this. I am seeing evidence of abscesses, which can be toxic for the whole body. Can kill a person if they don't get them out. With those gone, maybe a few fillings, he'll pick up in no time and be his obnoxious self... or should I say more obnoxious self." Doc chuckled while Ollie growled.

"Can you pull the teeth?" Sam asked. "How long will it lay him up?"

Doc considered. "If I'm right on the abscess, which I can't prove right now, then the holes will need to be packed. Maybe a week considering his age. That should make it safe to travel. We have an excellent dentist in town. I'd recommend him for the pulling. He is good at doing it almost never needs surgery to remove broken pieces."

"Thunderation, don't like the idea of losing my teeth," Ollie complained.

"Want to come back to the ranch?" Sam asked looking considerably relieved.

"All right. Dangnabit. I'll do it." And off the three went to find when they could get the teeth pulled.

"Well, that's a relief," Abby said, as she and Priscilla headed into the kitchen where Rose was making pie dough.

"James just got back from downtown," she told them putting the tea into a pot and pouring hot water over it. "And Cord asked if you'd be willing to have Aaron Robinson here for dinner tonight."

Priscilla frowned. "Of course, but is there a problem?" She

had sent James off with the buggy to get new locks after he dropped Grace at school, but wasn't surprised he had talked to Cord while there.

"No, it appears they worked out the custody. Mr. Robinson is leaving, but Cord wanted him to have the evening with Grace to reassure her that all is well."

Priscilla smiled broadly. "That's a wonderful idea. And I am relieved that got resolved without... er trouble."

"That just leaves what you are going to do about Martin Matthews," Abby reminded her as she accepted a cup of tea.

"Want me to try and read the leaves for you?" Rose suggested with a grin. "Too bad Connie left town."

"No tea leaves. I know what I'm going to do-- and now that Grace's custody isn't at risk, I'll do it. I will bring charges. I consider it unlikely I can get my charges heard in court, but I will then make sure the town hears what he did. I couldn't live with myself any other way. He might get off from the law, but he'll have to face the doubt of some at least. And if he ever steps across the line again, the law will get him."

"It will be an ordeal," Abby said, whom Priscilla knew understood how judgmental communities could be. Her running off with a gunfighter still had some of the *better* people in town turning their faces as she passed. Abby didn't care, as she didn't have to live with it. It would be harder to be here every day, but Priscilla had no choice-- not if she wanted to live with herself.

"It is the right thing to do," Rose agreed. "Your friends will stand with you."

"Possibly," Priscilla said as she sipped her tea, seeing a few leaves lying in the bottom of the cup. "Either way it doesn't matter. You two and Ellen will, and who else matters?"

"It could be hard on Grace, I suppose," Abby said with a sigh.

"You mean the children would tease her about me?"

"Children can be cruel."

"You think Cord needs to find a home for her with him?"

"I didn't mean that. Just keep track of what she's hearing. Then you can deal with it and help her if it happens."

"She's better off with us," Rose protested.

"I think so too for now," Priscilla said. "I agree. We'll keep track of how Grace seems to be with the children, whether they will come here for playing. If it seems to be a problem, we'll deal with it then." She tried to make her voice sound more confident than she actually felt.

She would do it. She would tell her story, but she didn't expect it'd be easy. Then, what would come after, she would just have to deal with as it happened. Women so often were blamed, for what men did in a world ruled by men. It did serve to make women stronger. She smiled at the slim consolation.

After a delightful evening with Grace's two uncles, where the little girl laughed more than she'd ever heard her and Davy added to the fun of the evening playing ball with Grace, Priscilla told James that he would need to hitch up the buggy after breakfast. James looked at her soberly but agreed.

That night when Cord used his key for the first time, after they made love, she told him her plans. "I'll come with you," he said.

"No." She put her fingers over his lips. "You know how Sheriff Adams dislikes you."

"He dislikes everybody."

She smiled kissing him again. "I thank you for the offer-- and if this goes to court, of course, you will have to testify."

She wasn't sure how that would go with the sheriff. Cord's testimony might be complicated since they were now lovers.

"If you are convinced this won't work," Abby said the next morning when Priscilla also refused her offer of coming for support, "why are you doing it?"

"Because Martin will do something again. I don't know what,

but he is a risk to others. I truly believe that. I don't want to feel I didn't do what I could."

"You are right." Abby gave her a big hug and waved her off with Davy in her arms.

At the sheriff's office, Priscilla tied up Jezebel, hoping he'd not be there. So often people said he was off drunk, but luck was not with her. There he sat at his desk smiling with the missing teeth and a grin that didn't mean he was smiling at all.

"Well, howdy, Miss Wesley. I kind of wondered if I'd be seein' you here eventually."

"Regarding my kidnapping you mean?" she drawled letting Georgia show through a little more than usual as she took a chair in front of his desk.

"Now was that what it was?" he asked with a smirk. "You want a cup of coffee while you tell me your version."

"Since it involved me, would there be other versions?"

"Well it might just be there would. So anyways, what did you want to say happened?"

She described her kidnapping, her learning it was Martin Matthews and finally how he had raced his team off leaving her there to die or so he hoped.

"Purty good tale," the sheriff said when she quit talking. She wasn't surprised he had not taken notes.

"It happens to be the truth. I would like to press charges."

"He said you'd be around."

She gritted her teeth against the angry retort. "He has every reason to lie," she said forcing a calmness she did not feel.

"So do you, Missy," Sheriff Adams retorted. "A lady," he hesitated over the word, "goes off with a man and then changes her mind, well it happens. So the next thing, she claims kidnapping to avoid having folks think poorly of her."

"I am not known for lying."

"Neither is Mr. Matthews. He has an upstanding reputation. He was sparking you. Everybody knows that. So you wanted him but then got scared. He says you drove him off. He figured you'd change your mind. He would've come back to see about that, but the snow kept him from it."

"That's his story, is it?" she asked smiling.

"Shore is. Backed up by Mr. Wright, I might add, who he told privately what had happened. He tried to go up there, to see if you changed your mind. Got attacked by 'paches. They figured you was killed and were plumb glad you turned up back in town safe and all. You want to tell me how you managed that? Had a little help?"

She suppressed her angry retort. "I would like to file a report regarding my accusations, regardless of what you do with it next," she said, as nothing that was being claimed was a surprise. "I expect you to keep the report on file also—because eventually you will need it."

The sheriff smiled slyly. "He rape you? If he did that, then I got something more I might consider, and there'd maybe be some proof if one of the ladies examined you." The look in his eyes bordered on lascivious.

"No, he did not rape me," she retorted. "Might I have a form to file my charges?"

"You might... So you come off the mountain same as you went up it?" He handed her the form as he looked to see her response.

She could not restrain the flush that came to her cheeks, and he chuckled. "Maybe he was disappointing as a lover and he didn't wanta admit it? There's real men might do better for a pretty thing like you."

"Sheriff Adams, can you give me a pen?"

An hour later she was back at her home, in the kitchen with Rose and Abby-- full of fury at the sheriff. She had expected him to disbelieve her. She had not expected he would then consider her fair game.

333

"If I have to," she said as she sipped the tea Rose handed her, "I'll go to the newspaper with it."

"It won't punish Martin and could make it more difficult for Grace if you do," Abby reminded her.

"That is the only reason I wouldn't do it. Grace is the priority in this. If she has any problem at school, I will put pressure on Cord to get a house for the two of them."

"And how would that be better for Grace?" Rose asked sitting at the table.

"I know but... I just don't want her to be hurt by any of this. Maybe she won't be, and we're worrying about something that won't happen. I mean I'm not her mother. She's just staying with us."

"Sure, that's all," Abby said with a laugh.

"When do you have to go back to the ranch?" she asked knowing how much she'd miss the energy of her friend, if not her insightful barbs.

"It won't be for a week at least. I know Sam is concerned about leaving Cord to face trouble. Ollie needs a week to recuperate from having three teeth pulled. Poor thing, but the calving starts in February. I think he won't have a choice soon."

"Wright is backing up Martin's lies. I don't know what's wrong with that man."

"Martin or Wright?"

"Both." Priscilla laughed. She smiled at them and knew she was all right with this. Inside her, something had changed. She felt a new empowerment. Perhaps Connie Sicilla had been right, and she had always had it in her. Whatever the case, it was there now. None of them could touch her with their lies, pressures, or expectations. She had gone past that. She was living with her own set of ethics. It was empowering.

"I forgot to give you this," Rose said going to the counter and handing her a letter that she quickly saw was from her mother.

Maybe not so empowered, she thought as she opened it. It

had been sent before she had disappeared. Her father had been ill but was better. They wanted to stay on in Florida, then visit friends again in Georgia before coming west possibly not until the next fall. Would that be a problem? Was she all right? Did she need them to return sooner? It was loving, sweet, and so supportive.

She had telegraphed them as soon as she returned to Tucson, but she needed to write a long, reassuring letter. The last thing she wanted was for them to return now. If they returned, she'd have to worry about them, and they'd be worrying about her.

She had things to resolve. They didn't just involve Martin. She would do all she could to make sure people in Tucson knew his true character, but he was no longer a problem to her, nor did she fear what he could do to her.

No, her concern was all for Cord. Was Wright a danger to him? She had seen the toughs in town as she'd gone in to file her report. They were arrogant and rude in the way they made crude comments as she walked past. Something would happen-- and when it did, how would Cord deal with it? Was he in danger? Could she handle it when gunfire erupted again? She would only know if it happened.

"How about if we go pick up Grace today," Abby suggested. "It's time the school saw more of you, I think."

Priscilla smiled. "Shall I have the buggy hitched up or want to walk?"

"Rose, could you watch Davy?"

"I'd love to."

"So why don't we ride down? You haven't forgotten how, have you?"

"Sidesaddle?" Priscilla asked with a grin.

"I don't. It makes no sense."

"All right. I'll use the saddle... Pants or riding skirt?" She giggled

"Let's give them one shock at a time. Riding skirt... for now."

CHAPTER 26

For the next weeks, Cord found his life falling into a comfortable routine, unusual for him. Time with his daughter at the Wesley house had led to a gradually building ease between them. It irked him that the legal system had refused to press charges against Matthews, but he could bide his time on that. One way or another he would nail him, but without doing something that ruined Grace's life or hurt Priscilla.

While he had heard the gossip regarding what had happened while Priscilla was away, most of it didn't touch him. He wasn't the kind of man people came to with rumors. Since Priscilla seemed happy and not concerned, he let it go.

The day Sam and family had left Tucson had surprisingly been depressing. He hadn't imagined he would grow so fond of a man but maybe the blood kin part mattered more than he'd ever known.

"You need me. You send word," Sam had said. "I'll be here as fast as Satan can get me."

Since Cord had known The Circle R calving season was starting soon, he wouldn't ask for help, but he had hugged his brother and smiled.

Now as once again he rode out of town with hope of nailing rustlers hitting the small herds to the north, he was in a good mood. Somewhere, someway he would nail Wright, and the crew he had hired didn't worry him. When Wright was arrested, the hard cases would disappear to find another paycheck.

It would also lead to Martin packing his bags, as no one else in town would hire him. Martin was sowing his own seeds of destruction in Tucson not only hanging with Wright but also his general behavior. He had talked to Jacob Spencer trying to convince him to file charges, but the old man refused to budge. It didn't matter. In time, Martin would step over the line with the wrong person-- and when he did, Cord would be waiting.

South of the Jamison place, he saw evidence of cattle being moved. He followed their trail, but due to the wind, lost the tracks in a sandy arroyo. On the hope he might pick it up again, he rode up the little canyon, watching for signs of cattle hair on branches or tracks near to the rocky banks. When he saw the huge boulder, which didn't look as though it belonged, he rode closer, pulled Jeb to a halt, and dismounted.

"Well I'll be damned," he muttered. The markings were etched into the stone. There was an owl and symbols that might've represented men. A few dancers and something like a snake or trail were alongside. He had seen such symbolisms on other rocks around Tucson, but this one was new to him. Clearly they had come from a people far more ancient than the current residents of the broad river valley.

He thought about bringing Grace to see these. No, first he'd take Priscilla. It was safe from any remaining Apache depredations, and she'd love them. Grace maybe later.

He rode on higher, edging around a sandstone ridge before he gave up hoping he'd find more cattle and horse tracks. The canyon was lined with saguaro, but on its bottom were cottonwoods, grass in their shade and ample underbrush, nothing that would hide a rustled steer. Wherever they had left the canyon, he'd missed it, or the rustlers had brushed out the sign.

Back in Tucson, he went into his office to see Rafe sitting on his desk.

"I swear I need to get you a desk of your own," he said except the office was too small for two.

"I don't mind using yours," Rafe joked.

"You know anything about those markings on the rocks north of town? On a big boulder. Petroglyphs, I think they call them."

Rafe shook his head. "Not my people. We got here from Mexico not that long ago, but there is talk of people who lived here before, long time ago. Got driven out when the rain stopped. Bad time."

"Owl up there on that one."

"Owls mean death."

"That's a pleasant thought."

"Just saying. Any sign of the rustlers?"

Cord shook his head. He was beginning to feel like a failure when it came to stopping the predations. Meade would be firing him if the reports and complaints kept coming in. Who cared if a woman was kidnapped, but cattle, now that was important, deporting Chinese because somebody wanted their leases, that mattered. Damn what kind of job did he have?

The other side of this was that he doubted Wright was rich enough to keep paying his unsavory crew if he didn't come up with something more to do with them. Penny ante rustling wasn't going to cover it. Something had to break.

Jamison came in through the door in a big hurry as usual. "Marshal, I saw you out our way. You got to arrest him."

"What evidence, Daniel? What would I use to get a judge to agree to a warrant?"

"There must be something." He frowned and stomped back out heading for the bar.

"Well that's going to help a lot," Rafe said with a grin.

"I am frustrated too," Cord admitted.

"You going to be at the Wesley's tonight?"

"Most likely."

"Good, then you can help Grace with geography. Man, I don't get that stuff."

"Her assignments are going to be beyond me too. Guess I should order her some books or something."

"Cord, you thinking of heading south to your ranch soon?"

"I don't know. Thinking is all I can do about it. I don't have the money to stock the ranch. Sam offered to give me a start on cattle but I can't take that from him. Even if I did though it'd be years before it'd pay off enough to have a family there. I sure couldn't take Grace down there." Nor Priscilla.

"Well if you go, I am thinking you'll need a hand."

"I thought you wanted to stay in Tucson."

Rafe shook his head. "Not any more. Ellen dumped me. Wants some guy with more prospects, I guess. That lets me out."

"Someone specific, who I'd know?"

"Probably. His father bought the Occidental. Going to upgrade it into Tucson's finest. I don't know. Just I can't blame her. I have nothing to offer her."

"Cowboying won't do it either."

"Nah, but I could prospect a little on the side. And getting out of town seems good right now."

"I wish I could help, but for now it doesn't look like I could support even myself if I went there, let alone pay a hand."

"Always comes down to money, doesn't it?"

"Maybe, but it's not like I can make much of a life for Grace up here either as a marshal. I don't want to start keeping a store."

"Badge does make a good target—especially with Wright just looking for an excuse, and when a sheriff who I can't say whose side he'd be on in trouble—if he could be found."

Cord rolled and lit a cigarette. "There's a lot of appeal in ranching. It's pretty country down that way. Not that many miles between my ranch and the Circle R. Still it'd be a lonely time for probably years."

"Cilla wouldn't go with you?"

"I wouldn't ask her. It's a three room adobe, not much of a house for any woman let alone one like her used to so much. What could I offer her there that she wouldn't have more of here?"

"You?" Rafe suggested with a laugh.

Cord thought then of the nights with Priscilla, her passionate responses and assertive love making. From a woman who knew little of a man, she now understood his body better than he did. Just thinking of her lush womanly curves, the beautiful face and long golden hair had him hot and wondering how long before nightfall. They had been careful to keep their relationship, such as it was, hidden. James and Rose, despite his always leaving before light, likely knew, but they had said nothing to him whatever their opinions.

It wasn't just the nights with her though. It was her loving way with Grace and helping others. The way she was interested in his life, the politics of the city. She was everything a man could ask for in a mate. He just wished he was the right man for her. He wasn't.

That night as they lay in bed after a particularly torrid lovemaking, he said, "Would you like to come out of town with me tomorrow? Go for a ride. A picnic."

"I'd love it. Buggy or horseback?"

"Horseback. I was up a canyon when I came across some petroglyphs. I thought you might like to see them."

"I'd love it. What kinds of drawings?"

"Symbols mostly. The canyon was pretty, steep cliffs, interesting rock formations. Very private."

She smiled. He knew she was thinking what he was. "Very private?"

"Looked that way to me." He imagined making love to her with the sky above. He wanted her naked and teased out of her mind. He knew just how he could do it and got hotter just thinking about it.

"I'll fix us some food and tomorrow you say?"

He struggled to get his mind on her words. "Later maybe we can bring Grace up. I wanted you to see it first." It and something he could not show her with his daughter there.

She smiled down at him bending to claim his lips as she ran her hand over his muscles. "Maybe I can scream a little?" she suggested laughing.

"Now I didn't have ulterior motives in mind," he said knowing he had.

"How disappointing."

In the morning Cord had told her to ride north out of town by herself, and they'd meet at Steam Pump Ranch to ride the rest of the way together.

James brought her mare around but had an uneasy look on his face. "You sure you don't want me to go with you?" he asked, as she came out of the house wearing her riding skirt. He had only been partially reassured when she'd ordered the ordinary saddle, not the sidesaddle. "Martin's still out there running free." He helped her mount.

"I think he's lost interest in me. Besides, I won't be anywhere there aren't others around," she said smiling down at him. Tied to the saddle was the tightly wound quilt, in saddlebags were fruit, bread, cheese, and bottles of water. If Rose and James suspected what was going on between her and Cord, they hadn't made comment.

She rode Jezebel out of town feeling relaxed with the wide

road and the mare's easy gait. Although she wasn't a talented horsewoman like Abby, she could ride well enough and even better astride. If it shocked a few proper ladies and gentlemen, they'd be shocked more if they knew the rest of her life. She had left behind proper with a flourish.

When she arrived at Steam Pump, he was waiting for her, standing in the shade of a huge cottonwood tree, letting his horse drink from a small tank. She reined up alongside, and Jezebel took a drink.

"It'll be dry out there," he told her as he mounted.

"I brought water." They put their horses back on the road north.

"Me too. It's not a lot of miles, but it is out of the way. Mostly the only other ones there will be cows."

"Sounds lovely."

"It's pretty country."

"Is it pretty where your ranch is?"

He glanced over at her before he answered. "Yes. It's wilder though beyond the Sierra del Pajritos. A long way from anything."

"Abby likes that life."

"Some women can adapt to it. For others it'd be torture. Likely comes from how sheltered they've been."

She didn't like the way he said sheltered, but she had to admit she wasn't sure herself. She felt she was growing in strength, but was it enough to ride through life beside a man like Cord O'Brian.

He pointed to a wide arroyo. "We head up there," he said. "It's easy riding until we get further up where the canyon narrows. There are a few narrow rock shelves but the horses can manage them. Glad you had the sense to ride astride."

She smiled at the compliment. "I think my days, of worrying about being thought a proper lady, are behind me."

"I ruined you?" He had what sounded like concern in his voice.

She laughed. "Abby. She taught me to value what matters and not worry so much what others think. It's beautiful up here, Cord. Those big trees have such lovely and unusual shapes." She frowned then as she saw a shape hurtle across the path ahead.

"Coyote," he said.

"Ah, trickster."

He nodded. "The one who plays games with fate." She heard the smile in his voice.

"And do you believe in fate, Marshal?"

"Sometimes there is no other explanation. Now whether coyote was involved, that's dicier." As they climbed higher, they came to sandstone steps, but Jezebel easily negotiated them. When he stopped and dismounted, she only saw a huge stone. A boulder that seemed could only have been set where it was by a giant god.

He reached up to help her down, and they ground reined their horses. "They won't go anywhere," he said as his gelding began to eat what grass was there. Jezebel wearing a bridle had less freedom to eat than the gelding's hackamore, but she gave it a try.

She looked more closely at the stone and saw for the first time the beautiful drawings. "Amazing," she whispered, as she walked with him to the base of the rock. "They're beautiful." She stopped when she saw the stick figure of an owl, clearly a great horned owl by the head shape and looking straight at her.

"What do you suppose it means?" she asked, uneasy as she remembered the owl was something Connie had seen relating to her hawk.

He shrugged. "Maybe a message only for them. Now, who could know."

"Rafe?"

"He said his people came to this valley much later. I asked around some-- but best I can understand, this is at least five hundred years old, and whoever did it has long been gone. My guess is they either represent magic or were a way to tell someone's story."

"This place has the feel of magic," she said as she turned back to him and went into his arms. She might have felt the owl was frightening given the vague warning but instead if felt reassuring. As though it was looking out for this place, a kind of sacred guardian. "It's a wonderful place. Thank you so much for sharing it with me."

"I thought we could... lie down for a bit. I saw a protected inner canyon just a bit farther up the arroyo. Shade right now so you won't get burned. We'd hear anybody coming."

She laughed as she threw her arms around his neck. "Will they hear me?"

"I'll muffle the sound if they might," he promised as he took her lips in a hard kiss. He thrust his tongue into her warmth. "You want me?" he asked.

"So much." They had never made love outside, and she relished the idea. "Think you can make me scream?" she asked.

"That sounded like a challenge." He picked up the reins of the horses and led them, past another sandstone set of steps. When they came to the small side canyon, she saw its privacy and even some grass in the hollows.

"It's perfect." When she reached to unbutton his shirt, he stopped her.

"No, I have something else in mind for today." He secured the horses.

"I am in your hands," she said as she handed him the quilt, and he spread it. He took a scarf from his saddlebag and held it up for her to see before he tied it over her eyes. With the blindfold, she felt the whole experience change. Instead of being in a canyon, she was within herself.

She waited as he walked around her, then came back to the front and began unbuttoning her shirt. He pushed it from her shoulders, leaving her shoulders bare and sensitive to the slight breeze.

She smelled a fragrance she couldn't identify, something sweet and at the same time pungent. With her sight taken, her other senses seemed aware of every little rustle of a bush, touch of a breeze and especially fragrance of the canyon, the rocks and even more of the musky scent of Cord—a mixture of maleness, his shaving soap, horse, saddle, dust. It filled her in a way she had never imagined.

He pushed the straps of her chemise from her shoulders, now kissing the skin he was baring, first the tops of her breasts and then the tips. She moaned against the sensations as he sucked on each nipple bringing them to rigid little peaks.

More, she wanted so much more from him, but he was taking his time and only slowly baring more skin and with each opening to the air, her body seemed more heated, more aware of each fleeting touch. Pushing down her riding skirt, he spoke for the first time. "Lift your foot." When she did, he pulled off first one boot and then the other, pulling off the leather riding skirt and stockings as he did.

She stood now on the quilt naked except for sheer white pantalets. His fingers and hands were all over her body, brushing against her sensitive points until he pulled off her last garment. She heard him move back from her. "Cord?" she whispered.

"Don't talk. Just let me look at you. So beautiful." He came around behind, his fully clothed body now brushing against her bare skin as he pulled the pins from her hair and let it fall over her shoulders. She swallowed against the sensations, as once again he was caressing her, this time pulling her back against his body. She felt the texture of his shirt, the roughness of his pants and those clever hands that were making her feel her body in ways she never had dreamed possible.

Soon she was moaning with the sensations, trying to turn to take him in her arms but he wasn't ready for that. He brought her again and again nearly to the peak but always stopped leaving her desperately needing him inside her.

Finally, he laid her down on the quilt, spreading her legs. She should have felt embarrassed to have him so intimately viewing her. Instead knowing he was standing over her had her body more heated than she'd yet experienced. She heard him removing his clothing, imagined the sight of his beautiful body as it would be revealed, then heard him putting on the protective sheath.

Blind as she was, everything around her was more alive, than she had ever imagined. Every sound, sensation, and then he was back, between her legs and caressing her, making her ready for him before he plunged into her. She knew she was making sounds, even screaming as she had teased she might, but nothing was real except hearing his groans, feeling him within, their moving together.

When she climaxed, it was almost immediately, but he wasn't ready for that and kept moving, stimulating. She learned she could climax more than once, then more than twice. When he finally found his own release, her flesh dissolved into pudding.

They lay in each other's arms, and then he pulled off the blindfold. It was awhile before she felt capable of speech. "That was amazing," she managed to whisper.

"You are amazing," he said, his voice hoarse. "I never knew anyone like you or anything like this."

After a time, they managed to find the energy to get dressed and eat the food, drink the water. They tied the quilt back on the horse. "We need to take this other places with us," she suggested as he finished securing her saddlebags.

The shots rang out loud but seemingly from some distance away. "What was that?" she asked trying to figure out from where they had come.

He boosted her into her saddle and vaulted into his as he took them back down the canyon at a fast trot. "When we get to the mouth of the arroyo, I want you to stay back until I find out."

That didn't prove necessary as just before the mouth, they saw the body of a man lying on his stomach, a horse standing not far from him. Cord leaped off his horse and ran to the body, seeing first the blood. Turning him over, she recognized Daniel Jamison. Only when he groaned did she know he was alive.

She took one of the canteens to Cord, then hurried back to her bags to find a scarf they could use for a compress on the wound. Cord tore open Jamison's shirt, lifted him a little and she saw two holes. One smaller in the back, the other larger in the front.

"Is he going to die?" she asked as she watched him press the cloth to the larger of the wounds.

"I don't know."

Jamison groaned and opened his eyes looking around without seeming to see anything.

"What happened?" Cord asked as he held the water to the young man's lips. He took some sips. Priscilla came to his other side and applied pressure with her fingers to slow the bleeding.

His eyes closed and then opened again. "Shot me in the back. Damn... I saw them with the cattle this time."

"Who shot you?"

"Wright along with two of his toughs. I thought... I tried to run. It was Wright with the rifle. I know it was."

"All right, steady yourself."

"Am I going to die?"

"Not if we can help it," Cord said. He turned then to Priscilla. "You'll have to ride back to Steam Pump and get help. I can't leave him here alone."

"And I can't ride as fast as you. I'll stay with him and keep pressure on this wound."

"Angel, I can't let you do that."

347

"You are wasting time. You can't do otherwise. Bring back a wagon. You know you can ride faster. Do it."

She saw he was torn between his duty and his fear for her but finally he nodded. He handed her his six-gun.

"You can't give me your gun. It's too dangerous for you to go unarmed."

"I won't leave you here without one, and I don't think you can handle a rifle, can you?"

She shook her head and took the gun. "Just hurry."

He ran to his horse and was leaping into the saddle at the same moment the horse began to run. She watched until he disappeared from sight.

"You will be all right," she tried to reassure Daniel as she moved to sit a little behind him, keeping the towel pressed hard against the wound.

"That damned bastard. He got me," he moaned. "I thought I'd get him but he got me."

"He hasn't gotten you yet. Now lie still." She lifted him a little, putting her arms around him to give him more warmth as she felt him beginning to shake. Blood was all over her shirt and skirt. She imagined it being Cord she held, as his blood spilled onto her. She let out a cry she couldn't suppress. It wouldn't be him. No, it couldn't be. She thought then of the owl symbol, but pushed the fear from her. She would not let that be a symbol of death for anyone—not today.

When she heard the horses, she thought at first that Cord was already back, but it wasn't. It was Wright and two of his men. The gun was beside her and she shifted enough to hide it under her skirt.

"Well, you do end up in some strange places, Miss Wesley," Wright said with a smirk.

"Would you get us some help? My friend has been hurt," she said hoping she could distract Wright long enough for Cord to get back-- then she feared what would happen when he did.

"He was was he? Looks like he's dead, but he isn't, is he, not if you're holding him like that."

She wondered if she could convince them Daniel was already dead. "He's..." With that Jamison groaned.

"Well, well now what do we do about this?" Wright asked leaning forward on the pommel of his saddle. "You look a little lonely out here by yourself... or were you?"

"I was just taking a ride," she said knowing if she reached for the gun, she'd be the one who ended up dead as the three men watched her.

"So you just came across this *accident*?" Wright asked, dismounting to come closer.

She thought about saying Cord had been with her-- but if she did that then they'd be waiting for him. "I was looking at the petroglyphs above," she said managing what probably looked like a grimace more than a smile. "Then I heard the shots and came back down to find Daniel lying here with all this blood and unconscious."

"Unconscious? He didn't say anything to you?"

"Nothing sensible. He seemed confused, delusional, mumbled something about Indians. Did you see any Indians?" She looked around as though frightened. Not hard to give that impression.

Now Wright was studying her, trying to assess her words. All she needed was to delay him. It wouldn't be long until Cord would be there with a wagon. Except if he brought a wagon, it'd take him longer. God, how long would it be?

"Miss Wesley," Wright said, "I think you're a lovely, little liar."

"How could you say such a thing? And you must send one of your men for help. Daniel is bleeding badly. I think he could die if he doesn't get a doctor and soon."

Wright gestured to the arroyo. "I see more than one set of horse tracks coming this way. You were with someone weren't you?"

She looked into his eyes and saw death. Not for a second would he hesitate to murder her. There was no sympathy in those snake eyes, only a coldness. The owl symbol had been right.

CHAPTER 27

C ord had raced to the Steam Pump, told the people there a wagon was needed for a wounded man and immediately headed back for the gulch. He felt a fear that wouldn't let up and took his Winchester from its scabbard as he rode, holding it in his right hand, ready to fire. He should have never left her.

Seeing two men on horseback, another standing beside Priscilla and Jamison's body, he didn't slow his pace until he was on top of them. Wright swung to face him as Cord took in Priscilla's terrified face. She was alive. He would keep her that way.

"What is this?" he yelled. The swirl of dust rose up around them as his mount plunged to a stop. He had his rifle pointed toward Wright, but he wasn't ready to use it, not with Priscilla in the line of fire. He again condemned himself for leaving her. What was Jamison's life to him?

Wright turned to face him, his gun in his hand but pointing downward. "Marshal, seems we have a problem here. A wounded man. Such a shame. Indians, I guess."

For a moment, Cord thought maybe this could be put off, that a shooting didn't have to happen, not yet, not with Priscilla in danger. Then Jamison began moaning. "He shot me." He pointed to Wright, his voice clearly understandable, nothing anyone could deny hearing. "In the back."

When Cord looked back at Wright, his gun was pointing at Priscilla. "Drop the rifle and get off your horse, Marshal or I will kill her. It'd be a shame, but you know I mean it."

Priscilla was in dire danger whatever he did, but Cord needed time for the wagon to arrive. He dropped the rifle and dismounted. The other two men jumped off their horses, grabbed him by the wrists, yanking his arms widely apart.

"I've wanted to do this for a long while," Wright said smiling as he advanced. The first punch caught Cord in the belly. He doubled with it before the second slammed into his jaw, lifting him back up. A beating, he could withstand if that was all it'd be. It wouldn't be, but with his arms held out, even by two smaller men, he had no choice but to take it until he got an opportunity to change the game.

Two more solid punches before the loud sound of a shot caught him almost as off guard as Wright who stumbled back. Cord didn't look toward Priscilla, as he jerked hard on the men holding him, pulling them toward him as they had also been taken aback at the gunshot.

With his right hand free, Cord slammed with the side of his hand at one man's throat, hard as he could, hoping to crush his windpipe, feeling satisfyingly solid contact before the man went down.

Reaching for his knife in the scabbard at his back, Cord sliced at the other, as the gunman started to reach for his revolver. The blade likely nearly decapitated him, but Cord couldn't look as he lunged for his rifle. Wright had been hit by Priscilla's shot, but he wasn't down.

As Cord got hold of the rifle, he felt pain as a bullet grazed his side. Rolling onto his back, he had the rifle up, pointing before Wright could get off a second shot. His bullet slammed the rancher backward, who struggled to rise and then collapsed in the sand.

Cord forced himself to his knees, almost afraid to look toward Priscilla. She was staring at him, the gun still in both her hands, but now pointed at the ground. He crawled to her, taking her in his arms.

"My God," he whispered against her hair. "Are you all right?"

"I am, but you are bleeding." Her voice sounded steadier than his.

"Not much, just grazed me."

She pulled up his shirt. "Are they all... dead?" She didn't look toward the bodies as she studied the gouge he knew he had in his side.

"Hopefully." He let out a breath. How easily it all could have ended otherwise. He had felt more scared than he ever remembered being. He'd faced bullets, danger but nothing like this where she could have been killed. He clenched his jaw as he rose looking toward where he thought he heard the wagon coming. He clenched his jaw at the truth he saw clearly. Whether he was on the ranch or acting as marshal, she would never be safe near him. He could never go through something like this again.

"Cord, you're bleeding. I need to bandage your wound."

He shook his head. "It's nothing. The wagon is here." The driver pulled to a halt a few feet from the carnage. The man on the seat beside him looked from the bodies to Cord.

"Pull your hat down over your face," Cord ordered Priscilla. "If we are lucky, they won't recognize you." That would take a lot of luck, but she didn't need more gossip attached to her name. If he could at least protect her from that, he would.

The older of the two men got down from the wagon. "Is that Richard Wright?" he asked as he stared at the bodies.

Cord nodded.

"What the hell happened here?"

"Wright was rustling cattle. Jamison caught them at it. He

tried to get away. He said they shot him in the back. He thought he'd lost them, but then fell of his horse. I heard the shots from farther up the canyon. He told me it was Wright, about the time he came on us. Wright and his men decided to make a fight of it. She got here when it was over."

"Well, you shore took care of it," the older man said with a whistle as he looked at the three corpses. These two old timers were of the type, who had long been on the desert, and learned to keep their mouths shut. They stuck to the jobs they were doing. Cord didn't think they'd be spreading gossip.

The real question was how much Jamison would remember. He'd deal with that later-- if Jamison survived. If he didn't, then Cord recognized he'd have a problem himself. These had been particularly brutal killings. One man's throat had been cut, a second slammed so hard he had suffocated, and a prominent citizen shot dead, there would be questions. A lot of them.

As much as Cord might've blamed Wright for what he had set in motion, he blamed himself even more. Priscilla could have been the one lying dead. He was the one who had put her at risk.

"How do you want to handle this?" the older man asked gesturing toward the corpses.

"You take Jamison to town in the wagon as quick as you can. Maybe we can keep him alive. Would one of you mind staying here with these bodies, while I send someone back for them and get the lady home?"

"We can do that," he said spitting out a plug of chewing tobacco as Cord helped him get Jamison into the back of his wagon.

"Can you ride?" Cord asked Priscilla as he walked up to her. "I think it'd be best if you can, but you decide."

She managed a smile but it wasn't easy. She saw by the cold tone of his voice and pain-filled eyes how he was taking it—not well. It had been so vicious and over so fast. She kept remembering seeing him held and beaten, and then picking up the gun and shooting hoping to kill Richard Wright. For the first time she understood a little of what Cord had always lived. Surprisingly she didn't feel any guilt. She would have shot again except by then Cord was in action, and she was afraid she'd hit him.

"My knees are weak, but if we go easy, yes. You don't have to take me all the way home."

"Yes, I do." His lips were set as he lifted her onto her horse and then mounted himself.

"I'll talk to you later," he said as the older man got up on the wagon seat and also headed back down the arroyo with the now moaning Jamison.

As they came out onto Oracle Road, she said, "You aren't blaming yourself for this are you?"

"Who else would I blame?"

"Richard Wright," she suggested, feeling steadier the longer they rode.

"Of course, but he didn't take you out and nearly get you killed."

"I made my own choice on that."

"Look, I don't want to talk about it."

"When we get to the house, I want to bandage your side," she said knowing he would want none of that.

"I'll have things to do. I can take care of it later."

"Cord, I need to do it."

He looked at her and nodded without any words. What was he thinking? They rode then in silence. She kept her hat down as Cord had suggested and was unsure if anyone she knew recognized her. She didn't care.

When they reached her home, James came out, a look at shock on his face as he saw the blood on her shirt and skirt, more on Cord's shirt. "Are you all right?" he asked as she dismounted.

"The blood is other people's. Cord, I want you to come in."

He was sitting on his horse looking down at her, his eyes hooded, not revealing what he was thinking. "Not this time," he said. "Tell Grace I'll be around as soon as I can." He turned and rode off leaving her angry and ready to cry even as she understood a tiny bit of what he was feeling.

"What the hell happened?" James asked handing Jezebel's reins to Ben.

"I'll tell you inside. Where is Rose?"

"Down at the market. She should be back in an hour."

"Let me explain it then, because right now I need a bath and to get out of these clothes.

Feeling nearly numb, Cord led Jeb into the stable, unsaddled and tended to the horse's needs—anything to avoid thinking. He had arranged for someone to pick up the bodies, stopped at the undertakers, notified the city attorney's office, Judge Emerson, and was left with nothing more he could do. A ride out of town would be out of the question until all the questions had been answered—a prominent citizen had been killed. The City Council might finally take an interest in what was going on. He expected the killings to lead to an inquest.

If he could, he'd keep Priscilla's name out of it. It might not be possible if Jamison remembered her being there and talked. He would be just the kind to talk. Otherwise, he felt confident the two old-timers would consider it no one's business. Since she had nothing to do with the killings, he saw no reason for her to be involved.

Walking into his office, he went to the back room, took off his shirt, poured water into the basin and began washing away the blood from his side. As he'd told her, it was a minor gouge, had stopped bleeding and didn't even need a bandage.

What he wanted was a shot of whiskey, but he needed a clear head for when the questions came. The one thing he wouldn't do was go back to Priscilla's. He wasn't able to talk to her about it yet.

For a time, he'd stay away, make sure her name stayed out of it, and then explain to her why they couldn't meet again.

No matter where he was, she would be in danger being near him. The fear he'd felt in that arroyo had been worse than any he'd felt in all his years of living by the gun. He never wanted to go through its like again. He loved her. That wasn't about to change, but he would keep his distance. He knew she loved him, but she would find another. His thoughts stopped there, as he couldn't let himself think of her with another man.

"What the hell is going on?" Rafe asked as he slammed through the front door and stood in the doorway.

"You mean the word isn't already out?" Cord asked as he put on a fresh shirt.

"You killed Wright and two of his men. Oh, it's out, all right? And Jamison is in the doctor's office getting patched up."

"Look like he'll make it?"

"That's what I heard."

Before they could say more, Sheriff Adams rushed through the door, for once not obviously drunk. "What's your explanation for what I heard?" he asked his face red from the exertion of hurrying there.

Cord sat at his desk and began rolling a cigarette. "I'll be filing a report."

"You can't go killing important citizens and not expect some questions. Judge Ames will want your story."

"Tell him to read the report." He lit the cigarette and met the sheriff's gaze with a cold look of his own. "You already know what Wright was up to though don't you?"

Adams huffed but didn't deny it. "Nobody could prove nothing."

"Well this time Jamison caught them at it, which was why he was shot in the back."

"And rather than bring them in, you killed them?" the sheriff asked in a sanctimonious tone.

"I preferred to stay alive," Cord retorted taking a long draw on the cigarette.

"You have any witnesses to this being self-defense?"

"I have a wound in my side and Jamison. That should do it."

"There will be an inquest."

"I figured as much. Sheriff, get on back to your office. I have a report to write."

The sheriff glared at him but turned and left. When he was gone, Rafe said, "What aren't you adding to the report?"

"Nothing that matters. Man, I hate reports."

At this point though writing it was at least something he could do—not so much a distraction as a job. This killing was worse than the three that had come before it-- not the doing of it. Adrenaline took care of the moment. It was the aftermath that was so hard-- this time enhanced by the guilt he felt over putting Priscilla in the situation, where she had to shoot a man to save his life. And there was no doubt that she had saved his life.

He thought again about the release he would get by going for a fast ride. He couldn't do it. He had a report to write, a story to tell, as he wanted it told. "Rafe," he said when he looked up, "how about checking at Doc's and find out when I can talk to Jamison?"

Rafe said nothing but left. Cord didn't know how his deputy suspected something more was involved. Maybe that damned extra sense they talk about. Whatever the case, the less people who knew the whole story, the better.

When Rose got back to the house, Priscilla had bathed and dressed in a cotton gingham dress. She'd managed to get her hair back up in a tidy bun and felt ready to face Grace if she came home with questions.

"I can't believe it," Rose said as she hurried into the kitchen, putting her basket of fresh produce on the counter. "The talk in the town is insane."

"About what?"

"Marshall killed three men. Good Lord Almighty, it's hard to believe even now. One of them was Richard Wright."

James had followed her in from outside. "They say why?" he asked looking at Priscilla as he asked it.

"Depends on who is talking," Rose said as she made coffee. "If it's the side likes the marshal, then it's rustling, that Wright was stealing cattle and got caught by Jamison who was shot. If it's them don't like the marshal, for how tough he can be, they say he was just looking for an excuse. The killings were brutal is what both sides say. Both sides are wondering what kind of man they got for a marshal could do that and to three men."

"I was there," Priscilla said. "Cord is trying to keep that out of the story. When I came home, James saw the blood on my clothes. It was that of Daniel Jamison. Cord and I had been riding down the arroyo and heard shots. When we got to him, he was hurt bad and babbling as much as talking, except he said Wright shot him in the back. I stayed with him while Cord went for a wagon. He made me keep his revolver. Before Cord got back, Wright and two of his men showed up."

"I knew you shouldn't have gone," James said with a grimace.

"I tried to convince Wright that Jamison had told me nothing, but then Daniel began babbling. Wright threatened me. That's when Cord got back. Wright made him drop his rifle or have me shot."

"Lord have mercy," Rose whispered stopping in the making of the coffee.

"Cord dropped it. Two of the men grabbed him, and Wright began to beat him. That's when I used Cord's gun to shoot Wright. I hit him, but moving as he was, it wasn't a good enough shot to kill. It did give Cord a chance to break away. Cord was so fast. I've never seen anything like how he reacted. He killed the two holding him in what seemed like seconds. Wright shot him as he was reaching for his rifle. Cord fired, and Wright was dead —so fast. One shot."

"So then he is holding out on you being there to protect you from more gossip," Rose said approvingly.

"Well he might find he's bit off more than he can chew without you there to tell the story," James said as Rose went back to measuring the rest of the coffee and putting the pot on the stove to brew.

"Our noble sheriff was walking around sounding pompous," Rose said with a sneer. "He'll make trouble over this if he can. The city council is finally taking an interest in the goings on—when it's over, of course."

"I'll tell them all what happened," Priscilla said.

"Why don't you wait a bit? See how this shakes out," James suggested. "If it's not necessary, then Cord is right. How would it look?"

"Like I care."

"But Grace will. The children could make it hard on her. Trust Cord on this. Give it some time, and see if he can handle it without you involved."

"I hate knowing that people would blame him," she said her first tears of the day rolling down her cheeks. "He blamed himself for my being there."

"Which is only right," James said.

Rose snorted. "Leave it to a man to give himself all the credit or blame. I say you're right for her to not say anything just yet, but Cilla is a grown woman and makes her own choices." She smiled.

"Actually," James said with his first smile. "I am kind of pleased myself. You shot him, huh?"

"Well it didn't stop him, but it did slow him," Priscilla admitted. "I meant to kill him and would have shot again except fear of hitting Cord. He really is something in a fight like that." She was surprised to realize it didn't horrify her but gave her a strange sense of pride.

"You're okay with shooting someone?" Rose asked with some amazement in her voice.

"Under the circumstances. He would have killed Cord and me too. If there had been an alternative, maybe, but there just wasn't." She drew in a breath and knew she really had changed in the last months.

"When Jamison starts talking, he might tell about you being there," James said more concerned sounding. "The more I've thought about Cord's decision to keep you out, the more I like it, but Jamison might make that impossible unless he dies."

"I really don't care," Priscilla said. "I'll do like you recommend and wait and see, but if Cord takes blame for this, I will go forward. I doubt Daniel will remember me. He was babbling, and mostly delirious."

As soon as Cord heard Jamison was awake and moaning in misery, he headed over to Doc's. "All right for me to talk to him?" he asked as Doc came out from the back room.

"If he makes sense, fine. He's still loopy from the chloroform. Rafe said you got shot too. You want me to check that?"

"Nah. It's fine. Just let me talk to him, and you better be there too. I don't want any accusations of my trying to prime a possible witness."

"You expect trouble over the killings?" Doc asked as he led him to the room where his patient was lying, moving restlessly against the covers.

"Never know," Cord said, as he stood by the bed. "Daniel, you awake enough to answer some questions."

The man opened his eyes and looked around as though mystified to find himself where he was. "I guess," he managed with a groan.

"What do you remember of today?"

"I was dead and in heaven. An angel came and took care of me."

Cord smiled. "Well you're not in heaven-- so tell me what you remember of what happened."

"I was out... checking the cattle." He glared at Cord. "Something you should have done."

"I was out there and fortunate for you."

"Oh yeah... I remember that... You ... wait I was shot first. I saw Wright with two of his men driving off my cows. I yelled at them to stop-- then when they turned with guns pointed toward me, I rode like heck to get away. They shot me. I think Wright but... somebody. I got hit... and stayed on as long as I could. I thought... I rode down an arroyo thinking I lost them but I... I must have lost consciousness. Next I knew, I was lying there, and you were there. I lost it again... heard shots but... No, I don't remember more. Just that angel."

"So you didn't see when I shot Wright?"

"No... You did? Did you kill him? Holy Jesus, I hope so. He tried to murder me."

"Yes, he's dead, and yes, I killed him. Rest now. You are going to be all right."

"I thought I was dead. Not so bad if that angel was the one with me," he said drifting off to sleep.

Back in the front of the office, Doc said, "I'll be sure and tell anybody what he said... leaving out the angel part, of course." He chuckled. "He'll likely forget that part when he's less loopy from the chloroform."

"Sheriff and maybe even the city attorney will be around."

"I don't think you will be blamed for this. Wright has been bucking for this end for years. His daddy didn't do enough keeping him under control. Spoiled the boy. Then when Aaron died, nothing but rustling and using it as an excuse to hire hard cases. You think his men might come after you?"

"I doubt it. They work for pay. Who'd make it worth their while? I don't think he had that many friends except Judge Ames and Sheriff Adams. Martin Matthews maybe."

"Wright used people. No friends. They will all be off the payroll now." Doc chuckled again. "Serve 'em right."

Outside the sun was just setting as Cord walked back to his office. He ran the events of the day through his mind. It had gone so quickly from heaven to hell. Hell had always been waiting for him, and it looked like it found him. Whether the town would want him as a marshal after this, he wasn't sure. What he did know is that when this was all straightened out, as soon as he could get a replacement into Tucson, he'd head for his ranch—with or without the money to stock it. He'd had all he wanted of being a lawman. He would not ask Priscilla to go with him. It would be no safer down there than with him up here.

As he thought about her, her beauty, how bravely she had stood by him, shot a man for him, he knew he'd been a lucky man to know that kind of woman. He would not be the one standing there when she died from a bullet meant for him.

At the office, Wong Chan was waiting for him. "Is there a problem, Mr. Chan?" he asked thinking it had been the day for them.

"I heard about the shooting, Marshal. Hope it won't mean trouble for you."

Cord shrugged. "So what can I do for you?"

"I had hoped to discuss with you this talk of immigration laws requiring trips back to China for papers."

"Yes, it is something out of Washington. I won't be enforcing any of them. Want a cup of coffee?" He supposed tea would be more desired, but he had none.

Chan smiled and took the coffee. "My family and I would not like to have to leave Tucson."

"If you can send for papers proving you immigrated legally, it'd be wise to do it as insurance, but I honestly think this will blow over. You and your family work hard and provide a lot of the food for Tucson. That will be forgotten when the next whatever comes along. Other than a few important people, most out here won't see it as their business."

"There has been some resentment of us."

"Human nature," Cord said as he lit a cigar. "If you have a problem though, you come to me."

Chan nodded. "I would like to become naturalized citizen," he said as he sipped the strong coffee.

"That would be good as you can speak for your people better than many."

"I learned from the Jesuits who came to my country. I speak Spanish also as for a while I lived in Mexico before coming north."

"With the Yaquis? Seems I heard that."

Chan nodded. "I want to make America and Arizona my home. Lin goes to school here now, and I appreciate that he can do that. I may need to speak for my family and friends."

"It is possible."

"Anything worth having is worth fighting for," Chan said as he put down the emptied cup. "But you know about that, don't you, Marshal." With that he was gone leaving Cord thinking fighting wasn't always enough. He would talk to Judge Emerson though and be sure that when he left Tucson, Wong Chan still had a friend in the legal system. It might be he would need it.

Martin Matthews sat at the back of the bar, a half empty bottle of whiskey on the table in front of him. He felt furious at the way life had cheated him once again. That stupid Wright, rustling penny ante stock and then bracing the marshal. What a fool. The question he had was what was he to do now?

Although Priscilla had told whoever would listen that he had kidnapped her, it hadn't carried any weight, not with Wright to back him. That was gone. How long could he last in the town? Damn that stupid man. He had ruined everything and ended up useless.

"You mind sharing the bottle?" Adams said as he came over and sat at the table.

"Get a glass and help yourself."

When he came back with the glass and poured himself a shot, he drank it in one gulp. "What you going to do now with Rich dead?"

"I am thinking about that. Who will get the ranch?"

Adams shrugged. "I don't know that he had kin. Distant maybe. Everybody's got somebody even him. Or maybe it'll go to the courts when taxes ain't paid."

"His hands leaving?"

"Like rats deserting a sinking ship."

"Why not you?" Martin asked with mild interest.

"O'Brian beat me up once. I want to wait around and see him get his."

"Been others hoping for that. Didn't work out so well for them," Martin said with a sour smile.

"Might be we can come up with something that would help that along."

"Like what?"

"Some think it was murder, that the marshal just killed 'em because he had it in for them. Caught them out there alone and they didn't have a chance."

"The ones who think that are the sleazy element in town, and you know it," Martin said, not unwilling to see the marshal get his but that seemed an unlikely hand to play out.

"We can start rumors. You never know."

"It's a waste of time."

"The Baileys are willing to talk against him."

"Look, their son went after O'Brian in front of a lot of witnesses. That isn't going anywhere."

Martin poured himself another whiskey with limited interest as Adams kept trying out various scenarios. It occurred to him that Wright had money at the ranch, money he could find. He would check that out.

He took another swallow of whiskey as he considered whether the proof he had of Wright's rustling would have any value now. Unlikely. He'd be smart to destroy that in case they looked further to see the books he'd doctored.

Then he wondered where Sally was. She had been avoiding him, but he needed her now and damn it all, he was not going to let her get away with treating him like dirt. Too many women had done that. He thought of Priscilla and felt his anger building. Women—damn them all to hell.

CHAPTER 28

T wo weeks had gone by since the killing of Wright. Although Priscilla had expected to see Cord, he had stayed away, seeing Grace after school, or asking James to bring her to him. She understood he needed time, but she was frustrated with his reasoning. She was more and more proving to herself that she did have the strength to be mate to a man like him, but he obviously saw it otherwise.

The inquest had come and gone with no one but Judge Ames interested in even asking questions. As soon as he was on his feet, Daniel Jamison had gone around town reminding people of all the bad things Wright had done. Any interest in replacing the marshal had disappeared— especially since there had been no more rustled cattle, with Wright out of the picture.

"What are you thinking?" Grace asked as they were both supposed to be studying her homework assignment.

"That the wildflowers must be blooming on the desert," she said less than truthfully although she had thought of that earlier.

"Could we go see them?" Grace asked with interest. "I could press some couldn't I?"

"You could, and I am sure James would take us. I remember a

place where there have been carpets of orange poppies in the past. I think other flowers too. Pressing them is an excellent idea. You could start a collection."

"Would Daddy come too, do you think?" Grace asked.

Priscilla smiled. "I suspect he'd be busy, but we could ask. Maybe you could surprise him with the pressed flowers. If you collect a lot, you can put them on cards and even letters you write."

Her eyes brightened with excitement. "Oh I'd like that very much."

They went into the kitchen to see if Rose had interest, which she did. An hour later they had hitched up the buggy and with James driving, headed west out of town. "I heard there are some petroglyphs out this way too," Priscilla said. "Could we stop and see them?"

"It'd be an easy break," James said. "I know the cliff you mean."

As they drove along the wagon road, Priscilla saw the tall rider coming toward them. She knew who it was, by the way he sat his horse, the hat pulled low. She wished they had not run into him like this, and yet she was eager to see him. It had been too long.

"Daddy," Grace cried as he drew nearer. James stopped the buggy and Cord brought his horse to a halt. He looked tired, but he smiled for Grace if not for her.

"You all heading out for a picnic?" he asked as he pushed his hat back on his head.

"We're on a hunt for wildflowers, thought maybe the other side of the pass. You been out there?" James asked

"I was, and you are on the right road. They're lush right now."

"You could come with us," Grace suggested.

"I wish," he said, "but I've been after someone and missed him. I heard he might have headed south of town-- so that's where I'm bound."

For the first time he looked at Priscilla, their eyes meeting for a few long seconds before he turned away. "Good luck," he said as he nudged his horse in the side and rode off.

They stopped first at the red rock cliff with a petroglyphs site, which was a short walk off the road. "Watch those barbs," Priscilla warned the excited little girl, as she wanted to skip ahead.

"Rattlesnakes are out too," James added as he told her she'd be walking behind this time. "And don't touch anything without asking first. Sometimes things have stickers that don't show. See that cactus, it jumps so don't brush it, or it'll end up in your leg."

The petroglyphs were high up with many different designs, some representing animals and people. Grace's favorites were those that looked like dancers with feather headdresses.

"How did they get up there?" Grace asked with awe.

"Someone who very much wanted to leave their story behind."

"How do you suppose they got them so high?"

"I guess they could use other rocks or maybe they had some kind of rope they made," James suggested.

"It might've been different when they were here also, perhaps more boulders in front," Priscilla added though she had no idea.

"It's so beautiful. They were good artists," Grace kept saying. "I want to draw some."

"Well, memorize the designs now. You can draw them when you are back at home," Priscilla said, forcing away the memory of other petroglyphs and Cord. "For now it is flower gathering time, don't you think?"

Grace was excited at everything she saw, as despite living in a desert, they didn't often come out into the terrain that could properly be termed desert.

Several hours later with many flowers to press, they were back at the house for Ben to put the buggy away. Inside at the table, they found the right books for Grace to use with sheets of newspaper to protect their pages.

"You find the prettiest ones," Priscilla explained, "form them as you wish and then put them between the pages. Pressure is what makes them last forever."

"Forever?"

"Yes, with both time and pressure, they will last forever."

"How long does it take?" Grace asked with wide eyes.

"Awhile."

As Grace worked on arranging her flowers, Rose gave Priscilla a meaningful look. "And how long you going to let this go on, girl?"

Priscilla didn't pretend she didn't know what she meant. "It's not all my choice," she retorted running the tip of her fingers over the satiny petals on a purple lupine.

"Isn't it? You know that man wants to be with you. Isn't it time, before it's too late, that you find what is stopping him?"

Priscilla nodded as she had been thinking along the same lines. Whatever Cord's reasons were for avoiding her, she'd had enough of it. She had given him time, but time wasn't fixing it. He would someday have to come to the house-- and when she had him here, he wasn't leaving without answers. What time wasn't solving, she felt confident pressure would.

With the first warm weather of May starting to remind Tucsonans what the word desert meant, Cord was glad to get his job done before it got hot. He pushed Clinton Adams into the cell before he removed his handcuffs.

"You got no right to arrest me," Adams complained, as he sat on the bunk.

"Tell it to the judge." Cord closed the door.

Rafe was looking out the window. "What's he in for?" he asked without much real interest.

"Ridge brought the charges-- theft at the Pedrales. Guess he doesn't like working much."

"Maybe he likes free meals," Rafe suggested still watching the street.

"What's going on out there?" Cord asked sitting at his desk.

"Nothing." He turned back to slump into the chair. "When are you going down to your ranch?"

"She out there with her new boyfriend?" Cord lit a cigar putting his feet up on his desk.

Rafe sucked in a breath and blew it out. "He's a slick one. That's all I can say for him."

"Slick as in suspicious?"

"I can't say that. Just slick dressing, well trimmed mustache, lacquered hair." He laughed without humor. "Not a strong man though. All he's got going for him is money. But then what am I saying? That's not ever an *all*."

"It does matter."

"Is that why you dumped Priscilla?"

"I didn't dump her."

"Tell it to the judge."

"I am doing what's best for her."

"And you?"

"By connection, yes."

James came through the door with a big smile. "Whatcha up to?" he asked as he looked to see if there was fresh coffee.

"Make it if you want it," Cord said.

"Nah, not that big a deal. I am here on a quest."

"And that is?"

"You are invited to our home for dinner tomorrow night."

"I'm busy."

James chuckled. "It's a party celebrating Grace getting all As."

"I'll talk to her about it later."

"And her birthday."

Cord frowned. "This is not her birthday."

"But we missed the last nine and so it's to make up for them."

Cord blew out the smoke and looked at him through narrowed eyes. James laughed. "You scared to come?"

"Might be."

James looked at Rafe. "You're invited too."

"Ellen coming?" Rafe asked frowning.

"She's been invited, of course. I don't know if she said yes."

"I won't be there."

"Grace likes you a lot. She will miss you."

Rafe shrugged.

"What about you?" James said looking at Cord. "You also going to disappoint your daughter?"

He hadn't seen Priscilla since that day in April when he had ridden past them on their way out to the desert. That is if he didn't count his dreams where he saw her every night. He knew he couldn't avoid her forever. "All right, I'll be there if nothing comes up." Mostly he didn't see himself as a coward—except where it came to her.

"Good. See you tomorrow." James grinned and waved as he walked out the door.

"You should come too," Cord told Rafe.

"Oh right, like the new convert is telling the unsaved what to do?" Rafe said with a sneer.

"Look, I don't like it either. I plan to stay as little time as possible, and you could do the same. Maybe Ellen won't be there."

"She will if it's for Grace. And maybe that boyfriend too."

Cord studied him through the smoke. "I can't argue with you. And I put in a request for replacements. It's just a matter of how long it takes to hire a new Deputy Marshal. When that happens, we're out of here. You can see how well you like starving down on my ranch."

Rafe forced a laugh. "We won't starve. I know how to snare rabbits. Always rabbits or lizards around." He stared out the window again.

Cord thought about being near Priscilla for an evening. It wouldn't be easy, but he needed to tell her how it was going to be. Not telling her to her face was cowardly. He didn't have to give her the reason. She would just argue with him. He would keep her safe and that meant a long way from him.

Preparing a special dinner for Grace's celebration took both Priscilla and Rose's afternoon. Grace had chosen the menu, which involved roasted chickens, mashed potatoes, gravy, salad of mixed greens and most especially a chocolate cake. Although James had said Cord agreed to come, if nothing arose. She felt nervous that he would find an excuse to stay away.

When dinner was on its way, she went upstairs and dressed in a striped cotton dress with a scoop neck and a bit of lace at sleeve and neckline. Downstairs she got the door herself when Ellen arrived.

"No boyfriend?" she asked as she had told Ellen she could bring a friend.

"I couldn't stand it another hour," Ellen said as she walked into the parlor. "I thought... Well never mind."

"James said Rafe wouldn't come."

Ellen sighed. "I had thought... well I might as well confess, since it was a terrible idea. I wanted to make Rafael jealous as I thought he'd then be asking me the big question."

"Ah manipulation, always a wise choice," Priscilla said as she poured Ellen a small glass of wine.

"So it seems. He just quit coming around, didn't want to compete for me. I guess he never cared that much." She frowned as she stared into the wine glass.

"Ellen, playing games is always a mistake. I suggest you talk to him as soon as you can, before he leaves Tucson, and you lose out."

"Oh like you are such an example of the direct approach," Ellen jibed.

"I have been giving Cord time. That has ended, and tonight he will be here. When he is, everybody will leave early. I hope... Then, he and I will talk."

"Where's Grace?"

"James is helping her with a homework assignment. That teacher does expect a lot from them. I needed to help Rose-- so James was elected to get that out of the way before company arrives."

The next knock at the door was Judge and Melissa Emerson. "Where's the birthday girl?" Judge asked and went into the den to see if he could help get this homework thing resolved.

"Will Marshal O'Brian be here?" Melissa asked.

"Unless something got in his way." Priscilla was beginning to have her doubts. Well if he didn't show up, she'd beard him in his den. One way or another, she had waited long enough.

The next knock at the door caused her to smile. He was here. When she opened it, he stood on the porch. She supposed his coming in the front door was supposed to be a signal to her that their relationship had changed. Her smile broadened.

"Marshal, how good to see you," she said as she stood back to let him enter.

He handed her a small wrapped gift which she set on a table. "For Grace," he said unnecessarily. He was wearing a white shirt, the usual gun belt and badge as a reminder of who he was.

"Now you don't need that heavy gun belt in here, do you?" she asked and smiling she reached out, untied the holster from his thigh and began undoing the buckle despite the fact that she was now being watched by everyone in the room.

"It's a habit," he said with a bemused smile as she deftly removed it from him and hung it over the coat rack.

"Nothing here will endanger you, I assure you," she said thinking that gun belt would not be the last thing she removed from the marshal before the night was over.

Outside in the dark, Martin Matthews had watched guests arriving at the Wesley home. It had been some time since he had lurked and watched Priscilla. This night, mere coincidence had brought him here. He had had other eggs to fry as the saying went.

The day that he had gone out to the Wright ranch and taken whatever he thought he could get away with, had been the day he turned his life around. Up until then he had been using his accounting skills to steal. At the Wright house he had taken whatever he wanted. He had laughed at how Richard had seen himself as so superior. Well, who was in the ground?

As he had walked through the rooms, he'd taken what money and valuables he found finally stopping at the gun rack. He knew Rich had just acquired a fine Winchester, Model 1886. His boss hardly had a chance to fire it before he was killed. He grinned as he took it along with bullets enough to supply it for some time.

From that day on, he had spent hours practicing out on the desert. It wasn't long before he could hit whatever he wanted within an inch. His nights had been filled in other ways.

As he had done with Rich, he began to go through people's homes or businesses. He was clever in how he did it. He smirked, thinking how stupid other burglars were. He didn't take all of anything. He took what wouldn't be missed or might have the owners thinking they had miscounted or misplaced. The rifle went with him, as a way to assure his safety, if he was caught. He never had been, and the hunting had been good.

Watching the marshal ride up to the Wesley home changed his trajectory. Stealing no longer seemed enough. He wanted revenge, revenge for the things he'd never had, for what he could never be.

With a growing rage, he had watched the handsome man walk into that house as a guest, a sanctuary he was now denied. He had seen the arrogance, with which the man stalked the

streets of Tucson or rode out of town and came back with innocent prisoners.

Cord O'Brian had everything Martin had ever wanted. The
strength, the power, and the way he could do anything, even kill
Richard Wright, and get away with it. As Martin stood in the
darkness, he knew he had something that the marshal did not—
the power to take his life.

Smiling as he leaned back against the wall of the house across
the street, he decided he would wait, as any good hunter did.
When the marshal walked from that house, at the end of the
evening, he would not yet know it, but he would be a walking
dead man.

Martin would finally get the revenge he had been seeking all
of his life. As he thought of his power, he felt a warmth surge
through his body. He reached for the small whiskey flask he
carried and took a drink. Tonight he was the hunter, and the
marshal was his unwitting prey.

As the evening wound down, Cord knew Priscilla was pleased
with how it had gone. He was too. He had bought Grace a delicate, gold charm bracelet with three charms already on it—a
heart, a cactus and a small flower. Grace had been thrilled and
immediately wore it jingling the little charms. No other gift
matched it in her eyes-- and when it came time for bed, she had
given him a big hug.

With the Judge and Melissa leaving with Ellen, Cord headed
for his gun belt ready to make his own exit. The opportunity to
tell Priscilla would have to wait.

"I want to talk to you," Priscilla told him. "Can you stay until I
get back down?" He turned back and lifted his hands in agreement as he watched her go up the stairs.

When she returned, she led him into the den. "We'll have
more privacy in here," she said.

That sounded like a safe place. When they were there, she

376

closed the door. He was surprised, when she shot a bolt, that it now had a lock. He moved across the room to sit on the edge of the desk waiting for whatever she intended to tell him. If she wanted to condemn him for leaving her without explanations, he deserved it. When she had said her piece, he would say his.

"You have been avoiding me," she said as she pulled the curtains closed, then moved to him, pushing his knees apart and pressing herself against him. "I tried to give you time to work this through." Her hands were now on the buttons of his shirt. He should have stopped her, but he didn't. He felt the buttons being undone, her fingers against his skin. She pulled his shirt from his pants and pushed it open.

"This won't work you know," he said hoarsely.

"Let me see about that," she said, undoing his belt buckle.

"You can't do that here."

She put her fingers to the buttons on his pants. He felt on fire with her touch, but he had to stop her. He took her hand and pulled it away. "You said talk," he managed.

"We will. After." She pushed his hands aside. In a moment, she had undone the buttons and pushed his pants away from his erection. By then he had lost the ability to say no or pretty much anything as she pushed his shirt from his shoulders. Pressing against his bared skin, she pulled his head down to where their lips met. Her tongue delved into his mouth. Whatever willpower he had had was gone as he pulled her up onto his lap, his swollen organ now against her hip as he began to caress her body, pulling her dress from her shoulders, baring her breasts.

"You know what I am wearing under this dress?" she asked as she shifted her position now to straddle him, lifting her skirt.

He knew now as he felt her bare legs, her skin against his. He managed to stop before he let her take him into her. "No protection."

"Oh that." She smiled then, left him for a moment and from a box on the desk retrieved a small package.

"Where did you get that?" he asked with what little sense he had left.

"I had James buy them for me two weeks ago," she whispered as she sheathed him with it. He might've wondered about that but lost the ability to think when she touched him again, caressing, kissing, tongue and lips arousing him even further.

He lifted her and laid her on the rug, coming over her, and entering with one swift movement. From that moment on, he was lost to the touch and feel of her, the burning intensity of having her hands on his buttocks, her nipples against his chest. Their climaxes came fast and hard and he collapsed to the side of her breathing hard and realizing they were still half clothed.

"God," he whispered sucking in and then blowing out the air and thinking he'd never known anything like how it was with her, and he never would again.

"Don't think that way," she said, seeming to read his mind, as she kissed his neck. "You are being negative about us."

"Angel, there can't be an *us,* and I have to go tonight."

She smiled. "Where's your horse?"

"Tied to the hitching rail?" he guessed with a faint smile.

"Not if Ben followed orders."

"This will not work," he said as he stood.

"Tell me more about it when we get upstairs. You are spending the night. Did I tell you that?"

He gave up knowing he wanted this one last night with her as much as he had wanted anything in his life. What difference could one night be? He watched her adjust her own clothing as he did his. Not that anyone would see them walking up the stairs, but it seemed the thing to do. He would tell her, explain to her why this wouldn't work, but he would stay until just before dawn as he had so many times before. Soon he'd be south of her, a long way from a temptation he clearly never would be able to resist if it was close.

CHAPTER 29

Martin had watched outside and grown more furious as he saw the marshal's horse led away by big Ben. Every service for that wretched man and none for Martin. He had a lot of people he'd someday pay back.

When the others left, he waited with his rifle ready. It was when the lights went off in the house that he understood—that trollop. Furious at being thwarted, he drank more from the whiskey bottle, realizing he had drained it. He would get the marshal somehow, someday but for this night, he was tired of standing and waiting, tired of being beaten once again.

He thought then of Sally. She had told him not to come to her. She didn't have a gentleman friend, she had claimed. She just didn't want to be with him that way again.

Who was she, a whore, to tell him such a thing? He felt a rage building as he threw the whiskey bottle against the wall watching it shatter. He needed a release, and she would provide it—one way or the other.

Holding Priscilla in his arms, Cord watched the eastern horizon turn pink behind the Catalinas. He felt her fingers now moving against his chest, his nipples, his belly and below. They had made love twice during the night. He felt sated, but it appeared she did not.

"You think I'm up to this?" he whispered as she grasped the proof that he was.

"After we talk," she said. "You are planning to leave soon, aren't you?"

"I usually do."

"I want you to stay not just tonight, but to keep clothing here and stay often with me if not all the time."

He realized she was offering a big thing to have a man sleeping over when they were not married. He wouldn't do it to her reputation, but he understood what it meant that she offered it.

"Cord, I am not saying this lightly. I mean it." She rose up on one elbow to meet his gaze with no doubt in her eyes.

"I know you do." The moment had come. He had to find the right words. "It cannot be, Angel. I won't let it be. You will never be safe next to me. If you don't understand that, I do,"

"Ah, so that's it. I will never be safe next to you, is that it? All right, I accept that. But you have to accept this. I will never be happy without you."

"You don't know that."

"Yes, I do. I want whatever I can have with you, Cord."

"I am going to quit the marshal's job as soon as they can get a replacement down here. Then I will be heading for my ranch, but it's no place for you down there. It's still dangerous, even with Geronimo no longer on the loose. I can't make a living on it for maybe several years if then."

"I don't care about that. I could go with you. I'm stronger than you think."

"I know that too. It's me. I'm the one not strong enough. I see you lying dead that day in the arroyo, and I can't do it."

"Then so be it. I will stay here and let you come to me when you can. I will do whatever it takes to be with you, as much as I can, but know this—I will never be happy without you near."

"And what will Rose and James think or Grace?"

"Grace is too young to understand anything but that her daddy is here when he can be. James bought a shirt. I told him who it was for. It's hanging in the wardrobe. In the morning, after breakfast here, when you leave, you will be wearing it."

He laughed then. "Your brand?"

"You might say that. It's not pink or lavender though." She smiled as she bent over him and claimed his lips with a searing kiss.

"You know this changes nothing," he said when she gave him air to speak.

She nodded and bent to kiss him again.

An hour later when Cord walked down the stairs, Priscilla was still sleeping. He wore his new blue shirt, his badge pinned to it. As he went by the coat rack, he put on his gun belt. He heard Rose in the kitchen. Unsure how she felt about him being there, he walked in anyway.

She looked up and grinned at him. "Coffee ready, Marshal. You like pancakes for breakfast today and some salt pork?"

"Sounds good." He poured the coffee and sat at the table as he tried to adjust his thinking to his new position in this family— and it was a family even if some were paid. "Mind if I smoke?" he asked before he rolled a cigarette.

"No problem at all." She handed him a dish for the ashes. "We'll have to get more ashtrays, I'm thinking." She chuckled.

Before Cord could respond to that, he heard a racing horse coming into the yard. He went out onto the porch as Rafe jumped from the saddle.

"Martin Matthews went nuts last night and beat Sally near to death. Doc doesn't know if she will make it."

"Martin in jail?" he asked as he decided breakfast was out and yelled for Ben to bring his horse.

"You spent the night?" Rafe asked as he looked with shock at the horse being led to them by Ben.

"Did anyone go after Martin?" Cord asked as he mounted. Rose came out the door yelling for him to wait as she handed him two biscuits wrapped in a small towel.

"I'll be back later," he said as he rode out. "Tell her when she gets up."

Riding out of the yard, Rafe said, "Some of the men went after him. He's got a rifle, Cord, and knows how to use it. He nicked one of them chasing him. He is heading up Sabino."

"Why the hell would he do that?"

"Likely he knows we'd cut him off at Oracle if he went that way, not going to work going south. I guess he thinks he can head over the mountain and go out the other side heading east. With the telegraph, he's not making sense anyway you look at it."

"I have to go by the office and get my rifle, ammunition, water, and I guess a bedroll if this is going to stretch out into a hunt."

"You spent the night at Priscilla's?" Rafe repeated more surprised by that than he apparently had been at Martin's revealed brutality.

"It changes nothing. When the new marshal arrives, I'm gone."

"Me too then. I just wondered."

At the office, Cord grabbed a jacket not for warmth as it was getting hotter every day but protection, in case he had to head into rougher country. Sabino had a wagon road part of the way up, crossing the creek several times if it wasn't in flood. After the wet winter, spring had been dry. He didn't anticipate there'd be any difficult fords.

"Hey Marshal, when do I get out?" Adams protested, his nose against the bars. "And when's breakfast?"

In the office, Cord told Rafe, "You hold down the fort, get food for that worthless excuse for a man. Go see if the sheriff will keep him on charges over there."

"I should go with you."

"You should stay here and make sure town stays peaceful."

"I told you he's got a rifle."

"I remember."

Cord went outside and mounted Jeb, nudging him into an easy trot. His mind was not on the manhunt although there would be time for that. Instead he thought of Priscilla, how beautiful she had looked lying in the bed, her golden hair spread across the pillow as it earlier had been spread across his chest. He knew he needed to put that from his mind as it could get him killed-- but until he got to the canyon mouth, he'd enjoy the memories. They might be all he'd ever have.

When he got up to where Sabino Creek cut off into the mountains, there were five men waiting. "We made sure he didn't sneak back out. Want us to go up with you?" Jace Winslow asked.

Cord shook his head. "It'll be better if I go alone and take it slow and easy, keeping him moving. Send a wire ahead to Tombstone and east just in case he gets out and heads that way.

"You expect that?" Jace asked with a frown. "I saw what he did to Sally. I don't want him doing it to some other gal."

"He won't.

As Cord worked his way up the canyon, he kept as much as possible to the side of the trail, watching for activity ahead but staying in the shadows and protected by the trees or cliffs where it was possible. Being bushwhacked wasn't on his agenda for how to go out and Matthews was not the type of man to face another squarely. A coward made him the most dangerous man to track.

About a mile into the canyon, he stopped, dismounted and listened again as he let Jeb drink and took some sips from his own canteen. The noise of the birds in the trees overhead told him that if Martin had passed this way, it had been awhile.

Sabino was always a wonderful place to spend time with multitudes of different birds, the huge cottonwood, Mexican blue oak, sycamore, and willows. Grass was lush enough to tempt Jeb who took full advantage of the momentary break. As they headed upstream, Cord walked in some of the roughest places. It wouldn't do to lame his horse.

There were only a few places that it would be easy to leave the canyon. He checked out one side canyon, looking for hoof prints. Seeing nothing fresh, he went back to the main canyon. As he rode slowly, he scanned ahead for movement.

Half an hour later he crossed the creek again aware suddenly that he was hearing no birds. It had become quieter than he ever remembered. He stopped Jeb again and listened. There was a kind of eerie stillness to the air. This didn't sound like the kind of thing that meant someone had been by ahead of him. More like an atmospheric stillness. He looked to the south to see if a storm was brewing. Nothing. The sky was clear and the air growing hotter.

Because he didn't want to miss a sign, he took longer than usual to reach the upper mouth of the canyon. Here the sides were steep, the creek curling among boulders and shaded with tall cottonwoods.

Again he dismounted and let Jeb nibble at what grass there was. Even though he had seen no fresh hoof prints, he knew his man was ahead. There was no place else he could be. Maybe by now Martin would be convinced no one was following and he'd make a mistake. Cord's problem was to be sure he didn't give him a target, as he mounted and again steadily moved forward.

There were times he'd have enjoyed riding up the canyon but not on a manhunt. Whenever Priscilla came to his mind, he forced the thoughts away. He wasn't sure what he could do about the relationship and right now any distraction was dangerous.

With the afternoon building heat, he stopped again to drink from his canteen, and it was then that he heard the roar, a rumbling sound as though a flashflood was coming. Dry as it had been, there could have been no flashfloods. Then he felt the earth move, frightening his horse. Behind him came the sounds of boulders crashing in the canyon. He didn't need to look to the nearby steep walls to know he wasn't far enough up the canyon to be safe in an earthquake, which was clearly what this had to be. He kicked his heels into Jeb's side urging him to a run.

His gelding panicked as the first rocks began to tumble off the cliffs above. Cord kept his stirrups when the first rocks hit him, one glancing off his forehead knocking his hat off, others hitting his shoulders and back. "Go," he yelled at the gelding, urging him to more speed. The rock, which struck his head and knocked him from the saddle, he hadn't seen coming.

Moments later with the dust rising all around him, Cord realized he was lying on the ground, rocks covering his right leg, his head dizzy from the blow. He had to get farther up the canyon, above the steep walls, or he could be buried where he had fallen. His right leg hurt making him unsure how badly it had been damaged in the fall from the horse-- or was it the rubble it was buried under?

Before he could do more than begin to throw off rocks, he heard laughter from higher up the canyon. He looked toward it and saw Martin balancing on a huge boulder and looking down on him a rifle in his hand.

"Always so high and mighty," Matthews screamed with the sound of excitement. "Could do it all. Well how about this, Mr. Hawk? Who's the predator now?" He laughed hysterically again as he lifted his rifle to make certain Cord understood what was about to happen. "I'm a crack shot now. Did you know that? You should. You know everything, don't you?"

Cord had faced death before and understood this was going to be his end—shot to death by a coward and unable to defend himself. Even if he had been able to uncover his gun from the rubble, Martin was beyond its range.

"Aren't you going to beg me, mister high and mighty," Martin screamed again as he brought his rifle to bear.

Begging would have changed nothing-- so Cord remained silent, no longer trying to remove the rocks on his leg as he watched Martin bring the gun to bear on his chest. In seconds all thought would be ended for him. He let Priscilla's beautiful face be the last in his imagination.

The movement of the earth again sent more rocks tumbling off the cliff. A few bounded off Cord's chest, but there was no gunshot. When the dust settled, he looked toward the big boulder. It and Martin were gone.

It took Cord a good half an hour to uncover himself, find his hat, assure himself that his gun was usable, and then get to where Martin had stood. His leg hurt enough, that he picked up a mesquite branch to use as a cane. Where the boulder had been, he could see it far below. It had rolled taking Martin with it into the lower canyon. He saw no sign of the man.

He stood a moment thinking of the irony. He had been dead, and Martin alive. An act of nature had changed the picture in an instant. He would not climb down to see if Martin had survived the fall. At this point, his own survival odds weren't good.

He was up a canyon, where below rocks and boulders were still falling, as the earth tried to find equilibrium after its shaking. His only choice was to go farther up, which meant a long hike to find the other route down. With a bum leg that wouldn't be easy, but he would have water half the way. Most likely, unless Jeb had also been caught by a boulder, ahead was his horse, and he began to walk.

The earth shook again, but this time he was able to keep his balance. Farther up the mountain, away from the tall cliff that had nearly buried him, the earth moving was less threatening. Another mile and he saw Jeb grazing under a mesquite trailing his reins. The gelding was still edgy from the unusual movements, but he let Cord mount. Slowly they climbed the mountain, watching for places the trail might've been shaken away. Twice they went down to the creek for water.

Cord looked to the sky, trying to determine what time of day it was. He'd been up this way before but a lot of what it looked like had changed. The main mountain road was two thirds of the way up. When he reached it, he could start back down. By then the sun would have set. Even with a nearly full moon, it would be too risky to travel once the light went.

The earth could have changed a lot of things with its shaking —not the least of which would be the old wagon road back to Tucson. There were a lot of boulders along the route, which could easily move again even without another quake.

He tried not to think about his daughter or Priscilla and what kind of damage might've been done to the Wesley home or the two he loved so much. He had looked back and seen what the shaking had done to Sabino Canyon, as it had thrown boulders bigger than houses from the top of the canyon to the bottom. Would Tucson still be standing when he got there?

All this time he had been determined to keep his ladies safe, but he had had no protection against what had happened. In fact, with Martin ready to shoot him, only the second tremor had saved his life. He gritted his teeth as he felt pain in leg, shoulder and head. He would not stop. Not until he was forced by lack of light. All he could think was that he had to get back.

When the quake hit Tucson, Priscilla was in the kitchen with Rose. "What was that?" Rose asked, as the floor rocked and threatened to throw them off their feet.

"Earthquake," Priscilla said. "Get out of the house."

"Like who can walk?" Rose complained, but they did make their way to the backdoor, and then into the yard away from the buildings. Priscilla felt like going to her knees to find stability as the movement seemed to go on forever.

All she could think about was where was Cord? The returning posse had said he had headed up Sabino after Martin. How far up? What would such a quake do to that narrow canyon? To someone in it? She tried imagining where he was. She visualized a protective light surrounding him, protecting, keeping him safe.

When the movement stopped, and they thought it was over, it shook again. By then Ben and James were out of the barns. The four of them stood in the yard looking at the buildings relieved that all seemed to be standing.

Priscilla looked toward the Catalinas. A huge cloud of dust rose from where Sabino was. Had he been crushed under the rocks, had the canyon totally collapsed? What was causing the dust, or was that smoke?

When the shaking stopped, they looked around the house. There were no cracks in walls or foundations. Inside a few things had fallen off shelves but otherwise it was as though nothing had happened.

"James," she said as she came outside dressed in a shirt, riding skirt, with a hat and boots, "please saddle Jezebel."

He looked at her with concern. "Going where?"

She knew where she wanted to go. She wanted to head up to Sabino and look for Cord. If he was buried under rock, she would find his body. She knew what she wanted-- she also understood she wouldn't do it. With all those big boulders, it'd be hours or maybe days before the canyon would be safe. She had to trust he'd get back to her. He wasn't dead. She would have known if he was.

"I need to get Grace, and then see what I can do downtown. There might be injuries-- Doc will need help."

"All right. I'll come with you." Five minutes later, they rode into town and saw that the most damage had been done to the older adobe buildings. A few had collapsed. When she got to the school, the children were out front, and the building looked to be untouched.

Grace came running. "Mommy," she cried and threw her arms around Priscilla the instant she had dismounted. "I was so afraid. Is our home all right? Where is Daddy?"

"The house is fine, and your daddy is away from town on work," Priscilla said tears running down her cheeks. She was thrilled to hear the word from Grace that she had never expected.

"When will he be back?"

"As soon as he can. For now, James will take you home. I need to go downtown and see if Doc Hadley needs help."

Grace nodded as James made room for her in the front of his saddle. Priscilla lifted the little girl up in front of him. "I'll be back when I am not needed," she said as she remounted and rode down to the doctor's office.

For the next few hours she helped with bandaging cuts, splinting broken limbs, and washing bruises and bumps. The people had been fortunate even if some of the buildings not so much. There would be some rebuilding required, but the Pedrales, courthouse, and major brick buildings looked fine other than bottles and glasses knocked off shelves.

When the stream of injured ended, with some sadness at Doc's telling her that Sally had died, Priscilla felt free to head for the marshal's office.

"Have you heard anything?" she asked Rafe who was taking supper to the prisoner in the back room.

He shook his head. "He'll be all right though. He always is."

"Yes, he will." She sighed and then remembered something else. "Rafe, I need to talk to you."

His expression was dour, as he closed the door between the cells and office.

"Ellen told me something."

"She's getting married, I suppose." His expression of gloom deepened. "I don't want to hear it."

"She's not getting married. She never wanted to be courted by that young man. She wanted to make you jealous."

Rafe exhaled heavily. "What?"

"She's young. She thought if you saw her with someone else, you'd propose. You hadn't, and she felt you needed a nudge. She told me yesterday. I told her to tell you, but I don't know if she will. She's embarrassed after my telling her what a foolish thing she did."

"You can't be serious."

"I couldn't be more so. Perhaps I am revealing a secret, but I feel like, after this quake, that such a thing just shouldn't be kept from you. I could see you were hurting over what you saw as her rejection. Try to understand that she also felt rejected by your not asking her to be your wife."

He cursed, mixed in with some words she'd never heard but assumed were Yaqui. After a long moment, he looked at her. "You sure about this. He didn't just dump her, and now she's trying to get back with me only to do this again?"

"If I wasn't sure, I would have said nothing. She's immature, but I believe she loves you. She made a foolhardy mistake. You will have to decide what you do with this information. I don't know if it all has changed how you feel about her."

"I only wish," he said glumly.

"Then talk to her. You know life can be over very quickly."

"You're afraid it is for Cord, aren't you, that this is what my uncle warned him about," he said not as a question.

"No, I feel he's alive. I just can't know for sure. Maybe I just feel him as I always do, and he is on the other side. I don't think so. I think he'll be back when he can."

"You have to be realistic," he said. "I rode up to the mouth of Sabino and it's changed-- huge boulders, the size of a house are now on the floor of the canyon, dust swirling still like a fog. If he was in the middle, when it hit, I don't think even he could have survived it."

"Then we have to believe he was not," she said fighting back tears. She would only cry when she knew there was no choice. For now she had hope.

That night she lay awake for hours as she thought over the last night he and she had spent, the feel of his strong body against hers. She remembered then the first time she had seen him. Oh she had seen him around town but it was just an anonymous person. That day, she had really seen him. She had been helping Doc Hadley and taken Martin Matthews into her home to recuperate from a gunshot wound.

What a foolish girl she had been back then as she had mistaken Martin's smoothness for strength. She remembered when Cord had walked into her home, spurs on his boots as he'd just ridden in from chasing down another lead regarding the stagecoach robbery. Dusty, tired from the trail, he had come to get more information from Martin, regarding Abigail's disappearance.

She grinned as she remembered the look of repugnance on Cord's face, when he had made no secret of his disdain for a man who would be laid low by a wound so insignificant. She had bristled at that. Who was he to tell Doc Hadley how serious a man's wounds were. Before he'd stalked out of the room that day, Cord had then given her that look, the one she had seen many times since, when he'd been frustrated with her.

After that, she had enjoyed their infrequent meetings and arguments—even though she hadn't known why. It had all changed on the railroad platform as they both waited for something that would totally change their lives in ways they couldn't have begun to imagine.

If something happened to him... She forced the thought from her mind. He was alive. He would be back-- what then? He was so set on their not being a family. There had to be a way to make him see that they were meant to be together.

She watched out her window as the big round moon rose higher in the sky. It sent a ghostly light over the mountains and the tree outside. She refused to see it as ominous. Cord would be back... She supposed it was an unlikely match, but it was the only one she could now imagine for herself. It was Cord O'Brian or no man.

She heard the hoot of the horned owl. No, it was not a sign of death. It was just an owl. She heard another owl, maybe two-- the sound was like laughter. Then the cry of a nighthawk as it swooped. She would put negativity from her. He was alive. She would accept no other outcome. He would return.

She got out of bed and picked Cord's shirt up from the floor where he had dropped it. Taking it into her arms, like a kind of teddy bear-- she fell asleep with the scent of him in her nostrils.

With morning she was dressed and downstairs when she heard James shout. She hoped against hope as she ran to the back porch. Cord was just dismounting, looking exhausted beyond measure, blood on his face, torn shirt and pants. When he saw her, he put out his arms-- and she ran to him like a bird returning to its nest.

"Thank God," she whispered. "I was so afraid."

He kissed her hair. "It came close."

She shivered, as she looked into his eyes. "But you beat it." She smiled then. "Are you hungry?"

"I could eat, but mostly just hungry to hold you. I was scared, Angel."

"It must have been terrifying up there."

"Oh that, but more fear it had been worse down here, and you were dead. Where is Grace?"

"Sleeping in this morning. She is fine, shaken a little that's all."

"I wanted to get to you right away but had to go up before I could come down, had to bed down up there or take a chance on breaking Jeb's leg and maybe mine. He's been through a lot too and needs water."

"I'll take care of him," James said patting Cord's back.

"Don't let him have too much right away. It was a dry ride off the mountain."

"Will do. Sure glad to see you back here, boy."

"Me too," Cord said with a little laugh. When Priscilla saw he was limping, she put her arm around him, insisting on helping him into the house. "Rock hit that leg but it mostly just twisted when I fell."

In the kitchen, she got him a glass of water, and then fussed over him, pulling off his shirt, washing his abrasions, and then bandaging the injury to his forehead. Rose began cooking him the breakfast he had missed only the day before.

"Martin is dead," he told her as Rose handed him a cup of coffee.

"You killed him?"

He shook his head. "It happened after the first quake. He had me. He knew it. He was up the canyon, high above me on a boulder, laughing, sounding demented. The first quake had knocked me off Jeb. I was half buried in rubble. He pointed his rifle at me. As far up as he was, no way I could get a shot off, even if I could have gotten my gun out from under the rocks."

"He changed his mind?"

"The earth moved again. When I could look, the boulder and Martin had disappeared. By the time I got up there, there was no sign of him, no movement below. I didn't go looking. He had to have been crushed as it rolled taking him with it."

"An act of providence some would say."

He smiled. "Well it was luck for sure and mine, not his. Was anybody killed down here?"

"The school wasn't damaged. Grace had questions about what

caused it, but mostly it was interesting to the children. In town some did lose their homes or had them damaged if they were adobe, some glassware broke, but overall, the buildings are fine. Injuries minor. The biggest damage was out where you were."

He looked at her then, and saw her with papers and tobacco as she began rolling a cigarette. "What are you doing?" he asked.

"Didn't you want one? Maybe you'd prefer a cigar," she suggested. "They are in the den, but I'd go get one."

"No," he said with a tired smile, "but why are you doing this?"

"I thought I should learn to do it," she said as she handed him a very well formed cigarette, and then flicked a match and lit it when he put it to his lips.

"Is there a reason?" he asked as he inhaled the smoke, holding it before he released it.

"Well when you come visiting, I'd like it to be maximum pleasure, master of this house and me."

Then he laughed. "Yeah sure on that last addition. Well, I had time to think, after the earth knocked some sense into me, and coming down off that mountain when I still wasn't sure if I would find you alive. I want you to marry me, Angel. Will you be my wife?"

"I have one question before I answer." She saw by the look on his face he was expecting it to relate to his gun or who knew what, but he nodded his acceptance. "Do you love me?"

He smiled. "I love you more than life itself."

"I love you too. And the answer then is yes. Right away. Tomorrow. I want to be your wife, but I admit I am surprised."

"I've been trying to control everything, but it didn't work. When the quake hit, I realized I wasn't in control of anything. A few minutes later, there was Martin pointing the rifle at me, and there is no way he'd miss. He had me trapped by the rock fall. Chance or fate stepped in. Who controls that? Whoever or whatever it is, it's not me."

Rose put his food in front of him. "Whatever it was did it," she said, "we're just almighty glad here that you came back to us."

"Are you sure about the marriage?" Priscilla asked as he began to eat. "I don't want you doing this and then feel trapped later."

When he looked at her, his smile was relaxed and more at ease than any she had ever seen on his face. "I am sure. Maybe you have the doubts now."

She bent to kiss him. "Rose, would you tell James to go get the judge before this man changes his mind—and when you get back, wake up Grace and tell her she's going to be a bridesmaid."

EPILOGUE

Circle O Ranch -- December 1889

"Mama, when will they be here?"

Priscilla grinned at Grace who was approaching a height that would soon have her looking up at her. "Anytime now," she said, as she had the last five times Grace had asked. The truth was she wasn't quite sure when they would arrive.

Ellen came in from the kitchen. "The pumpkin pies are ready or so Rose said." Ellen had a pregnancy bump out in front of her that made her look like a pumpkin herself as she plopped into a chair. "This baby has to be born soon, or I swear I'll take to rolling from place to place."

"Hopefully while Abby is here to help with the delivery," Priscilla said as she heard Jesse crying from his room alerting her that it was time for lunch.

"I'll bring him to you," Grace offered.

Priscilla opened the bodice of her dress as the hungry baby latched onto her breast and began sucking.

Two years earlier with three wagons loaded with goods, they

had all come to Cord's ranch despite Cord's reluctance to see her risk Grace or her life down along the border. It hadn't turned out to be as risky as he had feared. It had helped to have a good sized crew, as Ben, James and Rafe helped drive the herd they had purchased from the heirs to the Wright ranch. They had bought just a few hundred head to get the feel of the ranch land.

Cord had not wanted her to use her trust fund money, but his giving in on his pride had eased a lot of things, as they temporarily had brought in extra workers to expand the original adobe. She had loved the original structure as it sat beneath tall cottonwoods, mountains beyond, a small stream that most of the year flowed near the house. The charm was such that when they discussed how they could add on. It had stayed, as the core, to become a large kitchen with big cook stove, long table, ample counters and cupboards.

The living room, with a tall, beamed ceiling, had a massive stone fireplace-- rather like the one on the Circle R. Opposing it was a bookshelf wall now more half filled, with more books regularly added.

There added on enough bedrooms for company and their expanding family. The watering system was surprisingly effective with a mix of tanks and water towers. Using Sam's idea for pipes behind the cook stove, they even had hot water for baths.

Before leaving her Tucson home, she had decided which items she wanted to take south with her. They had loaded the wagons and taken sofas, sideboards, end tables, dishes, pans. Once they got settled on the ranch though, Cord had learned, as handy as he had been with a gun, he was equally adept with wood and built bedsteads, dressers, and cupboards.

Nearby, forming something of a compound, if there ever was trouble, they had built two smaller homes. One for Rafe and Ellen, the other for Rose and James with a bunkhouse near the barn where Ben and any hired men slept. In the center they had successfully started vegetable and flower gardens providing a lot of their own food.

The ranch had had a barn in pretty good shape, but they enlarged it to give them space for horse stalls, a milking stand which Ben happily handled, as well as one side for a chicken house. Corrals stretched down toward one of the ponds. One pasture was being cut for hay each summer to provide for those times when they needed to supplement the cows before calving.

They had decided to home school Grace, but found when they began, some of the Tohono O'Odham who lived in the region were interested in schooling for their children as well as a few families from across the border. That had expanded even more when Rafe's little brother, Gabriel, had decided he wanted to learn to be a cowboy and live with his brother. Instead of it being lonely out there, they discovered there was a community built around the needs of children. Talk of a possible mining camp beyond the ranch's land might bring more children in the future.

When she had gotten pregnant, she decided to have the baby on the ranch that would be her daughter or son's heritage. With Rose and the help of one of Rafe's aunts who knew much about birthing, she had had no difficulty when her time came. Happily having a baby had caused Cord to quit smoking as he said he didn't need it as much anyway and didn't want the smoke around the baby.

The added bonus had been when Sam also quit-- thanks to the competition still between them. That made Cord a favorite with Abigail. If the two men occasionally enjoyed a cigar behind the barn, nobody was the wiser.

Priscilla's parents had remained in Saint Augustine with a few reluctant visits west. Overall they had comfort and friends nearby which made Florida easier on their health. They put all of their Tucson holdings in Priscilla's name. Some she had sold, some she had put under the management of trustworthy people like Jason Ridge. It provided additional income as Tucson grew.

It was a security blanket they hadn't needed as was the monthly payment banked for Grace from her uncle's ownership of the Kansas ranch. The last time he had visited the Circle O, he was looking older and told Grace that he and her aunt had willed the ranch to her when they died.

Priscilla also saw the signs of aging in Rose and James, which made them the grandparents for the community, but told Priscilla that they would need to do less work, and someday be cared for themselves. She didn't mind that at all since they had spent so many years nurturing her life.

Jesse began to lose interest in the milk and started playing with the locket around her neck, a locket for which Joe Fox had drawn tiny images of Cord and another of Grace. She'd ask for one now of Jesse and Grace together.

"They're here," she heard Ben yell from the yard as she was fastening back her bodice.

Sam was driving the team as the wagon pulled into the yard with Abby, Davy and their toddler daughter, Alice. Ollie rode along behind on a horse, with Satan tied to the back of the wagon, as even with his growing age, he was still a stallion that only Sam could ride.

Priscilla looked up when she heard the scream of a hawk. It no longer was frightening to her but almost reassuring. Her hawk was with her. He was safe.

Cord came out from the barns, dusting off his hands as he had been forking out hay for the horses. The cows closest to calving were near the buildings, while the others grazed the nearby hills. They had gone light on the number once it was clear that a drought was on its way.

The Circle O had several reliable springs, which still had plenty of water. Any rain clouds that passed over their land were encouraged to drop moisture by the surrounding mountains-- so the drought wasn't looking as bad for their ranch land as farther north.

All that mattered to her was the tall man waving at the arrivals as he strode toward her, smiling and putting out his arms for the baby she was holding. He wasn't wearing a gun.

The End

This story continues years later Grace and Rafe.
"Arizona Dawn" explores the unintended consequences of local and national actions when unresolved emotion is involved.

The rest of the stories at Amazon.

http://www.amazon.com/Rain-Trueax/e/B006UX64X8

www.ingramcontent.com/pod-product-compliance
Lightning Source LLC
Chambersburg PA
CBHW060143260626
47160CB00001B/105